NEVERMORE

AURA COVE TEMPORAL TRAVELER
BOOK ONE

BLAIR BRYAN

WANT MORE GOOD BOOKS?

Scan the QR Code Above or Tap HERE to unlock my entire backlist & find your next great read!

🎁 JOIN MY BOOK CLUB

- **Read FREE Extended Sneak Peeks**
- **Unlock Exclusive Bonus Content**
- **Private Subscriber-Only Discounts**
- **Handpicked 5-Star Book Recs**
- **Delicious, Healthy-ish Recipes**

☞ **JOIN THE BOOK CLUB HERE**

bookclub.tealbutterflypress.com

PREFACE

Recently, Robert F. Kennedy Jr., now appointed as U.S. Secretary of Health and Human Services, made deeply troubling and harmful remarks about autism. Referring to it as a "preventable disease," he said, *"These are kids who will never pay taxes, they'll never hold a job, they'll never play baseball, they'll never write a poem, they'll never go on a date, many of them will never use a toilet unassisted."*

Not only are these claims offensive, they are factually and scientifically false.

Autism is a spectrum, not a sentence. While some individuals require more support, many autistic people live fully independent and meaningful lives. They fall in love. They start companies. They raise families. They pay taxes. And yes, some write poems that break your heart with their brilliance. To reduce this community to a list of assumed deficits is dehumanizing and unacceptable, especially from someone tasked with shaping national health policy.

This is why we need characters like Nevermore.

I wrote her to push back against these outdated, damaging narratives. Nevermore is neurodivergent because our stories (*and our heroines*) need to reflect the beautiful, varied spectrum of human experience. She doesn't move through the world like everyone else, and that's not just something we have to accept, it's something to celebrate. Her literal interpretation of the world, combined with her stims and repetitive behaviors, is a rebellion against the way people like Kennedy try to define others by limitation instead of possibility.

Parents of autistic children are rightly outraged. They want the world to know their children are not broken. They are not burdens. What they want from the rest of us is understanding. Patience. Respect. Not pity, and definitely not erasure.

My own encounters with autistic friends, family, and the moving stories in shows like *Love on the Spectrum* have opened my heart to the incredible depth, humor, and honesty that neurodivergent individuals bring to the world. They often speak with a honesty and emotional clarity that neurotypicals struggle to access. There's a kind of magic in their presence, a lens that reframes reality in the most unexpected and refreshing ways.

Nevermore exists because representation matters. She is not a token, she is a tribute. A quiet protest. A reminder that the world is not made better by conforming, but by including. We don't need to fix autism. We need to fix the way we *see* it.

XOXO Blair Bryan

For the minds that are wired differently and the hearts that hold them close.
The way you light up the world is nothing short of magic.

PART 1: MARCH 2024

CHAPTER I

PEREGRINE

BUCKSHOT.

Before you read another word, heed this warning: nothing can prepare you for the searing, bone-deep misery that rips through your torso when it breaks your skin. The initial impact stuns you into an instant state of shock, sending you sprawling backward. As the hellfire pellets scatter throughout your body, inch by agonizing inch, they are like a thousand little stabs in symphony crescendoing together into an apex of agony. In disbelief, you will be compelled to reach down for physical confirmation. When you glance down at your life-force slick on the pads of your fingers, warm and wet, you will find it's a sensation that is strangely not altogether off-putting. Then it unfurls, a dark crimson bloom seeping through your clothes. It's mesmerizing, watching the scarlet tide devour the real estate of your cotton t-shirt.

My imminent demise was precipitated by the

unfortunate underestimation of a little old lady. Technically speaking, "little" was a misnomer. For a morbidly obese seventy-year-old, Sheila was anything *but* little. She was also surprisingly agile as she navigated her cluttered home with the stealth and precision of a rotund feline on the prowl.

When she hit the bullseye on her first shot, I was reluctantly forced to concede Sheila possessed a commendable degree of marksmanship, but maybe that was giving her a tinge too much credit. After all, with a shotgun, one needs only to point in the right direction and hope for the best.

Mother always said, "Greed is the downfall of all mankind." And if she were still alive, she'd tell me I had no one to blame but myself. In all honesty, I was just too awestruck by the sight of it. I'd been planning this caper for the better part of two fortnights. It was a gift from the gods that landed in my lap after a chance encounter with Sheila's bitter and estranged son, Billy, at a dive bar I frequented. Over the years, I'd learned that slumming it with the locals often paid out handsome returns. You'd be surprised what the uneducated will say once their tongue has been loosened by alcohol.

According to Billy, (yes, you are correct in your assumption that a fifty-two-year-old man named Billy was as childish as the nickname implied) his mother was a doomsday prepper who didn't trust banks and believed the international financial system was on the brink of total collapse. When this happened, the world would revert back to using gold as its dominant currency. In preparation, she'd been hoarding gold bars for decades while she waited for this devastating apocalyptic event to happen. Since it hadn't yet, and likely never would, I was eager to relieve her of her burden.

Late one night, Billy bragged he'd be worth hundreds of thousands of dollars in precious metals when she died. It was a lazy pickup line he thought would green-light him into the panties of the bored blonde seated next to him. Unimpressed with his seemingly outlandish claims, she got up to leave, passing in a wake of cheap drugstore perfume. I waited patiently, letting the failure percolate from my perch three stools down, knowing with every passing second, he was becoming more ripe for the picking. When the time was right, I slid over and commiserated, "Women never see a good man when he's sitting right next to them."

"Damn straight, they don't," he agreed, his face twisting up into an ugly scowl. Then he chugged down the warm dregs of his Coors Light, setting the empty can on the sticky bar.

"Let me buy you a drink," I offered, barely able to stop the Cheshire grin from spreading across my face. I signaled to the barkeep, and he came running with the Jameson.

Four rounds of conciliatory shots later, a crucial ploy to ensure his recollection of our time together would be fuzzy, I seized my opportunity. He stood, swaying on his feet, and I absconded with his wallet when he turned to stumble off to the bathroom. It was a stained Velcro contraption that on the surface appeared worthless, with the exception of the plastic pocket that housed his driver's identification.

A few days later, after tracking down his mother, Sheila, on the internet, I pulled my car to a stop a block away from her front door. The home was situated on the outskirts of the affluent beachside enclave of Aura Cove. In the dark, I engaged in rigorous surveillance. The home was a classic seventies ranch, tucked into the end of an unremarkable side street. I was relieved to see it didn't feature an ocean view, greatly reducing the foot traffic. It was part of the original neighborhood of Aura Cove, built decades before greedy developers sliced up the coastline into multi-million dollar lots.

Sheila's yard was sparsely lit and covered with overgrown bushes and palm trees in a state of serious neglect. I'd had to tread carefully at first since those who were paranoid enough to remove the bulk of their financial assets from banks were often diligent about security. But one phone call to an acquaintance at a home alarm company verified that the blue logo on the sign stabbed into the ground near the front door was simply a decoy.

Over the next two weeks, I discovered that Sheila was a recluse. She relied on home delivery services with the kind of reckless abandon typical of Gen Z, who Uber for fast food. Every week, brown bags appeared on her front porch like clockwork, disappearing inside within minutes. You can learn a lot about a person by what they consume. Sheila, for instance, had a sweet tooth, an African Grey parrot, and didn't believe in tipping. After I handed her driver a generous fifty-dollar tip, he was more than happy to let me rifle through her bags, especially after being stiffed on his previous delivery.

By week four, it became apparent, in the interest of progress, that I would have to break a rule I had never broken before: entering a mark's house while she was still occupying it.

I took as many precautions as I could. On the eve of the full moon, I parked two streets away and used its natural illumination to navigate through connecting backyards to the rear of her house. I scaled the fence quickly and dropped onto the ground before scrambling toward the sunroom. At the back door, I pulled out my tools and, after only a few seconds of work, grinned with satisfaction when the interior mechanism disengaged. Then, I let myself in as quietly as possible, walking on tiptoes, and gently shut the door behind me. Once inside, I pressed my body into the shadows, straining to listen for movement, and waiting for my racing heart to recede. Then an unexpected rush of adrenaline filled me with brash overconfidence and encouraged me to take bolder risks.

Another downfall.

According to Billy, Sheila was fond of utilizing the ductwork to hide her treasure, and behind most of the vents in the house, gold bars and coins were tucked away. I started in the cluttered sunroom. Two sides of it were composed of glass where moonlight flooded in, tracing the lines of three dwarf lemon trees and other planters and buckets of vegetation. The air was musty with a slight citrus scent and buzzing with fruit flies. From the corner of the room, there was a rustling sound and a drowsy squawk that drew my attention to a large cage draped in a black sheet. During my month of surveillance, I learned there would be a large parrot sleeping inside.

"Who's a pretty boy?" the bird mumbled and churred between soft clicks and warbles. I froze in silence, waiting for the bird to calm back down, counting my breaths in the darkness. Eventually, he did, and I located the first vent, resting on my knees in front of it. Outside the house, I heard the ancient air conditioner power on. It squealed and hissed to life, the fan blades screaming in protest. I was grateful the loud rumbling helped settle the bird and disguised the electric whirring of my portable screwdriver.

After a few seconds, I had the vent grate resting on the floor, the screws squeaking as they rolled back and forth on the metal plate. I bent down, reached in, and patted around, feeling the first rush of euphoria when my hand connected with something cold and metallic. I pulled out the first two bars that caught a sliver of moonlight, and a satisfying grin spread across my face. In astonishment, I held the solid gold in my hands for a long moment, fantasizing about the down payment I'd make on a sailboat, already spending the windfall in my head. My literal ship was coming in, and it energized me to reach back into the ventilation duct to pull out more when my fingers brushed against the rough edges of something strange.

Completely engrossed in my pilfering, I pulled it out and was transfixed. I stared down at what looked like an exquisite golden sculpture of a miniature parrot barely three inches long. In my hand, the cold metal warmed to the touch, and I raised it to study the bird when a sudden shimmer of golden light stole my attention. I felt it vibrate in my palm, and then a flutter, as the wings flapped.

FLAPPED.

I shit you not.

Totally mesmerized, I cupped it in both of my hands, willing it to flap once more when, with a bang and a flash, the thunder of buckshot pitched me forward.

By the time I whirled around, Sheila stood mere steps away. She cocked the shotgun again, and I tried to dive for cover, but it was too late. When the second blast hit, I knew I was in trouble. I squeezed the bird in my fist. The wings were sharp, the edges cutting through my palm, but it was a minor annoyance and paled in comparison to the mortal wounds I'd already suffered.

"A bird in the hand is worth two in the bush," I mumbled under my breath, letting out an unsettling chuckle at the absurdity. I was quickly entering delirium, so I cannot tell you if what occurred next actually happened or was the final hallucination of a collapsing mind.

The golden bird began to flutter in my palm, tickling

the ridges of my hand until I released it into the air. It flicked its wings, sending a shower of sparkles drifting from the bird to the floor. Enamored with it, I struggled to my feet, stumbling forward as it flew toward the cage draped in fabric.

The shotgun cocked again, and I felt another shower of pellets explode as I fell forward onto the cage, ripping off the cloth and disengaging the lock on the door in one fell swoop. There was a metal clang as the shotgun fell to the ground and then a heavy thud when Sheila landed next to it. She was clutching her chest and moaning, her skin pasty and white. I staggered to my feet again, both hands covered in blood that was now dripping from my mouth in sputters and starts.

"Are you seriously having a heart attack right now? Why couldn't that have happened five minutes ago?" I let out a choked laugh as my blood dribbled onto the floor. In my last moments, as the circumstances became almost comical, my peals of laughter became even more unhinged.

"Uh-oh!" the gray bird squawked, taking in the scene of his caretaker on the ground as if he could understand what was happening. "Help, I've fallen and I can't get up!" he crowed, then repeated, "I've fallen and I can't get up!" The Life Alert commercial catchphrase resurfaced from my misty childhood memories, and I coughed out another coppery laugh. The bird had obviously been as overexposed to local access television as I had been.

The parrot splayed his wings, exited the now

swinging cage door, cawed at the golden bird, and then came to a rest on top of his cage. His eyes were unblinking, and he grew more animated and squawked louder as the golden bird flew closer to him. His soft head bobbed up and down in glee as the golden bird fluttered its tiny wings closer. "Gimme a kiss!" he chirped now that the golden bird was mere inches away. Then he jutted out his chin and spread his wings wide in what could only be described as an elaborate mating dance, while his flirty demand repeated in a sassy staccato, "Gimme a kiss!"

The golden bird whirred and chirped as it drew closer, and I couldn't tear my eyes away from the pair, now only a breath away.

As a final gesture, I reached one bloody hand toward my shimmering avian guide, desperate to flee the pain and take flight. Instead, searing agony flared, followed by a whoosh of ominous black light. There were screams I only recognized as my own as I drifted away, and then my soul took flight.

CHAPTER

TWO

"Welcome to the Free State of Florida." Nevermore chuckled dryly as she passed the gaudy declaration posted on the bright blue sign in the ditch at the state line. "That's ironic, coming from a state with one of the world's highest incarceration rates and who has been proudly revoking women's rights and LGBTQIA+ protections for years." Before she could fixate on the injustice and ruin the rest of her evening ruminating, her cell phone distracted her by vibrating in the holder attached to the dashboard of her white Sprinter van, breaking her train of thought. She quickly glanced over at it, seeing the caller ID read UNKNOWN.

"Nice try, but you don't fool me," she mumbled, reaching out to tap the red button that would send the caller straight to voicemail. To Neve, her cell phone was purely a necessary navigation device, not an instrument of interruptive communication with people who often had nothing to say. Everyone who knew Neve knew they would have to leave a message, and when she was ready to have a very brief, very factual conversation, she would return their call.

She was five miles away from her campground, a KOA that checked all the boxes she required. Clean showers, an adult-only section, and no pool. Pools were merely a toxic stew of germs that attracted families with noisy children like moths to a flame. Neve found it difficult to relax around children, with their incessant questions and propensity to swing from absolute joy to utter despair in a millisecond.

She rounded the final corner, executing a textbook hand-over-hand clockwise turn, and rolled onto the familiar gravel road, reducing her speed to exactly the fifteen miles per hour that was posted on the speed limit sign. Her fingers clenched the wheel as she scanned for the campsite she annually reserved online. Site 47.

During her first year as a solo nomad, she spent countless hours evaluating campground amenities. Her diligent research paid handsome dividends. Annually, when January 7th arrived, she could swiftly book a year's worth of reservations in just two hours, ensuring each campsite met her rigorous standards. Neve followed the same sojourn throughout the continental United States every year—Arizona by November and the Pacific Northwest by spring—hitting every National Park on the way. It was a route that never deviated. Neve was a creature of habit, finding the uniformity calming in its predictability.

She'd lived this way for over a decade, making a

living by selling her artwork directly to collectors. Her father had long ago warned her about the feast-or-famine lifestyle of a contemporary artist, but Neve was stubborn and found frugal ways to stretch the money she received from the rental of her childhood home and the infrequent commissions that came her way.

The nomadic lifestyle agreed with her. Neve found the solitude restorative. She always felt like she didn't fit in, as if the rest of the world had been given a rule book to which she'd never had access. Other people always knew the right thing to say when Neve often froze. By the time she'd formulated what seemed to be a correct response, discarding a slew of other options in her mind, they'd already moved on. It was a perpetual game of catch-up that left her exhausted and, as a result, Neve preferred to be alone.

At the age of forty-seven, she'd made the same trip twelve times, but still, the evening prior to a move, she would dedicate an hour to studying the map of the campground and refreshing her memory on the best route to her campsite.

"Right, right, left," she mumbled under her breath as she visualized the map in her mind. After the left, she spotted the wooden placard labeled 47 in bold green brushstrokes. It was a wide, level patch of green grass tucked between two towering pines with a neatly packed gravel landing pad.

She pulled into the campsite at a crawl, carefully aligning the van so the tires rested evenly on the ground. It took fifteen minutes of inching forward and back before she felt the balance settle beneath her. After years of practice, her gut knew when her home on wheels was level, and she'd learned to trust it.

Exhausted from the drive, Neve yawned as she turned off the ignition and clipped the keys to the green carabiner that dangled from the canvas loop of her messenger bag. She tapped it once for luck, connecting with the geode tucked inside. She wished she could pull out her charcoal pencils and sketch for a few hours, but seeing the sun sliding ever lower on the horizon, she forced herself to focus. Hooking up to water was her first priority, and she checked the gasket twice, then unwound the hose and threaded it onto the spigot, turning until it was tight. Then Neve tightened the hose once more, just to be safe.

Electricity was next. She uncoiled the extension cord, then froze when she noticed the filthy state of the electrical box. It appeared the previous tenant had used the edge to scrape off large chunks of mud from their hiking boots, and she was instantly disgusted.

"Humans ruin everything," she muttered under her breath as she contemplated her next move, hating the roadblock she'd encountered when she was losing daylight. "Rule 7. Keep our campground clean for everyone. Fail!" She made a mental note to discuss the infraction of the previous tenant first thing in the morning with the campground's owner, Chuck.

"Is it really that difficult to pick up after yourself?" She voiced the question as if she were traveling with a companion. Then Neve reached up and tightened the ends of her two French braids as she paced, feeling her tension rising. When they were snug once again, she forced herself to take in one deep breath, then imagined the frustration was like a red balloon filling up.

"What is the minimum that needs to occur for you to feel comfortable in this situation?" she asked under her breath, using the soothing cadence of Ms. Maplewood, the therapist her aunt required her to see weekly when she gained custody of Neve as a teenager.

She focused on answering the question as the red balloon she'd visualized neared its full capacity. When she uncurled her balled fist and metaphorically let it float away, the solution presented itself and the tension dissipated as Neve shifted into action. First, she snapped a photo of the state of the electrical box so she could show it to Chuck during their discussion tomorrow. Then Neve walked back to the van and pulled out her toolbox, taking the time to carefully chisel the hardened mud onto the ground before propping the metal door open with a Clorox wipe. She plugged the extension cord in with her other hand, avoiding touching the receptacle, and watched for the small green light that reassured her the connection was solid. Finally finished, a slight smile of satisfaction tipped up the corners of her mouth.

"Home, sweet home," she breathed. She climbed back inside and prepared a bowl of vanilla yogurt and nutty granola, eating it at the kitchenette before attaching her window coverings for privacy. Neve gathered her container of toiletries and took a shower just after the quiet hours began, knowing this would reduce the number of people she'd encounter in the public bathhouse.

The next morning, after a breakfast of two hard scrambled eggs, pineapple-orange juice, and two slices of bacon eaten at eight am on the dot, she completed her morning rituals. Digging out her cell phone, she scrolled through her texts and then listened to her voicemails. Just as she thought. Two messages from telemarketers requesting "just five minutes of her time." Blocking the numbers, she listened on, and the final message made her recoil in disbelief. Shaking, she listened to it a second time, then checked her watch, hoping to put off the return call. Seeing twelve hours had elapsed already, she let out a groan then redialed the number and waited, tapping her fingers on the space-saving convertible table, trying to ignore the obnoxious ringing in her ear and the anxiety growing in her belly.

"This is Officer Harrison Willey with Aura Cove PD," a warm male voice said at the other end.

"Officer Willey, this is Nevermore LaRue, returning your call." She forced a light, carefree tone, mirroring his, despite the turmoil churning inside her. On a whim, she added, "But you can call me Neve."

"Thank you, Neve. Then you can call me Harry," he offered, and she felt like it was a conversational win.

Before she could stop them, the next words tumbled out of her mouth, "Wait. Your name…is…Harry Willey?" Her eyebrows climbed up her forehead as she let out a soft groan. "My goodness, that's an unfortunate combination."

Harry chuckled good-naturedly on the other end.

"What?" Neve was puzzled.

"Let's just say I've heard that more times than I can count." He laughed again.

Neve wondered why he was laughing, feeling a hot flush of shame that she'd responded incorrectly, but she didn't have time to focus on it as the officer quickly moved on in a business-like tone. "You're the owner of record at 437 Manatee Lane?"

"Yes. That is true." She hadn't given much thought to her childhood home in years. Sheila's monthly rent payments came through PayPal like clockwork. She was the perfect tenant, never asking Neve to fix anything and paying every month on time.

He cleared his throat and adopted one of level-headed authority. "I was calling to inform you of an incident that occurred at your residence last evening. We responded to a report of shots fired and, upon arrival, located a deceased male in the sunroom."

"Oh, dear." Neve felt the first tremor of fear and she gulped. "Male? That's strange. There wasn't a man on her lease. Is Sheila okay?"

"I'm afraid not," he answered matter-of-factly. "She was also deceased. It's an ongoing investigation and, unfortunately, I don't have many definitive details yet. I can report a significant store of precious metals was found in the home, which indicates a possible motive for robbery.

It looks as though, instead of calling law enforcement, Ms. Bowker took matters into her own hands and shot the suspect at least twice before collapsing on the floor."

"Well, if Sheila shot him, he probably deserved it."

Harry let out a bark of unprofessional laughter that he tried to swallow with an embarrassed cough. "Sorry." It was another reaction Neve didn't understand; she was often baffled by conversation. "I can't confirm that suspicion at this time, but I *can* tell you that officials have secured the crime scene. Our detectives are on site and beginning their investigation, which includes processing the sunroom and surrounding areas for evidence. We've also called in forensic specialists to assist in our efforts and a team to canvas the neighborhood."

A shiver raced down Neve's spine under the relentless flood of details. "Okay," She heard herself answer, quickly overwhelmed and beginning to unravel. Neve had a hard time grasping the given information, unable to construct full sentences as the first waves of panic set in.

"I'm sorry to be the bearer of bad news," he continued with sincerity after interpreting her long pause as fearful. "But there is one more thing."

"More?" She didn't believe she had the capacity for more, and she tightened her grip on the phone, pressing it harder against her ear.

"We found a parrot inside the house. He appears to be alive and in need of care and keeps repeating the same phrase: Call Nevermore. I know this sounds strange, but he seems to be asking for you by name."

"What? Why on earth would he do that?" She racked her brain again, until she found the answer, "Of course. He's a parrot. That's what they do. Repeat things they hear. They aren't sentient beings."

"Animals are far more intelligent than we give them credit for," Harry added.

"What about her son, Billy?" Neve asked. "Perhaps he could provide care."

Harry let out a huff of disbelief. "Between you and me, Billy Bowker can't even take care of himself."

Neve pinched the skin between her eyebrows at the bridge of her nose, then tightened her braids again, eager for the conversation to end.

"Would you be in a position to provide for his care?"

"Me?" Neve shook her head so vehemently that the tips of her braids lashed her cheeks. "I don't know anything about taking care of a bird. Birds are dirty and loud. And, hello! Ever hear of bird flu?"

"Then, in that case, we'll need to contact animal control to safely remove the parrot and ensure it receives the proper care," Officer Willey said with resignation.

Letting out a heavy exhalation, Neve felt the weight of responsibility settling in. She'd been in the same position when she was fifteen, facing a placement with Child Protective Services when her aunt stepped up for her. Neve couldn't help but feel this was her opportunity to pay it forward. She let out a long huff of irritation. "I'm already going to have to derail my plans to go to Yellowstone to straighten out this mess and find another tenant. You might as well wait until I get there to make a decision about the bird."

"I was hoping you'd say that," Officer Willey said.

Then a realization hit her full force. "Wait, since a man was shot, there must be blood and other body fluids all over the house." The idea of it made her tremble, and she tightened her fists into tight balls and squeezed her eyes shut to control the surge of fear that accompanied it.

"That's a valid concern," he said. "To answer your question, yes, there are, but once we conclude our investigation, I can refer you to a crime scene cleaning specialist. They have extensive experience with handling situations like this and can take care of the cleanup for you."

Neve felt relief flood in. "It's going to take me a few days to get home anyway. I would appreciate the referral."

"And I'll keep an eye on the bird for you until then. Make sure he has food and water. He's pretty shaken up, dropping feathers like crazy."

"Oh dear, providing comfort and empathy are not my strong suits." She said, her unease growing as she started to rock back and forth.

"Let me know when you've arrived in Aura Cove. We'll have to release the property back to you. In the meantime, if you have any concerns or need further assistance, you can reach out to me directly. You have my number."

"Okay."

The phone call ended, and she stopped rocking, sitting still for several long moments, practically catatonic. Her breaths came faster, and she filled another red balloon in her mind, and another, and another. Before long, Neve was in the throes of a debilitating panic attack. Her thoughts spiraled. This was the second time blood had been shed in her childhood home, and the first time had almost destroyed her.

CHAPTER

THREE

FOUR DAYS LATER, in the early morning darkness, Neve arrived in Aura Cove and was standing on the driveway in front of her childhood home. Rather than going directly inside, she got to work tearing down the yellow caution tape strung between stakes in the front yard that had the potential to draw unwanted gawkers.

Years ago, she'd left it behind without a second thought, but now, being forced to confront the last place she'd seen her father alive, the trauma of those days came rushing back. Eyeing a For Sale sign two doors down, she had to admit the idea of putting it on the market wasn't unappealing.

"Hmm. I wonder if I would have to disclose it was a murder house? Surely, that would have them lining up at the door," she mumbled under her breath, already discarding the notion.

Unable to procrastinate any longer, Neve forced herself toward the front door that had been sealed with a crime scene notice. Black lettering declared: Police Line: Do Not Cross. She hesitated, gripping her key so tightly it bit into her palm. Every instinct screamed at her to turn around, sprint back to her van, and disappear down the highway.

With a sharp intake of breath, she punctured the seal and ran the key between the O and the L. The tape curled away as she cut, defeated. If only she could obey its warning, keep the door closed forever, and pretend none of this had ever happened. Obligated to see it through, she slid the key into the lock and turned the handle, grateful when the overpowering scents of bleach and industrial cleaning supplies infiltrated her nostrils.

"Much better than the alternative, I guess." she muttered under her breath as she stepped further into the darkened dwelling. Though it had been many years since she'd been inside the home, her muscle memory kicked in as she patted down the wall where the light switch resided. With one sweep of her hand, cool blue light washed across the area and made her gasp in shock.

Towers of cardboard boxes six feet high lined the hall and ringed the walls of the living room, making it feel much smaller than she remembered. One entire wall was dominated by metal shelves of neatly stacked, vacuum-sealed food pouches, all dated and labeled in scrawled Sharpie. On the bottom rack, dozens of water storage jugs lined several shelves, and on the top, rows of canned goods, from beans to pineapple chunks, were arranged in alphabetical order and lit by small motion-sensor LED lights. The collection of non-perishable food was so plentiful it resembled a small-town grocery store far more than a single-family home. While she appreciated the batteries and that the freeze-dried rations were stacked in neat, orderly rows, she wondered aloud, "Sheesh. How many batteries does one woman need? Clearly, there are no battery-operated appliances in here."

Next to a tattered recliner, a military-grade first-aid kit lay open on the coffee table as if Sheila had been interrupted while restocking it, and there was a huge army surplus duffle lying on the floor filled with boxes of shotgun shells.

Picking her way around the ammunition, she carried her messenger bag and leather portfolio down the hall. A soft squawking sound called to her, and she followed it, cutting through the clutter to the sunroom. She was grateful to see the room had been cleared out and only contained potted fruit trees and a hydroponic garden with blue grow lights where spindly greens were dying. Tucked into the corner, opposite the wall of windows, was a large bird cage that stood almost five feet tall. The sheet that covered it was balled into a pile on the ground and, from a perch on a branch inside, an African Grey parrot eyed her.

"Bwakkk!" he squawked as he flapped his wings, eager to command her attention. "Nevermore?"

Intrigued he called her by name, Neve gave him one small nod as she took tentative steps closer to the cage, which only served to make his cries louder and more agitated. He flapped his wings furiously, and Neve noticed two gray feathers drift down to collect at the bottom of the cage. What remained on his chest was drab and sparse, in contrast to the flash of colorful red feathers at his tail.

She reached out a hand and rested it on the door.

"Open sesame!" He clicked and bobbed up and down on his clawed feet, even more animated, his excitement palpable. He inched toward her, and she felt a shiver of fear shudder closer as she studied his powerful beak closing in. Her silence only made him crow louder,"Open sesame! Open sesame!"

She pressed her palms to her ears, the increasing volume making the wave of anxiety crest higher. "You want out?"

He bobbed up and down faster. Taking it as a confirmation, she reached one hand out and quickly twisted the door and flung it open. The bird took immediate flight from the confines of the cage and began circling the room. Gliding on his silvery gray wings, he executed several lazy circles before landing on her shoulder as if he belonged there.

"No, thank you," she said, swiping her hand at his clawed feet, eager to get him to disengage. "I am not a tree." She shrugged him off, and he alighted into the air once again, flapping away before finally coming to a rest on the top of his cage. His beady black eyes leveled on hers and stared at her unblinkingly. There was an almost human quality to the staring contest that made

Neve shift uncomfortably on her feet and choose a spot just above his head to focus on.

"Nevermore?" he squawked once. "Peregrine," he squawked and swiped an open wing toward himself, then he repeated the gesture. "Nevermore." He swung his wing to her, then squawked, "Peregrine," while swiping his wing back to himself.

"Peregrine? Is that your name?" Neve asked in utter astonishment.

He let out a slide whistle sound. "Ding! We have a winner!" He swished his wings.

In shock, Neve stuttered, "You… you can understand me?"

"I concur a second time." He opened his beak and vocalized a loud siren sound that made Neve cower away. Seeing her distress, he apologized, "Sorry for the volume! Can't be helped."

Curiosity winning out, Neve unclenched her shoulders and asked, "How do you know my name?"

"I was given a hint," Peregrine said, dismissing her question and focusing on himself. "Now that we have been properly introduced, I am in need of your assistance."

Neve let out a choked chuckle at the absurdity. "Great, he can speak in full sentences and he's got a better vocabulary than I do." She studied him in fascination, leaning closer but still striving to maintain a wide swath of personal space. Peregrine's ability to speak dumbfounded Neve. The sentences were well thought out, coming from a powerful black beak she was certain was strong enough to clip one of her fingers off at the knuckle. Reflexively, she curled them into her palms. The overwhelm rose like a wave, and she began to spiral.

Ignoring the bird's plea for help, she glanced around the room, trying to get her bearings, when her gaze locked on a dark brown stain that covered the concrete floor of the sunroom. It sent her reeling, peeling back the years to the day she was fifteen and had just come home from school, eager to tell her father about her perfect score on a biology test. Her heartbeat thrummed in her ears, as she dropped to her knees next to the cage before gathering her legs in a ball and rocking back and forth. Horrific images she'd thought she'd locked away when she was a teenager began to resurface in slow motion.

She remembered coming home that day from school and rushing down the narrow hall toward the sunroom, waving her test paper with the enormous red A scrawled on the top. The sunroom was her father's favorite room in the house, and she expected to find him there tending his bonsai tree with clippers or reading a report in the cracked leather recliner he loved.

"Dad! I have amazing…" Terror swallowed the rest of her sentence when she cleared the door frame and her gaze locked on a pool of thick, coagulated blood covering a large section of the sunroom floor. In shock, she dropped her paper and it floated down, seesawing back and forth until it landed squarely in the sea of red. Two dried crimson footprints were near the largest spill.

Splatters of red zinged across and spotted the walls, then dripped to the floor. The visual itself was horrific, but it was the metallic scent of death Neve would never forget.

A few minutes later, or maybe it was an hour, Neve lost all sensation and track of time as her body became paralyzed with shock. Eventually, in the distance, she could hear the whine of an approaching siren. She reached up to cover her ears and rocked forward and back, trying to self-soothe, jolting upright when two officers called out, "Aura Cove PD!" and then burst through the doorway. Neve was trembling in a ball, rocking in the corner, when a male officer held out his hand to her. She stared at it, knowing he wanted her to take it, but she couldn't make her hand obey.

His partner, a younger female, knelt down next to Neve, and in a tone far more soothing said, "I'm Officer Stiles. We're here to help you. Can you tell us your name?"

Neve blinked, the question finally registering. Then she swiped a hand across her cheeks and was surprised to feel wetness there. She chose a safe soft on the ceiling, one that was clear and just above the head of the woman. "Nevermore." Her voice cracked as she tried to comply.

"Nevermore, are you hurt? Can you stand and follow me to the kitchen?" Officer Stiles asked.

Instead of answering, Neve heard her father's words of guidance drilled into her head. "Can I see some identification?" Neve squeaked out.

"Verify, verify, verify." His deep baritone made her heart twinge. "Don't blindly accept the story you are given. You can't trust every person in a uniform."

The officer pulled an Aura Cove Police Department ID Badge out of her pocket and handed it to her. "I have to say this is the first time I've been asked for ID from a teenager. That's impressive!"

The token compliment confused Neve. "You're a cheery one, considering my house looks like the prom scene from Stephen King's *Carrie*."

The female officer's eyes bugged, surprised by the blunt observation. Before she could comment on it, they were interrupted by a shrill shriek.

"Nevermore?" A familiar shout cut through the awkward silence they were stuck in when her Aunt Talulah barreled through the door in a state of hysteria. Her wiry five-foot frame was covered in organic cotton from head to toe. A long bohemian skirt kissed the ground, paired with a peasant blouse. Her bracelets, an eclectic collection of amethyst, rose quartz, and tourmaline stones jangled together, snaking up her forearms. She claimed the crystals provided spiritual protection, a declaration Neve's father, Ellis, a research scientist, dismissed as heeby-jeeby nonsense. Cascading down her back, her long, platinum blonde hair shimmered, interlaced with lilac ribbons attached to a headband.

Aunt Talulah had the kind of presence that felt untethered, almost otherworldly as if she hovered above the earth rather than sinking into it. Despite her delicate frame, there was a strength in her gaze, and she radiated an ethereal, calming energy.

Talulah reached down, pulling her niece into the warm circle of her arms as Neve went limp. When a hug was forced upon her, Neve never knew where to put her hands. Should she wrap them around the waist or place them on top of the shoulders? It was always a conundrum where she narrowly avoided head-butting the unsuspecting hugger.

Neve felt her aunt stiffen when she caught a glimpse of the blood in the sunroom over Neve's shoulder.

"Are you okay?" Talulah asked. Then she pulled back, gripping Neve's arms as she looked her over from head to toe. Her skin blanched white as she bit on the corner of her lip.

Neve left the question unanswered as she stood at Talulah's side like a cast-off sock, letting her mind float away from the noise. She pressed her hands to her ears to block out the increasing chatter and began to rock. The voices around her muffled, but if she strained, she could still make them out. When the male officer started speaking, she felt herself tune out.

"Thank you for coming so quickly, ma'am. I'm Officer Daniels. I understand this is a lot to process, but I'll give you a rundown of what we know so far and then I'll need to ask you a few questions. If you're feeling up to it."

"Of course," Talulah agreed.

"The station received an anonymous phone call from

a woman who requested a welfare check be done at this residence."

"A woman?" Talulah asked. "Who?" she demanded, her eyes narrowing on the police officer.

"She asked to remain anonymous," Officer Daniels answered Talulah gently before continuing. "When we arrived, my partner and I found the front door wide open and entered the residence where we found your niece and a significant amount of blood in the sunroom. It gives us reason to believe someone may have sustained a very serious injury in this house."

"Serious? How serious? Are you... are you sayin'...?" Talulah's tone took on a high-pitched, terrified quality that recaptured Neve's attention.

At her side, Neve's rocking increased, and she began to wail.

"I'm sorry," Talulah apologized over the devastating tremor of Neve's sobs. "Mind givin' us a minute?"

The officer nodded and took several steps away to confer with the crime scene investigators who had just donned surgical booties and were carefully nearing the largest pool of blood. Flashes popped like a strobe light as photographs were taken of the scene, and the overstimulation made Neve even more agitated.

Talulah tugged her down the hallway, away from the incessant radio chatter.

"Honey bee, you're okay. I'm right here." Talulah's voice was soft.

Neve was stoic, refusing to make eye contact, though her wailing had quieted in proportion with her distance from the sunroom. After a long pause, she finally spoke, her voice a hushed whisper, "It's too loud, too bright, too red. I don't like these people." Talulah sat her down and brought her a glass of water.

After Neve drank all of it and was calmer, Talulah continued, "These people are here to help you," She turned toward Officer Daniels, who'd just returned, and asked, "Isn't that right, Officer?"

Before he could answer, Neve blurted, "No, they are not." Her tone was detached and almost robotic as she continued, "Statistically, police officers are more likely to imprison or fine you than they are to help you."

Officer Daniels frowned upon hearing Neve's blunt assessment of his profession. Talulah offered him an apologetic smile then turned toward Neve. "I need to talk to him in private for a minute, but I need to know you're alright, honey bee."

"I'm okay," Neve responded. "But I *am* hungry."

"We'll fix that, too, once I've had a word with the officers, okay?"

Neve nodded, then watched her aunt disappear back down the hall. Low voices carried down the hallway, and Neve could hear every word though they attempted to speak in hushed tones.

"Nevermore is overwhelmed, and I must apologize for her rudeness. She's always been a very straightforward child."

"No apologies necessary. She seems to be in a heightened state of shock, which makes sense given what she walked into," Officer Stiles reasoned, smoothing her partner's ruffled feathers.

"We just have a few more questions for you. With the amount of blood loss here, there is a possibility the injuries could be life-threatening. Who lived in the home?"

"Just my brother, Ellis, and you already met his daughter Neve."

"Until we get confirmation otherwise, we have to treat this as a critical situation. We'll need Ellis's contact information."

"Absolutely." She rattled off the digits of his phone number, and the officer scrawled them down on his notepad. "Though, a word of warnin'. It is often difficult to get him on the phone," Talulah said after a long pause, seeming to choose her words carefully. "Ellis is… very… driven."

"Driven?" Officer Daniel's lips straightened into a grim line. This was a man who was used to being lied to and, over the years, had developed a healthy sense of skepticism. "How so?"

"He's a cancer research scientist. When we spoke last, he mentioned he was writin' a paper that he felt was going to be revolutionary. He was testin' a new treatment protocol that had excitin' tumor reduction rates for certain cancers."

The officer scribbled notes into his notebook. "Where does he work?"

"He's a senior research scientist at NovaCure Pharmaceuticals."

After pausing to add this information, the officer's questions continued. "Was he seeing anyone?"

Talulah let out an ironic chuckle. "Do his co-workers count? My brother had a singular focus and thought any time spent outside of it was a total waste."

"That sounds pretty intense."

"It could be," Talulah offered. Then they were both distracted by a rhythmic banging sound. A pained expression transformed her features. "I need to get back to my niece. Is there anythin' else you need from me right now?" Hearing another thump, she turned and rushed down the hallway where she found Neve repeatedly banging her forehead against the wall. Her skin was already pink where it made contact with the plaster surface.

"Do we need to radio for a bus to check her out?" Officer Stiles offered, clearly confused by the child who seemed to be punishing herself.

"No, that's unnecessary." Talulah gently pulled her from harm's way into the center of the room, careful not to make too much direct contact. "If there is nothin' else right now, I'd like to remove her from this situation."

"I believe that's the best course of action. Our team needs time to process the scene and finish their investigation. We could get Child Protective Services involved, but I'd prefer to release her to a relative."

"I would never leave my only niece in the hands of CPS. I'm more than willin' to step in," Talulah said quickly, brushing off the ridiculous suggestion. "I've booked a room at the Seabreeze Inn near the square in Aura Cove."

The officer pulled out a business card from his shirt pocket and handed it to her. "If you think of anything else, please give me a call. We'll need you to bring Neve to the station in the morning to answer a few more questions. We'll also catch you up to speed with any further developments in the investigation. In the meantime, please continue to try to contact Ellis. We'll put a trace on his credit cards and canvas the neighborhood, but it's imperative we find him as quickly as possible."

At Talulah's side, Neve shivered. "I want my dad." She repeated under her breath as she rocked, trying to self-soothe, "I want my dad."

"I know, honey bee. I know," Talulah whispered, gently placing a light hand on her thin shoulder, knowing it was the only kind of loving contact Neve would tolerate.

The bird let out a piercing whistle, and Neve flinched in response, jolting back instantly from the memory of the worst day of her life to the nightmare currently unfolding in front of her. Seeing the dried blood stain a second time, she forced herself to shake off the cresting fear. Peregrine glided closer and landed on her shoulder again, and Neve batted him away with one irritated hand. "Please stop using me as a perch."

"My apologies," he squawked out, and after flicking his wings twice, landed on the back of a chair. "Flying. Who knew it was such a kick?"

"You're the strangest bird I have ever met."

"Ah, that's because I've only had avian genetics for a mere four days."

"What?" Neve shook her head to clear the absolute absurdity of a bird who could converse, not just mimic words he'd heard. "Since you seem to have the ability to think independently and speak in full sentences, I need answers."

The bird swept one feathered wing in front of himself and bowed deeply, an almost human gesture that bowled Neve over yet again. "Your wish is my command."

"What happened here?"

"I was simply retrieving some property from the sunroom when I was shot in the back. Not only once, but *twice* at close range."

His vague explanation painted him as the victim, but Neve didn't buy it. She narrowed her eyes. "I get the feeling you might be leaving out some key details, Perry. Can I call you Perry?"

"If you must," he huffed, turning his head to blink one intelligent black eye at her before changing tactics. "Very well, it will do me no good to keep the gory details to myself. What would you like me to disclose?"

"How did you know Sheila?"

"Though I was unacquainted with *her*, I had recently befriended her son, Billy."

"I'm confused. Why would you be in her home if you'd never met her?"

"Fine," he huffed, forced to concede as he was

backed into a corner. "I was relieving her of her gold bullion."

"This just keeps getting crazier and crazier," Neve muttered as astonishment crept in. "Gold? As in what leprechauns reportedly find at the end of rainbows?"

"Yes," Perry admitted. "I fancy myself a bit of an artist, not unlike yourself." He flapped one wing toward her portfolio case resting against the wall.

"An artist?" Her expression wrinkled up in disbelief. "Wait, do you mean *con* artist?"

"Potato, Pah-tah-to." He poo-poohed the distinction, seeming to shrug it off.

Neve dropped onto a chair as a prickle of knowing made her legs wobble and the hairs stand up on her arms. "Are you the man who died here?"

"Affirmative," he chirped, tipping his feathered wings up in a shrug-like gesture. Neve blinked several times, absorbing the onslaught of outrageous information that just kept coming.

"But how did you land in the body of Sheila's parrot?"

"That part is still very unclear to me. Hidden among her stash in the air conditioning vent was a gold bird that fluttered to life when I touched it. It was so mesmerizing I felt compelled to follow it to the bird cage. There was a final shotgun blast, and a blinding burst of light seared my vision. Then the air became heavy, thick with the smell of sulfur and I heard a low rumble. I felt myself being pulled down into a pit by cold, skeletal claws latching on and coiling around my ankles."

The bird shuddered and continued, his voice trembling. "The world above me dissolved, and the light dimmed to a distant, flickering pinprick, almost vanishing altogether, until the glint of the golden bird caught my eye. I knew instinctively, deep in my soul, that it was my only hope for salvation. The golden bird beckoned to me, and with every ounce of strength I had remaining, I wrenched myself away from the suffocating darkness. I catapulted through the void, spinning upward in one final, desperate attempt for freedom. When I awoke, I discovered I'd survived, but I'm now stuck inside the body of Sheila's bird."

"Perry, that's insane. It sounds like Sheila tried to book you a one-way ticket to Dante's Inferno and you clawed your way back."

Perry shivered and held up one singed feather as evidence. "It was real. I felt the heat."

"That's impossible."

"I would have said the same had I not lived through the last several days." Perry let out a loud squawk that started Neve. "Sorry, I can't help myself. The bird and I aren't always in alignment about how to remedy this bizarre situation. He can be annoying."

"You are both in there? Like a split personality?"

"More like a Siamese twin." His beak lowered until it was almost a scowl. "I seem to be trapped inside this creature, and I don't know how to get out. Perhaps you can help me?"

"I'm not sure you deserve it," Neve told him pointedly. "You made a selfish choice and are now facing the consequences. Considering you claim to have narrowly escaped hell, I would think you'd be more pleased with the outcome."

He squawked a chuckle. "You may be the most literal woman I've ever met."

"I prioritize facts over emotion," Neve explained with a shrug.

"But will you help me?"

"I don't know if that is possible. You *died*, Perry. There is no body for your soul to return to."

His wings tightened around his feathered body, and a crestfallen expression settled into his stance. They sat in silence until a box dislodged from the pile and fell to the floor, startling them both. A mountain of crudely printed newsletters, yellowing with age, slid out onto the floor. Neve bent down to pick one up. "WTSHTF…" she read the letters out loud. "What a nonsensical word! "Alex, I'll take Lost in Translation for $500," she attempted a joke, pulled from her days of watching *Jeopardy!* with her childhood nanny, Isla.

"It means when the shit hits the fan," Perry said. "It's a common phrase coined by the doomsday prepper community."

"Oh." Neve gathered them up and returned the stack to the box, ignoring the pouting bird. "At least you are useful and mildly intelligent."

"Mildly? My IQ is 142!"

"Is that high?"

"Everyone knows it is genius level! I'm in the top two percent!"

"Technically, that is incorrect. *I* was unaware it was genius level. And since most of your life decisions seem to lack basic common sense, I'd hardly label you a mastermind."

"If I had eyes that could roll, this is where I would roll them." His sarcasm was legendary as he strutted away.

"In that case, maybe I should call animal control after all. I can ask them to find a more suitable caretaker for you."

"Let's not get hasty!" he cried, quickly whipping back around. "Who knows where those public servant degenerates would send me? Animals are expendable. Humans eat them, for God's sake! Did we learn nothing as a society during the send-a-mouse-to-college heyday in the 1980s?"

Neve winced, sucking in a breath through her bottom teeth, remembering the donations her homeroom teacher would collect to send mice off to become laboratory test subjects. "Ahh. You might have a valid point. How about a truce?"

"What are your conditions?"

"I will provide a balanced diet. You will provide companionship *without* the snark."

He squawked, considering his options. "But most people find my sarcastic repartee delightful."

"I'm not most people."

"That much is certain." Perry held out the feathery tip of one wing, and Neve reached forward, offered a hand, and they struck a deal. One that would change their lives forever.

CHAPTER

FOUR

AT FOUR AM the next morning, Neve jolted awake, her pulse drumming in her ears. The camper van's interior was steeped in shadows, the faint glow of the moon casting silvery streaks across the interior. Blinking away the haze of sleep, she swung her legs over the edge of the bed and connected with the cool vinyl planks on the floor. Still groggy, she stumbled the few steps to the compact kitchenette, where she filled the coffee maker from the jug of water she'd filled the night before.

Her hair cascaded in soft waves down her back as she reached for her spray bottle, misting it with a light layer of diluted conditioner. With practiced ease, she divided it into two equal sections, her fingers weaving each side into neat, symmetrical braids. Once every strand was swept away from her face, she felt the tightness in her jaw unclench and was able to focus on her next task. Neve's morning routine had initially been suggested by her cognitive therapist. It mellowed the anxiety that perpetually hovered, ready to pounce at a moment's notice.

During the next thirty minutes, she sipped two cups of coffee from the only coffee mug she owned. It was covered in a repeating pattern she found soothing and had a smooth lip that was just the right thickness. When she was finished, she hand-washed the mug and tucked it back inside its home for use tomorrow, then turned to make breakfast. On the single gas burner, she scrambled two eggs for thirty-seven seconds, fried crispy bacon, and toasted a slice of bread golden brown before smearing on butter.

Neve enjoyed the same breakfast every morning. It was a habit that made grocery shopping predictable and kept waste to a minimum. Her relationship with eggs, however, was a delicate one. She could only tolerate their texture if they were fully cooked. The unwelcome squish against her teeth or surprise of a runny yolk had the power to derail her entire morning. To avoid that outcome, she overcooked them until the edges crisped and turned a deep golden brown. Gordon Ramsay would have been disgusted, but to Neve, they were perfection.

As she finished washing and drying her plate and silverware, the morning sun beat through the side windows of the van. Neve made the short journey to the house, eager to get started on the work that lay ahead as she got it ready for its next occupant. Neve depended on the rental income to supplement her commissions and knew it would do no good to drag her feet.

"The sooner I finish, the sooner I can leave." She gave herself an impromptu pep talk as she stood in front of the house. She hesitated on the front step, gripping the key to the new lock a locksmith had installed the night before a bit too tightly, as her eyes drank in the details that had escaped her yesterday. The rough coconut husk welcome mat she stood on read "Bring Coffee, TP, and Ammo—or Keep Out!" The glass of the front door had been reinforced with rebar, and there was a second deadbolt on the front door.

She slid the new key into the lock and pushed open the door with one hand. From down the hall, she heard a muffled squawk and the faint rustle of the bird's feathers. Ignoring him, Neve walked down the hallway to access the attic and glanced up at the rope coiled around two metal hooks. She wiped her damp hands on her shorts and unwrapped it, tugging down on the collapsible ladder. It creaked as if it hadn't been opened in decades, and the metal squealed in protest as she forced it down, making her shoulders tighten and clench protectively closer to her ears. She padded up the wobbly stairs and sneezed into the dusty air, feeling for the string of the lightbulb just inside the attic. Tugging down hard, the light flickered on a second before the rotted cord fell into a heap at her feet.

The warm yellow light from the bulb cast a nostalgic glow over the boxes stacked along one wall. Relics from her childhood lined another one, turning the attic into a moldering time capsule. She walked over to the bouncy horse she'd been told she'd adored as a toddler. Neve reached out and pushed its flank down, her fingers cutting a clean line through the dust. The springs squealed in protest as they made the plastic animal break out into a rollicking trot. Moving on, she made her way to the stack of boxes she and Talulah had carefully labeled and tucked away years ago.

"Why don't we store them for now?" Talulah had suggested after Neve turned eighteen and had decided she couldn't bear to live in the house, but hadn't been ready to sell it either.

Neve was dumbfounded by the suggestion. Keeping items she had no interest in seemed pointless, yet she perceived Talulah would feel better if she showed some attachment to her father's belongings. Keen to understand, she asked, "Why should I hold on to things just because Dad found them useful?"

"It's never a good decision to get rid of personal items when you are distressed. You might regret it later," Talulah reasoned as she sealed a box labeled Ellis Personal.

"I won't." Neve was resolute, her answer flat.

"Let's see how you feel in a year or two. Just in case you change your mind."

Neve doubted she would, but didn't argue. "Alright," she'd said, and so the boxes were stacked in neat columns and there they remained, untouched for decades. Now, an impressive gathering of dust bunnies frolicked on them and the boxes had shifted and settled. She reached out for one and picked at the disintegrating tape that had lost its usefulness years ago, squeezing it into a sticky ball. With a frown, she shook it off, dislodging the offensive mass that rolled to a stop at a wall of studs sandwiched with pink fiberglass insulation.

In the low light of the single overhead bulb, she pried open a box that was filled with spiral-bound notebooks. She pulled one out and opened it with a gasp. Her father's distinctive handwriting covered the pages in neat lines. On the front of the leather-bound journal, the year was branded into the hide. Neve paged through the first few yellowing pages, and an unexpected rush of emotion filled her at seeing the familiar letters and the slant of the I's and T's she'd recognize anywhere. She flipped through it, her eyes scanning the pages, but they were gibberish, filled with technical jargon, formula calculations, and diagrams that made little sense to her.

Beads of sweat broke out at her hairline, and she decided to take the box of journals downstairs to escape the heat that was already stifling. She stopped to count the rows of remaining boxes. There were fourteen total. As she headed toward the stairs, she determined it would take her a week to go through them all if she was willing to tackle two each day. Neve found numbers soothing, a predictable language that always had a correct answer. Math had rules and a sense of order that was far easier to understand than the messy, convoluted battleground of human emotion.

Neve walked the box down the creaky stairs and into the sunroom, setting it down on a TV tray. She planned to take a closer look at the journals after she fed the bird but noticed the cage was empty.

"Perry?" she called out, scanning the room for him.

"Finally, you decide to grace me with your presence," he scoffed from the top of the potted lemon tree that had camouflaged him. "I'm starving. I could really go for a breakfast sandwich from the Boardwalk Deli."

"Well, you will have to settle for ZuBird Natural," Neve said as she busied herself pulling out a small plastic scoop from the container of parrot pellets she found in the kitchen. After reading the directions, she filled the dish clipped to the side of the cage with the appropriate amount indicated on the label.

"Revolting!" Peregrine squawked his displeasure. "I've been subsisting on these burnt pellets for days. What I wouldn't give for a twenty-one-day aged ribeye and a glass of Montrachet."

Neve picked up the container and read aloud, "ZuBird Natural Parrot Pellets provide a healthy diet for African Greys who need a well-balanced and nutrient-dense food source, supporting their unique dietary needs and high intelligence."

"At least they got one thing right." He sniffed, raising his beak in indignation.

Neve chuckled despite herself. "It's official. ZuBird Natural Parrot Pellets has just officially confirmed your genius-level IQ."

He let out an irritated warble. Perry was moody but seemed to add a dash of humor to her otherwise solitary life. Remembering he'd made two food references in the span of five minutes, she thought it might be a way to win him over. "Okay, okay. I'll be making my weekly Wednesday grocery run later today. Do you know what is safe for you to eat?"

He preened in front of her as a look of bored resignation took over his features. "The safe route was never my forte."

"Let's consult the Google machine." Neve slid her phone out and opened a search tab. A few minutes later, after speed-reading four articles, she pulled her focus away from the phone and said with a grimace, "You're not going to like this."

"Pray tell what fresh hell awaits me."

"It says to feed you sixty percent pellets, twenty percent veggies, and twenty percent select fruits, with a few seeds and nuts mixed in."

Peregrine hung his tiny feathered head and let out an over-the-top, melodramatic sigh. "Great, I'm trapped inside the body of a vegan."

"Perry, there are worse things in the world to be," Neve said, feeling a sense of déjà vu trickling in. It was the same phrase Aunt Lu used to comfort her after she'd received her official autism diagnosis five years ago in her early forties.

That day, she remembered sitting as still as possible on the examination table. Each tiny movement made the paper under her thighs crinkle, an irritating sound that grated on her nerves and tightened the coil of tension growing in her chest. Just as she rose to her feet to escape it, Dr. Randolph breezed into the room with a sunny "hello," settling herself on a rolling stool.

It was time for her annual check-up. Neve had come prepared, notebook in hand, her questions written in her perfect penmanship, ready to tackle the appointment with a sense of control.

"Neve, do you have any questions or health concerns?"

She flipped open her notebook and asked a total of seventeen questions that Dr. Randolph patiently answered. It was the final one that made the physician pause.

"How does one go about getting a diagnosis for Autism Spectrum Disorder?"

"Why do you ask?"

"There's something different about me." Her gaze flicked to the doctor and then away as she continued. "I've always felt a few steps out of sync with everyone else. I struggle to read facial expressions, and when someone's actions don't line up with what they're saying, it completely throws me."

Dr. Randolph thoughtfully chewed on the inside of her cheek before answering. "Typically, a diagnosis would require a visit to a clinical psychologist, psychiatrist, or neurologist. If you are interested, I'd be happy to connect you with a colleague who focuses on late-diagnosis autism and the way it presents in females. She'd likely do a neurological assessment, take a detailed family history, and use a few diagnostic tools. But to be clear, there isn't one test that can confirm autism. It requires more of a holistic approach."

"Oh." Neve stared down at the notebook. "I do not like uncertainty."

"I understand," she sympathized. "Unfortunately, autism is a spectrum with behaviors that can vary widely from person to person." Dr. Randolph explained, "And, it presents very differently in women since they have the ability to mask behaviors to fit in and be more accommodating in social situations."

"Hmm." She carefully considered the doctor's reply. "Social situations were the worst," she admitted, her eyes glued to a spot on the floor as she was lost in the past. "I spent hours in my bedroom, rehearsing the right things to say. I wrote down questions on notecards and brainstormed conversation starters. I just wanted to be… normal."

"I bet that was exhausting."

"It was," Neve said, her voice a cracked whisper. She blinked several times, trying to absorb the information she was being given, but found the growing lump in her throat made it more difficult to swallow. "I thought you said it was anxiety."

"It could be, or it could be autism, or even both," she clarified. "Women are often misdiagnosed with conditions like anxiety and depression before autism is even considered. There just haven't been enough studies."

"It's not fair. Medicine always seems to fail women."

Dr. Randolph nodded her head in agreement. "It does, and I am sorry." The doctor's kind eyes settled on Neve with such sincere understanding Neve had to look away. "I will personally reach out to Dr. Monroe and see if she can get you on her schedule. A diagnosis might bring you relief and validate your experiences."

True to her word, a referral was given and Dr. Monroe saw her right away. After Neve answered an hour-long series of questions, she was given another pamphlet of documents to have a close family member complete. Aunt Talulah had dutifully returned them to the office, and six weeks later, Neve was brought back in for a follow-up.

After exchanging pleasantries, Dr. Monroe said, "There is enough evidence to support a diagnosis of Autism Spectrum Disorder."

"Oh." Neve laced her fingers together, casting her gaze downward. She let out a hot exhalation, feeling a heaviness set in.

"How do you feel?" Dr. Monroe prompted when the silence stretched out as Neve absorbed this new diagnosis.

"I guess, on one hand, I feel validated. But on the other, it's like I've been standing in a dark corner, shouting for years that something was wrong, and no one ever bothered to listen."

"That is valid. In medicine, it is sometimes hard to see the forest for the trees." The doctor nodded gently in agreement as she empathized with Neve. "Unfortunately, diagnosis is sometimes more of an art than a science. The truth is that several of the signs and symptoms you exhibit are present in other neurological disorders. But the greater truth is that you are a bright and highly functioning human being." Dr. Monroe leaned closer. "Now that we know, there are plenty of resources I can offer you. Cognitive therapy can help as well as behavioral therapy."

"Ugh." Neve let out a heavy sigh of frustration. "That sounds like torture."

"Nothing has to be decided today," Dr. Monroe added. "A diagnosis is simply a tool for greater understanding."

Peregrine's obnoxious squawk startled her from the past, and Neve covered her ears with her hands while he let out two more raucous squabbles.

"Must you make all that noise?"

"My apologies," he replied with a barking cough. "It's the other bird, but I will see what I can do to control it."

Neve studied the brown leather journal that rested next to Sheila's bug-out bag. Her intense focus drew the former conman's full attention.

"Ooh! What do you have there? Is that a secret diary? Let me guess… Are Sheila's sexual conquests detailed in it line by scandalous line?"

"Perry, you are giving me a serious case of the icks right now." Neve shuddered. "It's not Sheila's. The notebooks belonged to my father."

She slid closer and brushed her hand across the soft leather of the book on top of the stack. Perry's ridiculousness faded away as Neve muttered under her breath, "This is simply a tool for greater understanding." Pushing away her reservations about violating his privacy, she opened the book labeled 1989 and read the first entry.

January 14, 1989

Subject: Preliminary Findings on High-Dose Vitamin C and Copper Tripeptide Protocol and its Effects on Tumor Growth

Notes:

Tested high-dose Vitamin C and copper-containing tripeptide on cultured tumor cells (derived from HeLa cells). Initial results confirm a 30% reduction in cellular proliferation over 48 hours. Promising outcome but replication is needed.

Considering pathways of oxidative stress as the underlying mechanism. Reactive oxygen species seem to mediate apoptosis.

There was a detailed diagram of a tumor cell composed of shrinking circles and bubble-shaped protrusions with arrows pointing to mitochondria. Neve pulled the drawing closer, appreciating the attention he put into the shading of the medical illustration. It made the complex medical language easier to digest. She turned the page, and the next notation claimed her undivided attention.

Personal Reflection:

Ethical ramifications of using HeLa cells still plague me. If there were an alternative, I would seek it out, but there is none and so I am stuck waffling between my own conscience and the fact that a breakthrough could help millions of cancer sufferers.

N.L. (my child, female, age 12) spent the afternoon in my lab. Though she was completely engrossed in drawing molecules on the chalkboard, she managed to construct a stunning visual diagram of the Krebs cycle from memory! I noticed she rocks back and forth on the balls of her feet and bites on her bottom lip when focused, almost as if it helps her think.

I can't help but wonder if her intense focus is unusual. She doesn't make eye contact often and seems singularly focused on drawing. Maybe she's just obsessively quirky and awkward like her father? Her ability to absorb knowledge at this age is remarkable. Maybe I can steer and mold her into the brilliant scientist I know she could be.

The blatant longing for her to follow in his footsteps written in his handwriting made her adolescent frustrations rear back up. Neve's mind drifted to one of the last conversations she ever had with her father. It had been less of a conversation and more of an argument, and since he'd died, she never lived a day where she didn't feel a twinge of regret.

She'd just celebrated her fifteenth birthday, and her incredible academic prowess had landed her in the talented and gifted program. At her father's urging, she'd been allowed to take the PSAT exam early, and she'd just received her results and was eager to share them. She rushed home, finding Ellis seated in the sunroom with a stack of medical charts and an open journal in front of him. When he heard Neve enter, he held up one finger, then hastily scribbled a few more notes in the charts before closing them and turning to his daughter. Bursting with pride, Neve placed her test scores in his hand.

"Are these?" His eyebrows waggled as he scanned the document. "Wow. A 24! On your first try? That's incredible, Nomo! MIT and the Ivy's will surely come calling! With these grades, you'll have every door open to you. We need more brilliant female minds like yours in science."

Neve let out a long breath. She'd been bracing for this conversation for a while now, but she still felt unprepared. Her father wasn't used to an argument that didn't align with his own. Knowing it was now or never, she squared her shoulders and soldiered on. "If every door will be open to me, I'd rather choose another."

"What?" He set aside his pen and turned toward her, giving Neve his full attention. "We've been planning for medical school since you were in kindergarten!" He ran a hand through his hair. "But engineering would also suit you."

"No, Dad," Neve said, her voice small but sure. "*You've* been planning medical school. I want to go to *art* school."

"Art school?" He stared at her, dumbfounded, and his direct gaze burned into her, making her uncomfortable.

"Why is this a surprise? Ruben Angelica saw great promise in my work. If you had allowed me to attend École Artiste for longer than a year, I would have already had my first solo show by now, but instead, I've had to settle for summer workshops!"

"I'm sorry, but art isn't a career. You can't support yourself with paper and pencils. You need a degree. I won't be around forever, and you must focus on a sustainable career path. As a hobby, sure, drawing is a great stress release, but not as a vocation."

Neve's jaw clenched, and her shoulders tensed as she pleaded with him, "Art is my passion. It's the one thing that feels right."

"Passion doesn't pay the bills, Nomo."

"Stop calling me that. My name is Nevermore," she gritted out.

"Fine, *Nevermore*." He let out a heavy sigh. "Your doodling can be done on the weekends."

"Doodling?" She felt her anger rise. "It's not doodling! When was the last time you even looked at my work? You're so busy with your protocols and clinical studies, you don't even know what I am capable of. Ruben Angelica said I showed real talent and promise."

"I should have never let Isla put those ideas in your head," he bit out. "What happens when you're thirty years old and broke? Living off ramen and wondering why you didn't use your God-given talent for something worthwhile? You're brilliant! You could do anything, and you want to waste it on… on…"

"On something that makes me happy? On something that I am extremely proficient at?"

Ellis pinched the bridge of his nose. "Happiness is fleeting. Stability lasts. You can't just waltz through life doing whatever makes you feel good. That's not how the world works. It rewards breakthroughs. It rewards education."

"No. That's how *you* think the world works. I don't want to waste away in a lab following in your footsteps because I am too afraid to take my own."

"My footsteps would lead you to success, to security. To a future."

"They would lead me to a future where I am miserable."

He gazed down at the panel of test scores again.

"You want to throw it all away? Artists don't get paid what they are worth until they're dead."

"The money doesn't matter to me."

"Oh, I promise you, it will. Eventually," he mumbled under his breath.

"No, it won't!"

"I will not allow you to use your college fund for art school. Go if you must, but you will not have the support of my resources." He added, "When you come back to your senses and want to consider a more sustainable career path, then we can talk."

Infuriated, Neve let out an angry huff, then turned on her heel and slammed the door shut behind her, rattling the photographs in their frames. In her bedroom, she collapsed against the wall with a groan of frustration and slid down to the floor. The concept of having the next fifty years of her life already planned for her was too much to bear. A tightness spread through her body when she considered the path ahead of her. At that moment, she hated her father for being so singularly focused, so unwilling to listen and compromise.

For Neve, drawing wasn't a hobby; it was a lifeline, a language she was fluent in while she existed in a world that felt foreign. The moment her graphite touched paper, the chaotic buzz around her softened into an acceptable hum. Every line she sketched, every shadow she shaded, felt like freedom. It was her safe space where she could control every detail, every shape, and every reality on her own terms. It brought a sense of order to the world she craved.

When Neve worked, time melted away. In a world that was too loud, too fast, too bright, drawing was her sanctuary. It was the one thing that always felt right. It didn't demand explanations like her father did. It didn't make judgments like the people at school. It simply existed, waiting for her, welcoming her with open arms. Drawing was perfect in its solitary simplicity. It was her center. It was her home, and she wouldn't let anyone, not even her father, take it away from her.

CHAPTER
FIVE

LATER THAT EVENING, after the Helping Hands Food Pantry had emptied the living room of all the canned goods and bottled water stores, Neve peeled the plastic off Sheila's sofa and collapsed down into it with a sigh. There was the rustle of feathers, then Perry alighted near her elbow on a dead tree branch that was mounted upright in an orange bucket of hardened concrete.

On the coffee table sat a plate with an apple cut into nine equal slices and a glass of water. Neve reached out and offered a slice to Perry, then retrieved the purple geode from her father's messenger bag. It fit perfectly in her palm, and as she held it up to the light, it sparkled in the last rays of sun that streaked through the dirty windows. Surprisingly, the faceted stone tingled where it touched her skin, and she stared down at it, remembering the first time her father laid it in her hand when she was thirteen years old.

He had summoned her to his workbench in the

garage, where Neve perched on a steel stool, hooking the heels of her hiking boots onto the bottom rung.

"Close your eyes." Her father's voice had taken on a playful tone she wasn't accustomed to. Ellis LaRue wasn't one for games. This departure from his usually serious demeanor intrigued her instantly, but it was the next words that made a frisson of joy well up. "I have a surprise for you."

Neve quickly squeezed them shut, eager to receive it.

"Now hold out your hands," he directed, and she tentatively reached out, trying not to cringe and worry about the texture of the item he would place in them. She'd gotten adept at hiding her discomfort, especially in front of the kids at school who labeled her a weirdo and called her the Robot. The teasing increased each year, especially targeting the hiking boots she wore daily, even for gym class. The blisters on her heels from having to run track in them were a small price to pay in order to avoid direct contact with the germ-riddled cesspool found inside a junior high locker room.

The object he placed in her hands was round and about the size of a tennis ball, and she brushed the pads of her thumbs across the rough surface, trying to figure out what it was.

"You can open your eyes."

Neve stared down at an unremarkable gray rock, keenly aware her father was waiting for some type of positive reaction from her. She lifted it up and let the words slip from her tongue, even though they were a question. "Thank… you?"

Ellis chuckled, and his blue eyes crinkled at the corners. "What do you think it is?"

"It's a rock, Dad."

"True," he offered. "But what if I told you it's so much more than that?"

"It's a *gray* rock, Dad."

Another chuckle slipped from him, and Neve yearned to ask him what was so funny as the subtleties of humor were often lost on her. Ellis reached out for the hammer that hung from a hook on the pegboard behind his workbench. The pegboard of tools was her favorite part of the garage. Neve adored the organization of it. Each item had a home, a place it belonged, and she enjoyed helping him clean up and restore order when they were finished with projects. Ellis walked over to his gleaming toolbox, tugged open a drawer, and retrieved a chisel. Back at the bench, he grasped the chisel with a clenched fist and tapped on it with the hammer. It chipped and then, with a satisfying crack, the stone severed into two pieces, each falling open and onto the bench in front of them. Hidden inside the ho-hum gray exterior of the geode were thousands of bright purple facets that sparkled like diamonds in the sunlight.

"This is a good lesson, Nomo," he'd said, handing her half of the sparkling rock. "You can't always judge a person by what you see on the outside, and now we both have a reminder."

She stared down at it in awe, feeling a sense of

kinship with the rock. Most people would have walked right by the rock, preferring to collect ones that were more beautiful, having rings of petrified minerals on the surface. Her father had not. He'd been able to see beyond the average exterior to the gleaming treasure inside. Her father sometimes seemed like the only person who could see the same quality in her.

Ellis picked up the other half of the geode and held it up. "Two parts of one whole." Neve held her half to his, and when they connected back together, only the crack running around the outside remained. The geode tingled in her hand when it connected to its other half, and she jolted back as if burned.

Ellis's brow furrowed deeply as confusion set in. "Interesting. Did you feel that too? The tingle?"

Neve nodded solemnly. Her blue eyes were huge in her face. "Probably just static electricity discharging."

"That is a good hypothesis. How did you get so smart?" Her father grinned, stroking her cheek with his other hand, and Neve leaned into him, just barely closing her eyes. Her father's touch was gentle and the only one she didn't recoil from. He set his geode on the workbench, and Neve busied herself with returning the tools to their proper places. When they were finished cleaning up, Neve took her half into the house and into her bedroom, placing it on her dresser in a place of honor. There it sat until she'd had to pack it away the night he disappeared.

Neve closed her eyes to block out the pain that always seemed to accompany her memories of her father. When she opened them, it was Perry's excitable squawk that grounded her.

"Neve, where did you go just then?" His concern softened his intrusive question.

"Nowhere," she mumbled in response, being evasive as she set the precious stone on the empty coffee table. Neve gazed at it, feeling safer staring at the inanimate object than she knew she would be meeting the bird's eyes. She shuttered herself away, forcing Perry to change tactics. He settled on flattery, hoping it would draw her out.

"I do like what you've done with the place," he warbled.

"Thank you. It *is* nice not to be surrounded by gas masks and food rations," Neve admitted as she took stock of the freshly decluttered living room. "We've gained approximately seventeen square feet in this room alone." She drummed her fingers on the end table as a sense of restlessness cued up. It drove her to her feet, and she began to rock gently and wring her hands.

"What's got you so antsy?"

"Without the rental income from Sheila, I need to double down on my art commissions, and my agent, Lucinda, set up a meeting tomorrow at Elysian Atelier," she answered. "I'm hoping she'll take some pieces on consignment and maybe consider giving me a solo show."

"Ooh! That's a very prestigious gallery," Perry said. "Have you ever had a solo show before?"

"No." She cast her gaze down. "But it's vital to land

my first one before I turn fifty, or I run the danger of becoming irrelevant in the art world."

"It is? Who made that rule?"

"I did," she answered. It was a goal she'd first thought was attainable when she carefully wrote it down on the index card she'd taped to her visor when she'd purchased the sprinter van over five years ago. She'd sold just enough drawings to upgrade her conversion van and, after watching endless YouTube videos, was able to DIY the interior construction.

Neve had become accustomed to campground living with her Aunt Talulah, who was a traveling spiritual medium and gained custody of Neve when she was fifteen. They spent weekends and summers on the road together, often sleeping at campgrounds in a Volkswagen van that had been converted into a camper.

Neve tried to move back into her childhood home when she turned eighteen and became an adult, but there were too many ghosts there. Instead, she purchased her own Volkswagen van she modified into a home on wheels, and Talulah helped her find a renter. Between the rental income and her art, she was able to sustain a modest nomadic lifestyle for decades, which suited Neve perfectly. Now that her livelihood was in jeopardy, fresh fears cued up.

"I'm so nervous," Neve confided as she paced, chewing on her bottom lip.

A bellowed demand from Perry shifted her focus. "Question the premise!" he churred and then repeated, "Question the premise!"

"Great work, Perry! You unlocked the repetitive dialogue achievement," Neve muttered.

"I can't help it," Perry warbled. "It's instinctive! Damn this tiny bird brain!" He thrashed his wings in distress and, when he settled back down, added, "But truly, you put far too much pressure on yourself."

"I know he's not here to see it, but I want to make my father proud," she admitted.

Neve was on a mission to prove the career path she'd chosen would lead to the same type of success her father had commanded in his own. Her scribbled dream on that faded index card had once been forefront in her mind, but it shriveled over the years, like so many of her other dreams did after her father died. Securing a one-woman show now would give Neve the validation she craved. But most of all, it would prove to her father and to the rest of the world that she had made the right choice all those years ago.

The next afternoon, Neve was a bundle of nerves as she sat in the driver's seat parked in the lot, staring at the entrance to Elysian Atelier. She pulled the card out of her bag and stared down at it, willing the meeting to go according to plan. The idea of carrying on an entire conversation with a stranger was so daunting that she had spent the past two evenings meticulously crafting questions and rehearsing responses. She wanted them ingrained in her mind in case their conversation reached a dreaded lull.

Five minutes before their appointment, she gathered up her leather portfolio that contained her latest charcoal renderings and walked to the entrance. Her movements were precise but stiff, as though she were rehearsing each step in her head before taking it. Neve pulled the gallery's leaded glass door open, setting off a melodic chime that announced her arrival as she stepped inside. Counting the steps as she took them, letting the numbers distract her from the pit forming in her stomach, she'd just reached fourteen when her path forward was blocked by the hammered copper desk where a pretty receptionist was seated and speaking on the phone in a hushed tone.

While she waited, Neve's eyes darted around the space, taking in the clean white walls, the carefully arranged paintings, and the minimalist sculptures sitting on well-lit pedestals. Every object seemed perfectly curated and intentional. The gallery was modern and sparsely furnished, with benches featuring sharp lines and dramatic silhouettes. Its sophisticated colors captivated the eyes, but Neve was terrified to sit on any of it.

"Can I help you?"

Neve hesitated a moment before stepping forward to speak to the receptionist, rehearsing her response in her mind. "I'm here to see Lisa Tremaine. My name is Nevermore LaRue, and I specialize in hyperrealistic drawings. I have a one pm appointment to discuss the possibility of representation or hosting a solo show at this gallery."

The receptionist tilted her head, intrigued by the depth of Neve's direct and straightforward reply. "Of course." She stood and added, "Please follow me." Neve was led into a bright office with wide windows and a low-slung desk with a mid-century modern chair. She sat down and pulled the portfolio onto her lap like a baby, afraid to let it rest on the floor.

A few minutes later, the door swung open. Hinged in the center and nearly twice the width of a standard door, it made for a dramatic entrance. Lisa strode over confidently, dressed in white from head to toe with chunky silver jewelry. Her silver hair was cut into an ultra-short pixie cut, and her thick black glasses framed dark blue eyes the color of denim. "I'm Lisa Tremaine. It's lovely to meet you, Neve. Hyperrealism is a challenging style. I cannot wait to see your pieces. Lucinda speaks so highly of your talent."

Lucinda was tasked with coordinating with galleries and selling Neve's charcoal hyperrealistic drawings. She believed in Neve's talent, but the market was especially tough lately, and Neve had been living lean and filling her financial gaps by taking on commissions of pet portraits. It felt a bit like selling out, but it paid the bills.

Lisa patted the desk, inviting Neve closer with a warm smile as she scrutinized her with curiosity. "Let me take a look."

Neve hoisted the portfolio up onto the desk and unzipped it. Then she sat back down, her back ramrod straight. Encased in their archival protective sleeves were twenty of her latest pieces. Lisa stood, cupping her hands on her incredibly sharp hips as she leaned closer and studied the first one.

Lisa chewed the inside of her bottom lip, narrowing her eyes as she appreciated each line in silence. She gently flipped the page by the edge and drank in the next one, slowly making her way through all twenty pieces without so much as a word. With each passing second, Neve felt her anxiety grow and a flush of heat walking up her torso. It was always difficult for her to be vulnerable enough to open her artwork up for criticism. She hated this part of the process that left her feeling completely exposed to a virtual stranger. To keep it in check, Neve focused on the floor tiles in front of her, daring to flick her gaze up each time she heard Lisa turn a page.

When she was finished, Lisa gathered the portfolio in her hands and set it back on the coffee table between them, opening it to the first page. Then Lisa took the chair across from Neve and leaned forward, her eyebrows lifting in genuine astonishment. "Your work is… just… remarkable," she finally said, tracing her fingers along the edges of the sleeve, careful not to touch the artwork itself. "You've captured every detail —the straight lines, the shimmering reflection of the sunset in the windows, and the way the light bends. It's astonishing. How long does a piece like this take you to create?" Lisa asked, tapping the next page where a detailed rendering of Hotel Ambrosia captured every brick, gargoyle, and piling with impressive detail. Her positive critique made joy crackle through Neve. She swallowed her fear and felt her jaw unclench. When it came to discussing her artwork, she could speak endlessly and without preparation. It was the one topic of conversation that always flowed naturally.

"Approximately ninety, eight-hour days," Neve replied earnestly. "I track my time on an app and work in two-hour increments with a fifteen-minute break in between. It's the optimal schedule for the focus required to do the piece justice."

"Impressive. Your precision shows in the work. Are architectural renderings your only subject matter?"

She felt her hope fizzle and looked down, avoiding eye contact. "I have also recently delved into animal portraits." She pulled her sketchbook out of her messenger bag and offered it to Lisa. A smiling photo of a boxer with a tennis ball in his mouth was so vivid you could almost feel the fuzz of the ball and the drool on his tongue. "Exceptional," Lisa murmured as she considered it. "Your work is extraordinary. Truly. But have you shown your work in any galleries of our caliber before?"

"No," Neve said, shaking her head. "I've been focusing on perfecting my technique. But Lucinda researched your gallery extensively and says your emphasis on contemporary realism aligns with mine."

Neve reached into her messenger bag and pulled out a neatly typed packet, which she handed to Lisa. Each section was meticulously organized, with bullet points, timelines, and proposed budgets.

Lisa skimmed the document, then looked up at Neve, her admiration deepening. "You're incredibly thorough. This is more detailed than some professional proposals I've seen. Tell me, what would your ideal collaboration look like?"

Neve straightened her posture into an even more upright position, her head tilted to the side as she considered the question before answering. "I want a solo show," she said. "A full exhibition with proper lighting and high-quality frames. There should be printed programs with artist's statements for each piece, and I'd like to ensure the work is priced appropriately for its value."

Lisa's lips twitched in amusement at the comphreshive answer, but she didn't laugh. "I admire your clarity. It sounds like you have a strong vision for how your work should be presented."

Neve nodded vigorously. "Yes. Presentation is crucial because the conditions it is viewed under influence how people perceive the art. It must be perfect."

Lisa glanced again at the drawings laid out on the table. "Your work deserves nothing less. However, hosting a solo exhibition is a significant undertaking for both the artist and the gallery. There's marketing, logistics, and the matter of ensuring the right audience attends. Have you considered how you'd help promote your work?"

"I, um… The truth is… I struggle with promoting my work. That's why I have Lucinda. I am an artist, not a marketing expert."

Lisa chuckled at her very blunt response. "While I can understand your expertise does not extend to promotion, we usually require the artist to have an established fan base on at least one social media platform."

"Oh." Neve's bubble burst and she turned to the portfolio and began to run the zipper down the length of it to close it. Lisa reached out one well-manicured hand to prevent her from closing it all the way. Confused by her response, Neve was forced to meet her gaze.

"Here's what I propose. Let's start by featuring two or three of your pieces in our Emerging Artists' wing. Next week, the Ruben Angelica show opens and we anticipate drawing record crowds. It'll give your work exposure and help us gauge audience response. If it's successful, then we can discuss plans for a solo exhibition."

"Ruben Angelica?" Neve asked. "My childhood nanny was one of his muses, and she took me to meet him when I was young. He was the first adult to truly take me seriously and recognize the potential in my work. Ruben was responsible for my acceptance to École Artiste."

Lisa let out a delighted gasp of surprise. "How incredible! Now that you mention it, I can see the influence. There is a meticulous attention to detail in your renderings that is reminiscent of his paintings. The texture in your shading is definitely a nod to his brilliance."

"Thank you." Neve was pleased by the praise. "That is the highest compliment you could ever give me. He was a legend!"

"Yes, he was. The most prolific modern painter in Florida's history. Ruben insisted on excellence and handled every aspect of his own career, from negotiating with private collectors to setting up shows and private auctions. He actually bequeathed two of his paintings to the Tampa Museum of Modern Art, and they are on loan for our show as well. Considering your personal connection, it would be a full circle moment to debut your work next to his, don't you think?"

Neve's brow furrowed, her hands flexing into tight balls as she considered it. "While it is not my initial preference," she said carefully, "I believe this is a great opportunity for me. May I have input on which pieces are selected and how they're displayed?"

"Of course," Lisa said. "Your input is vital."

Neve exhaled, her shoulders dropping from her ears to their natural resting place. "I find this proposal acceptable. Thank you."

"You may also be interested to know TMOM is giving an award during the event to one deserving up-and-coming artist. It's a five-figure grant that will allow the recipient to focus exclusively on their art, as it includes lodging and a monthly stipend. I believe you have a real shot at winning it."

"I agree." It was easy for Neve to have bold confidence in her work. "Winning is a definite possibility, though I can't say that with certainty, as I don't know the caliber of the other artists competing."

"True, but you can't let that stop you. And who knows what other doors it may open?" Lisa smiled warmly. "I will forward you the details. I'm excited to work with you, Nevermore."

Over the next hour, Neve helped Lisa choose the three pieces that would debut at the show and sent them to be framed. When they were finished, Neve drifted out of the gallery on cloud nine. She was going to have her artwork debuted next to Ruben Angelica's. He'd been one of the first to see artistic greatness in her and was one of the reasons she'd pursued a career in the fine arts. The opportunity was a bucket list moment, and she couldn't believe her luck.

CHAPTER

SIX

THE NEXT MORNING, Neve was back in the sunroom after breakfast, the stack of journals still sitting where she left them. Part of Neve wanted to dive into them and get a better understanding of the father she never knew as an adult, while the other part was the scared child who wasn't sure she could handle more of his clinical observations of her behavior as if she were one of his experiments.

Deep down, Neve was still the little girl who yearned for his presence. Having lived without him for decades now, she'd elevated him to saint status in her mind, and she was afraid to discover anything that would taint her memory of him.

She cut open another dusty box, this one filled with his clothing. A blue button-down was on top, riddled with moth holes. Neve shook it out into the air and sneezed at the particles of dust dancing in a stream of warm morning light.

From his cage, Perry sneezed three times in quick succession.

"Godzilla!" Neve shouted out after the third one. It was Talulah's quirky version of *Gesundheit*. When he sneezed again, Neve said, "Now you're just doing it for attention."

"I would do no such thing!" he chirped back, outraged at her accusation. "It's all the dust." Perry continued to complain as he preened his greasy feathers with his beak. "It makes me so itchy!" He expressed a loud chirp of displeasure, then picked at the feathers under his wing that hung exceptionally flat. "There is a white ceramic vessel under the sink in the guest lavatory." Perry shook out his feathers with a rustle, then bobbed up and down on his perch, getting more animated.

"How do you know that?"

"It's strange. The bird and I, our souls, seem to be intertwined. I still have all my human memories intact, but there's also this other consciousness. I am fully cognizant of the bird's life with Sheila. I know things I shouldn't and have memories that aren't mine. It's deeply unsettling."

"Weird," Neve said, her tone one of confused perplexity. She walked down the hall to the guest bathroom and rooted around under the sink. "I found it! What do you want me to do with it?"

"Fill it with warm water, silly girl. It is time for my bath!" Neve filled the bowl at the sink, testing the temperature on the back of her wrist. It took several moments to walk the heavy container back to the sunroom without any of the water sloshing over the side.

"Where should I put it? In your cage?"

Perry let out a long, exasperated whistle of a sigh. "Of course. Why shouldn't I hurl my precious bird brain against these prison grates? Brilliant idea."

"Don't be such a drama queen, Perry."

"It's the only way I can seem to get what I want around here," he huffed, inching back up his perch, throwing a temper tantrum that Neve found ridiculous. After he was through whining, he made a valid suggestion, "I need more space. The cage is too restrictive. How about the coffee table?"

"See? Was it so difficult to ask for what you wanted?"

"I guess not."

Neve lowered the heavy bowl onto the coffee table and moved her father's journals to a haphazard pile on top of the box. When she opened his cage, Perry took flight immediately and glided to it, perching on the edge of the white ceramic dish. He let out a low warble of delight, then a mix of clicks and soft whistles as he hopped into the warm water. He splashed, sending droplets flying in every direction, several of which landed on Neve, who took a step back, staring down at them on her hand in repulsion.

"Hey! This is supposed to be your bath, mister! Not mine." Ignoring her, Perry dipped his beak in, sucking up water, then sprayed it on his chest while he used his powerful wings to flick more of it to his feathers. Tiny, crystal droplets clung to his red tail feathers before cascading down, refracting the light into tiny rainbows.

He spread his wings wide and shook vigorously, and the water dropped back to the dish gently like rain. A sudden flap of his wings sent a misty spray outward, accompanied by a sharp, gleeful squawk that echoed through the room. Neve frowned in mild irritation, but her attention was quickly diverted by the trill of her cell phone. The ringtone revealed it was her Aunt Talulah calling. They had a standing monthly check-in, and with all the recent distractions, Neve had completely forgotten about it.

"Hello," Neve answered, cradling the phone between her ear and shoulder.

"Honey bee!" Talulah was soft-spoken, a calming presence in her life ever since she could remember. "Where are you today?" She was well versed in her niece's nomadic lifestyle, knowing the circuit she typically made. "Arizona?"

"Actually, I had to come back to Aura Cove. I'm at Dad's house."

"What?" Talulah questioned, "Why?"

"There was an issue with the tenant."

"Sheila?" Talulah had an incredible memory. "She's been the perfect renter. What happened?"

"She's dead."

"Oh." Talulah let out a surprised yelp, then quickly recovered. "I guess I'm not too surprised to hear she made her transition. She *was* gettin' up there, honey."

"It wasn't a peaceful one." Neve said with a frown. "She confronted a thief during a home invasion, shot him dead, and then, for the grand finale, had a heart attack."

There was a sharp intake of breath that let Neve know Talulah received her message but didn't know how to respond to it. After a long pause, her aunt offered, "Let me move some things around. Chakra and I can be there in a few hours." Chakra was her fluffy Samoyed dog that traveled with her.

"I don't think that's necessary," Neve said. "The Aura Cove PD was nice enough to help me find a crime scene cleaning company, and they took care of the mess."

"Oh, dear," Talulah grumbled. "I can't stand the idea of you there alone. I'm comin'."

"But I'm not alone," Neve informed as she flicked her gaze to Perry perched on the edge of the dish again, his feathers slightly ruffled and soaked to a dark sheen. He fluffed himself out with a loud whoosh, scattering water everywhere. His claws clicked softly on the dish's edge as he preened his wet feathers, nibbling and smoothing each one into place with an audible rustle, interspersed with quiet, satisfied clicks of his beak.

"You're not?"

"Sheila had a bird, an African Grey named Perry. Turns out, he's quite a companion."

A whir of delight came from Perry at her unexpected compliment.

Talulah chuckled, a light tinkling sound. Then,

remembering her visit to the gallery, Neve quickly blurted, "And I have some good news! Three of my pieces were selected to be included in the Emerging Artists' wing during the Ruben Angelica show."

"Really? That *is* fantastic news! How long does it run? I'll come see it."

"I know what you're doing," Neve said, her tone accusatory.

"What?" Talulah tried to feign innocence, but it was paper thin.

"You're coming to check up on me under the guise of attending my show. But I'll have you know I am doing as well as can be expected under the circumstances. I handled it all by myself. I've been getting it ready for my next tenant. I even ventured up to the attic and found some of Dad's old journals."

"You did?" Talulah's tone was somber, and Neve heard her swallow hard.

"It's strange to read what he's written after all this time. I know it's a violation of his privacy, but I was curious," Neve admitted. "There are notes about the experiments he was working on before he died and…" she paused, then shame crept into her voice, "even notes about me."

"Oh." Talulah's voice was low. "I bet that was difficult to read."

"Yes and no. In a way, it brings some peace. There are glimpses of him that help me see him so clearly. Details I've forgotten." Her tone shifted to a heartbroken whisper. "After all this time, I'll never understand why he's never tried to make contact with you."

"Remember, dear, I am merely a conduit and give a spirit a voice. The soul has to want to connect. Ellis has to initiate the contact."

"He's never reached out? Never asked about me?" Neve still had a hard time wrapping her head around the fact that her aunt was a famous medium with a direct channel to the afterworld, and the one person Neve wanted to speak to more than anything refused to come through.

"I wish it were different, too, but I don't think it is a good idea to open old wounds. Beatin' yourself up like this is not the answer. Your father is gone. Let' im rest. If he wanted to communicate with us, he would've."

"What if he is still out there? We never found his body."

"Neve, you can't keep punishin' yourself like this. I know you would like closure, but the truth is sometimes you don't get it. Life leaves a paper trail, and he hasn't used a credit card or a bank account for over thirty years. He's gone, and we both have to accept that."

Neve felt her frustration rise in her chest in the form of heat that made her clench her fist at her side and gently rock forward and back on the balls of her feet.

She shook her head no as Talulah continued to reason with her, begging her to understand. "You have a life to live. Why waste your time diggin' through the past when it won't change anything? Focus on your art. Ellis would want you to."

"That's not true. Dad *never* wanted me to be an artist."

Talulah let out a heavy exhalation before she continued. "That response came from fear and his misconception you'd become a starvin' one. I know, without a doubt, he would be proud of the life you have built for yourself." Talulah continued pleading her case.

After Neve listened to a five-minute diatribe on why she should focus forward, she finally asked, "Are you finished trying to convince me to move on?"

Talulah let out a morose chuckle. "I suppose I am."

Neve went straight to the heart of the matter with her usual directness. "Are you telling me not to read his journals because you are afraid of what I'll learn?"

The silence on the other end dragged out to an uncomfortable length before Talulah answered in a small voice, "No, I'm not. You have a tendency to hyper-fixate on things, and I don't want to see you miss out on opportunities in your own life because you are focused on your father."

Neve let out a heavy exhalation, clearly frustrated by the circular conversation they were stuck in.

"I can't stop you though, can I?" Talulah finally answered.

"No," Neve answered truthfully.

"Then at least keep me informed of what you find. If I can help, I promise I will."

"Can you try to reach Dad on the other side again?"

"If I say yes, can we change the subject?" Talulah muttered, defeated.

"We can." Neve was relieved by her request.

Then, without skipping a beat, Talulah asked, "How long are you stayin' in Aura Cove?"

"I'm not sure yet. Originally, it was only going to be for a few days, a week at the most. But the show changes things, and now, I've got my hands full learning how to care for an African Grey parrot."

Across the room, Perry let out a squawk of irritation as he continued to fluff himself, his clean feathers rustling.

Ignoring him, Neve continued, "I guess I'm going to stay as long as it takes to go through the boxes in the attic. I've put it off for far too long. It's time to face the past."

"Be careful with yourself, sweetheart. Diggin' up the past is dangerous, and you might not like whatcha find," Talulah warned. They chatted a bit longer, then Neve hung up the phone, proud she had stood her ground. Talulah was always overprotective, sensing danger for Neve around every corner, but this time there was an urgency in her tone that made the hairs on the back of Neve's neck stand up, and she wondered what her aunt wasn't telling her.

CHAPTER
SEVEN

FIVE DAYS LATER, Perry chirped and stroked his wings. He bit at his feathers, preening himself while he perched on top of the cage in the sunroom.

"Do you have to groom yourself right now?" Neve asked, her irritation slicing through the silence where she was engrossed in her laptop. On the screen, she was reading an email from an enraged client whose vitriol coated each word. The commission she shipped the day before never arrived, and the delay was made worse because the drawing was supposed to have been a focal point of decor at a surprise fiftieth birthday party.

Neve entered the tracking number, her fingers twitching as she clicked through the pages. After a few moments, the screen confirmed her worst fear: the package was stuck in Kentucky, despite the client having paid for next-day air.

"Ugh! You can't trust corporate America!" Neve muttered under her breath, clearly distressed.

A frustrated groan escaped her lips as she stared at the screen, wondering if a simple email response would suffice. The thought of making a phone call and engaging in dialogue with an irate customer shot a wave of anxiety straight through her. Confronted with any kind of high-pressure situation, her mind often went blank, words slipping away as apprehension took hold. Maybe Lucinda could call on her behalf and smooth out the rough edges? Neve forwarded the email with a short note and crossed her fingers.

"Why so glum?" Perry said.

"The commission I shipped yesterday never arrived. Apparently, next-day air means whenever they get to it in Kentucky." She reached down and tightened the ends of her braids, and Perry swooped closer, perching on the arm of a chair.

"Neve, my dear, it seems there is some negative cusp energy affecting you. Have you considered the cosmic implications of the upcoming planetary event?"

"What are you talking about, bird?" she muttered with a frown creasing her brow, eager for him to stop talking so she could focus.

"Mercury shifts into retrograde tomorrow for the next twenty-one days."

"So what? Astrology nonsense is more Aunt Talulah's wheelhouse." Neve discounted his suggestion without looking up from the screen. "She's a spiritual medium. You know… Haley Joel Osment? I see dead people?"

"Stop right there! Talulah LaRue is your aunt?" He

whistled in shock and his tiny jaw dropped. "I used to watch her videos on TikTok!"

"I'm not surprised. Three years ago, a video from a reading went viral, and now she does readings all over the country," Neve said, still distracted by the screen.

"I can't believe I didn't put it together until now!" Perry let out another squealing squawk, then quickly apologized. "Sorry, my bird twin takes control whenever I get too excited. He's the type of chap who loves to stare at his own reflection and is driven by his most basic instincts."

"That's got to feel weird."

"It does." He brushed it aside with one flap of his wing and whistled again, practically fangirling. "Holy cow! *You're* related to Talulah LaRue! Will I get to meet her someday?"

"You seriously buy into all that born-again spirituality and Mercury in retrograde nonsense?" Neve asked. "Dad never did, and I'm not sure I do either."

Perry's feathers made a ruffling sound as his tone turned teasing. "Oh, of course you don't. And yet..." Perry paused, his eyes two black beads gleaming on either side of his head, "You seem distressed as you sort through your email correspondence."

Ignoring him, she punched a key and the computer's screen turned bright blue, spilling cold light onto her cheeks. Irritated, she punched the control keys harder and let out a groan as Perry alighted behind her on the back of the sofa.

"Oh! The dreaded blue screen of death," he chirped

with glee. "*And* a missing shipment? I'd call those Exhibits A and B! Mercury in retrograde is famous for causing technological glitches and headaches related to miscommunication. Does any of this ring a bell?"

"Merely a coincidence," she dismissed. "Computers glitch and shipments get lost all the time."

There was a crash in the attic.

"Ah, right on cue! Did you pile the boxes too high, or..." He strutted across the back of the sofa, smug and self-satisfied, "Could it be the cusp of Mercury acting out again?"

Neve rolled her eyes and stood, striding down the hall with a scoff. She yanked the attic stairs down and climbed up, her feet creaking on the old wooden steps. As she reached the stacks of dusty boxes, a disheveled pile of yellowed newspaper clippings and medical journals caught her eye that had been scattered across the floor from the overturned box. Frowning, she gathered them up, straightening the brittle pages into a neat stack before setting them atop a nearby box.

The article on top stopped her cold. Her father's winning smile beamed back at her, and a sharp pang tugged at her chest. It was a group photo of young scientists in the lab, taken in 1990 when she was thirteen. The headline boldly declared, "Cancer Breakthroughs. Meet the dream team chasing the cure!"

Neve carried the box down and set it on the coffee table. She picked up the photograph again and held it closer to her face, studying it closely. The resemblance was there. They shared the same eyes and the same wave of mousy brown hair, though hers was streaked with gray now. He'd been gone so long, she couldn't remember what his smile looked like when actual joy crossed his face. The photograph felt like a gift. In it, he looked so carefree and full of hope for the future. His eyes shone bright with analytical curiosity. She wished she'd gotten to know this version of her father before he devolved into the paranoid and distracted version he became in the months before he died.

"What happened to your father?" Perry asked, peeking at the photograph over her shoulder.

"The police believe he was attacked in his home by someone he knew. There was no sign of a struggle, no fingerprints or DNA. Just blood. So much blood." Neve murmured the last part. She set down the photograph and wrapped her arms around herself, trying to self-soothe. "The human body cannot survive losing more than two liters of blood. When you lose thirty percent of your blood volume, it leads to rapid heartbeat and low blood pressure, and you require immediate medical attention. When you get to two liters, it's organ failure, unconsciousness, and death."

"Oh… that's why…" Perry's words drifted away as understanding lit him up from the inside out and he hopped closer.

"I've spent a lifetime running away from… this." She waved her hands at the box of newspaper clippings.

"And my unfortunate demise brought you right

back." Perry let out a morose chirp. "For that, I'm truly sorry."

Neve lifted her eyes filled with tears to meet his.

"Did they ever find his remains?"

Neve shook her head no. "After seven years without contact or any activity on credit cards or checking accounts, you can petition the court to declare a person legally deceased. Aunt Lu took me on the road with her, and I've rented out the house ever since. She was convinced someday I'd want to return here and persuaded me to wait to dispose of his things."

She sank back into the cushions of the couch, eyeing the box, wondering what other secrets it held. "Now they seem like pieces to a puzzle that might answer some questions." Neve was lost in thought for several minutes, and Perry hopped closer. A brush from the feathers on his wing brought her out of her melancholy memories. Neve scrubbed her face with her hand, then glanced down at the watch on her wrist.

"Dang it!" She jumped up. "This trip down memory lane is going to make me late!" Before he could ask any more questions, she ran out of the house only to return twelve minutes later wearing a long prairie dress that she'd paired with her hiking boots and a light denim jacket.

He chirped, "Where are you going all dolled up?"

"Tonight is opening night for the Ruben Angelica exhibit at Elysian Atelier. The largest private collection of Ruben Angelica's artwork is on loan, and three of my pieces have been selected to be shown in their Emerging Artists' wing." She rocked forward and back on the balls of her feet, thrilled to have her artwork shown next to an artist of his caliber.

"I'm confused," he admitted, tucking his wing in close as he side-eyed her choice of footwear. "Is the gallery at the top of a very tall mountain?"

"Very funny." Neve looked down at her feet. He wasn't wrong. "Mingling is going to be hard enough for me. I dressed for comfort."

"Ah, that was probably wise."

"This night could be pivotal in my career. I'm in the running for a fellowship that would provide for food and lodging for a year and give me the support needed to focus on my work."

"But what would that mean for me?" Perry asked, ever the self-preservationist.

"I don't know," she admitted truthfully. "But there is no sense in speculation right now."

"Speak for yourself." He was miffed. "I've built my life on speculation."

"And you can see where that got you," Neve blurted. She scooped another cup of pellets into his tray that Perry sniffed at and then cut him off several slices of cucumber as a peace offering. He happily crunched on them as she gathered her keys together and slid them into a small crossbody wallet. "Don't wait up."

"I never do," he warbled as she left the room and pulled the door closed behind her.

Neve slid into the driver's seat of the van and cruised the short distance to the square in downtown Aura Cove. Antique street lights cast a warm glow over the sidewalks as twilight deepened and their soft light pooled on the tumbled cobblestones. Small groups of well-dressed men and women strolled past the rows of charming shops lining the main street. The walkways were dotted with potted trees and lush plants, giving the area a beachy boardwalk vibe. Her gaze drifted to the candy shop across the street, Kandied Karma, where a white-haired woman shot her a warm smile as she flipped the sign to "Closed."

Neve eased the sprinter van into the last parking spot, tucked the keys back into her bag, and followed the brick-paved sidewalks toward the gallery with an impressive stone front. There was a different kind of tension zinging through her limbs. Though her artwork would be exposed and on public display, there was an element of anonymity that made the reveal easier.

The gallery was filling up, and servers wearing purple button-down shirts and bow ties passed carrying trays of hors d'oeuvres and flutes of champagne. Neve helped herself to a glass and sipped at it, letting the alcohol lubricate her rusty social wheels. She melted into the crowd, preferring to people-watch from the outer edge of the room. As the noise in the room intensified, her tension grew. It was obvious some guests were in love with the sound of their own voices.

A flamboyant man, with his hair slicked back and a bright purple jacket dusting his bony shoulders, had just delivered an air kiss on each cheek of a nearby man. Neve would never understand why two kisses were required when one would suffice. He pointed enthusiastically at Angelica's most iconic piece on loan from TMOM, Inheritance of Grace, a striking portrait of a flaxen-haired mother and daughter that had made him a household name. Something stirred in Neve as she studied the painting from afar. There was a familiarity she couldn't quite place.

"Look at that precision," he said, his voice dripping with exaggerated admiration. "The almost oppressive fidelity to reality. It's as if Angelica distilled the very marrow of the mother-daughter bond into the canvas itself. Don't you think?"

The younger, more attractive man at his side shook his head and swiped another flute of champagne from the handsome server in front of him. They exchanged a wink, and Neve watched the interaction with great curiosity.

"Lance, this is not hyperrealism. It's an interrogation about the sacrifice of motherhood and its effects on modern culture. You can feel the weight of her selflessness and utter devotion in every shadow and highlight. Each pore, every glimmer of light, is a manifesto. Truly, Ruben was not just a painter, he was the cartographer of human emotion."

"Yeah, a cartographer of whatever you said." Lance took a slow sip, his eyes lingering on the waiter's retreating form. Neve eavesdropped on the rest of their conversation as she found listening easier than participating. She scanned the other side of the room to get her bearings and to choose her next group to hover around when her gaze connected with Lisa's. Neve forced an awkward smile and then ducked away, silently hoping to avoid another painful interaction.

"Oh my God! Is that Ana Castanova?" Murmurs around her intensified, and there was a parting of the crowd as the wealthy celebrity strode into the gallery. Dressed in a smart red suit that was expertly tailored to her hourglass figure, she oozed confidence and old money. Neve studied her, wondering what it felt like to walk into a room and own it.

To center herself, Neve patted down her crossbody bag, searching for her good luck charm. She had tucked the geode inside, but as she unzipped the bag and tried to pull it out into her sweaty hand, it slipped from her grip and clattered to the floor. Then, to her utter horror and amazement, it bounced and rolled, skidding across the travertine to land at the toe of Ana Casanova's boot. Neve rushed over to retrieve it, but Ana had already leaned down to pick it up. The stone glittered in the gallery spotlights when she held it up in the light.

"Captivating, isn't it, darling?" Ana cupped the stone between her palms, and Neve swore she saw it brighten and throb in tune with her quickening heartbeat. "Let me guess, it's a good luck charm from someone special… your father, perhaps?"

Neve gasped at her accuracy, eager to have the geode back in her possession. "Yes," she whispered. "How did you know?"

"Just a hunch," Ana said with a wink. She leaned closer and lowered her voice an octave. "You are smart to keep it close." Neve's gaze locked on the geode, and she only relaxed when Ana placed it back in her hands. "Never let it out of your sight. It's special. You never know, it might be the key to your destiny."

The stone vibrated in confirmation, sending shockwaves through her body. After Neve tucked it safely back into her bag, she turned to thank Ana, but her mind went blank. She was physically unable to put more than two words together and her brain spun out, trying to recall the list of conversational topics she'd prepared.

"Relax, darling, these events are positively dreadful. But I promised Lisa I would make an appearance. What about you? Why are you here?"

"I have three pieces in the Emerging Artists' wing."

"Do you now?" Ana queried. "I fancy myself a bit of a collector. I will be sure to check them out." When Ana turned to grab a flute of champagne from the tray being passed, Neve took the opportunity to duck away and make her way further down the wall of Ruben's paintings. It was far easier than trying to make small talk with a celebrity. Ana Castanova was intimidating.

Neve turned the corner into the Emerging Artists' wing. Soft notes from a young woman plucking the strings of a harp drifted in the air and dampened the more abrasive chatter from guests in the space, making it easier for Neve to concentrate. Standing in front of her three pieces was a small group of five people. They were pointing at her work that had been framed in thick black frames with creamy white mats.

One man removed his glasses and leaned so close to the glass that his nose nearly brushed it, his eyes transfixed on the image mounted behind. Neve's heart raced with a mix of desperation and fear, longing to hear their conversation but dreading the vulnerability of it all. She took a cautious step forward, and when he shifted aside, her eyes landed on a small purple sticker beside two of the three pieces, indicating they'd been sold. A wave of relief washed over her. She glanced around the room in awe, wondering who in the crowd had treasured her artwork enough to purchase it.

"There you are!" Lisa said, appearing at her side. "Two of the three are spoken for, and I just heard Ana Castanova is seriously considering the third. You must have made quite an impression on her." She paused, then added, "Nevermore, I believe you have earned your right to have a solo show."

"Really?" Nevermore's heart leapt.

"It was simply serendipity to include your pieces during the Angelica event. Your personal tie to the master has made all the difference."

Neve was crestfallen. "Oh. I thought they'd been purchased because of the artistic merit of my work."

"I've been in this business long enough to tell you it doesn't matter." She held up her flute of champagne to toast. "This is a win, and I truly hope you see it that way." Not understanding her intention, Neve awkwardly reached for Lisa's glass, taking it out of her hand. Lisa pinched her lips together to suppress a smile as an uncomfortable silence stretched over them both. Neve stood flat footed, clutching the stem, not sure what to do with it. A soft groan escaped when she fixated in horror at the red lipstick print on the rim. Thankfully, a server appeared at her side and offered Lisa another glass.

Neve felt relief flood in when Lisa was pulled away by another patron. She rushed in the opposite direction and set the glass down on an empty serving tray. Then she brushed her hands together and made one more pass around the gallery, dawdling long enough to soak in the beauty of each of Ruben's paintings. She reveled in his masterful use of color and repeating impressionistic patterns. The layers were painstakingly applied with a palette knife, forming a thick, textured style that defined Ruben Angelica's work.The layers were painstakingly applied with a palette knife, forming a thick, textured style that defined Ruben Angelica's work.

His paintings commanded the eye, not giving a viewer the opportunity to meander or lose focus from the story he was telling. They were an inspiration, and viewing them was sustenance for her soul.

Before she slipped out, she allowed herself one more stroll through the Emerging Artists' wing. She caught Ana Castanova's eye from across the room, and the elegant woman raised her champagne flute, seemingly in celebration, just enough for Neve to notice. Confused, Neve turned back to the wall where her pieces were displayed. All three of them now had stickers indicating they'd been sold. She drifted out the front door, her feet barely touching the ground. So what if they were snapped up because of her childhood connection to the master? Or because she was too clumsy and tongue-tied in front of a celebrity? The money they brought in would spend the same.

CHAPTER 8
PEREGRINE

Like anyone else on the planet, I've long had recurring dreams about flying. Dream analysis by any head shrinker will try to distill the desire into a metaphor for your daily life. If there is a sense of urgency or fleeing, you must be trying to escape stressful or overwhelming situations. If you are soaring effortlessly, you may be trying to manifest freedom in your waking life.

Now I can tell you from experience, those dreams didn't even scratch the surface of the unbridled joy felt when I soared on my new wings through the salty sea air for the first time. A wing and a prayer? I'd never been much for the latter, but these wings? Who knew they'd deliver on every promise?

With two flaps, I was airborne into the sky above the ocean. My bird consciousness took over, showing me the ropes, and easing me into the wild blue yonder. Effervescent and light, I found gliding was as instinctive and natural as breathing. With a mere flick of my red tail feathers, I learned I could shift directions. Spread out before me like a fantastic buffet, the open sky beckoned. It was an endless expanse of air that fanned out to the horizon, and soaring through it, I'd never felt more free.

Two more powerful winged thrusts and I shot even higher, then floated down, riding the wave of air. I was adrift in a sea of euphoria, and my options felt endless. Should I tilt and glide the current down or shift and ride the updraft?

What a rush! I would compare it to a runner's high, where a burst of adrenaline pushes your body to its limits as every cell works in conjunction with one goal in mind. Flying *is* pure magic!

What were the perks of being a parrot? Free room and board, of course, though the meal plan left much to be desired. The burnt parrot pellets that made up over half of my diet were revolting. Bitter as hell, slightly nutty, and lacking a certain umami, they were a foodie's worst nightmare. What I wouldn't give for smoked salmon and crème fraîche with a dusting of caviar! And forget the seductive allure of sugar. It's now off-limits and toxic to my delicate avian system. I fear that now, instead of dreaming of flying, I will fantasize about ten-layer chocolate cakes dripping with ganache. What a reversal!

So far, Neve has been a reliable companion, though she's different from most women I've met. In my prior life she might have been the ideal mark, but after escaping the bowels of hell, I feel the stirring of a conscience. Which, if you'd known the depths of my selfish, depraved soul prior to this existence, should come as quite the surprise.

A trip to the beach to let off some steam had been my idea, but after taking my first flaps into the salty breeze, from a perch above, I can see Neve's shoulders finally receding back to their normal place instead of crowding around her ears.

It is vital that I endear myself to her as all of my basic needs require human intervention to be met. I must prove my worth now more than ever, especially since she mentioned a business opportunity yesterday that would exclude me. To be honest, it's left me verklempt.

Exhausted from my first sea flight, I chose the bent bow of a palm tree near Neve to roost. She was sketching the pounding surf on the grounds of an elaborate hotel. Clouds were gathering, and the breeze picked up. Engrossed in her work, Neve didn't notice the first droplet. The sun was now fully behind a wall of clouds when I glided down to rest on the sand near her.

Her hand was smudged with charcoal and there was a graceful elegance to her movements. Her anxiety was replaced by a calm confidence I'd never seen her exhibit before. Lost in her work, serenity had settled in. I got the sense drawing was the only time she felt safe, understood, and completely comfortable.

There was a low rumble of thunder in the distance, and I felt a surge of energy gathering. I didn't want to interrupt her, but perhaps it would be necessary. After my next lap, of course.

CHAPTER
NINE

THE STORM CLOUDS GATHERED, flitting toward the sun, softening the light that traced the elaborate architecture and trickled down the elegant lines of the building. The last rays of the sun separated the grand hotel from the palm trees and lush landscaping that surrounded it. Neve squeezed the pencil tighter between her fingers, wanting to get the shading just right before the light changed. Her gaze flicked between the building and her sketch, completely engrossed in her work until the clouds engulfed the sun completely. The drastic shift in illumination shattered the spell her art had cast over her, leaving her momentarily dazed as she stumbled out of it. Neve glanced up at the building wall of black storm clouds and felt an electric shift in the air.

"Perry!" she shouted as she turned back and feverishly shaded, darkening the sky by gliding her pencil sideways over the area to develop the base density. "This is your five-minute warning! A storm is coming! We have to leave soon!"

Digging in her bag, she pulled out the silver tin, pressed the pencil she was using back into its resting place, and then selected one a bit softer. It offered the smoothest lead and was exactly the one she needed to add the last few lines to the drawing. She jumped when the first raindrop landed on her shoulder, quickly shut the sketchbook, and tucked it safely inside the messenger bag to protect it. Water and paper should not mix.

Neve stood and pawed inside the bag for her keys when her fingers brushed past the geode, which felt warm to the touch. Confused by its obvious shift in temperature, she pulled it out of the bag and held it up in front of her face, studying the sparkling crystalized interior. She remembered Ana's advice: "Keep it close. It may hold the key to unlocking your destiny."

A solitary ray of fleeting sunshine struck the face and made the purple stone glow. Neve was transfixed by its beauty, enthralled by the spectacular prisms created by the facets of the stone that cascaded across her skin onto her fingers.

There was a rustle of feathers and, from her peripheral vision, she noticed Perry alight on the blanket at her feet. His feathers brushed against her ankle when his soft, contented chirp transformed into a warning squawk. The rumble intensified, thundering through her ears. Goosebumps flashed down her limbs, and then a blinding flash of light accompanied by a loud crack pitched both Neve and Perry backward onto the sand. She gripped her fingers around the geode, gasping for air.

Instantly, Neve's ears started to ring, and she shook her head back and forth, trying to escape the irritating noise. There was a powerful jolt as a bright white spark jumped from her to Perry, to the geode, and back again. Neve smelled singed feathers and, in her mouth, a bitter, metallic ozone aftertaste made her scowl.

"I can't see." She voiced her fear and used her free hand to cover her blind eyes. Disoriented, she felt her muscles spasm and fully contract as the wall of white consumed her consciousness, and she felt herself slip into it. The last thing she heard was a painful, muffled squawk from Perry. She tried to turn toward him when a searing zap into her ribs made her gulp for air.

Later. She resolved to help him later. Right now, she just needed to close her eyes and protect them from the searing light. Neve curled into the fetal position as a wall of mind-splitting sensation overload crashed over her. Reflexively, she covered her ears with her hands and rocked back and forth to soothe the pain. The movement didn't have its usual calming effect, and terror instinctively made her rock faster.

She flopped back with relief when the sound was muffled, then her surroundings morphed into complete silence. Grateful for the break in stimulation, Neve felt her muscles unclench as she drifted into a white sea.

PART 2: MERCURY IN RETROGRADE
APRIL 1989

CHAPTER

TEN

WHEN NEVE'S eyes fluttered open, there was a tingling sensation throughout her body, and it took several long minutes for her vision to acclimate to her much darker surroundings. The stillness was eerie but welcome after the audio onslaught she'd just endured, and she rolled onto her back, feeling the soft nap of velvet against the skin underneath her.

Gradually, all of her senses returned, and she realized something was cutting into her palm. Letting out a cry, she loosened her grip and gazed down, her eyes registering a shard of the geode, but the color was a vibrant celadon instead of its usual amethyst. The stone was warm to the touch, and its surface was sharp and tinged with the rust color of dried blood. Underneath the crystal was a single, downy gray feather that slipped from her palm and floated to the floor. "Perry?" She whispered his name before she felt goosebumps prickle, racing up her forearms. From a few feet away, a man cleared his throat, and she felt her skin crawl. She was being watched.

"Isla, *ma choupette*, please hold your pose," a deep male voice with a hint of a French accent, encouraged from the shadows. All at once and with complete horror and mortification, Neve glanced down at her bare torso, fully illuminated and shamelessly exposed beneath the unforgiving glare of three harsh spotlights. They surrounded the pedestal where the chaise lounge cradled her, turning her into a spectacle. Every curve of a body she didn't recognize was laid bare. She was chilled to the bone and the cold air made her pink nipples stiffen. Neve quickly wrapped her longer arms around pillowy breasts to cover her nakedness.

Isla? The name was oddly familiar, hiding on the fringes of her memory, blocked by her current humiliation. Panic flooded Neve, consuming all her internal resources, and the lingering embarrassment flamed her skin lobster pink. She heard chair legs screech against the floor as her vision acclimated, and she registered a sea of easels fanned out in front of her. Behind each one, a student sat on a stool sketching. Sketching what? She stood up and then realized she was completely nude. The students were sketching her!

Letting out a little yelp, she attempted to step down but instead tripped in her heels and fell back onto a crushed velvet settee. The fabric was mortifyingly soft against her bare bottom. She heard the man who had spoken from the shadows striding closer, and she scanned the platform around her, searching for something to hide her nakedness. At her feet, a satin robe was puddled on the ground, and she reached out to pick it up and hastily put it on, drawing the tie around her trim waist. She shoved the geode into the pocket of the robe as havoc stormed through her. This body? Whose was it? *It's not mine!* Neve started to spiral when she felt a tingle of intuition tell her to take a deep breath.

All is well.

She received the dreamy thought as though it was whispered into her very soul, and it brought her great comfort. Neve didn't have time to identify the source before she heard the man's deep baritone voice say, "Let's take a break." She had never been more grateful to hear those words. Neve got to her feet again and teetered down off the pedestal she'd been elevated on.

The room grew brighter as lights were turned up, and Neve gasped when she saw the man. She'd recognize that face anywhere. It was the same one smiling from the program from her exhibit at Elysian Atelier. Though, in that photo, he'd had a shock of curly white hair. This man's was coal black. Was he Ruben's son? The genetic resemblance was uncanny and added to her overall feelings of malaise.

He was tall and lean, with a chiseled jawline covered in thick stubble. His eyes danced with mischief, and his thick, curly hair was combed back from his prominent forehead, though a few wayward curls framed his inquisitive dark eyes. When she locked eyes on him, there was an animalistic magnetism she couldn't deny.

She felt warm hands grasp her own and was surprised that her usual initial reaction to recoil from touch hadn't surfaced. "Isla, the agency said you were comfortable with nudity. You were doing so well. Don't get modest on me now." Neve retracted her hands from his and forced herself not to wipe them down the front of the silky robe. Why did he keep calling her Isla?

"I'm sorry, I'm not feeling well. I need to use the bathroom."

"Sure, darling, but we have one more hour together, or I am going to have to renegotiate our agreed-upon rate with you."

Unsure what that meant, Neve quickly nodded and rushed to the exit, scanning the hallway of the art center for a bathroom. When she saw a stick figure with a skirt, she heaved a sigh of relief and barreled through the swinging door into a bathroom lit by overhead fluorescent lights.

A bank of mirrors was installed with vanity globe lights ringing it, and when Neve glanced over at her reflection, she did a double-take. A well-endowed, tall, leggy blonde wearing the same mint-colored robe she'd just put on stood in front of her. She raised her hand and the woman in the reflection did the same. With a gasp, Neve stepped closer and leaned in, marveling at the smooth, dewy skin on her high cheekbones and the long black eyelashes that surrounded her brown, almond-shaped eyes. Her cheeks were flushed pink, and when she brushed her fingers across the planes of her cheekbones, the stunning blonde in the mirror did the same. It was unnerving.

"What in the actual hell is happening?" she mumbled softly, even more perturbed when her reflection mimicked every twitch of her lips as if her words were dubbed. The door creaked and a young woman walked in. She stopped in front of the mirror next to Neve and pulled out a Bonnie Bell Dr. Pepper Lip smacker and, after pulling off the lid, circled her full lips several times. Her oversized, off-the-shoulder sweatshirt featured the Guess logo and provided a peek of an electric blue sports bra. Acid-washed jeans were tapered and cuffed at her ankles, and brilliant white LA Gear tennis shoes donned her feet. It was a retro look that transported Neve right back to the late 80s.

"Great costume. It's so retro!" Neve heard herself say, surprised she'd actually initiated a conversation with a stranger.

"Like, what?" Crisscrosses of bewilderment twisted up the girl's forehead.

"Is it 80s dress-up day or something?" Neve asked.

She blinked like Neve was speaking in a foreign language. "Girlfriend is buggin'," she muttered under her breath as she rooted through her purse, producing a trial-size can of Aqua Net. Neve watched her gather a chunk of hair from the side of her head and then spray it down with a cloud of hairspray. Then she turned the vent of the hand dryer up and the hot air hardened it into a crisp wing. She washed her hands and retrieved a pack of Bubblicious grape bubblegum, spending a few minutes unwrapping a lavender wad of chewing gum before offering the pack to Neve.

"No, thank you," Neve said.

"You must hear this all the time, but you are, like, drop-dead gorgeous and it has been so gnarly to work with you."

"Gnarly?" Neve asked. "Are you trying to tell me I'm twisted and difficult?"

The girl giggled. "No, silly, you know, like, totally awesome!"

"Oh… thank you," Neve replied awkwardly. She was stunned. She'd never heard those words outside of the Valley Girls books a librarian forced on her as a child. Even more shocking was her comfort in speaking with a stranger while maintaining eye contact. There wasn't the build-up of uncomfortable energy that normally accompanied her interactions with others, and the novelty of it added even more layers to her discomfort.

You're okay. Breathe with me.

There it was again. Neve glanced over her shoulder, searching for the source of the impromptu pep talk, but there was no one else in the bathroom.

The girl glanced at the Swatch watch on her wrist. It was colorful with a bright purple strap and pink and lime green face. She remembered begging Talulah for one just like it on her sixteenth birthday.

"I better get back. He locks us out if we aren't on time. I had to practically offer my firstborn to get into Ruben Angelica's advanced oils class. My parents will kill me if I don't get an A." She rushed out of the bathroom and left Neve at the sink.

"Ruben Angelica," she repeated, still staring at her reflection in shock and awe. Her thick hair was curled with the outrageous volume of decades passed. Piece by piece, the clues were coming together, and the first inkling of truth surfaced as she stared at herself. "How is this even possible?" she blurted into the air. "Perry?" she called out, not expecting an answer. "I must be dreaming." She slapped one cheek. "Ow," she howled, shocked by the instant sting of pain from the palm of Isla's hand. Neve dug her fingernails into the heels of her hands where they made red half-moons and began to tingle.

"It appears I am fully awake. Perhaps it's a lucid dream?" she asked her reflection, who stubbornly refused to answer at first, but when she finally did, it sent chills down Neve's spine.

It's much more than that.

"What is?" she asked, her trepidation growing as she had the unsettling realization her mind was now dually occupied.

Go back.

Resigned that she would have to return to the classroom, Neve steeled her resolve. She twisted the tap, ran a finger under the water, and brushed the curve of her brow with one pinky. Taking a deep breath, she squared her shoulders and began the walk down the hallway. Ruben was standing at the door holding court, with several students gathered around him in a half-circle and hanging on his every word. Seeing her, his eyes lit up, and he turned to the group and said, "I need a word with the lovely Isla. Please go inside and get settled at your easels."

Neve felt a smile turn her cheeks up. He strode closer to her, like a panther stalking his prey, his intensity making her cheeks flush red again. "I'm not feeling well." She started in with the best excuse she could come up with under the circumstances. There was no way on God's green earth she would get back on that stage naked.

He cocked his head to the side and studied her. Then, surprising her, Ruben reached out and brushed the back of his knuckles against her cheek, an unnerving sensation that made her center tingle with desire that equally confused and tempted her. "I am sorry to hear that. What do you propose we do about the hour we'll lose together then, hmm?"

"Um… I'm open to ideas." Neve was bewildered, hearing herself answer in a timbre that was infinitely sweeter than her own. She was *not* usually open to ideas. Most people's "ideas" were useless rubbish.

His gaze warmed her from the inside out, and she felt the novel sensation of ease filling her. It was not her normal state. Could it be borrowed from Isla? She'd read about pretty privilege, but seeing the presence of it actually being confirmed in front of her was eye-opening.

"I am hosting a gathering at my home tomorrow evening. It is a roundtable artist salon where I've invited the crème de la crème of Florida's contemporary artists, and I'd like you to attend as my guest." Her hand was cradled between his warmer ones, and the feeling of attraction was intoxicating.

"Fully clothed?" Neve needed the confirmation and couldn't stop herself from asking the question, but then was compelled to add a playful wink that felt decidedly more Isla.

"To start," he said with a devilishly handsome grin. He scratched at his jawline, cupping his chin in his hand as he studied her. "Then we'll see where the night takes us." He pulled a card from his pocket and handed it over to her. "Seven o'clock?"

"I'll be there." She squeezed the card in her hand before asking, "Um… where are my clothes?"

"Darling girl, you *must* not be feeling well. They are in my office. Down the hall, the first door to the right." He took a step closer and bent down to kiss her cheek goodbye at the precise moment she turned her head to glance at the path leading to his office. Her lips collided with his, plump and soft, shooting a blush of awkward heat through her.

"Sorry!" she blurted, her cheeks on fire as a chuckle escaped him, and he shifted to try to kiss her other cheek goodbye.

"Two," Neve said the word aloud.

"Yes, two kisses, *mon amour*," Ruben said. "It is customary in my country."

"Of course."

"I must get back. *À demain.*"

Neve watched him stride confidently away and had to fan herself with her hand. His accented English dripped with Parisian sex appeal. It was as though he was dusting his instructions with cinnamon. A hint of it here, a touch of it there, and it had the unusual effect of making her weak in the knees.

Neve slipped the high heels off her feet and padded down the linoleum barefoot to his office. Lit by a small lamp, the ambient light spilled onto a Jansport backpack that felt familiar. She unzipped it and found neatly folded clothing inside, determining it was hers. She pulled on the DayGlo tank top and white, tapered-leg, skin-tight denim that hugged her curves, then a pair of ballet flats.

A calendar on the wall next to his desk caught her eye, and she leaned closer to study it. It yawned open on April 1st, which was marked off with a neat black X. Neve pulled it off the wall and flipped it closed so she could see the cover. The confirmation took her breath away.

1989. She was stuck in 1989.

CHAPTER

ELEVEN

BEFORE HER PANIC COULD CREST, and wanting to slip out the door before the painting class was excused, Neve rifled through the backpack. Inside Isla's wallet, she discovered a bus pass. Hope welled up as she realized the power of the card in her hand. She quickly dressed and rushed out of the building and down the sidewalk. Neve knew exactly where she was, and she also knew Bus 271 would let her off a few blocks from her childhood home.

On the bus, she spent the entirety of the ride reasoning with herself, pinching her skin, and trying to talk herself out of the reality that was confirmed by every passenger surrounding her. Some were listening to their Walkmans, wearing corded headphones instead of AirPods. All were sporting some sort of late-eighties fashion in DayGlo colors, bold logo t-shirts from Coca-Cola and Benetton, and pegged jeans. Her gaze drank the scene in, trying to process the flood of incoming information, drifting up to a photo of an egg in a cast iron pan where bold yellow letters declared, "This is your brain on drugs." Seeing it brought on a wave of pure nostalgia.

"Any questions?" Neve mumbled the rote response she remembered from the campaign under her breath. The message had been beaten into her psyche, thanks to after-school specials and the parodies that followed for years later.

When Neve glanced out the window, the rows of boxy gas guzzlers and grocery-getter station wagons only reinforced the evidence that was becoming impossible to ignore. The McDonald's on the corner sported a vintage green roof, obnoxious yellow arches, and loads of brown bricks, and the Chick-fil-A that moved in next to it in 2015 didn't even exist yet.

On the bus, there wasn't a single person staring down at an iPhone. No one was taking a selfie or engaging in FaceTime. Instead, they were reading books or people-watching. Neve felt her heart pang for the simplicity she remembered from her childhood. Back then, neighborhood kids were sent outside to play, riding bicycles with banana seats and tucking packs of candy cigarettes into the rolled sleeves of their T-shirts.

At her stop, she turned and began the short walk to her home. A teenager riding a bike zoomed past her in the darkness, probably trying to get home before curfew, and she had to jump into the grass to avoid a collision.

Neve hurried, eager to ring the bell and find her father waiting for her on the other side of the door. She yearned to be closer to him, but being trapped inside the body of a stranger, she knew their reunion had the potential to be messy, and was unsure how to navigate it.

When the house came into view, she froze. Neve hid in the shadows, standing in the darkness outside it. She saw it with fresh eyes as a sensation of déjà vu crashed over her. The house stood still, dark against the night. The ever-present ache of her father's absence sharpened, twisting in her chest. He'd been gone for decades in her present, but here, in 1989, he was *alive*. Her father was inside the house, somewhere under the roof she'd had to replace after Hurricane Ivan. Her heart galloped in her chest as she fought between her desire to rush to the door to ring the bell and the instinct to remain hidden.

Neve wasn't there to interfere. Just to see him, to lay her eyes again on the face of the father she'd loved and had missed so terribly it made her heart ache. The front windows were dimly lit, and she strained to catch glimpses of movement through them, but there were none. Neve swallowed, the lump catching in her throat as she slid around the side of the house to the sunroom, her father's favorite room in the house.

A whimper escaped her lips when she caught her first glimpse of him through the glass. There was her father, Dr. Ellis LaRue, seated at his desk. He was poring over documents, his lips moving as he read through them with a pen tucked into the crevice behind his ear. His unmistakable profile was softened by the warm glow of the lamplight he favored. His face was fuller than she remembered, and he radiated health and vitality.

Neve couldn't breathe. Her chest felt tight, and at her sides, her fingers curled into fists as if grounding herself could anchor her there. She acknowledged the prickling sensation on the back of her neck and the slight static hum in her ears accompanied by lightheadedness that always came with sensory overload. She couldn't tear her eyes away, and her vision started to swim. She let out an astonished chuckle as she wiped the tears away with the pads of her thumbs. Alive. Her father was alive.

He was speaking to someone. Neve dared to step closer and caught a glimpse that sent her stumbling back in shock. Her hand shot to her mouth, her pulse pounding in her ears. Through the glass, she saw her younger self, just twelve years old. Her breath hitched as she watched the girl, small and gangly, clutching a sketchbook. Her shoulders were hunched inward like armor, one hand tracing repetitive circles on the corner of the page while her foot tapped up and down.

The girl sitting there didn't know yet about the years of misunderstanding, the labels that didn't fit, and the constant feeling of being wrong when everyone else was right. She didn't know how many times she would be forced to hear the word "difficult" whispered during parent-teacher conferences. She didn't know how hard she'd have to fight to figure out why she was the way she was, and that the answer wouldn't come until she was in her forties.

Neve stood there, feeling everything all at once. The ache of recognizing her years of loneliness, the bittersweet tang of knowing she'd survive it, and the overwhelming urge to gather the child in her arms and tell her she was enough.

On the cushion, the girl laughed, the sound muffled by the glass, but Neve felt the memories returning as a multi-layered sensory flood that made tears well at her lashes, blinding her vision.

When she blinked them away, her father's stern gaze through the window paralyzed her. Neve froze. Her father's expression hardened as he crossed the room toward the screen door that let out a squeal of protest as he stepped closer.

Hide.

A warning came directly from her intuition, delivered in Isla's sweet tone.

"Who's there?" His voice boomed as he threw open the door. The screen door slammed into the ill-fitting frame as he stepped closer, peering into the darkness. "Hello? I know there is someone out there." Neve pressed herself into the shadows next to the house. Holding her breath, silently begging him to turn around and head back inside, Neve stumbled further away. She should have been more careful, should've remembered how sharp her father's instincts were.

A beam of light from a flashlight blinded her. Then, before she could decide whether to run or attempt to explain herself, he said, "Isla? Did you lose your key again?"

Neve's throat went dry. Her mind raced as she came crashing back down to earth and her rational thinking returned. He didn't recognize her as the older version of his daughter. He saw someone else entirely, someone he already knew. Isla again. Oh yes, that's why the name sounded familiar! Isla was her childhood nanny for a short time when her father's frequency of business travel ramped up. She'd slipped into Isla's body somehow after the lightning strike. Dumbfounded and afraid, Neve felt herself nod yes in answer to his question.

He let out a heavy sigh and pinched the bridge of his nose. "You must be more careful. This will be the second time I have to have the locks changed in a month." He started to pace in front of her, clearly agitated. "It's dangerous and I have a child at home." Waves of frustration rippled from him, and she was anxious to calm him down.

Neve felt his disappointment crash over her.

Backpack.

Unsure of what else to do, she pulled Isla's backpack from her shoulder and felt a nudge to unzip a pocket. "Wait…" she said, digging through the contents, when the sight of the keyring made her heart leap. She pulled it out and shook the keyring, making the keys jangle together with a winning grin. "Ta-Da!"

Seeing the keys, Ellis's tightened jaw unclenched, and Neve watched his shoulders relax.

"Dad?" A small voice stole their attention.

"It's okay, Nomo," he said, "It's just Isla." Hearing

her childhood nickname for the first time in decades made tears prickle, and she blinked them away, swallowing hard against the lump forming in her throat. Until that moment, she'd forgotten her father was the only one who called her Nomo. It was a detail she'd packed away because it hurt too much. Neve forced herself to smile at the young girl standing there clutching her sketchbook to her chest, focused on a spot on the grass in front of her.

"Come on, kiddo," Ellis said, tilting his head toward the back door. "Let's go back inside. Isla can help you get ready for bed."

"Okay," she answered as she darted past without so much as a glance, disappearing through the door behind him.

And Neve was left standing there, wondering how to process the events that just transpired. How many nights had she lain awake in the VW camper, on the road with her aunt, as a teenager, desperately wishing for this very reality? A reality where her father was alive and tucking her into bed every night? The child was safe now, but Neve knew in just a few years, they would all be forever changed.

Was Neve brought here to warn them? Or was she being given a second chance to change the trajectory of their lives, and if she did, what would be the long-term repercussions?

CHAPTER 12
PEREGRINE

EVERY INCH of my body burned with exquisite agony. I cautiously opened one eye and jolted up in shock when I saw the metal bars. Jail! I was incarcerated. Panic surged through me, and a wave of dizziness made my vision blur. Reality crashed back in as I flicked a wing, feeling the brush of my feathers against the enclosure. I was a bird. A jailbird! A squawk tore from my throat as I thrashed in a panic, flapping wildly for several minutes before I managed to steady myself and regain control.

I glanced around to get my bearings. It wasn't *my* cage. That was the first thing I noticed. My current residence was a gilded monstrosity with bars too close together, a thick metal perch that was too slick, and there was no bell for me to ring. I hated it. Draped over the cage was a dark cloth that was unfamiliar, too. I hopped over and tried to grasp it in my beak and yank it off, to catch a glimpse of my surroundings, but it was too heavy and I couldn't get the leverage I needed. Instead, I decided to use my words.

"Nevermore?" I squawked, testing the waters when I heard movement rustle behind the curtain. Seconds later, the darkness lifted and a stocky woman of Latina descent leaned close. Her deep brown eyes were curious yet friendly, and the lines on her plump face were carved into folds of skin spotted by the sun. She folded up the fabric and laid it on an elegant side table as I took in the rest of the room.

The air smelled like lemon wood polish, and dust bunnies danced in the air thanks to the feather duster wielded by the woman in front of me. The walls were paneled in rich mahogany, gleaming under the dim light of an ornate crystal chandelier. Two walls were filled with bookshelves that stretched to the ceiling, laden with leather-bound books that smelled of ancient paper. They weren't books meant to be read. They were trophies, their spines embossed with gold, a visual testimony to the owner's intelligence. Many were in too pristine of a condition to have ever been opened. I was certain if I was able to take a closer look, I'd find a few first editions in the mix.

At the center of the room sat a massive desk, its surface smooth as glass and gleaming in the light. It was carved from a dark slab of wood, with intricate detailing along the edges, and adorned with tiny vines and leaves that seemed to twist and writhe if you stared too long. On top, papers lay in neat piles, weighed down by a crystal globe that caught the sunlight pouring in from the arched windows. The light danced across the walls in fragmented rainbows, but the room remained eerily vacant. Large paintings on the sidewalls were lit by spotlights and practically glowed, giving the library an art museum ambiance.

The chair behind the desk was a gleaming throne of leather and brass, its high back curving to swallow whoever sat upon it. Opposite the desk, a tufted sofa stretched in front of a low coffee table made of glass and iron. The decor was traditional and timeless, even the rugs. Persian, I'd guess. They featured patterns comprised of wool yarn so intricate they made my head spin. The result was a masculine study that screamed opulence and wealth.

Across the room, the sturdy maid continued to dust the carved plaster sill of an arched window. Singing in Spanish and twirling while she dusted, it appeared as though she gained immense satisfaction from her work. I studied her as she spun around the room like a whirling dervish. How could she eek so much joy out of a mundane life of servitude?

When I grew bored watching her work, I screeched louder. I fluffed up my feathers and flapped my wings furiously, hoping to gain her attention first, then, perhaps, freedom. The maid barely whisked her eyes over, engrossed in her duties.

My thoughts began to spiral. Where was Nevermore, and how did I get here? I thought about the last time I'd seen her. One second, I was soaring through the salty air of the gulf. The next, I'd landed on the towel next to her, when a stray bolt of lightning shot down from the gathering storm clouds. It leapt from the geode, through Neve, and then through me, completing its circuit. There was a flash of white and then I drifted away. Did the same fate befall Nevermore?

You would think after what happened with Sheila and inhabiting this bird body, nothing would surprise me anymore. But this was the second unexplainable supernatural event in my life in a short period, and it could not be easily rationalized.

Control your environment. It was the golden rule of my previous human profession. Following it, I could go into any situation and extract the outcome I desired from my mark using manipulation and control. The maid's blatant refusal to acknowledge my presence made another surge of panic rush through me, quick and electric. I thrashed my wings, clearly agitated, and the clang of the cage bars echoed through the room. It didn't matter. No one came running. Now that I'd been demoted to pet status, I could see I would have to adjust my approach.

"Calm down, calm down, calm down," I muttered to myself, pacing along the perch. I didn't like the feel of it under my claws. Too slippery. Whoever owned this cage had no idea what a parrot required in his domicile. I fluttered to the floor of the cage, pecking at the latch. It wasn't one I recognized. Sheila's cage at Nevermore's had a simple hook latch I could open with my beak when I couldn't motivate a human to do it for me. This one was a twist lock, shiny and smooth, and no amount of pecking and poking would make it budge. I squawked in frustration, throwing my whole weight against the door. Nothing.

One question circled in my mind on repeat: Where was Neve?

The maid strode closer to the cage to see what all the fuss was about. "How you say, Nevermore?" she asked, her Spanish accent thick and her grasp of basic English grammar weak.

"Where's Nevermore?" I demanded, loud and sharp. The maid cocked her head as if trying to interpret my vocalizations, but she didn't answer. When I squawked again, I was elated to see a man, presumably a cook because of his pristine apron with the name Amos embroidered on it, poke his head through the doorway. He was a burly black man with a sunny disposition. His skin was dotted with moles and freckles, and his teeth were straight, white, gleaming squares framed by his full lips.

"Why the ruckus, Rosa?" he asked, closing the distance between us as he entered the room.

"He say, where's Nevermore?"

"Nevermore?" Amos let out a burst of a laugh. "He done lost himself. Fool thinks he's a raven." He wagged his smug finger at me and I wanted to chomp it off.

"Perhaps he angry birds?" Rosa suggested.

Angry birds? If she only knew the goldmine that would turn out to be in two decades! Still, I was offended by the reference, and I wouldn't have any of it! "Angry?" I echoed, my voice high and mocking. "I'm not angry, I'm apoplectic! I am livid! I am incensed! A weak mind employs a weak vocabulary!" I paced and swished the confines of the cage, waiting for my insults to land. My word choices were far better than theirs. They had a certain cadence. Seemed more accurate. More important.

"Apop-what?" Amos laughed heartily with Rosa. "Lord, Ruben must be working overtime on the vocal training with this one!" He shook his jovial head, a pudgy bald circle atop his stocky body. "Maybe he's hungry," he said and pulled a shiny apple from his pocket. He bit into it before removing the offensive bite from his mouth and offering it to me. To me! It was repugnant! I would have been less disgusted if he'd given me a wet kiss on the mouth!

"No, thank you!" I snapped as I preened my feathers. How dare he offer me a bite of ABC (already been chewed) apple!

"Suit yourself, but I'll leave it here in case you change your mind." He twisted open the cage's bar and tossed the rest of his half-eaten apple into the food tray, then closed the door before I could escape.

Frustrated, I climbed back up to the perch, my claws clicking against the smooth metal. The study was eerily quiet now. Rosa had long since finished her dusting and moved on. The only sounds were the distant hum of the air conditioning, bursts of the vacuum cleaner, and the occasional creak of the wood battling against the Florida humidity. I was a prisoner in this strange house with its cultured marble floors, crystal chandeliers, and gothic library, and I didn't know why.

As the sun dipped below the horizon, casting long shadows across the room, I made a decision. I didn't know how I was going to get out of this cage, but I had to find a way. I was certain Nevermore needed my assistance.

CHAPTER

THIRTEEN

Neve jolted upright, disoriented by her surroundings. She sat up in the bed and rubbed her eyes as the truth started to trickle in. "That's right," she whispered to herself. "It's 1989. I'm in the guest room at my childhood home, and my father is alive and right down the hall." She felt a zing of giddy joy at the prospect of seeing him and bounded out of bed. But her vantage point was higher, and she felt an internal wobble as she adjusted to Isla's longer legs.

You're safe, Neve. Take a breath.

"This dual consciousness experience is wild," Neve mumbled under her breath in Isla's sweeter timbre as her equilibrium returned.

Through the walls, she heard the indistinct murmur of voices. Normally, Neve cherished her morning solitude, but Isla's social butterfly tendencies were hard to ignore. The contrast set off an internal tug-of-war that felt unsettling. In a small act of compromise, she slipped into the shower in her ensuite, letting the water drown out the noise and her own indecision. Neve lathered up the pink bar of soap and brushed it across Isla's long limbs and down the length of her tight abdomen. This body was as flawless as any she'd ever seen in magazines, but the greatest transformation was the lightness of being that accompanied it. Compared to yesterday, a looser sense of ease replaced her usual rigidity. Neve was a literal person, tethered to logic and the certainty of cause and effect. Yet inside this conventionally beautiful body, there was a shift. There was an unclenching as the scurrying thoughts in her mind slowed.

"Is this how the rest of the world experiences life?" Neve wondered aloud as she rinsed the shampoo from her hair, the suds tracing lazy tracks down her bronzed skin. Normal. It was such a polarizing word. When Neve was younger, it was all she longed to be. She suppressed her stimming, forced herself to make eye contact, and mimicked small talk, but masking was exhausting. Over the years, she'd come to accept and eventually embrace her neurodivergent differences, and now, it appeared she was participating in an out-of-body experience to test that hypothesis.

Neve pulled a towel from the hook and wrapped it around herself, catching a glimpse of Isla's long legs extending much farther into the foggy air than hers ever did. She wiped away the steam from the mirror and smiled at her reflection. Neve felt a fizzy sense of joy that was alarming at first. The longer it remained, the more settled she became in it. It was as if she were in the changing room trying on a new identity and a new consciousness altogether.

"I'm Isla Warner," she whispered to her reflection, testing out the words on her tongue, as she finger-combed her long wet hair. Then she let her towel drop to the floor as she palmed the crown of her head, rubbing in soothing circles. Neve twisted back and forth in front of the mirror. She was fascinated by Isla's tanned skin, plump breasts, and shapely waist. Her own body was thinner and angular, and she was unaccustomed to the softness of Isla's curves.

She tugged open the dresser drawer and picked through the clothing offerings, pulling on Isla's *Frankie says Relax* t-shirt because it would be a visual reminder. Neve pulled on a frayed pair of cut-off jean shorts and then tucked the sliver of the glowing geode into the pocket. When she was ready, she opened the door and padded out to the kitchen where her father and her twelve-year-old self were already gathered.

Ellis sipped his coffee, eyes skimming the newspaper, while young Nevermore methodically scooped up one kernel of Cap 'N Crunch at a time, raising each piece to her mouth from the brimming bowl in front of her.

"Eggs and toast?" Neve asked, hearing her words in Isla's much softer voice, and she had to gulp down her nervousness when her father's gaze diverted from the newsprint to meet hers.

"Yes, please," he said. "I know it's your day off, but

I was hoping you could help me with Nomo for a few hours. I've got to get to the lab and work out the final dosage of the protocol before we start animal testing."

"I can do that," Neve answered more quickly than usual, nudged by Isla, who was eager to please. "However, I do have plans for the evening."

"I will make sure I'm home by three pm." He shot her a quick smile then folded the newspaper as Neve studied him. He was distracted. When she was a child, she hadn't noticed it, but now, seeing him through adult eyes, Neve could see the gears of his mind on a continual spin. He was physically present, but seemingly in two places at once. She longed to reach out to him, to tell him to linger longer at breakfast and play a round of chess with Nomo before rushing back to the lab. But she couldn't bring herself to say the words.

Neve pulled out the cardboard carton of eggs and slid two slices of sourdough into the toaster. She cracked the eggs into a bowl and whisked them into a soft scramble. A few minutes later, she placed a steaming plate of sunny eggs in front of her father and sat down to eat across the table from him. After breakfast, she wiped down the table and added their dirty dishes to the empty dishwasher. When the kitchen was restored to order, she sat down next to the girl, careful not to touch her.

"What would you like to do today, Miss Nevermore?"

"Can we go to the aquarium?"

"Of course," Neve agreed, Isla nudging her to the

organizer on the refrigerator where she found their season tickets. "Your dad bought us a season pass. Why don't you get dressed and we'll go?"

Nevermore nodded and scurried away to her bedroom, emerging ten minutes later. She was dressed in leggings, a long-sleeved shirt, and her trademark hiking boots.

"It's going to be ninety today. Maybe you should change into shorts."

"No." Nevermore set her slim shoulders as a scowl turned the corners of her mouth downward. "I want to wear *this*."

"I understand, but you might…" Neve's explanation died on her lips. She intimately knew that Nevermore needed a barrier between herself and the world. It didn't matter if the temperature soared to triple digits and came with off-the-charts humidity. It was more important to keep the barrier intact. She glanced down at Nevermore's feet, and Isla encouraged her to offer the child a compliment. "I like your boots."

"They are comfortable *and* practical," the child said with a curt, self-satisfied nod, holding up the brush and elastics. "Can you braid my hair again like you did yesterday?"

The geode in her pocket shot a tingle of warmth to her upper thigh. The request caught Neve off guard. This is where it started, the origin of her adoration of French braids. Isla had braided her hair for the first time on a whim, but over the next few months, it would become a daily obsession until Isla finally taught her how to do it for herself.

As Neve gathered the keys to the car Ellis bought for her to shuttle Nevermore around, she had the disorienting sensation of being in two places at once. Her hands moved on autopilot, double-checking that the season passes were tucked inside Isla's billfold, while her mind floated elsewhere. Neve's analytical brain was consumed with finding reason, and she was distracted, noodling on questions she couldn't answer. It seemed the longer Neve remained trapped inside Isla, the more comfortable she felt in the other woman's skin. But there was also the sensation of pieces of herself slipping away that was unnerving.

Lost in thought, she handed her Walkman over to the child, who snatched it eagerly from her hand and slipped the headphones over her ears. Without a word, they climbed into the car and set off down the familiar road leading to the Aura Cove Marine Rehabilitation Aquarium.

As she drove, Neve stole glances at Nevermore. It was an uncanny thing, viewing her childlike self from a different perspective, and she couldn't stop staring. In the seat next to her, the girl paid no mind to Neve's lingering gaze and tapped her fingers to a rhythm only she could hear. When they pulled into the parking lot, Nevermore's excitement was so palpable it burst from her in restless blips of motion. Rocking and tapping. Begging to be released.

Neve led Nevermore into the aquarium and beelined

to the octopus tank, knowing it was the child's favorite. She situated Nevermore far away from strollers filled with other children, banging and pawing at the tank. Neve stood transfixed, awed by the sensation of experiencing joy through the eyes of her younger self.

Blue streaks swirled across the child's face, the specular highlights casting a rippling glow on the small darkened room in cool blues and dark purples. She hovered close to the glass, entranced by the flowing movements of Willa, the vibrant orange Pacific octopus that inhabited the tank. Elegant and graceful, Willa glided closer to the girl, who tentatively reached out one hand and let out a giggle of delight when the octopus reached one tentacled arm toward her. It reminded Neve of Michelangelo's' fresco, *The Creation of Adam*. The movements of the cephalopod were hypnotic, and Neve crouched down next to the girl to marvel at the liquid way Willa navigated the waters.

Nevermore reached up to pull the headphones off her ears and let them encircle her neck. "They have three hearts, you know," she said, her voice a mix of awe and authority while she stared at the animal. "Two pump blood to their gills, and one pumps blood to the rest of their body. And their blood is blue because it's copper-based, not iron-based like ours. Isn't that rad?"

Neve did know. These were facts she'd memorized from the book her father had gifted her on her twelfth birthday. She'd become obsessed with sea animals, and he'd always loved to fan the flames of her curiosity. Knowing the child was bursting with information and desperate to share, Neve indulged her. "Why do you think they need three hearts?"

"Because they are always moving, just like me!" the girl exclaimed, her busy hands flapping as she spoke. "When they swim, one of their hearts stops beating. But when they're crawling around like that," she pointed as the octopus curled one of its arms around a rock, "all three hearts get going again."

Neve grinned and jumped in to offer her own fact to the excited child who was already rushing headlong into another. Their voices overlapped as they tried to share the exact same fact at the exact same time. "Did you know they are smarter than dogs and cats?"

"Jinx!" Neve said. "You owe me a Coke!"

Nevermore's enormous blue eyes widened. Jinxes were taken very seriously in her eyes.

"What else do you know?" Neve gave her an encouraging nod, prompting the girl to continue.

"They can open jars, escape from their tanks, and even play. Once, I read about an octopus that squirted water on a light switch until the lights went out because they were too bright. How cool is that?"

"Pretty cool," Neve agreed, glancing at the octopus as it slithered into a crevice, its skin shifting to mimic the texture of the rock. "I see why you love them so much. They're clever like you."

The compliment made the girl twist back and forth as if her body couldn't contain her joy. "I like them because they can hide away from people when they want to, or they can be super social." She flicked her gaze at Neve, a rarity that made Neve's heart clench in her chest. "They aren't stuck being what everyone else wants them to be."

Neve's throat tightened. She felt Isla's desire well up to reach out and place a hand gently on the girl's shoulder but decided against it. Instead, Isla's voice grew soft. "I think that's an incredible way to view the world."

The janitor wiped the glass with a soft cloth. He'd overheard every word of the conversation, and it had made a soft smile spread across his face. "Your daughter knows a lot about octopi."

"Isla is my nanny." Nevermore was quick to set him straight. "My mother is dead. She died when I was a baby."

Neve gasped. The factual yet detached way she delivered information had never bothered her before, but this time, seeing it from an outside perspective, she felt a stab of shame. The janitor's jaw dropped. He was stunned speechless and quickly departed them, pushing his cart of cleaning supplies into a darkened hallway.

Completely unaffected, the child shrugged, her gaze returning to the tank. Neve guided Nevermore through the rest of the exhibits and then to the overflowing gift shop, where she chose a small plush octopus, hugging it to her chest. Her excitement carried over to the car ride home as Nevermore's words spilled out in rapid bursts.

Neve listened patiently, asking questions that made the girl's enthusiasm shine brighter. She remembered what it felt like as a child speaking about a topic she loved. She was compelled to recall all the pertinent facts and share them with any person who showed an iota of interest. Nevermore rattled them off all the way home. It was a deluge of information, and Neve indulged her, knowing it was rare when Nevermore felt understood.

Later that evening, after a hot shower that made her skin lobster pink, Neve rifled through her closet, vetoing dress after dress. Each one was tighter and showed more skin than the last. At the very end, a conservative little black dress awaited, and when she pulled it over her long limbs and felt it fall over her skin, she was relieved that it at least seemed to cover most of her cleavage.

She stared down at the crimping iron. The moment her fingers brushed the rod, all the times Isla used it previously flooded into her consciousness, pushing away the self-doubt and softening her inexperience. She remembered Perry's revelation about having a bird Siamese twin. At the time, she hadn't understood it at all. Now that she was living it firsthand, it made more sense.

Twenty minutes later, her hair was seared into crimped compliance, her lips were slick with gloss, and she slid the tube and the green geode into the tiniest handbag she'd ever seen. The stone was glowing even brighter. Neve wondered if the change was a message of some kind. Unable to decode it, she walked out of her bedroom to see Ellis reading to Nevermore in the sunroom. He stopped short when he saw her in the doorway, and Neve shifted from one foot to another on the balls of her feet, feeling a flush of embarrassment from his focused attention.

"Take the car."

"I couldn't. I promised I would only use it for driving Nevermore."

"I insist," he said, adding, "The idea of you walking to the bus stop alone in the dark doesn't sit well with me."

Neve felt relief rush in, accompanied by a sweetness she wasn't prepared for over his concern. This was the type of fatherly energy she didn't know she longed for, and it overwhelmed her so much she had to fix her gaze on the floor.

"And take this," he said, striding closer and thrusting a fifty-dollar bill in her hand.

"You already pay me more than enough."

"A woman needs cash in case of an emergency," Ellis insisted. "There are those who would take advantage of a situation if given the opportunity." He pushed it closer, and she reluctantly took it, folded the bill, and put it in her purse.

"You're getting it back tomorrow," Neve said, and Ellis chuckled as he ambled away.

"Have fun. We won't wait up, will we, Nomo?"

"Bedtime is at 8:30," the girl declared. "Not 8:31."

"Yep. 8:30 sharp, you're right," Neve confirmed with a small wave as she left them cozied up in the sunroom. She stole one last glance at them in the amber-colored light, listening to the patient timbre of her father's voice as he answered each of Nevermore's questions without complaint. She closed her eyes, committing the memory to the most important part of her brain, and then forced herself out into the cooler evening air.

Twenty minutes later, she pulled up to a security intercom in front of iron gates flanked by lush tropical landscaping and several palm trees. When she was admitted access, the doors creaked open with a mechanical groan, revealing a winding cobblestone driveway, already filled with cars. She parked, retrieved her handbag, and started down the drive, her slingbacks tapping against the stone as she approached the mansion.

It was a sprawling Mediterranean villa with a roof of clay tiles and so many turrets it reminded her of a castle. Vines crept up creamy stucco walls, their green tendrils framing enormous arched windows lit from within, and Neve could see flashes of movement from people inside.

Neve hesitated at the double doors; their deep mahogany surface was intricately carved and studded with leaded glass with wrought iron scrollwork sandwiched in between. She rang the doorbell and could hear it echo inside. A minute later, a fifty-something maid opened it, flashing Neve a warm smile. Dressed in a black uniform with a white apron and orthopedic shoes, a name tag on her chest identified her as Rosa.

She cocked her head at Neve and asked, "Are you here for dinner party?"

"Yes, I'm Isla Warner."

Rosa clapped her hands together. "Mr. Ruben be so happy! He tell me to bring you to him as soon you get here."

"Oh!" A burst of surprise left Isla's full lips. Neve was bowled over by the special treatment. Ruben's favor shored up her confidence that typically wilted in social situations, and Neve was grateful as she thrust Isla's shoulders back, pasted on a smile, and followed Rosa as she snaked through the crowd. The house buzzed with small clusters of people, each deep in conversation, wine glasses and champagne flutes in hand. Their glasses never seemed to empty, thanks to three servers who endlessly circled with refills.

Neve overheard bits and pieces of pretentious conversations as she grew more accustomed to walking in heels on Isla's long legs. "Investing in fine art isn't just about beauty; it's a tangible asset that appreciates over time. It's a strategy that prominent families have utilized to preserve their wealth for generations."

Enya's *Orinoco Flow* played softly in the background, its new-age soundwaves mingling with the scent of linseed oil and jasmine in the air. A magnificent curved staircase twisted upward, with a handmade wrought iron banister. Covering the walls was a collection of enormous canvases. Some were mounted in gold leaf frames while others were merely leaning against the walls. Ruben's collection of museum-quality art was eclectic and extensive, and Neve longed to linger and study each one.

"Isla! *Mon chéri!*" Ruben exclaimed, his French accent making his words ooze with hypnotic sexiness as he crossed the room with an entourage of onlookers in tow. The movement made the silk scarf draped loosely around his neck flow behind him. His smile was broad and genuine, and his dark curls tousled as he pulled her in for a hug, depositing kisses on each of her cheeks. He was barefoot, wearing loose linen pants cuffed at the ankles and a peasant shirt that was so splattered with dried paint it almost became a canvas itself.

Unsure of herself, Neve slipped off Isla's heels and kicked them to the side, dodging glances from the small group gathered around Ruben. The tiles were cooling underfoot, and the relief from the pinching footwear was instant.

"Bravo, darling! Yes! Please, make yourself at home." Ruben clapped his hands together, his gaze warm as it fixed on her, and the corners of his eyes crinkled. Instead of feeling like she was under a microscope, Neve felt a surge of unexpected heat well up in her core from his focused attention.

Seconds later, the rest of the crowd gathered around them began to remove their shoes. Under his spell, Neve took a tentative step toward Ruben and tripped on a pair of wedges, pitching her forward. He caught her by the forearms, and Neve tingled from where his hands touched her bare skin. Isla's self-deprecating laugh burbled out in a high-pitched peal of delight. When she was safely standing by his side and his arm was protectively slung around her waist, Ruben produced a small bell from his pocket and rang it, summoning Rosa.

"Could you please gather the discarded footwear and see that it is organized by the door for my guests? It's become a trip hazard."

Rosa quickly dipped her head yes in response and got to work while Ruben led Neve to a vintage velvet sofa in the solarium. The rest of the group filtered in, following him as if he were the pied piper. Ruben seemed to feed off their attention, getting sustenance from it rather than feeling drained. He popped the cork on a bottle of wine, pouring the contents into two wine glasses and handing the rest of the bottle off to a server to pour for the other guests. He picked them both up and offered one glass to Neve.

Cradling his own with his long fingers, once everyone had a glass, he lifted his to make a toast. "To unceasing curiosity and beauty in all its forms." Ruben reached forward to tap her glass. He shot her a roguish wink, and Neve felt herself blush with pleasure again. The gesture seemed intimate like he'd shared a tantalizing secret. Internally, Neve was a rollercoaster of emotion, and she seesawed between the obvious attraction Isla felt for Ruben and her own natural logic and social awkwardness.

Eager for relief, Neve took a step back and took a sip of her wine, watching him enthrall his other guests. She was grateful the physical space calmed the roar of emotion coursing through her. Farther from him, Neve found she could take full breaths again, and her heartbeat slowed down to a more manageable pace. In this calmer state, she studied him from afar.

His easy confidence was charming, and he appeared humble. Ruben didn't once mention his work unless directly asked about it, and even then, he seemed to answer their questions as concisely as possible. He introduced other topics of conversation, shining the spotlight on his favorite contemporary artists and which cafe to find the best coffee in Paris. When he mentioned David Bowie, Neve was shocked to discover Isla must be a raving fan, as she could now speak intelligently on his music, though she'd never cared about it before. The duality of her consciousness filled her with a sense of awe and wonder. She was learning new things every minute about the woman whose body she inhabited, and she could feel Isla's more relaxed and confident countenance calm her social anxiety.

Ruben was magnetic, the kind of man who made everyone feel like they were the center of his world. He knew how to work a room and weave stories and playful anecdotes that captivated the crowd, and it seemed to energize him. Surprisingly, Neve found herself clamoring for his attention along with the rest of his guests, unsure if this was Isla's influence or her own curiosity. Around her, the room tilted toward him, every smile angled his way. And still, somehow, Neve leaned in closer, feeling herself getting swept away into the spotlight of his focused attention.

After an hour of laughter and conversation, he stood

abruptly and whispered in her ear, "Come," his eyes sparkling with mischief. "There's something I want to show you." Goosebumps sent a chill through her when his breath brushed across her collarbone. Neve didn't pull back when he grabbed her by the hand and led her up the winding staircase and then down a long hallway. It was a gallery of original artwork, some she recognized from her Art History class in college, and a few she remembered from his exhibition in Aura Cove. She longed to linger, but Ruben tugged her down the hallway too quickly, eager to have her to himself. Being the subject of his undivided attention was a heady experience. It sent Isla swooning as her own besotted thoughts spiraled. The dual experience of intense attraction sent her reeling.

They climbed a hidden staircase and arrived at a heavy oak door on the other side of the mansion, its surface marred with streaks of paint. He pushed it open to reveal a studio loft with an entire wall of windows. Candles and small lamps illuminated the room, and Neve drank it in. Paintings in various stages of completion lined the walls, while jars of brushes, tubes of oils and acrylics, and scraps of canvas cluttered every available surface.

And there it was. His masterpiece. In the center of the room, bathed in a single spotlight, was an immense canvas, nearly as tall as Isla herself. The painting was propped on a towering easel and clearly still a work in progress, yet it already hinted at the brilliance of the original she'd seen at Ruben's show in Aura Cove. The skin of the woman's graceful back glowed against the burgundy draped fabric that bound together a mother and a child, their heads tipped toward each other, lost in a blissful moment of connection.

"What do you think?" Ruben asked, his voice low and filled with a vulnerability she'd never heard before in a man. He circled her, hungry for her feedback, savoring her reaction, her sharp intake of breath.

Neve stepped closer, her eyes tracing the bold strokes of color that were his signature, encompassing deep blues, fiery oranges, and stark ivory highlights. The composition was a study of curves, with the bold color palette and layers of stippled impressionistic texture his work was known for. The paint was thick, applied by a skilled hand wielding a palette knife, and she felt an almost irresistible urge to reach out and touch it. While the woman's face was practically finished, the features of the baby were just beginning to emerge from the layers of paint.

"Inheritance of Grace," she whispered.

"What did you say?"

"That's what you should call it."

"*Fantastique!*" He bounced on the balls of his feet, joy spreading across his features, and Neve felt another flash of searing heat from his positive reaction. He brought her hand to his lips and kissed the top of it. "We are a perfect team!"

"It's extraordinary," she breathed, stepping closer and letting her eyes drink it in inch by inch.

Ruben offered a shy smile, his expression fighting

between pride and insecurity. "It's not finished yet. But when it is, I think it will change everything."

"Who is she?" Neve asked, her gaze fixed on the woman in the painting.

"I can't believe you don't see the resemblance," he said, a slight blush creeping up his neck.

"See what?"

"She's… you. Or, at least, how I see you when you become a mother."

Neve turned to him, startled. "Me?" She felt his eyes boring into her as if she were on display, and the vulnerability made her heart race.

Ruben ran a hand through his dark curls, suddenly bashful. "There is something about the way you carry yourself. It's as if magic runs through your veins. I can't stop thinking about you."

He stepped closer, and Neve's breath caught in her throat. Isla's laugh escaped in a burst as her nerves got the better of her. Neve had never been pursued so intently. It felt heady and dangerous. To calm the storm of emotion welling inside her, she turned back to the painting, trying to reconcile the figure on the canvas with the body she currently inhabited, finally admitting there was an undeniable resemblance.

Ruben's expression grew serious. "I believe it has the potential to be the most influential piece of my entire lifetime. When it's finished, it will travel the world. Museums, galleries, and private collectors will clamor for it, as entranced by your beauty as I am." He grabbed her hand and twirled her body into his, and

Neve let him. He was warm and inviting, his eyes dancing with joy as an unspoken energy zinged between them, making her giddy. Combined with the tipsiness from the wine, she felt her inhibitions melting away as his whisper brushed across her neck and caressed her earlobe. "It might take decades before people really see the importance of this piece. Art has a funny way of waiting for its time."

"It's true. Someday, museums will be fighting over it." Neve let the future slip from her tongue loosened by wine, glancing up at him, getting lost in his eyes and finding the eye contact more than tolerable. "You will have sold-out shows. People will line up to see your work, and you'll achieve immortality. Someday, this piece will sell for millions at auction."

"Is that so?" He grinned and nuzzled her cheek. "I love *your* vision of *our* future," he murmured, his face dipping so close Neve felt dizzy. She took a small step backward, trying to regain control of her emotions.

As if sensing her hesitation, he broke the silence with a laugh and struck his forehead with the palm of his hand. "*Mon Dieu!* I've scared you, haven't I? Talking about destiny and art like a madman."

"Maybe a little," she admitted, grinning. Neve pulled away from him and took another step toward his palette and brushes, skimming her thumb across the horsehair tips of a fan brush. "Can I watch you work?"

"My process requires total dedication. Knowing you are in the room would be intimidating, and I need the freedom to explore and create without judgment."

"I understand," Neve said, clearly disappointed.

"I will make it up to you in other ways." He drew her into his arms and grazed his full lips across hers. A shiver shot down Neve's spine. She leaned closer, finding Isla's lips parting, becoming instinctively obedient. She smoothed her hands over the broad line of his shoulders and melted into a puddle of warm butter under his touch. Sparks ignited behind her eyes and fireworks burst in brilliant silence. It was her first kiss, albeit borrowed in Isla's body, but somehow it felt safer there. She'd always wondered what it would feel like to kiss a man, and now she knew. It was fizzy, like the champagne Talulah liked to sip on special occasions. It was a fluttering sensation and a freefall of bliss that edged toward pain, and she swallowed the overwhelming desire to squeal with pleasure. What a rush.

The sound of chimes made them both resurface from the smitten bubble they were ensconced in. "Ah, yes, I promised my guests I would dazzle them with something special. We will pick up where we left off afterward? Perhaps we can enjoy a nightcap?"

"Um… possibly." Neve was suddenly shy and grateful for the diversion as she fought an internal battle about what would come next if Ruben continued his pursuit.

"Could you inform our guests I will be with them momentarily?"

Relieved, Neve nodded and made her way down the hall and back to the main staircase.

"Ruben has a surprise in store for us in a few minutes!" she called down from the landing. "Gather around. You won't want to miss it."

At the base of the stairs, the crowd thrummed with anticipation, their voices buzzing with the clinking of champagne glasses and short bursts of laughter. When Ruben walked out to meet Neve on the landing, he raised a hand for silence, his gaze sweeping over the sea of admirers as he bathed in their adoration. With a dramatic flourish that seemed more in line with a Penn & Teller Magic Show, Neve and the rest of the guests burst into applause when a large object covered with a dark velvet drape was wheeled into the room. Ruben disappeared behind it and when he reappeared, perched on his arm was a sleek African Grey parrot with feathers like polished silver. The bird blinked, clearly unamused by the sudden attention. More applause covered the sharp gasp from Neve as her hand flew to her mouth.

Could it be?

With a grin, Ruben bent closer to whisper a command to the bird.

"Ruben Angelica is the next DaVinci!" the bird squawked, and the crowd burst into more spontaneous applause as Ruben beamed. Without hesitation, the parrot continued, "Genius, he's a genius."

Compelled to know the truth, Neve took a step closer, tentatively offering her arm as a perch for the bird. He hopped over and squawked even more loudly as he climbed up the length of Isla's forearm.

"Perry?" Neve whispered, swinging him closer to her torso.

"Bwakkk!" His eyes narrowed as he got more agitated.

"It's me. Neve," she whispered, burying her face into his feathers to mask the words. Perry did an about-face, jutting his feathered head back, and Neve's heart leapt. "I'll find a way to get you out of here," she promised as Perry nuzzled into her hair. "So much has happened…" Neve was desperate to talk to him but was interrupted by Ruben's showmanship.

"Seems the bird has exquisite taste in women." Ruben smiled, then tried to guide the bird's attention back to him. "Say, 'Ruben Angelica is an artistic genius!'"

Perry, emboldened by finding Neve, let out a shrill whistle and flapped his wings indignantly.

"Ruben Angelica is an egotistical asshole," he whistled, and the crowd fell awkwardly silent, giving him the opportunity to level another insult. "Ruben Angelica is a talentless hack." Neve flinched, knowing Perry had a flair for the dramatics, but fearing Ruben's reaction to it.

The crowd gasped. Some applauded, assuming it was part of the act. A burble of laughter shot up from the crowd, and a voice said, "Oh, snap! That bird totally roasted you." The words echoed through the space and drew laughter from the crowd again.

Ever the show-off, Perry launched himself from Neve's arm, his wings pumping furiously as he soared up the two-story room to perch on a plastered column near the skylight. Delighted with his performance, the bird crowed from on high.

Ruben stormed over to the cage and tapped it, demanding his return. The clang of the metal as it hit against the collection of rings on his fingers made Neve wince. His over-the-top theatrical charm was quickly dissolving into thinly veiled irritation, and she could feel the tension rising.

"Come here, you stupid creature!" he hissed, staring up at the parrot who let out a bored squawk.

"You're the one who's *trés stupide*!" Perry blurted with glee as he left his perch and circled the room, swiping closer to where Ruben and Neve stood.

"He doesn't mean it," Neve said, trying to play peacemaker.

"Of course he doesn't. He has a brain the size of a walnut," Ruben snapped, jumping up in a failed attempt to reclaim the bird. He landed on Isla's foot, twisting her ankle, and Neve crumpled to the ground, letting out a yelp of pain.

Hearing Neve's cry, Perry circled closer, flapping his wings wildly, feathers flying. "Still bigger than yours!" he screeched, swiping at Ruben with his beak. Perry dove in attack mode, as the onlookers scrambled for cover. Champagne glasses spilled. A man in a bowtie tripped over a pedestal, sending a sculpture crashing to the ground. Satisfied with the chaos he created, Perry darted higher and glided above Neve and Ruben as he figured out his next move.

He circled one more time before hovering directly above Ruben's head, and then he deposited a generous blob of green and white excrement on the artist's shoulder with a chirping chuckle. When it landed, Ruben's face twisted into a scowl as he stood frozen in place in shock. Neve barked her laugh into her palm, climbing to her feet and hobbling to a banister as pandemonium broke out.

"Don't worry, sir. That's supposed to be lucky!" Amos offered from the dessert table covered in crystal that he was protecting from the rush of guests seeking a safe place from the crazed bird.

Ruben turned to him, incredulous, his eyes threatening to pop out of their sockets. "Lucky? LUCKY?" he screamed, his tone shrill. He gestured to his soiled shirt. "I was just shat upon by that winged menace. If this is luck, fate has a twisted sense of humor!"

"For real, it blends right in with the paint splatters on your shirt. Call it a two-toned masterpiece, my man."

Ruben rolled his eyes at Amos and let out a hot huff of frustration while Perry circled, beating his wings again, squawking in what sounded suspiciously like laughter.

He glanced up at his shoulder again, sighed, and gave a small, self-deprecating chuckle. "Perhaps a collaboration with the bird is in the cards?" Ruben joked in a booming voice, finally getting his emotions under control and trying to save face. He straightened and flashed a practiced grin as his easygoing host persona slid back into place.

"What a great idea! With those feathers, he practically has his own brushes built in!" Neve added with Isla's beaming smile and a playful shrug, eager to take some of the heat off Perry.

The crowd erupted in laughter and applause. Even Ruben couldn't resist cracking a rueful grin. He reached over for Neve as the crowd began to disperse. "*Mon chéri*, please forgive me. I hope I have not hurt you."

"Just a bit of a sprain." Neve rotated her tender ankle, wincing in pain as she hobbled the first few steps. She was relieved when she heard Isla wave off his concern and even more relieved when she limped to the door and said, "But I think we better call it a night."

CHAPTER 14
PEREGRINE

THE NEXT MORNING, phantom fingers tapped the metal bars of the cage where I lay weak with hunger. I had been exiled without snacks and had reluctantly returned to my roost after the stunt my bird twin pulled at Ruben's party.

Disdain filled me for my dual occupant. He'd taken the controls and forced me to debase myself in front of a crowd, and the embarrassment still made my feathers flame. It was bad enough that I was a prisoner in his bird body, but to share it with a vile creature who preferred to fight his battles with excrement felt punitive.

The dark cloth over the cage obscured my view as I opened one drowsy eye. Then a shaft of morning light infiltrated the cage as the fabric slid down the metal bars of the enclosure. A curious, elfish female face leaned in, filling the space and shooting me a wide smile, exposing crooked white teeth and a smattering of freckles across a dainty upturned nose. Her blonde hair fell down in waves to her shoulders, and her baby bangs were separated from the waves by a thick red headband. She was of slight build, wearing a long shift dress splattered with paint.

A human! A new one I hadn't met yet! I started to rustle and flap and screech out a greeting as I sized her up.

"Rise and shine," she sang, seemingly thrilled to see me.

"Open sesame," I said as I bobbed and weaved my feathered head. "Bwaaak! Open sesame." I watched her hand drift to the cage door, reaching out when Rosa appeared.

"Time for breakfast, Camille," Rosa said. "You no be in library. Ruben no like. The bird in time-out."

"Time-out?" Camille asked as a concerned frown twisted up her features. She seemed familiar with the concept. "He's been trapped in there all night. Can't we let him out?" she asked, clanging her fist on the cage three times, almost as if she felt compelled to do it. She repeated the question a few more times as she crossed the room, walking on her tiptoes. Rosa grabbed Camille by the hand to lead her away, when she made a frustrated yelp.

"*Ay! Dios mío!!*" Rosa said under her breath as Camille became more agitated and started to let out distressed yips intermixed with tears. She wrung her hands together, pointing at me, making a scene.

"No!" she shouted. "I am not leaving! I want to have

breakfast here, with the bird." Her stubbornness amped up as Rosa tried to calm her with soft words in Spanish. None of it worked. Camille dug in and doubled down in both volume and quantity. From the cage, I squawked in solidarity with my new best friend.

Rosa sighed in defeat, briefly left the room, and then a few minutes later returned with Amos, who was carrying a breakfast tray. The sight calmed Camille's rising hysteria instantly.

Well played. I stuck one wing out and bowed, staring at the slight woman who'd successfully manipulated two grown adults into getting what she desired.

"Over here, sweetheart," Amos said, setting the tray down. I eyed it greedily. Sunny eggs, a bright green apple, and two slices of bacon. He handed her the roll of silverware. "All the usual suspects."

"Yep. Eggs, apple, bacon," she said, naming them as she took her inventory, then she turned the plate a quarter turn and picked up a strip of the meat.

Bacon. I would never taste its smoky deliciousness again. Famished, I watched her settle in and start eating. I leaned closer, the insides of my stomach rubbing against each other, causing a growling noise while I watched Camille chew.

"Gimme a bite!" I chirped and clicked, delighted when Camille laughed and darted over to my cage on her tiptoes with the slice of bacon in her hand. I was salivating at the sight of it.

"Bacon! Come to Peregrine. Yum, yum, yum!" I

cawed as I bobbed up and down, encouraging her with short phrases, careful not to draw too much attention to myself. Amos let out a chuckle and reached out to trade an apple for the bacon, and my heart dropped. Cockblocked by the cook. There would be no bacon for me.

"He might love it, but he can't have it. Birds eat nuts and healthy fruits like apples."

Camille pressed the apple through the bars of the cage, and I pecked at it greedily, devouring most of it in a rapid succession of tiny chomps from my beak. Beggars can't be choosers. She watched me eat, tucking her fingers out of harm's way as the apple disappeared. Over the next five minutes, I felt my good senses return as my blood sugar normalized. I chirped and cooed in thanksgiving and nuzzled her soft fingers through the rungs of the cage with the top of my head.

"He likes me," she said, pleased as punch. The fine collection of crow's feet crinkled at the corners of her eyes as she stroked the feathers on my head through the bars of the cage.

"He does," Amos confirmed with a warm smile.

The door opened and Amos jumped to gather the dirty plates and silverware as Ruben strode in toward us. I felt Camille's fingers tremble the closer he approached. With great regret, she pulled her hand away and laced her fingers together in front of her.

"Camille, please step away from the cage. The bird is unpredictable. We cannot take the chance of him hurting one of your precious fingers."

She raced away on her tiptoes, letting out anguished

cries and a huff of frustration. "You treat me like a child when I'm thirty-two years old!"

He ignored her outburst and turned to Rosa. "Take her to the studio." After Rosa led her away, he smacked the cage with the back of his hand, sending me flapping to the opposite corner in an act of self-preservation.

Ruben narrowed his eyes as he studied me through the bars. I let out a series of nervous clicks and whirs. His forehead frowned and his brows scrunched together into one bushy black line. Propping his chin on his hand, he continued to stare me down, his lips curled with disgust. As much as I didn't want to, I forced myself to offer him an apology. The first attempt was garbled. I tried again. "Sorry."

The word startled him and he leaned closer, intrigued. "What are you sorry *for*, bird?"

"Poopy party! Poopy party!" I rocked my body side to side, hopping from one leg to the other, choosing to respond in my companion's more staccato idiotic phrases. I was an expert at reading a room and understood my typical haughty indifference would not bode well in this situation. I danced in cadence with the words, a comical performance that Ruben found oddly entertaining. I added the words, "Oopsie poopsie!" Then I gave another loud squawk and a round of flapping my wings. I knew once more might do the trick, so I repeated, "Oopsie poopsie!" and fluffed up my chest with a whir.

It worked. Ruben's scowl was replaced by a wide

grin and a warm, boisterous laugh. "Quite the comedian, aren't you?"

I bowed deeply, swiping a wing across my body in response.

Rosa returned, and in the distance Camille's cries were muffled. "Camille very sad. She fall in love with bird too quick."

Ruben waved her concern away as if it annoyed him. "Good. When we're finished working for the day, spending time with the bird can be her reward."

"The bird is Peregrine!" I cawed, tired of hearing them call me "the bird" in a tone that dripped with disdain. "Peregrine is the bird!"

"Peregrine, huh?" Ruben repeated. "Of course it is." He leaned closer. "A word to the wise, Peregrine, if you can't control your bowels, you'll be headed to the taxidermist."

I chirped and ducked my head, letting his ice cold threat sink in. He turned to Rosa, his lips curled into a smirk as if he'd not just made a threat against my life. "I must get back to work. Please see that lunch is served in the conservatory by one p.m." He sniffed the air. "And clean out that cage. It's revolting."

At last, I would be freed from the confines of the cage while she cleaned it. "Ruben is an artistic genius!" I added, showing my gratitude. Ruben chuckled as he walked away, hands tucked behind his back. He whistled a little tune. I mimicked it, eliciting another soft chuckle of amusement from him, and then he disappeared down the hall.

CHAPTER

FIFTEEN

BACK IN AURA COVE, Neve limped out of Isla's bedroom, following the hum of the morning news broadcast. Still drowsy from sleep, she detoured over to the neat kitchen, making a pot of coffee. Pouring two cups, she hobbled down the hallway and into the sunroom where Ellis was working in the morning sun with the television on. Seeing her pained shuffle, he stood and rushed to her side, relieving her of both of the cups, and she hopped on her good leg over to a chair to sit.

"Did you hurt yourself last night?"

"Just a silly sprain, a party injury, I guess you could call it," Neve responded without overthinking. It was the strangest sensation to just let the words roll off her tongue without carefully considering if they were the right ones first. Then it was accompanied by a burst of self-deprecating laughter, another of Isla's influences that astonished her.

"Ah, to be young and foolish again." Ellis shot her a quick smile of gratitude as he took a sip of the coffee she'd made. "Strong enough you could almost chew it. You know me well."

His praise made warmth rush through her, and she locked it away, wanting to remember it forever. Neve took a breath to steady herself before asking, "Is Nevermore awake?"

"Not yet," he said. "I need your help this morning. My sister is coming by any minute. Can you keep Nomo occupied elsewhere while we chat?"

"Of course." Neve stared down at the stack of legal documents piled high on the coffee table. Curious, she squinted, trying to make out some of the words, becoming frustrated when he covered them with one of his scientific notebooks. Neve bit the inside of her cheek just as a soft knock sounded at the door. She stood to answer it, but Ellis interrupted her.

"I can get it."

Stubborn, Neve said, "It's better when I don't let it stiffen up too long. My father taught me to push through pain."

"Well, he must have been a very smart man," Ellis said, wrapping his long fingers around the cup and turning back to the paperwork.

"He was," Neve whispered, saddened by the past tense as she hobbled away with tears in her eyes. She'd always found the transformation from *is* to *was* devastating; it had the ability to send her reeling each time it came up in the middle of an average day, often without warning. She shook it off and ambled to the door, relieved that the movement did seem to loosen the stiffness in her ankle.

But when she opened the door, Neve was unprepared to see her beloved aunt radiant and in the prime of her early thirties. Her bright gray-blue eyes sparkled with intelligence in her smiling face, and the gap between Talulah's front teeth was endearing, a flaw she'd always embraced. Talulah wore her long hair loose, a cascade of platinum blonde that caught the sunlight streaming through the palm trees at the entrance of the house.

The cloud of lavender enveloping her aunt made Neve close her eyes and inhale deeply, unlocking a flood of childhood memories. She leveled her gaze on Talulah's face, noting her skin was glowing and smooth and her crow's feet were barely noticeable. Talulah radiated light and joy, and Neve was astonished to experience the breadth of it anew through Isla's eyes, knowing in a few short years, the devastating loss of her brother would dim it.

Talulah offered a greeting, "Hello, Isla. Ellis is expectin' me."

Neve tucked her trembling hands behind her back. They wanted to reach out, to fling her body into Talulah's arms and hold her close. Neve wasn't a hugger, and Isla's physical knee-jerk reaction confused her. She adored Talulah, but Neve wasn't typically comfortable expressing emotion through touch. However, in Isla's body, she seemed to crave it, and

Neve had to tamp the desire down as words caught in her throat, knowing it would only lead to danger and confusion.

"Of course, he's in the sunroom," Neve offered and watched her aunt's thin frame practically float down the hall. Talulah wasn't yet the woman who'd been forced to forgo her own grief to help her niece navigate hers. She was buoyant and carefree.

Neve tried to give them privacy and stay away, but under the guise of starting laundry, she found herself edging closer to the open door of the sunroom. Focusing on the low voices of her father and aunt, there was a soft shuffling of paper as Ellis sorted through the legal documents. Neve hid just out of view, watching their interaction with great interest, praying Nevermore would stay asleep long enough for her to learn something.

"Sign here," Ellis said, his voice subdued as he pushed a stack of legal documents toward Talulah and flipped through the pages. "And here. And… here."

"Wait." Talulah hesitated, the pen she'd been given hovering over the page. She glanced up at her brother, her eyes graying with concern. "This isn't just a grocery list. It's your *life* and Nevermore's. Please tell me why you feel such urgency to establish legal guardianship documents now."

Ellis rubbed his temples, the exhaustion in his movements visible. "It's something I should have taken care of years ago. I need to make sure there are resources in place for Nomo if something should happen to me…" The rest of his words died on his lips as Talulah reached out and gripped his hand in support.

"Don't be silly. Nothin' is going to happen to you," Talulah interrupted, her direct tone cutting through the air.

"I know, but this job may be the death of me. The lab's a pressure cooker, and I'm a single father. I need to make arrangements just in case…" He drifted off again. "Honestly, I could use the peace of mind. It's been in short supply lately."

Talulah leaned closer. "I agree. It *is* important to have a contingency plan." She paused, squeezing her fingers around his wrist, connecting with his quickened pulse. "But a stressed heart beats its way to an early grave," she said softly. "You're runnin' yourself into the ground, and I don't think you even see it."

Ellis looked away, his jaw tight, but she pressed on. "You're barely sleepin', and you've got Isla practically runnin' the household while you're locked away at the lab or buried in your studies. It's not sustainable. If you burn out and a heart attack sends you to an early grave, what happens to Nevermore?"

"But I'm doing this *for* her," he murmured, his voice rough.

"I know you are," Talulah said gently. "But what if the *way* you're doin' it costs you everything? You can't plan for Nevermore's future if you're not a part of it. You need to take a break, a real one." She laced her fingers together and leaned closer, her expression imploring.

Ellis's hands balled into fists on the table, his knuckles white. He stared at the papers in front of him, his voice barely above a murmur. "You don't understand. I can't stop. If I don't finish this work, the whole project collapses. And if that happens… what kind of legacy is that for my daughter?"

"She doesn't need a legacy," Talulah said, her voice soft but firm. "She needs a father who sees her. Who understands her."

Ellis's shoulders sagged, and he let out a shaky breath. For a moment, he looked older than his thirty-nine years, the weight of his burdens etched into every line of his face. "What if I *don't* understand her?" he finally admitted, the words tumbling out like a confession.

Talulah tilted her head, her brow furrowing. "What are you talkin' about?"

Ellis hesitated, his eyes darting down the hall where Nevermore slept. "She's… different. Have you noticed? She doesn't look at me when we talk. Not really. It's like she's focused on something else and looking right through me. And the other day, I dropped a plate on the floor where it shattered, and she just froze. Then Nevermore covered her ears with her palms and started rocking. I tried to comfort her, but she pulled away like my touch was too much."

Talulah's lips parted in surprise, but she stayed silent, letting him continue.

"And it's not just that," Ellis added, his voice tinged with helplessness. "She's so… particular. About her clothes, her food, her routines. If something's out of place, she shuts down. Yesterday, I used one of her pencils without thinking, and she refused to go to sleep until I put it back in the case."

"Ellis," Talulah said gently, her heart breaking at the vulnerability in his tone.

"I don't know what to do," he admitted, his voice cracking. "She's brilliant. The way she explores the world through her drawings, it's like she can see every detail through a microscope. But sometimes it's like she's not even a part of this one. What if… what if something's wrong with her?"

Talulah reached for his hand, her touch steadying. "Nothin' is wrong with Nevermore. She's unique. You said it yourself; she just sees the world differently. Maybe all she needs is for you to meet her where she is and help her figure it out."

Talulah squeezed his hand tighter, her eyes locking with his. "Stop bein' so hard on yourself. You don't have to have all the answers right now. You're a scientist. You know how to adapt. You experiment. You find a way."

Ellis exhaled, his eyes glistening. He nodded slowly, then whispered, "I'll try."

"Good," Talulah said, her voice resolute. "Because she needs you. Just as you are, not some unattainable perfect father. Not the man with all the answers. Just her dad."

A faint shuffle of movement near the doorway made her pause. Talulah's gaze flicked toward the shadow in the hallway. "Isla," she called out, her tone direct. "Is there somethin' you need?"

Neve felt her cheeks flame in mortification as she took a few steps inside the sunroom. "Sorry, I didn't mean to eavesdrop, but I heard you mentioning Nevermore, and I think I have a suggestion that could help."

Ellis straightened, his jaw tightening. "Isla, this is a private conversation."

"I understand." Neve tried to offer a smile to deflect the tension. "I only wanted to help. Nevermore's drawings *are* extraordinary, and I may have met someone who could help develop her skills. I've been doing some modeling for Ruben Angelica." Again, the words tumbled out with ease, and Neve let them.

"The artist?" Talulah interjected, clearly already acquainted with his work.

"Yes," Neve continued, gushing as Isla's excitement grew inside her. "Perhaps he could evaluate her work? Speak to her about a future career in the arts?"

"That's not necessary," Ellis said, a stiff edge to his tone.

But Talulah jumped in, her eyes narrowing on her brother. "Actually, it *is* necessary. Nevermore has a gift. She could create a life from it, but she needs someone to nurture her talent. And let's face it, you're not the person for that. You don't have the time *or* the patience."

Ellis flinched as though struck. He opened his mouth to argue but then closed it, his jaw ticking and his

Adam's apple bobbing when he swallowed. His next words were strained as if they were physically painful. "I will give it some thought."

"Fair enough. I'll go see if the little miss is awake," Neve said, disappearing back down the hallway. At Nevermore's door, she pressed her forehead against it, getting her bearings. What she'd just overheard sent her bobbing in a sea of turmoil. There was so much to process.

Her father was afraid he was failing her. It was the first time she'd even considered the possibility. In her mind, he loomed as large as an action figure, always protecting her. She'd never considered he was susceptible to other human emotions like fear, regret, and insecurity. To see her father waffling on his decisions and questioning his parenting from Isla's vantage point was sobering. It left Neve feeling confused and questioning every memory from her childhood.

CHAPTER

SIXTEEN

THE NEXT MORNING, after dropping Nevermore off at school, Neve hurried home, her pulse quickening with anticipation. With Ellis at work, it was the first full day she had to herself since arriving, and she refused to waste it.

A week had passed since she'd woken up in the past as Isla, yet she was no closer to uncovering what had happened to her father. Meanwhile, Ellis remained blissfully unaware of her true identity, burying himself in research and doting on Nevermore on the few nights he was home.

As impossible as it seemed, she'd finally acknowledged the truth. She'd traveled to a different time, and every television show, movie, and book she'd ever read on time travel all pointed to one fact: Neve was put here for a reason, and if she wanted answers, she had to figure out what that reason was before time ran out.

In her pocket, the sliver of geode tingled. Neve intuitively understood it was a guide of some sort, a temporal key that unlocked a crucial moment in the past. It was valuable, and since she'd landed, she'd heeded Ana Casanova's advice to keep it close at all times.

With little else to go on, Neve thought through the facts. Somehow, Perry had traveled back to 1989 with her. He was currently stuffed into a gilded cage a mere twenty minutes away at Ruben Angelica's home. Why? It didn't make any sense. Why were they separated? The geode tingled again, glowing brighter, but revealed nothing.

In frustration, Neve let out a heavy exhalation and decided to solve that riddle later, in favor of the one that had consumed her since she was fifteen. Neve had a hunch the answers she needed were hidden somewhere inside these four walls. The house held secrets and, being given this second chance, she was focused on unearthing them all.

She padded down the hallway barefoot. The humidity made the floor sweat, and she wrinkled her nose, jonesing for her trusty pair of hiking boots. Normally, the moist sensation would have stopped her cold, but she felt Isla's influence gently propelling her down the hall.

The Florida sun filtered through the pristine windows of the sunroom, casting dappled light on the heavy wooden desk. Neve hesitated in the doorway, inhaling the scent of old leather and the tang of mildew lingering in the air. Neve ran a finger across the edge of Ellis's desk, its surface littered with papers, notebooks, and technical drawings. She reached down to pick up one of his notebooks from the tidy stack in the desk's corner. She flipped through it, noticing his handwritten observations were stacked in neat rows, the data organized in straight columns. Neve paged further, and his penmanship appeared strained as if he were cutting the words into the paper. He scribbled notes in the margins, and there were small doodles as if he struggled with the protocol in his mind and was trying to unlock the answers. The tiny drawings intrigued her and made her feel more connected to him. The last page of the book made her gasp. It was a recognizable sketch of twelve-year-old Nevermore. Her head was bent toward the paper, engrossed in her drawing, her brow furrowed.

See? Your father saw you. Truly saw you.

Isla's thought was intrusive whispering through her mind, cutting through her memories and gutting her with tenderness. The softer version of her father she encountered through Isla contradicted what she thought she knew.

Time unraveled as she pored over his latest journal, each entry pulling her deeper into the intricate workings of his mind. His meticulous notes revealed an intellect both razor-sharp and endlessly curious, paired with a relentless work ethic that left her in awe.

As a child, she had only glimpsed fragments of his world, but now, each page unveiled hidden layers of his life she had never known. The chance to understand her father on such an intimate level felt like an unexpected gift. His mind was a machine of logic and analysis, yet in his moments of raw brainstorming, she recognized flashes of creativity that felt familiar, mirroring her own. She closed the journal and placed it back where she found it. It was a start, but she yearned to know more.

Neve walked down the hallway to his bedroom, standing outside the door for an hour before she breached the threshold.

Careful.

Ignoring Isla's warning, her curiosity won out. She opened the door and let herself into the modest bedroom. The brass ceiling fan squeaked over a queen-sized bed that was neatly made and pushed against the wall. A nightstand to the left of it held an alarm clock with large red LED numbers and a dusty stack of books on molecular biology.

In a wooden case, on top of a rattan dresser, there were two dress watches gleaming in silver and gold, and next to them was his Mensa membership ring. Neve gently lifted the ring from its resting place, her fingers brushing against its cool surface as she examined it. The silver band was adorned with small diamonds, their intricate pattern forming the modern M shape with the world icon perched above it.

She slipped the ring onto her finger, but it was too loose. Without thinking, she slid it onto her thumb, where it fit snugly. The ring pulsed where the metal met her skin. A subtle, electrifying tingle seemed to spread through her and a wave of desire swept over her. She felt an uncontrollable craving to keep it. The urge was overwhelming, and without hesitation, she embraced it.

"Perry must be rubbing off on me," she muttered, hating herself a little as her gaze locked on the ring, considering her next move. The diamond chips winked in the light and mesmerized her as she stared at it.

Please don't do this.

Isla begged her to return it, but instead, Neve slipped the ring off and slipped it into her pocket. When it connected to the geode, a shiver of electric current shot through her and she yelped. She braced for another searing jolt as she squeezed her eyes shut and pulled them both out into the palm of her hand. A wave of dizziness overcame her and her ears started to ring. There was a *whoosh!* that sent her reeling, and she felt her breakfast churning in her belly.

Neve heard Talulah's lilting voice in her head, from all the readings she'd witnessed as a teenager while she traveled from state to state with the medium. "Objects hold energy. I use them to tap into the spiritual realm."

The shift in energy was undeniable, and Neve couldn't ignore the sense that the two objects were somehow connected to her purpose, but their proximity was making her violently ill. Her head pounded and a clammy sweat dampened her brow. Desperate for relief, she yanked them apart, quickly placing the ring back in the box. The moment they were separated, the dizziness and nausea that had consumed her began to lift, leaving her breathless with relief.

She spent the rest of the afternoon in her bedroom,

curled up in bed, trying to sleep off the lingering effects that felt like the aftermath of a brutal hangover. The fog in her mind slowly lifted, but one thing was clear: she needed to see Perry again. He was the only one she could trust to help her make sense of it all.

CHAPTER

SEVENTEEN

A FEW DAYS LATER, after finally wearing her father down, Neve drove to Ruben's with Nevermore in the passenger seat and her portfolio balanced on her lap.

The child had thrown a fit when Neve had tried to get her into the red dress Ellis had purchased for the occasion. While Isla's gentle persuasion spilled from her lips, Neve had to bite back a grin. She already understood exactly how the confrontation would play out.

In her bedroom, Nevermore had whined and cried, yanking at the neckline. "It's too tight and itchy. I hate dresses!" She stamped her foot on the ground and then flung her body onto the bed, clawing at the zipper resting against the back of her neck. "Get it off me!"

"You never get a second chance to make a first impression," Neve heard Isla's voice reason as if it mattered, her tone pleading. "And you look so pretty in it."

"*You* can keep pretty. I'll stick with talented," Nevermore countered. "Pretty is overrated." Seeing her nanny's crestfallen expression, the child quickly added, "No offense."

"None taken," Neve mumbled, letting out a weighty sigh in defeat. She felt Isla's frustration, but secretly Neve was proud of the preteen who had just made a very logical and reasonable argument. "Okay, fine. Go pick out what you want to wear, but I reserve the right to veto."

A few minutes later, Nevermore returned wearing a pair of long black leggings and a soft cotton tag-less t-shirt. On her feet was a pair of laced-up hiking boots, and seeing them made Neve chuckle. The girl's hair was sectioned off neatly and braided down either side of her head with long satin ribbons at the end of each tail.

"Gotta learn to choose your battles," she whispered to herself for Isla's benefit, hoping to head off her objections. From the dead silence within, it appeared Isla had been worn into compliance.

They drove down the freeway in blissful quiet, and by the time they'd pulled up to the circular drive, any lingering irritation had long since burned off.

Nevermore glanced through the windshield in awe of the sprawling mansion as the car slowed to a stop. "Whoa. Is Ruben Angelica a gazillionaire?"

"That's rude," Neve corrected. "The correct usage is, Ruben Angelica has done quite well for himself."

"You're acting weird," Nevermore said. "You

haven't been the same since that night Dad caught you outside in the dark when you lost your keys."

Neve gasped in surprise. "What do you mean?"

"Your voice is different. Before, it was softer, and you laughed more."

"I'm sorry. I've been a little preoccupied. I will work on it," Neve said, making an excuse as she gathered her backpack. She was astonished at the young girl's perception. Though the child preferred to keep to herself, and getting her to contribute to a conversation was like pulling teeth, it was obvious she didn't miss a thing. Neve reached over and tried to grab the portfolio by its handles.

Nevermore let out a low growl and squeezed her hand on it tighter. "Mine." She said a single word.

"I'm trying to help you," Neve reasoned.

"I don't need your help." Nevermore clenched her narrow jaw, and Neve had to turn away to hide the smile threatening to spread across her features.

After a lengthy negotiation, Nevermore allowed Neve to carry the heavy portfolio up the concrete steps to prevent it from dragging on the ground. She encouraged the child to press the doorbell that set off a flurry of chimes behind the heavy door. A few minutes later, it opened and Rosa looked at them inquisitively with a pleasant expression on her face, her eyes sparkling.

"Rosa! It's so great to see you again. This is Nevermore, and we have an appointment with Ruben at three," Neve told her.

"Yes. He say you coming. Follow me, he in studio." Rosa turned and led them into the great room. They had to hustle to keep up with the maid's muscular legs. Neve scanned the room and listened for Perry, hoping to lay eyes on him.

Not right now. Focus on Nevermore. You can find the bird later.

"Isla!" Ruben's warm voice boomed from the landing of the staircase before he floated down it with a wide smile. He kissed both of Neve's cheeks and then turned toward the child. "And you must be little Nevermore," he added with a hint of amusement, his eyes focused on her face. When he leaned down presumably to kiss her cheeks, Nevermore dodged the contact, hiding behind her nanny.

"Looks like someone is a bit bashful," he said as he stood to his full height, ignoring the slight.

Nevermore scrunched up her brow. Neve could tell the intensity of Ruben's gaze was already too much for the child to bear. The girl didn't meet his stare; instead, she focused on the small, abstract painting on the wall next to him. It was a burst of color, bright oranges and cool blues, that swirled into something vaguely recognizable.

"Isla has told me so much about you," Ruben continued, trying to bond with the child, his voice warm and encouraging.

Nevermore shot her a look. "You lied to him. I'm *not* little."

"I didn't say you were." Neve sighed in defeat and

shot Ruben an apologetic half-grin. "Nevermore is a stickler for the truth."

Ruben reached out and patted Nevermore on the head, a gesture that made the girl duck away again. Then he bent down to her level and asked, "Would you like to see my studio?"

"Yes!" Nevermore's excitement was palpable.

She cheerfully trailed behind Ruben, heading up the ornate staircase, but suddenly stopped short, her expression shifting to one of dismay as she stared at a large painting. Neve, who was bringing up the rear, nearly collided with the young girl and reached a hand to the rail to steady herself.

"This is Rembrandt's signature," Nevermore said, pointing at the corner of the painting with one skinny finger as she squinted at the portrait. "But it's not his work. The light is all wrong. His signature style has a warm glow like the subject is lit from within. This one is too dark."

Ruben stepped back toward her, his voice a little too smooth. "Ah, yes, well, Rembrandt was known for his masterful use of light *and* shadow. It's called chiaroscuro, where the artist creates depth using stark contrast between the two."

Nevermore mulled his explanation over as she continued to scrutinize the painting, her eyes squinting at it. "No," she muttered with a defiant shake of her head, refusing to accept his answer. "Nope. No way."

"This self-portrait was from his private collection, a practice painting, if you will." Getting more exasperated, he added, "Every canvas can't be a masterpiece!"

Nevermore wasn't convinced, and Neve turned toward the child, who continued to make an argument against its authenticity. "It's *not* Rembrandt. The brushstrokes are too thin. Rembrandt's were thick, almost like he was painting with a palette knife." She waved her finger toward the painting while tugging on the end of one braid with her other hand.

Ruben hesitated, then laughed awkwardly as he explained her objections away with a shrug. "Everyone's a critic. But believe me, it has been authenticated and *is* a Rembrandt original. It's very valuable, actually. You're just not used to seeing original art as it should be displayed."

Nevermore rolled her eyes and frowned. Neve considered the child's blunt observations for a moment but was distracted by the warmth of Ruben's fingers cupping around her forearm. He took her elbow and guided her up the rest of the stairs, leaving Nevermore to trail behind. At the top of the landing, Nevermore hesitated at a Renoir that hung under museum lighting. Her eyes lit up for a second, recognizing the piece from a book she'd brought home from the library. Then she leaned in closer and balled her hands into fists at her hips, thrusting her shoulders back in defiance.

"Isla, remember this one? It was in the book we checked out from the library last month, but the colors aren't right. I can tell by the way the reds blend with the pinks. Renoir liked to layer his paints, allowing ample drying time in between, but this one looks like it was slopped together in a rush."

Ruben winced as a flash of irritation passed over his features, and he palmed his face in frustration. "Well, the reproduction in books doesn't convey the quality of the original. I'm sure that is what you are getting hung up on." His smile tightened, and Neve could feel the agitation mounting as he continued to explain, "Renoir's work has always been a bit exaggerated, especially with the brushstrokes. It's part of his charm." He turned toward Neve and spoke out of the side of his mouth, thick condescension coating every word, "A child couldn't possibly understand the nuances of technique the same way a professional artist does."

Nevermore growled, and Neve turned toward the girl, trying to silence her with a glare, but Nevermore didn't catch on at all. Instead, her eyes narrowed, and she continued her argument, "Look at the shadows under her chin. There's no depth, no softness. Renoir *loved* soft shadows. Whoever did this didn't even bother to get the light source right."

Ruben glanced over at Neve with a wink and another tight shrug, then slid his gaze over to the angry sprite and said in a resigned tone, "You're very perceptive, Nevermore." When she didn't respond, he turned on his heel and quickened his pace.

The girl nodded to his retreating form, seemingly proud of herself yet oblivious that the air was thickening with tension. In an effort to steer the meeting in a more positive direction, Neve grabbed Nevermore's hand and rushed her down the hall toward his studio, hoping the child would not stop to examine any other paintings. Thankfully, even though Nevermore yanked her hand free, she remained silent.

Once inside, he took the portfolio case from Neve, set it on a wide workbench, and unzipped it. Making a show of consulting the gold watch on his wrist, he stated, "Let's take a look. I have another appointment coming soon, so I only have a few minutes to evaluate your work."

Neve felt a knot form in her belly. The act of sharing her art, of opening this very private part of herself to another person, was never easy. It was made infinitely more difficult witnessing her younger self being critiqued by a master for the first time. In tandem with her rising anxiety, Nevermore gripped the ends of her braids and shifted back and forth on the balls of her feet.

The first drawing in the portfolio was an architectural rendering of the Tampa Bay Art Museum. The building was instantly recognizable, and the attention to detail so awe-inducing that it was like viewing a black-and-white photograph.

Ruben stared at the charcoal drawing for a long time, his expression unreadable. The seconds stretched, and Neve felt a flutter in her chest. She glanced at Nevermore, whose gaze was locked on Ruben, eager to hear his opinion. The quiet stretched out for several more minutes before he finally spoke in a low voice. "You're very talented," he said, his tone sincere. "There's a confidence in your work. An attention to detail that most children your age never possess." He flipped the page to the next drawing of an ocean reef with an octopus curled around the coral.

"You have a real gift," he whispered as he flipped another page.

Nevermore blinked, surprised by the praise. At her side, Neve swallowed against a lump in her throat. She wasn't prepared for the emotional reaction that was happening inside her body. Her recollection of the meeting was lukewarm at best. She remembered Ruben liking her work, but experiencing it again through Isla's eyes was a vastly different experience.

Neve watched Nevermore wrestle with it, too. A life-changing, monumental event was unfolding, and they both grappled with the overwhelming rush of feelings accompanying it. No one had ever told her she had a gift, not like that. Not in a way that made her feel like she wasn't just some stupid kid scribbling with a pencil on a piece of paper.

Ruben went on, his tone shifting to a more business-like one. "There's something profound here. A depth to your work that is remarkable. I know a few places, and a few people, who could help you build your skill set. With the right guidance, you could go very far, young lady." When he zipped the portfolio closed, Neve leaned toward Nevermore, her eyes flashing as she silently mouthed the words "thank you."

Catching on, Nevermore uttered a curt, "Thanks." Then, without hesitation, was bold enough to ask, "Who are these people and where are these places?"

But his entire focus had already shifted back to wooing Isla, ignoring Nevermore completely. The sensation was like a free fall. Neve remembered the sting of dismissal from her childhood and she watched Nevermore's confidence crumble away as she was disregarded.

Ruben continued talking to the woman he believed was Isla, shooting her a tempting grin. "She's young. Her talent now barely scratches the surface of what she could be capable of with the right instruction. I could put in a good word for her at École Artiste."

"You'd do that?" Neve asked, her tone unconsciously softened by Isla, who batted her eyelashes, an odd mating gesture that felt surreal to Neve. She'd read about women doing such pandering things in books, but never once had she felt the urge to try it herself.

"Of course," Ruben replied, leaning closer, his gaze becoming more hypnotic. "I see her potential and want to help her realize it."

At her side, Nevermore let out a cheerful shout that made them both jump. Neve let out a burst of a giggle and thrust a quick hug on Ruben as Nevermore bounced back and forth on the balls of her feet.

"Yes. Help me realize my potential," the girl said, vying for his attention.

Snubbing her again, Ruben flashed a winning grin at Neve. "It's nothing. She deserves a chance to grow and learn. And if she's ready, I'd be more than happy to open the door."

Neve nodded thoughtfully, her gaze flicking between Ruben and Nevermore. "I think she would appreciate that very much."

Ruben's smile softened further, and he turned back to the girl. "I can tell that you're special. I have a gift for discovering raw talent and I am never wrong."

"False," Nevermore blurted. "You are mistaken about those paintings."

Neve winced. She knew it was the last thing he wanted to hear. Her younger self hadn't quite grasped the subtlety of adult conversation. She would get better at it, but not until she was well into adulthood.

A flicker of irritation cropped up on Ruben's face, and Neve let out a pained chuckle, her mind racing for ways to distract him.

I'll take it from here. Follow my lead and you'll get to see Perry again.

She felt Isla's resolve strengthen and the urge to lean close enough to brush her breasts against his arm. Fighting against her disgust at the ingratiating gesture for the greater good, Neve worked through it and laid on the charm, Isla's voice oozing with overt sexuality. "I'd love to continue our conversation over dinner tomorrow night. Just the two of us."

The close contact worked, and Ruben flashed her a naughty grin. "I think I can make that work," he said graciously as he steered them back down the hall, down the stairs, and to the front door with a rushed goodbye.

Neve walked Nevermore silently back to the car, laying the portfolio on the back seat. She pulled out of the drive, down the private lane, and through the iron gates before she allowed herself to let out a squeal of excitement.

"Did you hear that? École Artiste? He said he's going to pull some strings at the school and get you in!"

"Should I be excited?" Nevermore asked.

"Uh… yeah!" Neve teased, a playful grin tugging at her lips. "It's only *the* premier fine arts school on the entire East Coast."

Nevermore blinked slowly, digesting the information. Her brows furrowed, then relaxed as a tentative smile crept onto her face. She looked up at Neve, her voice small but hopeful. "But the bigger question is… will Dad actually let me go?"

Neve let out a heavy sigh of resignation. The girl had a point. She understood exactly how stubborn their father could be. "You let *me* worry about that," she said, soft but steady. "I'll find a way."

CHAPTER

EIGHTEEN

THE NEXT EVENING, the hum of a familiar car engine rumbled as her father parked his car in the garage. It sent vibrations through the house where Nevermore sat cross-legged on the living room floor, staring down at her latest drawing. Her pencils were fanned out around her in a semicircle, organized in levels of hardness. She was distracted, pulling apart then kneading her art gum eraser, lost in thought.

Nevermore had been despondent since they'd returned from parent's night at her school, where her drawings had been a focal point of the Spring Showcase. Neve's heart dropped when she observed Nevermore standing on her tiptoes in the school hallway, scanning the crowd for Ellis, only to be disappointed.

"Finally," Nevermore muttered, not looking up as she rubbed the white eraser over a smudge on her paper, then blew the shards of it away.

Neve glanced at the bereft child from the sink in the kitchen where she was washing green grapes in a colander. She would have to leave in the next fifteen minutes to make it to Ruben's on time for her dinner, but it was hard to leave Nevermore in her current state. She was briefly tempted to put her leggings on, pop some popcorn, and be the buffer between Nevermore and Ellis, but Isla nudged her forward.

This opportunity could change her life forever. We must go.

Hearing footsteps approaching, Nevermore groused, "He's exactly one hour, twenty-seven minutes, and forty-two seconds late," the child calculated, using the digital watch on her wrist.

"Nevermore," Neve said gently, "that's not helpful."

The sound of the front door opening cut her off. Nevermore shot up from the floor, pencils abandoned. She darted toward the foyer as Neve trailed behind her, wiping her hands on a dish towel.

Her father stepped inside, his sports coat slung over one arm and his briefcase in the other. His tie was loosened, and his face looked drained and pale as if he'd used up every ounce of his energy just driving home.

"Hey, Nomo," he called out as he set his things down, not yet glancing her way.

Nevermore folded her thin arms across her chest, standing perfectly still in the hallway. "You were supposed to be home earlier."

Her father turned toward her, his brow furrowing. "I

know, honey. There was an emergency at the lab I had to attend to.”

“You forgot about my showcase,” Nevermore interrupted, her tone devoid of accusation and dripping with blunt honesty.

He blinked, taken aback. “No, I didn’t forget. I just… couldn’t… get away.”

“Nevermore,” Neve cut in, a warning tone in her voice, “how about we let your dad settle in before we bombard him with what he missed?”

“It’s fine,” her father said, though the tightness in his jaw suggested otherwise. He rubbed his temple and sighed. “I’ll make it up to you, Nomo, I promise.”

“You can’t make it up,” she said, her tone clipped. “The event is over. My teacher is taking my drawings down tomorrow.”

“I’m sorry.”

“Sorry is not good enough,” she replied. “If my art were one of your lab reports, you would have made seeing it a priority.”

Her father ran a hand through his hair. “That’s not fair.”

“Fair doesn’t matter. Facts do.” Nevermore turned on her heel and stomped back toward the living room.

Neve followed, throwing a sympathetic look over her shoulder at Ellis. “She didn’t mean it like that. She’s just hurt.”

“I know,” he muttered, loosening his tie further. “Believe me, I know.”

Nevermore was back on the living room floor,

silently sketching the outline of a clock tower. Creating precise lines and accurate shading, she was consumed with replicating line by line of the rich detail she recorded in her mind during a visit a week prior.

"Your dad's trying," Neve said softly, sitting beside her on the floor. "You know that, right?"

Nevermore shrugged without looking up.

Neve glanced at the watch on her wrist. "I have to leave soon. Ruben's expecting me for dinner."

"You're seeing him again?" Nevermore's question was laced with suspicion.

"I have to if we want a shot at getting you into École Artiste," Neve murmured. She knew she would have to choose the right time to broach the subject with Ellis, and tonight was not the night.

"He's icky," Nevermore said bluntly, gripping the pencil harder in her hand. "He talks too much and doesn't really say anything."

Neve let out a snigger that was decidedly Isla, then offered the child an explanation Neve didn't agree with. "Men often do that, thinking they're being charming."

Nevermore shot her a blank look. "It's annoying."

"I agree with you. Most of them are," Neve said with a conspirator's chuckle, getting to her feet and picking up her handbag. "Don't give your father too much grief. He loves you."

Nevermore frowned, ignoring Isla's plea as she continued to sketch. Then she offered a piece of her own advice without looking up. "If Ruben tries anything weird, choose violence. Punch him in the face. Poke out his eyes. Then go for the jugular."

"Wow." Neve was taken aback by her detailed instructions. "Where did you learn that?"

"Dad took me to a self-defense class. He said all women need to learn how to protect themselves."

"Smart man," Neve mumbled as she pulled the keys from her handbag, and Ellis walked down the hallway toward his bedroom to change his clothes. "Your father is exhausted. Try to be nice. Remember, we are going to need to get his approval if Ruben can get you an interview at École Artiste."

At the prospect, Nevermore's scowl lifted, and she reluctantly agreed. "Okay. Fine. You have a point."

Twenty minutes later, Neve stepped into Ruben's home and was immediately enveloped by the rich aroma of gently simmered red wine. She was shown to the dining room by Rosa and sat at the table for a few minutes alone. Compelled by a desire to touch the geode to center herself, she opened her handbag. Inside, it was nestled in tissue paper, and light pulsed through it like it had a heartbeat. Mesmerized, she pulled it out and cradled it in her palm. Why was it pulsating? Was it a warning or a sign? Not having a pocket to put it in, she tucked it inside the confines of her bra, and the stone synced with her heartbeat. The sensation was comforting and put her nerves in check.

Glancing around the room, she took in the gold leaf candlesticks and elaborate place settings with more silverware than she'd ever seen in her life. Tiny spoons and three-pronged forks were laid delicately across the top of her decorative charger plate. Panic set in as she wondered what they should be used for. Then she remembered she had learned to blend in at school by mimicking the behavior of those around her. Tonight, she would do the same.

"Isla," Ruben greeted her warmly, appearing from the door leading to the kitchen with two glasses of red wine. His tailored shirt was unbuttoned at the collar, where a glimpse of his tanned chest peeked out, and his roguish curls framed his smiling face.

"Ruben," Neve said, accepting the wine with a careful smile.

"To beauty," he toasted, raising his glass.

"And to whoever is cooking dinner, it smells magnificent," Neve said, jutting her chin toward the kitchen.

Ruben chuckled. "I decided on French tonight, inspired by the years I lived in Provence. Coq Au Vin. It's my grandmother's recipe, and I even made it myself."

From down the hall, Neve's heart leapt when she heard a rustle and a defiant squawk. "The results are in! That is a lie." Neve almost choked on the wine, having to clear her throat before she could speak.

"Ignore the stupid bird," Ruben said, waving a

dismissive hand in spite of his cheeks pinking up. "They repeat whatever nonsense they hear. Pay him no mind."

"You're the dummy." Perry's insult echoed down the hallway.

At her breastbone, the geode vibrated, and anxious to see Perry again, Neve slid closer and batted Isla's long eyelashes at Ruben, then gushed, "I've always wanted a bird."

"Well, then." Ruben shot her a devilish grin, then pulled out a bell and rang it. Within seconds, a man appeared. "Amos, can you be so kind as to bring the bird to the dining room? It seems our guest is quite taken with him." He turned to Neve, reached down, and grasped her hand in his own. "And I am quite taken with her." He pulled her hand to his warm lips and kissed it. The act sent a shockwave of electricity flowing through her. It silenced her analytical mind as her cells ignited with an attraction she'd never felt before. It was impossible to concentrate on anything else, and she felt her usual skepticism and common sense drift away. A hum of energy circuited through her, radiating from the geode and toward her limbs.

"You're different, you know. Most women are so… predictable. But you, Isla, you're like a rare painting. Each time I see you, I discover something new."

Neve pulled her hand from his to break the spell and took a sip of her wine. This feeling of infatuation was strange and new. She understood the concept of romance theoretically but had never been the recipient of it. Now that she had, it left her feeling untethered and a bit breathless.

Before she could respond, Rosa appeared at his side.

"Mr. Davenport call. He on line one, or you want me take message?"

Ruben frowned, glancing at Neve with regret before standing. "I'm sorry. This is important. It's a collector I've been trying to pin down for weeks."

"Of course," Neve said, gesturing for him to go, eager to be accommodating to give the headiness she felt in his presence a chance to dissipate.

Neve waited until he disappeared into the kitchen, and she overheard the low murmur of his voice. Then she stood when Amos rolled a dolly with the gilded cage into the dining room. Inside, Perry was chirping and squawking, and she was so relieved to see him, she rushed straight over to the cage.

Perry bobbed with excitement, flapping his wings. Neve quickly unlatched the lock and offered her arm that he hopped onto without hesitation. Then he climbed the length of it, tucking the top of his head into the curtain of Isla's hair, and cooed with delight. His feathers tickled and Neve laughed, brushing the top of his head with the pads of her thumb.

"Are you okay?" she asked.

"Now that you're here, I am," he churred, grateful for the reunion.

"How did we get here?" Neve asked.

"I don't know. One moment I am gliding over the

ocean spray, and the next we're stuck in 1989. It feels like a fever dream."

"More like a nightmare," Neve added. "But somehow, we ended up in the same timeline, *together*. That's got to mean something," she suggested, glancing over her shoulder. She reached in, pulled the geode from its hiding place, and grasped it between her thumb and forefinger. Seeing it, Perry let out a long, appreciative whistle.

"What is that?"

"It's a piece of Dad's geode that made the journey with us. When I woke up in 1989, I was completely nude, holding this and one of your feathers."

Perry let out a wolf whistle, and Neve pushed the top of his feathered head away. "Pervert." Neve rolled her eyes and continued. "It's reactive. It seems to be a talisman of some sort. At Dad's, the glow was getting brighter by the day, but now I can feel it pulsating with energy."

"Surely, that must have some significance. Keep it close until you discover what it means."

Behind the door, Ruben laughed, and Neve tucked away the geode for safekeeping and whispered, "Ruben is charming. Why do you hate him so much?"

Perry flinched and snapped his wings. "Because I used to *be* him."

"What? You can shape-shift, too?"

"No, you silly, literal being!" Perry teased. "I used to be *like* him. Self-absorbed, using women to stroke my ego. Ruben is in love with Ruben."

"But he's advocating for Nevermore," Neve reasoned. "He sees value in her work and wants to send her to École Artiste. It's an opportunity that changed her life! Changed *my* life!"

"We must be careful," Perry warned. "Altering the past can have significant ramifications in the future."

"Are you talking about the butterfly effect?"

"Exactly."

"But what if it is a good… no, a great ramification? Who would it hurt?"

"That's the thing. We won't know until we get back, *if* we get back!" he squawked.

Neve let an anxious exhale slide between her teeth. She'd never considered the possibility they would be stuck in 1989 forever.

"People like him do not do anything that doesn't directly benefit themselves. I can't put my beak on it, but something feels off. There's another…"

Before he could finish, Rosa came through the door and set a bread basket on the table, shooting a suspicious glance at Neve and the bird before leaving. Perry squawked in warning, shifting into simpler words in case they were overheard. "Upstairs!"

Perry flapped his wings again, louder this time as if to give her a nudge. "Hidden away!"

Neve leaned toward the bird, her curiosity piqued. "What is hidden away?"

"Go now! While he's busy!"

She hesitated, her gaze flicking toward the door where Ruben's voice still echoed in the air. Curiosity gnawed at her, and she quickly padded up the staircase on the tips of her toes, careful not to make a sound. She felt the geode guiding her as she rushed down the hallway and to a back stairway. The stairs creaked under her weight as she ascended, her breath coming a little faster with each step. At the top of the landing, she could make out a few notes of classical music. The familiar scent of turpentine and linseed oil grew stronger the further she went.

Afraid of what she would find, her heart began to thrum in her chest in communion with the vibration of the geode. Each step closer increased the tension welling in her belly. Her hand was on the knob of the closed door. She tried to turn it, and her heart dropped when it was locked.

"Mr. Ruben will not like you poking around here."

Neve whirled around in time to encounter a suspicious Rosa, who was staring her down.

"I'm sorry. I took a wrong turn looking for the bathroom," she tried to explain, but Rosa was wary as she reached out to grasp her hand and pull her away from the door.

Neve's breath hitched in her chest. Her heart pounded so hard it felt like it might burst. The geode seared the skin over her heart. Her vision blurred, and her hands began to tremble. A faint shimmer of light flickered as she felt her body drawn toward Rosa's, pulled by a magnetism she couldn't deny. Neve inhaled a weighted breath, and then she was engulfed by wisps of white light. They surrounded Rosa, dancing in a specular funnel before surrounding them both.

The tingling started in her fingertips, spreading heat up her arms like wildfire. Her skin prickled and her muscles spasmed uncontrollably. Her bones cracked and snapped as they twisted into an unrecognizable shape. Rosa gasped in terror, falling back as Isla's body contorted into a ball, and she howled in agony.

There was a piercing wail as the wisps hovered, then raced over them and rushed to the floor. When she finally exhaled, they disappeared, and then the world went white.

CHAPTER

NINETEEN

THE FIRST THING Neve noticed when she woke up was the mind-splitting headache. It wasn't just a dull ache either, but felt like a jackhammer had been chipping away at the delicate tissue behind her eyes. She groaned, rolling onto her side, and that's when the second realization hit her—her body. It was heavier, more achy, and completely unfamiliar.

Ay! Dios Mio! What happen?

Neve's eyes shot open, and she stared at the ceiling fan spinning in hypnotic circles above her. "Isla?" she croaked from a mouth as dry as the desert. The name spilled from her lips in a soft Spanish accent. Her heart began to race as she tried to piece together where she was, and she inhaled a deep breath. The room smelled faintly of lavender and lemon furniture polish, and the bed beneath her was smaller than the one she'd been sleeping in at her childhood home.

No Isla. Mi nombre es Rosa.

Again, Neve understood the conversational Spanish effortlessly when she had never spoken a syllable of it in her life. Swinging her heavy legs over the side of the bed, she froze in shock, drinking in the sight. Her legs weren't Isla's long, tanned, slender limbs. They were thicker, ropy with muscle, with faint blue varicose veins tracing a map she didn't recognize. She patted her stomach where the ridges of her perfectly flat abs had dissolved into the softened abdominals of a menopausal woman. Her hands trembled as she drew them close to her face to take a closer look. Her fingers were rough and calloused, her nails blunt and unpolished. She felt wetness dripping from her nose, and when she brushed at it with the tips of her fingers, she was astonished to see blood.

Neve stumbled on her shorter, stocky legs to the small mirror hanging on the wall of her ensuite bathroom, paralyzed by the reflection.

"Ay! Ay! Ay!" she whispered, her voice hoarse and slightly familiar. It had a choppy, melodic Hispanic accent that hinted at her Latina heritage. It felt natural coming from Rosa's lips, but definitely wasn't Isla's anymore, nor her own.

Neve patted her thicker cheek. Her dark brown eyes were now framed by crow's feet and laugh lines. Her skin, a warm caramel tone, was weathered and scarred by pockmarks, and her coal-black hair was peppered with gray. It brushed the tips of her shoulders, and she rubbed at the crick in her lower back that let her know she was moving too fast so soon after waking.

Rosa's hands flew to her face, tracing over the unfamiliar features reflected in the mirror as panic bubbled in her chest. "This can no be real," Neve muttered in broken English, shaking her head, slow to comprehend the truth reflected in the mirror. Isla's light countenance had completely disappeared, replaced by the robust strength of Rosa.

She'd shifted again! Her mind whirred on this discovery. Was she destined to jump from person to person, trying on their soul in some sort of new age changing room, discarding it like a pair of pants that didn't fit? Was this her life from now on? The concept was difficult for her to accept. It felt like she was splintering into pieces and the sensation was destabilizing.

A burn on her chest ached, and a poking sensation led her to reach into her cotton brazier and pull out the geode. The heat was cooling off, but it shone like a beacon, but a beacon to what?

She left the bathroom and staggered back to her bed, the exhaustion making it difficult to stand for long periods of time.

A soft knock at the door startled her. Before she could respond, it creaked open, revealing a tall, burly African American man in a clean apron. His chocolate-brown skin gleamed in the morning light, and his deep-set eyes crinkled with concern.

"Rosa, you're finally up," he said, stepping inside with a tray of food. "You okay? You don't look so good."

"I…" She hesitated as panic set in. He was the cook, but she struggled to put a name to his amiable face. Her gaze landed on the name embroidered on the apron. Amos. "I fine! No worry, okay?" she finally answered, her voice wobbling with relief.

"Hmm… fine? Girl, you anything but fine," he said, setting the tray on the nightstand. "You were complaining about a headache yesterday. Maybe you're coming down with the flu?"

Neve looked down at the tray that held a steaming cup of coffee, a small bowl of carefully diced fruit, and buttered toast with a ramekin of honey. It smelled divine and made her stomach growl, but then she was struck with a wave of nausea.

"Maybe you should take the day off," he suggested, his tone softening. "You work too hard as it is."

"No!" she said, her response harsher than she intended. Neve was afraid if she took a day off, it would arouse suspicions. "I fine. *Un minuto nada más!* Please, just one second, okay? I need breath."

Amos studied her for a long moment with narrowed eyes, then shrugged. "Okay, suit yourself. Ruben's got guests coming for dinner tonight, so it'll be a busy day, but don't push yourself too hard." He turned and left, closing the door softly behind him.

Neve sank back into the pillows, her head in her

hands as the truth came flooding in. Ruben. She was now the maid at Ruben Angelica's mansion. Somehow, she'd shifted into Rosa's sturdy body, leaving Isla's lithe one behind. How? Her thoughts spun out as she tried to come up with a factual answer. She yearned to speak to her father about it. Surely, his brilliant scientific mind could solve this quantum debacle, but as Rosa, she no longer had a connection to him. Her heart dropped as grief set in. Even though Ellis was alive and well in 1989, she couldn't reach him anymore. As Isla, she'd been given a second chance to soak up his time and attention. As Rosa, she wouldn't have the luxury, and the truth gutted her.

Eat, Muñeca.

Taking Rosa's advice, Neve turned to her breakfast and ate every morsel, allowing herself to wallow for a few minutes before forcing herself to stand and face the new reality she'd been dropped into. There had to be a reason bigger than what she could comprehend that brought her here. Determined to figure out what it was, she pulled open the closet to find several simple shift dresses hanging on hangers sheathed in dry cleaner's plastic. On the shelf above, white aprons were folded into a neat stack, along with black socks and compression hosiery.

She wrestled with a pair of compression tights, yanking them up her thick calves and tugging them over her dimpled thighs. Every movement felt foreign as her body now carried weight in places it hadn't before. When she finally wrenched them into place, they were constrictive, and she had to push past her rising tide of sensory irritation.

Rosa nudged her, calmly whispering, *You need. For feet.*

Neve forced down her desire to yank them off and stuff them deep inside the trash can. Instead, she tucked the glowing geode shard into the pocket of her apron and stepped out into the hallway. The soles of her thick orthopedic shoes squeaked on the polished marble floors as she beelined toward the back staircase, straining for Perry's familiar squawks and chirps, when Rosa's escalating anxiety stopped her dead in her tracks.

This not way. I late. Ruben no like when I late.

With a heavy sigh, she reluctantly turned around and followed the faint buzz of activity down the stairs. Behind the swinging door to the kitchen, she could hear the clatter of dishes, the murmur of voices, and the occasional outburst of laughter. She proceeded into the kitchen where, at the island, Amos was slicing vegetables into cubes with the precision of a surgeon. His *mise en place* was a culinary wizardry to behold.

"There you are," he said without looking up. "We need to set the table for twelve, and don't forget to polish the silver. Also, Ruben is trippin' about the current cleanliness of the chandelier and wanted me to pass the message on to you."

Neve's mouth went dry. Polishing silver? Wasn't that a task that had been rendered obsolete in the twentieth century? She didn't even know where to begin.

I help. Get the cart.

"Of course," she said, trying to sound confident as she tried to relinquish control. Letting Rosa take the lead, she found herself being nudged past Amos and padding to a closet. Inside, she found a small cart stacked with cleaning products, a cordless vacuum, and a mop holstered to the back. She pulled it out and rolled it toward the dining room. Drawing a finger across the windowsill, she wrinkled her nose at the thick coating of dust that covered it. Blood rushed to Rosa's cheeks as she flooded with embarrassment.

Looks like I miss spot.

"At least Ruben is no expecting perfection," Neve reasoned as she gazed out the window overlooking the sprawling Xeriscape garden where rocks and prehistoric-looking tropical plants filled beds shaded by palm trees.

A dreaded crystal chandelier sparkled overhead, and the long mahogany table gleamed underneath. She unfolded several large beach towels over the table and sprayed the cleaner marked "Chandelier Sparkle" over the crystals. She read the bottle and made the sign of the cross, hoping it would live up to its bold claim of spotless, no-scrub shine. "It say so easy, it almost too good to be true!" Neve felt herself chortle with delight. It was a strange sensation made all the stranger because Neve had never chortled in her life.

She sprayed the sparkling crystals until they dripped down onto the towels, then picked up the feather duster and a can of Pledge and began to dust. The frown on her lips slowly receded as she discovered the work was oddly satisfying, and she was shocked to learn her usual ultra-diligence against germs had taken a back seat while she resided in Rosa's body. She worked quickly through the room, finding the mindless tasks of cleaning and polishing a balm to her overactive mind, and she was grateful for the shift.

After an hour, the aches in her shoulders and lower back intensified, and she found herself muttering curses under her breath in Spanish.

By the time Neve finished cleaning the room, her arms felt like jelly. She moved on to the silver, carefully polishing each fork, knife, and spoon until they gleamed, closely following Rosa's directions whispered inside her mind. When she returned to the chandelier, she was pleasantly surprised to see the grime had dripped down to the towel, and all that remained was a shiny fixture that looked brand new. Neve balled up the dirty towels and tucked them into the hamper on the cart. Next, she vacuumed the great room, scrubbed the marble staircase with a combination of vinegar, rubbing alcohol, water, and a few drops of lavender, and arranged fresh flowers in vases. By the end of the day, her muscles screamed in protest, and by the time Amos called her back to the kitchen to help prepare hors d'oeuvres, she was ready to collapse from exhaustion. Neve was bone weary and her feet were swollen.

"You're moving slower than usual," Amos remarked, handing her a tray of deviled eggs to garnish.

"I okay, all good!" Neve snapped, then immediately felt Rosa's guilt rush in.

He held up his hands in mock surrender. "Alright, alright. Don't bite my head off."

"*Lo siento*," she apologized, feeling terrible for taking her frustrations out on the man who seemed to be Rosa's friend.

"Your blood sugar is low. Eat this." Amos handed her one of the rejects, and she popped it into her mouth without delay, relishing the smooth texture of the cool filling on her tongue.

By the time Ruben's guests arrived, Neve's feet were barking. She carried trays of champagne and appetizers anyway, smiling politely at his guests, going through the motions as Rosa. She'd been hoping to see Isla, but the model was not in attendance. It did sting, however, when she witnessed Ruben putting the same tired moves on another woman. Perry was right. Women *were* interchangeable accessories to men like Ruben. Unwittingly, she'd almost become one of his conquests. The thought made a shiver race through her, and she thanked her lucky stars she'd dodged that bullet. While he flirted and carried on, Neve fantasized about sprinkling itching powder onto his clean sheets and inside his tighty-whities for betraying Isla. Rosa chuckled at the thought, at first feeling slightly tempted by it before coming to her senses.

You funny! But I need job more than you need payback.

Her heartfelt plea forced Neve to reconsider. When

the evening finally wound down and the last guest left, Neve dragged herself back to her small bedroom. She collapsed onto the bed, her body aching in ways she'd never imagined possible. Staring at the ceiling fan, she let out a long sigh. She didn't understand why the shift had happened, but one thing was certain: she had to discover what she needed to learn to leave this life of servitude behind, because being Rosa was exhausting.

CHAPTER

TWENTY

THE FOLLOWING AFTERNOON, heavy rain battered against the tall windows of the study, streaking the glass in long, silvery rivulets. Thunder rumbled in the distance, and the wind howled through the dense palm trees that surrounded the sprawling property as a tropical thunderstorm raged. Inside, the mansion was quiet, save for the distant ticking of a grandfather clock and the soft chirps and warbles from the bird. Perry was silent in the gilded cage, eyeing Ruben seated at his desk, lost in thought. His fingers were steepled under his chin as he gazed at a half-finished painting resting on an easel.

At three pm, there was a break in the rain, and Rosa nudged Neve to quickly gather the mail from the locked box before it started up again. As she sorted through the envelopes and ad circulars, her eyes snagged on one letter near the bottom of the pile. It was a formal, cream-colored envelope addressed to Martin DuBois c/o Ruben Angelica with the mansion's address handwritten in an elegant script. With no return address, it immediately piqued her curiosity. The geode in her pocket tingled and guided her to lay it on top of the pile alongside a silver letter opener that resembled a 16th century dagger.

Neve walked the tray to the study where her heart leapt when she saw Perry in the cage. Seemingly uninterested in her, he was focused on grooming his feathers. She ached to run to him but would have to wait until they could be alone. Dutifully, she carried the tray to Ruben's desk and set it down. "Mr. Ruben? Your mail."

He glanced over at it, then stiffened. Neve watched as his eyes narrowed and he pulled the cream envelope into his fingers and turned it over in his hands. He stared at it for a long moment, his expression pinched. Then, without another word, he slid the silver dagger through the seal, pulled out the folded paper inside, and shook it open. Neve watched his eyes scan quickly over the page, and as they did, his face drained of color. Ruben let out a slow, shaky breath, then crumpled the letter into a tight ball with his fist. His lips parted as if to speak, but then quickly closed as he reconsidered, swallowing hard.

"Rosa," he said, his voice low and cold, "Please give me some privacy." She hesitated only a moment, not wanting to leave Perry's side, before he spat, "Now."

Across the room, Perry let out a warning chirp but remained otherwise silent, picking up on the increasing tension. The sudden urgency in Ruben's voice sent a chill down her spine. Neve quickly nodded and backed toward the door, but she was intrigued. What was in that letter? Who was Martin DuBois? She reached into the pocket of her apron and fished out the geode that quivered in the palm of her hand, its glow illuminating her face in the dim hallway. It felt like the stone was trying to tell her something. She hesitated just outside the cracked door, and the geode shook violently, rooting her in the spot. On the other side of the door, she heard Ruben's heavy footsteps move across the study. A minute later, she heard the faint clink of ice hitting the bottom of a glass.

"Boozing it up already?" Neve whispered to herself. Whatever was in that envelope had rattled him. She leaned closer to the gap in the door and heard the soft click of a phone number being punched into the desktop phone. Ruben fell back down into the chair and swiveled to face the window, giving her a chance to step closer. Neve strained her ears to hear bits of his conversation, pressing herself against the wall, limiting her breath to shallow gasps.

"Pick up," Ruben muttered. His voice was hushed, and Neve could only make out fragments. A few minutes later, he slammed the receiver down and rattled off a string of colorful French words that were so laced with venom they had to be obscenities. He rose to his feet, the highball glass still gripped in his hand. With a final sip, he rattled the ice cubes in the empty glass, then, in one swift motion, hurled it against the wall of the study. Neve flinched at the sharp, deafening crack as the crystal shattered, the jagged shards scattering across the floor.

"ROSA!" he shouted, and it startled her. She backed away from the door, trying to calm her hammering heart, then waited the few seconds it would have taken her to walk up the stairs before she opened it.

Terror made her voice waver. "Yes, Mr. Ruben?" She studied him. His shoulders were tense and his whole body was stretched tight with tension.

"I've got to get back to Camille. Can you take care of this mess?"

"*Si*." She nodded as he strode away. Neve waited until his footfalls were swallowed by silence, then quickly crossed the room. She rushed over to the cage and leaned in close to whisper, "Peregrine, bird-man, it me." Her choppy English confused him.

Perry hopped closer, and his head jutted toward her, then cocked as if he was questioning what he'd heard.

"*Ola!* Perry, *Soy yo,* Neve," she hissed at him in bits of Spanish, glancing over her shoulder.

"What? Nevermore?" he screeched and bobbed, clearly excited to see her.

"Technically Rosa, but *si*."

"Goodness gracious! Now, this is what I call a considerable visual decline! Isla was an absolute vision! Rosa? Not so much!"

Rosa rolled her eyes at his insult and smoothed the front of her apron. "Hopefully this body only borrow, too. I want return to my real one." Neve was surprised at how true that statement felt.

"Wow." Perry was stunned by the development. "My flabbers are significantly gasted! How did you…?"

"I not know," Neve explained. "One second I run up stairs, then *whoosh*… white light… and I wake up inside Rosa."

He paced back and forth on the perch as he listened to her explanation. "Now that we are both in the mansion, what have we been sent here to do?"

"I keep asking same question."

"More importantly, how do we hasten our return home?"

"That one, I been afraid to ask," she said, utterly perplexed as the next words came out in a long sigh of defeat. "I not know."

They were quiet for a long moment, each lost in the gravity of the situation. Eventually, Neve said, "This no feel random to me. It feel very… how you say… purposeful?"

"Does it?" Perry needed more convincing.

"Nothing is chance. There is reason for everything. We just need find it," Rosa said with conviction, and her accent thickened. "Last night, you say hidden away, Mr. Peregrine. What you mean?" Neve felt wetness and a prickle inside her left nostril.

"You're bleeding!" Perry chirped, waving his wing at her now.

Neve swiped under her nose with her index finger, shocked to see more red blood there. "This body. I in here, but Rosa is, too. Are you having same experience?"

"Minus the blood," he said. "Perhaps it's the unfortunate side effect of two humans inhabiting a body at the same time?"

"Maybe." Neve tried to clear the highway of her mind that felt too heavily trafficked. "I learning first two days after a shift are worst." Wanting to stay occupied to keep her mind off the internal tilt-a-whirl, she leaned closer. "Hidden away? What is hidden?"

Perry glanced behind her in both directions before he whispered, "Not what… *who*."

"*Ay! Ay! Ay!* I remember!" she blurted. "I run up back stairs, my hand on door knob. I turn, but it locked. Rosa catch me, I shift."

Perry went on, his voice steady but laced with disapproval, "There's a woman Ruben keeps locked away in the other wing like some kind of secret. Her name is Camille."

A wave of lightheadedness washed over Neve. Her knees buckled slightly, and she stumbled toward the nearest chair, collapsing into it before the room could tilt any further.

Perry's expression shifted, concern flickering in his gaze. "Are you okay?"

Neve was disoriented, and then a trickle of knowing infiltrated the gray areas in her memories. "She no secret. I know of her. She live here for years. She is artist Ruben has been mentoring from Pathways of Light."

"What is that?"

"It a group that help people with mind delays and

troubles, make them fit in society and support they self. Ruben be they biggest helper for almost ten year."

"Sure, he is. That Frenchie, he's a giver!" Perry's sarcasm was slathered on thick.

"Mr. Ruben *is* giver!" Neve heard herself exclaim in his defense, the words tumbling out before she could stop them. Rosa was absolutely certain Ruben had good intentions; however, Neve had more reservations, a nagging sense that things weren't as simple as they seemed. "Seems Ruben man of many secrets!" Neve said, half to Rosa, half to herself, her voice tight with suspicion as she reached into the trash can, pulled out the wadded ball of paper, and smoothed it flat with one lined palm.

"It say," she read slowly, sounding out the first few words before Perry cut in.

"Bring it to me." His tone was demanding, and she felt Rosa's cheeks pink up in embarrassment.

"You be nice bird," Neve scolded him as she walked the letter over to the cage and held it in front of him. Perry splayed his wings excitedly before reading it aloud,

Do not ignore me. Honor your promise and wire $250,000 to this account in the next seven days or I'll tell the media everything.

M.

The word 'everything' was underlined so furiously the pen cut through the paper, leaving a hole in it. There was no signature, just that single innocuous initial. M.

"Ooh! The plot thickens!" Perry whistled with delight, rocking from one foot to the other. "It takes a con to recognize one!"

Unconvinced, Rosa's hand waved his smug glee away, but Neve's curiosity won out. "We must find out. Who is M?"

CHAPTER
TWENTY-ONE

THE NEXT MORNING, every muscle in Neve's body ached. She let out a whimper as she rolled off the bed and onto Rosa's swollen feet. In the small bathroom, she showered, letting the hot water unclench her tight muscles. Then she dried off and tapped three ibuprofens into the palm of her hand, swallowing them without water. Her joints creaked and tendons popped as she made her way over to the closet for a clean uniform. Once dressed, she added a white apron, popped the geode into her pocket, and sat on the edge of her made bed to pull on her shoes. Neve was half-heartedly vacuuming the travertine, inching closer to the back staircase, when she felt Rosa's fear well up.

Wait. You no go now. Later you take lunch. You see.

Rosa's clear instructions made her pause. Neve was just a visitor in Rosa's body, and she reluctantly decided it was selfish to risk the woman's livelihood to get answers, so she yielded and spent the next few hours cleaning the guest bedrooms. At lunchtime, she climbed the back staircase with the lunch tray in hand and padded down the hall. Outside the door, she set the tray on a small table and paused to adjust the delicate porcelain cups. The hearty scent of French Onion soup wafted up to her nostrils, and her stomach growled. Under the stainless steel cloche, a turkey sandwich on rye with peppered bacon and a stoneware crock of soup with a mountain of broiled gruyere cheese waited. It smelled heavenly, and Neve couldn't wait to get back to the kitchen to enjoy her own bowl.

The door was opened just a crack, and the hushed tones of a conversation drifted through it, halting her movements. There was a dramatic shift in Ruben's voice, a velvet undertone of coaxing authority that rooted her to the spot.

"Camille," Ruben said, his tone low and measured, "we're approaching the deadline. The gallery is expecting the collection next month, and there's still so much to refine. These two new pieces, they're good, but we both know that, with a few modifications, they could be great."

"But they *are* finished," came a soft, hesitant voice. Neve didn't recognize it at first, but then it slowly registered when she received a hint from Rosa.

It Camille.

Neve leaned closer as Camille tried to argue. "They are exactly what I envisioned. They are great *right now.*" Her insistent declaration was tinged with a quiet uncertainty that made Neve's heart ache.

"Great? Oh no, *ma chérie*. Not quite," Ruben continued. The faint scrape of wood stretcher frames against the easel accompanied his words. "This one, for instance, the colors are too muted. It needs to grab hold of the viewer's eye and never let it go!" His footsteps echoed closer, and Neve's heart galloped in her chest.

"And this one… the composition is too…" He hemmed until he seemed to find the word he was looking for, "…derivative. It's decent, but it won't command a premium price at the auction."

There was a long pause, and Neve envisioned a cunning jackal circling a wounded animal. She pressed the door open ever more slightly, angled to get a better view of the studio, and finally laid eyes on Camille. She was wringing her hands, her large, expressive eyes darting between the painting and Ruben's imposing figure.

"I wanted to convey *tenderness*," Camille argued quietly. "The color story is essential to reinforcing this emotion."

"And…" he paused, shifting to a pandering tone, "it's lovely," Ruben replied, softening to a croon. "Truly, it is. But you must remember what we agreed upon. You're not just painting for yourself anymore. You're painting for the world! And with my assistance, you will reach the highest heights in the contemporary art community. Do you know how hard it is to achieve mainstream success as an artist while you are still alive? Nearly impossible. I have opened my home to you and invested my time and energy because I see your potential for greatness. I can't help you if you don't follow my advice."

Camille blinked a few times and focused on her fingers laced together in front of her.

Neve leaned closer, craning her ear to hear more, but all was silent. After a long pause, Ruben finally said, "Don't pout, *ma chérie*. It's unbecoming. If you follow my advice, the art world will fall in love with you. Isn't that what you want?"

"Yes," she whispered. "More than anything." Camille's words twisted with a longing that broke Neve's heart. She'd long felt the same yearning. Recalling his interest in young Nevermore's portfolio just a week ago, she wondered if she was witnessing a premonition of her own future. His rigid control and manipulation were alarming and drove her into immediate solidarity with Camille.

"I can make it happen," Ruben insisted, his voice firm now. "But only if you trust me." She heard steps coming closer, and Neve straightened up and slid behind the door, holding up one balled fist. Before she could knock, the door opened and Ruben offered her a winning smile.

"Ah, great timing, Rosa. Camille could use some refreshment."

Neve nodded in agreement, set the tray down on the low table, and glanced at Camille. The young woman sat perched on the edge of a chair, her wide eyes fixed on Ruben with a mix of irritation and acceptance. Her fingers were smudged with paint, her sundress dotted with flecks of vibrant color. She bit on the corner of her lip, keeping her eyes cast down.

"We were just discussing the upcoming auction."

"Of course, sir," Neve replied, bowing her head slightly. Her heart ached for Camille. There was a fragility there that Neve felt driven to protect. She busied herself setting the plates down and pouring tea. When she handed Camille her saucer, their eyes met briefly before Camille's darted away as if it required too much effort to maintain the gaze.

"Thank you, Rosa," Camille murmured, her voice barely above a whisper. Ruben turned his attention back to Camille.

"Now, after lunch, how about you get back to work? We have a lot to accomplish, and not much time to do it."

They eat now. Then you take plate.

Neve withdrew quietly and walked back to the door, waiting for them to finish, grateful it gave her an opportunity to listen in. She forced a bored look onto her face and glanced around the room, noting the tidy piles of canvases and easels holding two paintings that seemed vaguely familiar. She wracked her brain standing there while they ate lunch, trying to recall where she'd seen them, but Rosa's memories were overlapping her own and muddying her thoughts.

Camille stirred her spoon through the rich broth of the soup in front of her. "Yum," she said, bringing a spoonful of soup to her lips. After two more spoonsful, she grinned with delight. "Rosa, can you tell Amos his French Onion soup is my favorite?"

"Of course," Neve replied. "You make Mr. Amos happy."

Camille grinned and rocked forward and back on the legs of the chair she was seated on. "Yum." Camille took another sip before taking a bite of her sandwich. She set her spoon down and leaned back into the chair as a puzzled expression settled on her features. She cleared her throat as her cheeks turned a shade of pink. Then, two more times, she cleared her throat.

"Camille," Ruben said in between bites as he slurped up the soup. "Drink some water. That sound is making me lose my appetite."

She scratched at her throat and took another small sip from the spoon. Then she coughed quietly as if she didn't want to draw attention, and took another sip of water. A few minutes later, Camille let out a small moan of distress. She raked her fingernails at her throat and tugged at the collar of her shirt, frowning as she shifted forward and back in her seat. The blood rushing up made her cheeks flush a dark crimson.

Ruben stopped spooning the soup into his mouth, slamming the utensil down hard on the table. "Seriously, Camille, stop that incessant noise!" Ruben scolded.

Ay Dios Mios! Trouble.

A whisper from Rosa commanded Neve's full attention.

"Maybe the soup was a little too spicy for me?"

Camille asked, her voice more hoarse than it had been minutes ago.

He tilted his head. "It shouldn't be. Amos knows you prefer foods that are a bit more bland. But if it's too much, I can have Rosa bring you something else."

"I feel dizzy," Camille said, fanning herself with her hand.

Ruben rose from his chair, flinging his cloth napkin next to his bowl. "You look flushed. What's wrong?"

"Could I lie down for a few minutes?" Camille fanned her hot cheeks with her hand.

Ruben's irritation at the request surfaced quickly, then disappeared when he noticed Rosa watching him from the corner.

"Is it food, Mr. Ruben?" Neve took a step forward and asked in Rosa's broken English, "Is it allergic reaction?"

Ruben cursed under his breath. "Get Amos in here now!" he shouted, his voice carrying down the stairwell and spurring Neve to rush out of the room on Rosa's sturdy legs.

"Amos!" she shouted over the railing on the landing. "Come quick! Ruben need you!"

A few seconds later, Amos's heavy footsteps bounded up the staircase with Neve trailing close behind. He burst into the room with a look of alarm. "Sir?" he asked, his eyes darting to Camille, where a faint rash was walking up her neck.

"Did you do anything different?" Ruben demanded,

pointing at their almost empty dishes. "She seems to be having some sort of reaction."

His brow furrowed in uncertainty. "It's the same French Onion soup recipe I've used for a year, sir. Beef broth, a bit of red wine, some stock, and Worcestershire sauce."

"Rosa, please take Camille back to her bedroom and call the doctor. Amos, you're with me. I need to see every bottle you used today." Neve shifted uncomfortably, her eyes darting toward Amos, who was clearly shouldering the brunt of the blame. She gathered up Camille and walked her back to her bedroom, administering a dose of Benadryl she found in the medicine cabinet. When she was certain the girl was out of harm's way, she called the doctor from the study, gathered up the plates, and returned them to the kitchen where Ruben was on a rampage.

"This is a huge setback that could have been avoided!" he snapped, his voice icy and a blue vein throbbing in his neck.

All the ingredients Amos had used to cook their lunch were sitting on the counter, and Ruben was studying each one. He held the bottle of Worcestershire sauce up. "What does this say right here?" His eyes widened as he roughly shoved the bottle toward the cook, pointing at a line of tiny type on the bottom of the label.

Amos pulled his reading glasses from his pocket and settled them on his face before he read aloud, "May contain shellfish." He handed the bottle to Ruben, then wrung his hands, his usual confidence utterly shaken. "I didn't know..." The cook's voice faltered as guilt washed over his face. "It's a different brand..."

"How could you be so stupid?" Ruben tossed the container into the trash and then paced the room. Fury surged from him in waves. "This cannot happen again," Ruben said, his voice steely. "For the next month, you will serve Camille the same three meals every day. Eggs and bacon for breakfast, a chef salad and an orange for lunch, and chicken Alfredo for dinner."

Amos nodded, seeming to shrink.

"Do not deviate from this menu! No substitutions. No new ingredients. Do we understand each other?"

"Yes, sir," Amos whispered, his jaw slack and his expression grim.

Ruben turned on his heel and strode out of the kitchen as silence engulfed the room.

Amos palmed his face, then turned to Neve. "Tell me Camille is okay," he begged.

"She be fine. Doctor coming soon," Neve assured. "But why Ruben so mad?"

"All he worried 'bout is hittin' that deadline. Ain't even ask how she was, not once," Amos muttered as he started to clean up the mess on the countertop. Neve worked alongside him, relying on Rosa's intuition to guide her. His regret was palpable, and he muttered under his breath, beating himself up for making the mistake. In her pocket, the geode shard hummed, and

Neve felt deep inside her bones that Ruben's anger was motivated by a deeper, darker reason, and she vowed not to rest until she got to the bottom of it.

TWENTY-TWO

THE NEXT AFTERNOON, Ruben leaned against the island in the kitchen, raking one hand absentmindedly through his unruly curls that were smudged with cerulean blue paint. Across from him, Amos stood at the stove, stirring a marinade of honey, lime, and garlic. Neve entered, balancing a tray of dirty dishes from Camille's lunch, and she walked on eggshells past Ruben to the sink.

The citrus-infused air between them was thick with tension that Neve was desperate to escape. She had just set the tray down in the sink and was about to slip away when Ruben suddenly stepped into her path, cutting off her exit.

"How did you know?" he asked, his tone laced with curiosity, as his dark eyes held hers for a beat. "About Camille, I mean."

Neve pushed her hands into the pockets of her apron and cupped her fingers around the geode. It pulsed with energy and tingled in her closed fist, and Neve found the sensation oddly comforting. "She scratch her throat," Neve said in Rosa's choppy English. "My nephew… I see before. They grab the neck, eyes get big. I know. He almost die." Rosa's revelation stunned even Neve.

Ruben studied her, his arms crossed over his chest. "Thanks to Rosa identifying the early signs of anaphylactic shock, a tragedy was averted." His lips were set in a hard line as he shot Amos a disparaging glare.

Neve swallowed the lump in her throat, then glanced over at Amos, who nodded sadly and lowered his chin, still blaming himself.

"You not know," Neve tried to reassure the cook. "It not your fault."

"Hmm," Ruben hummed from the back of his throat. For a few seconds, he oscillated between blame and forgiveness. Then, with a resigned exhale, he let it go. "In any case," he said, his tone becoming razor sharp, "I hope you learned something from this."

"I did." Amos was steadfast. "Sir, it won't happen again. I swear. I'll stick to her meal plan, no exceptions. You got my word. I'll double-check every ingredient."

"Good." Ruben nodded. "But I also decided we needed a contingency plan." He glanced down at his watch. "There is a new cutting-edge injector that can be used in an emergency. It cost me a bloody fortune, but Dr. Brenner should be here any minute to show us how it works."

The doorbell chimed before he could offer any further explanation.

"Right on time." Ruben clapped his hands together and turned to Rosa with a welcoming smile. "Can you show him to the kitchen?" Then he turned to Amos. "Put that on the back burner. This matter needs your full attention." Amos turned off the stove and quickly washed and dried his hands as Rosa led Dr. Brenner into the kitchen.

"Alton." Ruben shook his hand warmly, then gestured toward the countertop where Dr. Brenner set down his briefcase. He was middle-aged with an athlete's build, and his hair was cropped close to his head in a Caesar cut. The doctor opened the latches of his case and pulled out a pen-like device with a flourish. The label on it was in bold capital letters with clinical markings.

"This is an EpiPen," Dr. Brenner said, holding it aloft with reverence. "It's a miracle of modern medicine, but it's not something you can just pick up at any local pharmacy." He paused, letting the weight of his words sink in. "I had to pull considerable strings and call in some favors to obtain one for my dear friend, Ruben."

"*Merci,*" Ruben said, studying the medical device with quiet fascination.

"It's so small," Amos said, astonished.

"It is, but don't let the size fool you. It packs a wicked punch. The EpiPen delivers epinephrine to open the airways, buying enough time to seek proper medical treatment in the event of a severe allergic reaction. Without it…" His eyes flicked to Ruben, who shifted uncomfortably, already imagining the alternative. "Let's just say you don't want to find out." The doctor paused, letting the gravity sink in before he continued, "Now, to administer a dose, all you need to do is remove the safety cap and grip it firmly in your hand. Then, jab the needle into the outer thigh, through clothing if necessary, and hold it there while you count to ten." He demonstrated the motion, stabbing through the air with it, landing on his own thigh with the cap still intact. "Afterward, you *must* call 911 and seek appropriate medical attention."

Dr. Brenner handed the EpiPen over to Ruben. "Store this in a safe, easily accessible place where everyone in the household knows where to find it. Seconds can make the difference between life and death when a person is in active anaphylactic shock."

Ruben paused, surveying the kitchen. His eyes landed on the glass-fronted cabinet near the door. It was eye-level, central, and impossible to miss. He crossed the room in purposeful strides and opened the door, clearing a space among the fine China and crystal decanters. Carefully, he placed the EpiPen inside.

"Here. This is where it stays. If anything happens, everyone knows where to find it. I want each of you to remember this spot. Understand?"

"Yes, Mr. Ruben," Neve said, and Amos echoed.

"Dr. Brenner, thank you for the house call. I'll walk you to the door."

Neve watched the two men walk away, and Amos turned back to the stove without a word. "Are you okay, my friend?"

Amos turned toward her with a woeful look. "Ruben runs hot and cold, man. You'd think I'd be used to it by now. Dude's got that artist temperament, but ain't no good sweatin' it."

The telephone on the wall rang, and Neve crossed the room to answer it. "Angelica residence." She was surprised to hear a voice she recognized, and it sent shivers down her spine.

"*Ola*, Rosa!" Isla's sunny cadence greeted her warmly. It was light and melodic as if she didn't have a care in the world. "I was hoping to reach Ruben. I don't know if you remember, but Nevermore and I came for a visit and he offered to put in a good word for her at a local art school. Nevermore has been driving me crazy asking about it every day," she confided with a light-hearted chuckle.

"Of course," Neve answered, and she felt her heart swell with love for Isla's persistence.

"I wanted to follow up and see if he had any luck."

"Let me see if he is available."

"Thank you very much, Rosa."

Neve walked to Ruben's study and knocked on the door. "Isla Warner is on line two."

He clapped his hands together and rubbed them briskly before picking up the handset and saying, "Isla, *Mon Trésor*. Great to hear from you." Neve left the study but hovered outside the door, listening and watching the interaction from behind a crack in the doorjamb.

Inside the study, Perry let out a loud squawk. "Ruben, is that your wife on line one?"

Neve heard an embarrassed chuckle rise from Ruben, and she pinched her lips to contain the grin that wanted to spread across her face.

Ruben forced a stilted laugh, then explained, "I can assure you I am unmarried. The bird is a joker."

"Ruben's the joker!" Perry parroted back, his tone sing-song and filled with heaps of melodic snark.

Ruben covered the bottom of the handset with his palm and hissed at the bird, "Shut up or it's off to the taxidermist for you!"

"Help!" Perry chirped. "Save me, dear Isla. Ruben's threatening to end my life." Two slide whistles added the perfect amount of panache to his delivery.

Ruben choked out another awkward laugh, and then there was silence as he listened, then purred, "*Mais non! He's quite the exaggerator.*" Neve had to press her lips together to contain the burst of laughter trying to fight its way out. Perry had birdie-balls the size of Miami.

"Ruben has syphilis!" Perry blurted, not letting up. There was a clang as Ruben pulled the loafer from his foot and flung it at the cage. When it hit the metal bars, Perry ducked, then flapped his wings and let out a distressed warble.

There was a long stretch of silence before Ruben spun away from the bird to face the wall of windows as

Isla spoke. Then he answered in a gentle voice, "I need a bit more time, my sweet. I have an honorary spot on the admittance committee, and our annual enrollment meeting happens in a couple of months. I should have more information then, but in the meantime, I'd love to invite you to the auction. I am unveiling a collection of my latest work and would love to see you there."

There was another silence.

"*Très bien!*" he rejoiced.

Perry whistled and then squawked, "Frenchie has a rash on his wiener!"

Ruben's chair screeched against the floor as he whipped around to face Perry in his cage, and Neve's heart pounded in her chest. Enraged, Ruben said a hasty goodbye and slammed down the phone, then stormed to Perry's cage where his shrill squawks and cries intensified. "That's enough out of you!" he groused, scowling as he gathered up the heavy cloth and flung it over the cage. "You're lucky Isla has a soft spot for you or you'd be gone already!" Then, he bent down to retrieve his penny loafer and slipped it back on.

Hearing his footsteps approaching, Neve scrambled away from the door and quickly descended the staircase, her heart pounding.

¡Ándale!

Rosa's warning echoed in her mind and spurred Neve to pick up her pace. She couldn't afford to be caught eavesdropping when Ruben was already in a foul mood. At the bottom of the stairs, she paused just long enough to catch her breath, then slipped silently into the shadows, vanishing before his voice reached the landing.

CHAPTER 23
PEREGRINE

LATER THAT EVENING, after my punishment was over, Amos pulled the velvet cloth off the cage and doled out my evening sustenance. I chirped with delight and cooed at him, thankful for the buffet of fruit and seeds he'd provided, along with a scoop of pellets that were far worse than the ones Neve fed me at Sheila's. Sure, bird pellets had come a long way in the last thirty-five years, but I still turned my beak up in disdain, savoring the satisfying crunch of real nuts instead.

After I'd finished, I preened my feathers with my beak, smoothing them into place after the afternoon's festivities. An icy shiver raced through me, remembering the seething rage in Ruben's gaze during the phone call. His emotions swung like a pendulum from one extreme to the other, and it occurred to me, in the interest of self-preservation, I might need to dial back the insults. I let out a depressed chortle, saddened because it was my only form of entertainment and I would dearly miss it.

The doorbell chimed its festive ditty, chasing away the gloomy remnants of a tropical thunderstorm. I stopped preening and tested the door of the cage, pressing against it with my beak. Luckily, Amos hadn't secured it properly. Eureka! I was free at last. I slipped into the cool air with barely a flutter, careful not to draw attention to myself since I was already the bane of Ruben's existence. Just inside the foyer, I perched on the limb of a driftwood sculpture, safely out of sight.

The bell chimed again and I watched an aggravated Ruben stride over to the front door and press his eye to the peephole.

"*Mon Dieu!* This day will be the death of me!" he cried, muttering a string of French curses under his breath as he laid his forehead on the heavy wooden door, stalling. "How in the world did she find me?" Ruben mumbled under his breath. When the doorbell rang a third time, he let out a hot exhalation between his gritted teeth and ran a nervous hand through his black curls, still twisting in anxiety in front of the door.

She? Cue the DRAMA! This was going to be interesting! I quivered with excitement at the prospect of tantalizing insights this visit might yield, hoping it would help Neve. Finally, I had found a way to contribute to our mission!

Then the knocking began, demanding and persistent. *BAM! BAM! BAM!* Whoever was on the other side was relentless and would not be ignored. Heaving a final sigh, Ruben turned the deadbolt and slowly opened the door.

A woman stood there, drenched but smirking, sexiness dripping like venom. Her black trench coat clung to her hourglass figure. Rain trickled from her long dark curls to her shoulders, and her red lips were dangerously full. She had the kind of plump bottom lip I used to love to nibble when I was a human.

"*Mon coeur*," she purred, her French accent curling around the words like a wisp of smoke. She made a tsk-tsk noise with her tongue and offered him a sexy pout. "Aren't you going to invite me in, Martin?" Her accent made the name ooze with far more sophistication than its bland Americanized version.

Martin? Who in the hell was Martin? This was getting more interesting by the second!

"Oh," her plump lips pursed together. "That's right, you want to be called Ruben now." She then questioned his surname. "Angelica, is it?" Her lips were twisted into a mocking smirk. "We both know there is nothing angelic about you."

Ruben's jaw tightened, and his hand gripped the edge of the door. "What are you doing here, Margaux? I wired you your money."

"Is that any way to greet your beloved ex-wife after *five... long... years*?" She arched an impeccable eyebrow, her red lips curving into a pout. "I've traveled so far, and in such terrible weather. Surely, you could at least offer me a drink."

Ex-wife? Now she had my full attention. I hopped

closer, drinking her in. At closer glance, the cracks in the foundation were showing. Fine lines puckered around her lips, and when she smiled, a network of lines connected her features. Her limbs were sinewy and taut, though the skin had lost some of its elasticity. If I had to guess, I'd put her age just under the big 5-0. She took care of herself, knew how to apply makeup, and chose flattering fashion, but there was a harshness to her. A trace of bitterness she'd tried to camouflage by wearing pretty things exuded from her, though this realization did little to dissuade my desire to indulge in her delights. God, solitude was a cruel mistress.

"We have nothing more to say to each other," he said, attempting to close the door. Margaux pressed one strong arm against it and sidestepped him without waiting for permission to enter the house.

"You always were such a terrible host," she said, shaking off her coat and tossing it onto a nearby chair. Underneath, she wore a sleek black dress that clung to her like a second skin. Margaux turned to face Ruben, tilting her head and drinking in his opulent surroundings. "You're doing quite well for yourself, I see. Big house, fancy cars, not to mention your tortured French artist act." Her smile widened, becoming more predatory by the second, but it never reached her eyes. "How quaint," she purred with condescension.

"What do you want?" His voice was low. I had to flutter closer to hear him.

"Straight to business, as always. You've lost none of

your charm." She walked back toward him, her stilettos clicking on the tile floor. When she was close enough to touch, she leaned in, her husky voice dropping to a whisper. "We need to talk about the forgeries."

I jutted my bird head back. Wait. Did she just say forgeries?

I watched his Adam's apple make the slow journey down the length of his throat as he gulped. Ruben was afraid.

"There's nothing to talk about. You've been compensated. Fully, I might add, and besides, I destroyed the evidence years ago," he said, dragging her toward the door. Margaux would have none of it. Her chuckle was quiet but cut like a razor blade through butter. She yanked her body away from him and whipped around with a wave. "All except for a few, I see." She waved one lined hand at the collection going up the staircase. Her discerning gaze swept the room, lingering on the walls, drinking in the artwork Ruben loved to show off at his dinner parties.

Savoring the moment, Margaux pulled a folder from her handbag and raised it in the air with a knowing smile. "I've recently been in touch with a journalist who's eager to interview me about my wrongful conviction. He's developed quite a compelling theory involving a silent partner and a cover-up that might strike a chord with you. I promise, you'll be riveted. His preliminary investigation was very thorough."

Ruben's silence spoke volumes. He ripped the folder

from her hand and began to rifle through it. A grim frown puckered his lips and his jaw ticked as tension settled around his shoulders.

"Where did you get this?" he asked, his voice tight.

"You've never been very good at the paperwork, *Mon Coeur*. That's always been my area of expertise." She stepped closer and pressed him into the wall, pulling the folder from his hand and pressing her lips to his. Her fingers walked down his chest, landing below his waist as if they belonged there. "This little exposé could ruin you. Luckily, I was able to head it off at the pass." She pressed her full breasts against him, and I heard him moan. "I've always had your best interests at heart." She delivered a series of soft kisses to his neck, and he closed his eyes and swallowed hard. Finally getting his wits back, he pushed her away and crossed the room, but not before I caught a glimpse of his desire tented in his cuffed linen pants. Margaux chased after him, cornering him directly underneath my perch.

"I'm legitimate now. I've made my own way," he argued, turning away from her, but she grabbed his arm, her red nails threatening to break his skin as a scowl furrowed her brow into deep creases.

"Yes, I'm well aware you are Ruben Angelica, beloved modern impressionist and one of the highest compensated living artists in the world." She spat it out like an accusation. "While I've been rotting in jail for the last five years, taking the fall for our failures, you've been living in the lap of luxury," she accused, closing the gap between them and the wall. "Where is your sense of loyalty, your gratitude?"

"Gratitude?" he repeated, yanking his arm away from her grip and folding his arms across his chest.

"Yes, gratitude! If it weren't for me, you would have been the one in prison. Fortunately, I'm here to offer you a choice."

"A choice?" His voice was thick with disdain.

"Work with me again." She stepped closer, her eyes locking onto his. "We were good together, *Mon Coeur.* The very best. And with your talent and my business acumen, we could be unstoppable."

"And if I refuse?"

Her smile turned cruel. "Then I'll show the world exactly who you are. The journalist? He's already very interested in telling my story." She cleared her throat and corrected herself. "Our story. Imagine what he'd do with proof that your precious career was built on lies. I could bring the art world to its knees with one tiny, little phone call."

This was getting interesting. I longed for popcorn to accompany the viewing of this scandalous, impromptu documentary. I. Was. Riveted. I couldn't wait to fill Neve in on this new development.

Ruben clenched his fists, his nails digging into his palms. For the briefest of seconds, I felt bad for the man. Margaux was an unapologetic cougar and poised to devour him.

"You're a monster," he seethed, his voice barely more than a hoarse whisper.

"Perhaps," she said, her lined lips curling in triumph as she pressed closer until their faces were inches apart. "But you've always *loved* monsters."

Before he could respond, she closed the distance between them, her lips crashing against his. It was a kiss filled with anger, lust, and years of unresolved tension. Her hands tangled in his hair, pulling him closer as if she wanted to swallow him whole.

They broke apart, both of them gasping. Her lipstick was smeared, and his eyes blazed with desire.

"Still so easy to manipulate," she said, her voice dripping with mockery as she dabbed the corner of her lipstick with the tip of one red fingernail.

"Get out," he growled, recovering quickly, his voice vibrating with barely concealed rage.

"Oh, I'll leave," she said agreeably, stepping back. "But not without a promise. Think it over, *mon coeur*. Work with me, or watch everything you've built here crumble to dust."

She picked up her coat and slung it over her shoulder. With that, she was gone, the door slamming shut behind her. He stood there, his heart racing, his mind a whirlwind of fury and fear. The tropical storm outside gathered strength and battered the windows, mirroring the inner turmoil currently building inside Ruben.

He turned to look at the paintings on the wall, the forgeries that could destroy him. Cursing at himself, he tore one off the wall and slammed it to the ground. I watched the frame crack open, sending the canvas flying across the marble. I ducked behind the tree, afraid he would take out his frustrations on me. When he walked away, I glided back to the cage and hopped inside. It was obvious, in Ruben's current state, that I was safest behind its bars. But one thing was certain, this house just got a lot more interesting.

CHAPTER

TWENTY-FOUR

THE NEXT MORNING, Neve pushed her cart filled with cleaning supplies into the library at the crack of dawn. She rushed over to the cage and tugged the velvet cloth away. Sunlight caused Perry's drowsy trilling to stop abruptly, and he stretched out his wings, fluttering his feathers until they settled.

"What took you so long?" he groused, eyeing his empty food dish, hoping Neve would take the hint.

"I busy," Neve explained. "Mr. Ruben change clothing more than RuPaul at drag show. But I bring gifts." From the pocket of her apron, she pulled an apple and a paring knife and cut it into pieces.

"If you think you can get back in my good graces by offering me an ordinary apple, you are sorely mistaken," he huffed, turning away and offering her his red tail feathers. "I'll have you know, Amos gave me chunks of dragon fruit yesterday." He turned up his beak and folded his wings together in an oddly human gesture of defiance.

"I am not Amos. You get what you get and you no throw a fit!" Neve scolded. She reached into her pocket and pulled out a container of natural nuts and seeds, giving it a gentle shake to rouse his interest. It rattled just enough to command his attention, and his head swiveled toward her. Without waiting for his permission, Neve unlatched the cage and poured the mix into his food tray. The moment the nuts clattered against the metal, he hopped over, plucked one up with his beak, and crunched it, moaning with delight.

"There, drama king. Now you done with your tantrum, we be friends again?"

"I suppose that will suffice," he said between bites. When the dish was empty and the apple was gone too, he finally settled enough to dangle his tawdry tidbit. "I've got scorching hot goss!" He sang the phrase and added a jaunty slide whistle.

Confused, Neve's forehead wrinkled. "Hot goss? What that?"

"A tantalizing tale? An alluring account of a lurid encounter?" he added and then, seeing her blank expression remained unchanged, muttered out of the side of his beak, "Never mind, Nevermore."

His clever wordplay tickled his funny bird bones, and he rolled onto his back, cackling with glee, thoroughly amused by his own wit and charm. He could almost hear Neve blink as his joke fell flat. It was completely lost on her, so he plowed ahead.

"You'll be interested to learn, Ruben entertained a female caller late last night."

"He did? Who?"

"M! I believe I made the acquaintance of the mysterious M!" Several shrill, ear-shattering squawks cut through the silence, compelling his wings to puff and flap. A single feather drifted down to the bottom of the cage before he was able to get himself under control. "My apologies, but I'm powerless to control it. I seem to be afflicted with a severe case of avian Tourette's."

Neve offered him Rosa's muscular forearm, and he hopped out of the cage onto it. "Cougar alert!" he blurted with a squawk, then alighted into the air with another brash whistle and took a victory lap around the room, pumping his wings to expel a burst of frenetic energy.

"What? Where?" Neve glanced over both shoulders and rushed to hide behind the desk, afraid she'd see a wild cat closing in. She always believed she was a realist with a healthy amount of common sense, but this jaunt back to 1989 had proven anything was possible.

"Not the cat, Neve, the mature, sexy woman." Perry swooped around the perimeter, then slowed to a stop before landing on the soft headrest of the leather tufted sofa. "Blackmail. M is shaking Ruben down!" He coughed, then apologized, "Again, my apologies. I can't let myself get too excited, or I lose my ability to articulate." His feathers caught the light as he puffed up with indignation. "My avian twin makes his presence known when my excitement gets the better of me. I will try to control it."

"Explain yourself," Neve said, getting impatient. "And no using words from urban dictionary, *por favor*."

"Okay, fine," he said from his perch on the sofa. "Ruben's former wife, Margaux, managed to locate him, and his enthusiasm for the encounter was, shall we say, underwhelming? She insisted they discuss..." he paused, letting the tension build, raising one wing to the side of his beak before he whispered, "...the forgeries."

"Forgeries?" Neve's head snapped back in astonishment and she pursed her lips, considering the accusation. She paced the room, thinking aloud as the pieces clicked into place and a realization came like a bolt of lightning.

"I was right," Neve whispered, more to herself than anyone else. "When I bring Nevermore here like Isla, she tell Ruben they fake, good ones but still fake."

"Vanity, it will trip you up every time!" Perry bobbed in agreement. "He couldn't destroy the paintings because they were too beautiful, too perfect. Ruben used them to fool his fancy guests into thinking his art collection was authentic. They were evidence of his wealth and success. 'Oh, look at my priceless treasures,'" he mimicked in a pompous tone. "Art is the only investment that always appreciates. Puke."

Neve staggered to a chair and scrubbed Rosa's face with her hands. "*Ay caramba.* But he so talented, why someone like Ruben Angelica throw all away?"

Perry sighed, "Oh, dear, sweet Nevermore. Not

everyone follows the rules to the letter as you do. It's easy. He was looking for a payday when his art was taking too long to produce one."

"Hmm." Neve considered it.

"And…She called him Martin. He isn't Ruben Angelica after all!"

"Martin?" Neve was perplexed. "Martin DuBois?" she repeated under her breath, remembering the name on the envelope. Ruben used an alias. Why?

"There you are," Ruben barked through the doorway. Neve jumped and picked up Rosa's feather duster, attempting to look busy while Perry flew away to safety.

"I have an unexpected guest arriving this evening, so I need you to prepare the guest room. I've also removed several paintings from the walls and put them in the garage. They need to be destroyed."

"But why?" Neve asked, hoping to draw the truth out of him.

"I don't have time for your questions!" His abrupt tone silenced her request and made her shrink. "Cut them from their frames and have Amos bring me the stretchers to re-use."

"But…" His glare made her swallow the rest of the sentence.

He took a step closer, his tone turning even more threatening. "Do what you are told, Rosa, or I will have to find someone who can."

Neve felt Rosa's terror swell inside her, and it coupled with her own anger to form an intense wall of emotion. Her nostrils flared as she let out a hot exhalation, clenching her jaw to stop her actions from putting Rosa in jeopardy. "Yes, sir," Neve finally gritted out.

Without another word, Ruben stormed away, slamming the door behind him. An hour later, she was cutting the canvases from their frames. The sharp carpet knife she'd been given sliced through the artwork like a hot knife through butter. She pulled at the loose canvas, tearing it off its stretcher frame. On the concrete floor of the twelve-car garage and parking pad, a discard pile was growing.

The next painting was significantly heavier. She slid it against the wall for support before carefully cutting away the backing. To her surprise, she found a kraft paper envelope tucked inside. Neve tugged it free and unfastened the clasp. When she reached in and pulled out a thick stack of bills tightly banded together, her breath caught and she couldn't suppress an astonished gasp.

Mucho Dinero!

Neve gripped the cash in one hand, her other shuffling through the bills, and her eyes widening as the hundreds flipped by. The total was staggering. It had to be well over ten thousand dollars, more money than Neve had ever held in her hands at once. The geode in her pocket seared her skin and sent an electric tingle circuiting through her as she heard Rosa's instructions.

Hide for now. Behind bench. Mr. Ruben never use tools.

Heeding Rosa's advice, Neve tucked the money behind a pile of weed-whacker parts and a jumble of screwdrivers, resolving to return for it later.

Ruben came to check her progress in the late afternoon. "Is that all of them?" he asked, crouching down to inspect her work. He flipped between three of the loose canvases with a somber look on his face.

"Yes, Mr. Ruben."

He stared down at them as if appraising his brushstrokes with a discerning eye. Letting out a heavy exhale, his tone downshifted low and his delivery was ominous. "You realize what you've done, don't you?"

He placed the cut canvases back on top of the pile and leveled his gaze on the housekeeper, folding his arms across his chest.

"I do what I was told."

"No, Rosa." He nodded sadly. "It's much more than that. It's destruction of evidence." He leaned in, intimidating her. "And now, you're an accomplice, whether you wanted to be or not."

Neve's voice trembled in fear. "Evidence of what?"

"A crime."

Neve felt the blood drain from her face as Rosa's fright peaked in her belly.

"Don't even think about going to the police," he advised, his tone steely. "You are a Hispanic maid with little more than a green card. Your word would never stand up against that of a respected figure in the art commmunity."

Neve was stunned, grasping instantly what this

meant for Rosa, and she felt a wave of nausea roll through her.

He picked up a square from the forged Renoir. "It's such a shame. Do you understand the level of expertise it takes to create a replica of one of the most iconic paintings in the world? Not to mention, practically needing a degree in chemistry to get the paints and solvents just right to mimic the materials used centuries ago? It's a delicate, time-consuming process, and I was excellent at it. They would have gone undetected if my ex-wife hadn't been so greedy." He threw it down on the ground and began to pace. "Margaux kept pushing the boundaries, wanting to cut corners and produce more and more and more." His hands gesticulated wildly as his anger rose.

Neve's brows knit together, confused by the loss of control he was describing. She made her decisions logically and with a clear head. It was hard to understand everyone didn't function that way.

"She was a glutton. Her appetite… for everything…" He stopped pacing long enough to make direct eye contact. Neve shuddered in repulsion, easily interpreting what he was leaving out. "…was insatiable."

Speechless, she felt the nudge from Rosa whose fear was escalating with her own.

He need calm down. Tell him good thing.

"And you become one of most important artists on East Coast." Neve forced herself to utter the compliment, grateful for Rosa's guidance.

"I have, and now that she's resurfaced when I am so close to the pinnacle of my success, I cannot let her sabotage everything I have worked for."

"But why you do it?" Neve asked.

"Because I was destined to live a life far better than the one I was given." He glanced around the expansive garage where his fleet of luxury cars were parked on a decorative parking pad. Walking over to a canary yellow Corvette, he swiped one hand down the length of it. "This was the first splurge I made when the money started flowing in."

Ruben walked over to the sexy black Bugatti parked next to it. He slid into the seat and closed his eyes, leaning back into the headrest.

"But your talent wasted, making copies when you could make own art. You see now, yes?" It was the only question that felt unanswered.

He shot her a wry smile. The sting of regret made him flinch as he shrugged his shoulders and slid back out of the leather seat. "*C'est la vie.*" He slammed the door shut, then walked away, and Neve was grateful for the solitude. She felt Rosa's tears prickle at her lash line and shook them off. Now was not the time to curl into a ball in the corner. It was time to channel the outrage storming through her and strengthen her resolve.

Ruben Angelica was not worthy of the pedestal she'd put him on. He was a fraud and an imposter. She felt Rosa nudge her to gather up the discarded Renoir and roll it into a cylinder, tucking it away with the money, just in case.

With a steady hand, she pulled the geode from her pocket and its green glow was electric. The stone pulsed in the center of her palm, sending a surge of energy and filling her with a new purpose. Neve hadn't been sent to 1989 to reunite with her father. She'd been sent to expose the truth about Ruben Angelica.

CHAPTER

TWENTY-FIVE

RUBEN WATCHED the headlights of the sleek black town car he'd sent to fetch Margaux emerge from the mist and snake their way up the drive. Fog had rolled in from the sea, and it swallowed the surrounding palm trees and sandy beaches whole. The hulking, gray landscape matched his current mood. He raked one hand through his curly hair, then chewed on the nail bed of his thumb.

The car slowed to a stop, and he watched the driver open the door where a stiletto emerged at the end of one long, honeyed leg he'd used to spend hours worshipping. He knew every freckle on her skin by heart. A frown spread over his features as he felt his body respond to hers against his will. She'd had this effect on him since they'd met, and he'd been foolish to think the attraction waned. It simply had lain in wait, lurking about, waiting to be reignited.

Margaux climbed out and stood, peering up at the sprawling mansion with a smirk muddying her sensuous lips. She was enjoying this, and he felt the bittersweet burn of sexual tension and hot angst fuse together in his gut. He knew he was playing with fire, and yet he was powerless against it. The danger was intoxicating.

The doorbell chimed. He swallowed the rest of the amber-colored whisky in his cut crystal glass and made his way to the door, turning Rosa away with a resigned mumble, "I've got this one." The truth was, he didn't have it at all, and a pained chuckle burbled up and out of his lips.

When he opened the door, she stood on the portico, pulling off a pair of gloves. "Margaux," he said, each syllable clipped and ice cold. He spit out a frosty greeting. "Welcome back."

Margaux met his gaze, her lips curving into a slow, tantalizing smile. "Don't sound so thrilled. You might want to give your staff the impression you missed me." She boldly strode through the door, leaving Ruben to deal with her luggage and tip the driver.

Returning after the driver pulled away, Ruben shut the door with calculated restraint, the resounding click echoing through the cavernous foyer. As he drank her in, his eyes narrowed just enough to assess the lines on her face. It had been five years she'd spent locked in a French prison and it changed her. There was a stiffness in her gait. Margaux's body had always been a master class of curves, but the time inside chiseled her sexy edges into harsh points. She was thinner, her lips quirking down now instead of up, set in a rigid line. Her skin had suffered from the lack of anti-aging products, camouflaged now by concealer and powder that settled into the fine lines. From a distance, she was still flawless, but up close, he took pleasure in inventorying every physical imperfection, trying to talk himself out of the attraction he still felt.

"You changed your look," she remarked, taking in his dark hair that was slicked back and his piercing dark eyes that darted toward her like twin daggers.

"Let's be clear," he said, his tone hostile and menacing. "This isn't a vacation. You're here because I can't trust you to keep your mouth shut." His gaze dropped to her trademark crimson lips, and he felt the familiar wicked urge to ruin them surge up from the depths of his depravity. As if plucking the thought straight from his mind, she caught her bottom lip between her teeth. Her well-trained tongue darted between her lips then disappeared again, and he was forced to train his gaze elsewhere.

Margaux glanced around the grand foyer, taking in the sweeping staircase, the glittering chandelier, and the now empty walls. Pointing at where the art used to hang, a gleeful chuckle of victory escaped her as she clicked her tongue at him.

"Sweet, *stupide* man. Too little, too late." She stalked closer, closing the distance between them, and he felt the magnetism he'd always felt in her presence. She snaked her arms around his neck and leaned in, and he felt himself harden in response. He cursed his weakness for a split second before he gave in to it. Her lips were soft and yielding, her kisses becoming more fervent as she stirred with passion under his fingertips.

He pulled back from the edge of delirium and mumbled, "It's fitting in a way that you're here."

"How so?" Her head tilted to the side, and he felt a tingle of anticipation.

"It's classic Sun Tzu, *The Art of War*. Keep your friends close and your enemies closer."

She breathed into the sliver of air remaining between them, drawing him in hypnotically. "Which am I, *mon coeur?* Friend or enemy?

"That remains to be seen," he whispered, curling a tendril of her hair around his finger. He tugged it down and relished the gasp of pain that dripped from her lips.

Margaux still took his breath away, but she was more dangerous now than she'd ever been. She knew too much about his past. Margaux had been his wife and his willing accomplice, selling his forgeries to gullible art collectors in Europe. It had been a lucrative business that paid handsome dividends until he'd tired of toiling away in his studio making copies. In frustration, Ruben conceived an easier path forward, but he'd needed a scapegoat. In order to realize his new dream, he'd had to leave the past and Margaux behind and reinvent himself in America.

It had worked. His new identity in the art world, Ruben Angelica, was hailed as a contemporary artistic genius, and he was forging his immortality, show by show. He couldn't afford to get sidetracked now by a romp down memory lane, no matter how satisfying it would be.

Ruben untangled himself and took a step away from her. It would be easy to let himself get carried away and pick up where they'd left off, but he would not allow it. Instead, he shot Margaux a smirk. "Enemies implies we're equals, and I assure you we are not."

A flash of rage burned in her gaze and then quickly dissipated. He watched her delicate nostrils flare, enjoying the exchange far more than he should have. It took a second before she could respond with an appropriate comeback. She turned to him, cocking her head, and shot him a devious grin. "*Non*? If we are not equals, then what are we? Because the last time I checked, *you* are the one bending to *my* terms."

His lips twitched and sarcasm snaked through his response. "And what a joy it is to have you remind me."

Letting out a little peal of laughter, she followed him deeper into the house, her heels muffled now by the Persian rugs that stretched across the floors. Ruben's strong silhouette cut through the dim light as he led her to the library. He poured himself another drink, but didn't offer her one.

"So," he said finally, settling into the leather armchair behind his desk and regarding her with a calculated calm. "What exactly are you hoping to accomplish by rekindling your obvious lust for me?"

A rueful chuckle rang out as Margaux perched on the edge of the tufted leather sofa, crossing her legs with lady-like grace. "Paying my debt to society has emptied my coffers. The funds you wired helped, but I need to rebuild my financial resources after losing so much time."

Ruben's upper lip twitched in disgust. She cocked her head at him as she pulled the hem of her skirt up to offer him a glimpse of her black garter belt. He closed his eyes to steel himself against it, then reopened and forced his eyes up to meet her gaze.

"Since my release, I have thrown myself back into my work. I've met two new collectors who are practically salivating for their next acquisitions." His jaw tightened as she leaned forward slightly, allowing him a glimpse of her breasts, and dropped her tone to a purr. "I figured we could rekindle… the business and… perhaps… more."

Ruben's laugh was low and humorless. "Surely, you remember I am not the masochist here. You are."

She arched a brow, her devilish grin never wavering. "Keep lying to yourself. Your hands still tremble when we touch, and I can feel the effect I have on you. We had something great together and we can have it again."

His gaze darkened, and for a moment, the air between them crackled with the weight of their past. It would be so easy to surrender to his desire. In the bedroom, Margaux's skill was unmatched, and no other woman had ever claimed such power over him. Ruben was engaged in a tug-of-war between his cock and his brain. Was the past always doomed to repeat itself? He shook the lusty thoughts off. "No. I will not let you tear down the new life I have built."

"*Mon coeur?*" She murmured, "You misunderstand." She gazed at him, her expression unreadable. "I don't want to tear anything down. I want to help you build something new."

"I don't want your help, Margaux." He waved one hand behind him. "As you can see, I am doing quite well on my own."

Her lips curled into a scowl. "This life was subsidized by the one we built together. You owe me."

"I don't owe you anything," he bit out.

Her eyes softened, just for a moment. "That's not true." The vulnerability in her timbre caught him off guard. For a moment, he felt the guilt rush in. He saw the woman he'd fallen in love with all those years ago. But then, just as quickly, her mask shifted back into place.

Dismissing his temporary lapse of judgment, he stood to leave. "It's late. You should go to bed."

"Yes, we should," she purred, her voice dripping with desire. Their eyes locked, the sexual tension between them crackling like a live wire. Then Ruben turned and walked away, leaving her alone, but not before muttering over his shoulder, "Rosa will show you to your quarters." Then Ruben congratulated himself for walking away, heading down the darkened hall as the familiar twin aches of desire and resentment coiled in his chest.

CHAPTER

TWENTY-SIX

Late that night when the house was still, Neve slipped out of her bedroom and up the staircase to the study. She neared the cage and pulled off the velvet cloth.

"Perry," she hissed, trying to wake him. He warbled in response. "PERRY!" she whisper-shouted.

"Don't touch me there, Isla," he chortled, then let out a soft chuckle.

"Eww!" Neve grimaced and twisted open the cage, eager to draw him out of whatever erotic dream he was having as fast as possible. She stroked his wing with the tips of her fingers, and he jolted, then opened his eyes.

"To be unceremoniously yanked from the depths of a sumptuous carnal delight into this dreary banality of wakefulness is an offense so egregious that even the gods themselves weep at the injustice."

"Good see you too, bird man." Neve glanced over her shoulder, listening for any sound of footsteps.

Hearing none, she whispered, "Listen. I find envelope full of cash in back of one painting Ruben tell me destroy."

He let out a low whistle, and Neve shushed him. "How much are we talking?"

"Over ten thousand dollars."

"Whoa." His head snapped back. "What did you do with it?"

"I hide it," Neve said. "In my underwear drawer."

"No offense, but that was an astute choice. With a derrière like Rosa's, it would be the very last place anyone would deign to search."

"Tone down misogyny a little, yes?"

"Fine." He hopped onto Neve's forearm, leaned in close, and whispered into her ear, "I bet there are more. Search all the paintings in the house. Ten thousand dollars will go a lot further in 1989. Cash will come in handy if we're ever forced to make a hasty exit."

"Okay. I will." She nodded, already mentally cataloging which rooms in the mansion had framed artwork. "What you think about Margaux?"

"I don't know," he replied, eyes narrowing thoughtfully. "She's definitely got an agenda. I just haven't figured out what it is."

Down the hall, a door creaked open. Neve froze, her pulse quickening as a flutter of fear gripped her chest. She held her breath, straining to catch the rhythm of approaching footsteps over the thrum in her ears.

"Get out of here," Perry whispered urgently. "It's not safe."

In a blur of motion, he flew back to the cage. Neve rushed to drape the cloth over it, hiding him from view just as the footfalls grew louder. Without another second to waste, she slipped out the door of the study and moved swiftly down the hallway, her feet silent against the cold tiles.

She reached the powder room, twisted the doorknob with trembling fingers, and ducked inside. The door clicked shut behind her, and she leaned against it, barely daring to breathe. Minutes passed like hours. Neve counted to one thousand for several long agonizing minutes before the silence outside convinced her it was safe. Afterward, she crept back to her bedroom, but even once the door was locked behind her, her nerves remained frayed. It took over an hour of staring into the dark, her thoughts circling like vultures, before her mind finally settled enough for sleep.

CHAPTER

TWENTY-SEVEN

MARGAUX SPENT the next several days padding through the house in bare feet, while Ruben sequestered himself in the studio, sunk into one of his brooding moods. He declined every one of her advances and left her alone for long stretches of time while he painted around the clock.

To pass the time, Margaux roamed the estate, slipping quietly in and out of rooms, her curiosity deepening with each locked drawer and half-closed door she encountered. The maid hovered around, her presence unavoidable and her watchful suspicion rippling through the halls. Margaux knew the game. If you wanted to understand the dynamics of a household, you started with the staff. But Rosa was too loyal and becoming too wary, so Margaux pivoted to Plan B. The Cook. Men always spoke more freely when their hands were busy and their guard was down. And Margaux had a knack for getting men to talk.

A week into her stay, Margaux sought Amos out, wandering into the kitchen with calculated casualness. Her plan was simple: stay close, build trust, and wear his defenses down one day at a time. He was at the sink, rinsing strawberries and humming to himself, when she lingered in the doorway just long enough for him to notice.

"Can I help?" Margaux offered, careful to keep her tone light, almost innocent like the question had sprung from genuine curiosity rather than calculation.

"Oh, no, ma'am," he said quickly, not looking up from the sink. "I've got it under control."

"You know," she went on, brushing an invisible speck from her silk sleeve, "I've always wanted to learn how to cook. My mother was dreadful in the kitchen." She gave a soft laugh, letting it drift between them.

Amos hesitated, his hands briefly pausing in the stream of water. Then he turned off the faucet, shook the colander twice with a practiced flick of the wrist, and set it down beside the sink.

Margaux took a few tentative steps closer, the quiet pad of her bare feet inaudible on the tile. Her eyes sparkled with mischief, but her tone had a playful edge. "I bet Ruben told you to keep an eye on me."

Amos stopped cold. He reached for a dish towel and dried his hands with deliberate care, avoiding her gaze. But he didn't answer. He didn't need to.

Margaux smiled, satisfied. She tilted her head just slightly, letting her dark hair fall over one shoulder. "Wouldn't it be easier to do that if I were right by your side?" she said sweetly, her voice like honey. She shot him a dazzling grin as if it were the most logical idea in the world.

For a moment, the only sound in the kitchen was the slow drip of water from the faucet and the distant tick of the grandfather clock in the hall. Margaux didn't move, letting the silence stretch, knowing full well that discomfort could be just as persuasive as charm.

He let out a laugh. "Aight, you got a point. If you want to learn, I can teach you a few things." Amos pointed over to the shelf under the countertop. "Aprons are over there."

"You won't regret this!" Margaux enthused and rushed over to put one on, tying the strings behind her waist.

He handed her a bowl of clean strawberries and, with a paring knife, taught her how to remove the hull. They worked in companionable silence for a while, and when she was finished, he had her clean the romaine and spin it dry.

At lunchtime, he glanced at the clock, cursing under his breath.

"What's the matter?"

"Ruben wanted lunch served at 12:15 sharp. I better hustle or it will be late."

"Is there anything I can do to help?" she asked, and when he answered no, she let out an exasperated sigh, careful not to sound too melodramatic. "Between you and me, I don't know how you do it!"

"Do what?" Amos asked, glancing over his shoulder

with mild curiosity as he carefully arranged Camille's salad onto a piece of bone white China.

"Deal with Ruben," she said, lowering her voice slightly and stepping closer, as though she were confiding a secret. "He always has to be in charge." The words rolled off her tongue with practiced ease, softened by the disarming grin she flashed him.

Amos let out a burst of unexpected laughter. "True story." His hands moved with mechanical focus as he wiped a stray drop of dressing from the rim of the plate, but Margaux saw the faint tightening at the corners of his mouth.

"We struggled with his control issues our entire marriage." She kept her eyes pinned on the countertop for a beat, then lifted them with calculated vulnerability. "To be honest, he doesn't deserve another chance, yet I want to give him one anyway." She made her voice waver, just enough to betray a hint of insecurity as she forced a film of tears to blur her vision. "Does that make me pathetic?"

Amos paused in the middle of wiping down the counter, the cloth stilling in his hands. He studied her for a quiet moment, then set it aside and turned to face her fully. "Of course not, girl," he said, settling his warm gaze on her. "It makes you human."

Margaux nodded sadly, then turned back to dry the cutting board, letting the silence do the rest. She hoped it would be enough to stir sympathy in him. When he moved closer and dropped into a conspiratorial tone, her heart swelled with triumph.

"You know what always makes me feel better?" he asked, his lips curling into a slow gin grin.

"What?"

"Gumbo. And it's one of Ruben's favorites."

"It is?" she said with a laugh, widening her eyes just enough to seem genuinely surprised. "I had no idea. Will you show me how to make it?"

"How about I get the ingredients at the market and we'll make it this weekend?"

"*Oui!*" Margaux flashed him a winning smile.

Amos's fingers flew as he finished lunch preparations in time and left to deliver the tray to Ruben. When he returned to the kitchen, his usual sunny disposition returned with him.

On Friday, Amos schooled her on the finer points of Cajun seasonings. He taught her how to make a roux, stirring it until the muscles in her forearms tingled from overuse, coaxing the dark brown color from flour and butter.

Margaux chatted away as she cut vegetables and sautéed them in the pan, peppering her more intrusive questions with innocuous ones.

"I thought gumbo always had shrimp in it," she said as she diced an eye-watering onion. "Not that I want to spend my afternoon cleaning and deveining them." She grimaced as the thought of it made her shudder and bile rise in her throat.

Amos hesitated as if searching for the right words. "Usually, it does, ma'am. But..." He trailed off, and Margaux noted the careful pause. "...Ruben's got a few folks… close friends who have, well, certain dietary restrictions."

It was a vague reply that piqued Margaux's interest, and she waited for him to elaborate while he kneaded the pasta dough with steady hands. The dough was soft and pliable beneath his palms. He dusted the board with flour, then stretched and folded the dough again before feeding it through the hand-cranked cutter. The long, golden ribbons spilled out in perfect strands. Finally, he added, his voice low but matter-of-fact, "He said, if I want to keep my job, I need to keep seafood the hell out of this house."

"Wow!" Margaux said, drawing out the word with exaggerated disbelief. "I know Ruben can be intense, but that was just rude. He shouldn't speak to you that way!" She leaned back slightly, arms crossing over her chest in mock indignation. She paused just long enough to let the shared grievance settle between them, then leaned forward again, lowering her voice into a clandestine whisper. "Can you keep a secret?"

Amos nodded and leaned closer, waiting in expectation for something juicy.

"Sometimes Ruben scares me," she confided in a hushed whisper, biting her lip for his benefit.

"Me too," Amos admitted under his breath and then let out a somber chuckle before returning to his Alfredo sauce. He opened the glass front cabinet and pulled out a storage dish when the red label of the EpiPen caught her eye.

Curious, Margaux dried her hands and crossed the

room a few minutes later, pulling it out of the cabinet. She held it up and asked, "What is this? Some kind of candy thermometer?"

"Not quite." He walked over to her and gently pried it from her hands, holding it with kid gloves. "It's called an EpiPen. We keep it on hand for emergencies."

"What does it do?"

"It helps keep the airway open in the event of an allergic attack."

"What an innovation! My brother has a peanut allergy. Would this help him if he was having a reaction?" Margaux asked.

"It could mean the difference between life or death," Amos said, his voice steady but tinged with seriousness as he placed the pen back in its spot and gently closed the cabinet door. "But we aren't supposed to touch it until Mr. Ruben tells us to. Understand?"

"Of course." She nodded, then sniffed the air with a sudden gasp. "Oh no! I think our roux is starting to burn!" Desperate to shift his focus, she half-heartedly stirred the pan with a bamboo spatula. Amos chuckled, quick to move to her side and take over. She lifted her shoulder and breathed in the pungent scent of onions and garlic. After lunch, she would take a long shower to wash the stink of the kitchen off her skin and spend the rest of the day exploring. Margaux wasn't built for kitchen duty.

Later that afternoon, while Rosa was on the other side of the property, Margaux let herself into Ruben's study. She stopped at the bar cart to pour herself a drink and let it sit on his desk. Bored and wanting to snoop, she tugged on the drawers of his desk, most of which were locked. Margaux rooted around the top drawer, looking for a set of keys among the pens, pencils, and paperclips, finding nothing.

"He locked it up and threw away the key," Perry squawked to life from his perch in the cage.

"You sure are a clever boy, aren't you?" Margaux cooed, walking over to the bird.

Perry whistled the first line from the chorus of the new Milli Vanilli smash hit, "Girl You Know It's True." He ducked and bobbed along to the beat, then sang out, "I love you!"

Margaux clapped her hands and chuckled, *"C'est trés bien!"*

Perry chirped and whirred, bouncing up and down with delight, thrilled with his own performance. "The key! The key!" he blurted, his squawk high with glee.

Margaux arched an eyebrow, questioning him curiously, "Do you know where it is?" Then, receiving no immediate answer, she took a slow sip of whiskey. She strolled down the length of the bookcase, her fingers trailing absentmindedly across the spines as she read them.

"Warmer," the bird chirped.

Taken aback, Margaux took another step. "Colder." She whirled around, amazed at his ability to articulate.

"Are you playing hot and cold with me?" From the cage, Perry let out an excited confirmation squawk and thrashed his wings in response.

To test his accuracy, she quickly reversed directions, and he churred, "Warmer!" Two more quick steps in the same direction made him squawk in a shrill warble, "You're on fire! You're an inferno!"

Margaux stared at her fingertip in astonishment. It had come to rest on the worn leather spine of *The Key*, a dark, twisted Japanese novel from the 1960s that eerily mirrored the power struggles present in her own marriage. When she and Ruben had lived together, he used a hollowed-out copy to stash his keys, passport, and other valuables inside, hiding them in plain sight.

A thrill shot through her. With a delighted gasp, she pulled the book from the shelf. The cover creaked as she pried it open, exposing a small box nestled inside the carved-out pages. On a ring inside the box were seven keys. She quickly inserted them into the lock one at a time, twisting with no luck until number six. It turned easily with a satisfying click.

One by one, she rifled through the drawers where his paperwork was filed neatly away into green folders labeled in handwritten capital letters. She whipped through the first few folders straight to the one labeled bank statements. Margaux pulled out the stack of papers, almost an inch thick, and set it on top of the desk where she paged through it. She expected to see the balance growing every month during the years she rotted in her cell. Instead, it told a very different story.

Ruben was cash-poor. He was living on credit, month to month, only barely scraping by.

Frustration blossomed in the pit of her stomach as she continued to flip through the papers page by page, painting a full picture of his bleak financial situation. When she got to the bottom of the stack, she returned the papers to their appropriate file folder and grabbed the next. Two hours passed in a blink as she took stock of his disappointing investment portfolio, several bank accounts around town with low balances, and the titles to his fleet of luxury automobiles that were leveraged to the hilt. Ruben had built a house of cards, juggling creditors that could come crashing down around him at any moment.

She'd sipped on the whiskey to soothe the growing unease in her belly and then poured herself another. The folder labeled Life Insurance held another strange curiosity. Inside was a life insurance policy in the amount of two million dollars for Camille Sinclair with Ruben Angelica declared the sole beneficiary.

The sound of approaching footsteps startled Margaux from her thoughts. Perry chirped and cried, "Danger, Will Robinson! Danger!"

Confused by his cries, but taking heed anyway, panic set in as Margaux hastily returned the papers to the envelope. Her hands trembled as she slid the drawer shut and locked it. Seconds later, she returned the key to the book and barely got it back on the shelf before she rushed through the opposite door, just missing Ruben.

CHAPTER

TWENTY-EIGHT

The soft clinking of metal against metal echoed faintly as Neve polished the silverware while standing at the breakfront in the dining room. Spread out on a towel were several piles of forks and teaspoons, and she let her mind drift as she zoned out while rubbing the tarnish off each one.

A few minutes later, Margaux entered the room, interrupting her peace, and offering her a warm greeting. "Hello, Rosa." She flashed her a captivating grin, raising two wine glasses and a bottle of wine like an invitation. Neve couldn't deny there was a magnetism about the woman as if she sucked all the air out of the room. While Neve preferred to live on the periphery, it was obvious Margaux thrived front and center.

Neve returned the pleasantries, knowing that was what was expected of her. "*Ola*, Ms. Margaux." Her gaze flicked to the woman and then back. Margaux was too perfect. Her hair was sky high, a masterpiece concoction of back-combing and Aqua Net, and the exaggerated shoulder pads of her red jacket lent her the geometric angularity that made the 80s power suit popular. Margaux set the bottle and glasses down with a flourish, then expertly twisted the corkscrew and uncorked the wine. The cork freed with a raucous pop and then, without waiting for it to breathe, she poured herself a glass.

"Don't you think it's time we've gotten to know each other better?"

"Uh… *si*?" Neve answered in Rosa's Spanish, her tone timid and questioning.

"Have a drink with me." Margaux drew lazy circles on the rim of her crystal glass with her finger as she watched Neve work. Then she swirled the wine in the goblet and took a long sip, letting out a content moan of pleasure. "C'mon," she wheedled. "Ruben's wine cellar is fully stocked. I know he'd never miss one tiny bottle." She poured another glass and slid it over to Neve by the base.

"*Gracias*, but I cannot," Neve said, turning it down. "I have work to do."

"I won't tell if you won't." Margaux smirked and offered her a wink. "One little sip won't hurt you." She took another long swig before continuing. "You *must* try it. The man has impeccable taste when it comes to wine."

This is bad idea.

Neve hesitated, hearing Rosa's warning, then set the polishing cloth down and picked up the glass, taking a small sip, hoping it would appease Margaux and she would leave. It was full-bodied and complex with a cherry finish and surprisingly took a little of the edge off of the coil of worry that was building inside Rosa's body.

"How long have you worked here?" Margaux's chummy tone was perplexing. It heightened Neve's defenses, and she decided to engage as little as possible.

"About two years? When Mr. Ruben buy this house and move in," Neve offered as she turned back to polish the silverware. She counted the remaining pieces, hoping the conversation would wrap up before she got to the end of the task.

"And how have you found working for him?"

"No better, no worse than my last boss." Neve intentionally kept her answer ambivalent, not wanting to draw any further attention to herself.

"But his temper…" Margaux's shoulders quaked as if a shiver had cycled through her. "When he's under pressure like he is right now, Ruben can be a powder keg, capable of exploding at any moment."

Neve had already witnessed his volitile mood swings, but a small part of her was skeptical of the warning. Margaux wasn't her friend, but she sure seemed to be confiding in her like one. Perhaps she had an ulterior motive. Neve narrowed her eyes at the woman, searching for clues.

"I want to tell you something, but I'm afraid you'll take it the wrong way," Margaux said softly, choosing her words carefully. After a long pause, she leaned closer and whispered, "You need to be careful around Ruben. He isn't the man he pretends to be." Her teeth were stained a deep red from the wine, and Neve nervously ran her tongue over her own, fearing they looked just as terrible.

"He not?" Neve's eyebrows knit together in confusion.

Margaux made a show of looking over both her shoulders before continuing. "No. He's very dangerous." Her eyes darkened, and she took another long sip, the redness on her lips and tongue deepening. "I was trusting and obedient once like you are, and I paid the price. Ruben has a history of leaving the dirty work for other people."

"How?"

"We were business partners, but I was naïve and didn't see what he was doing until it was too late. I spent five years in prison while he vanished with the money we made and started a new life in the United States."

Neve feigned an expression of shock on Rosa's face. He'd already confessed this to her, but she was determined to keep Margaux in the dark until she understood her intentions.

Margaux's tongue clicked. "Aren't you curious why Ruben locks himself in his studio behind closed doors for days at a time? What is happening up there?"

"He not lock himself. Mr. Ruben is just private man," Neve tried to reason with her, defending Rosa's employer because she knew how much Rosa needed the job. "His work demand total focus."

"Perhaps." Margaux let out a hollow chuckle, and a long silence stretched between them. She tugged up the sleeve of her jacket where a silvery-white scar appeared. As her glass was now empty, she poured herself another. "I found something else you might find interesting in his study."

Neve leaned closer. The geode in her pocket tingled, and she felt a surge of energy flow into her from it. "What?"

"A life insurance policy for two million dollars written on someone named Camille Sinclair, where he is named as the sole beneficiary."

Neve's stomach flipped as Rosa's panic flooded in and she took over, her lips pursed. "You are not to go in his study. Mr. Ruben very clear." She took another small sip of the wine, hoping it would help the maid relax.

"Don't play games with me, Rosa. Who is Camille?"

"She's not what you think. He help her. She artist and he mentor."

Margaux's eyes darkened as she considered it, folding her arms across her chest.

"Camille shy. She prefer solitude of her suite. She eat, breathe, sleep, paint."

"Wait... she lives *here*?" Neve could see Margaux grappling with the accidental revelation. A flurry of emotions played across her face before Margaux shuttered them away, one by one.

¡Dios mío! Neve felt a dizzying surge of regret, as internally, Rosa realized she'd said too much.

Margaux drummed her fingernails, then offered a piece of advice, "If I were Camille, I'd watch my back."

"Why you say?"

"When a man takes out a large life insurance policy on a woman, she should get very nervous," Margaux answered, letting the implication hang heavy in the air.

Footfalls echoed down the hall, and Neve jumped like she'd been seared by a cattle prod. The accusation left Neve spiraling as unanswerable questions circled in her brain.

Margaux straightened, her expression smoothing into a neutral mask. "Think about what I said." She nodded once, then lifted her glass in a toast and headed back to the kitchen with the rest of the bottle, giving Neve a lot to think about.

CHAPTER

TWENTY-NINE

Two nights later, it was time to make her move. Margaux took a long bubble bath and then rubbed scented oil into her skin. She pulled on a black satin robe, garter belt, and a pair of sling-back heels she knew made her long legs look fantastic, then clipped a white handkerchief to the end of a fireplace poker.

In the hallway, she heard Bret Michaels crooning the opening notes of *Every Rose Has Its Thorn*. She followed the music, humming along as she let herself inside his study. With a playful grin, she waved the makeshift white flag back and forth, inching closer to Ruben's desk, hoping the grand gesture read more adorable than desperate.

Ruben chuckled when he saw the white flag, and she felt a wave of relief loosen her limbs. Leaning the fireplace poker gently against the wall, she sauntered to the gilded cage and began to untie her robe, unaware she'd just given the bird an unintentional peep show.

From inside the cage, Perry let out an enthusiastic wolf whistle. "Hey, sexy lady!" he squawked, feathers ruffling with delight. The bird's over-the-top reaction made Ruben chuckle again, despite his best efforts to keep a straight face.

"There," Margaux purred in a sultry whisper, turning to face Ruben. "Was it so difficult to be nice to me?" The words dripped from her tongue like warm honey. She inched closer, her gaze locked on his, and deliberately let the robe slip from one shoulder to reveal the soft curve of one of her magnificent breasts.

"Boobies!" Perry chirped again, clearly enjoying the striptease as he released a raucous whistle of delight. "Wowie! Zowie!"

Margaux let out a throaty laugh as she pulled Ruben into her arms for a long, wet kiss. "You've been working so hard. Maybe it is time for a break?" She folded her body against him in the way she knew he craved. Her fingers moved slowly, unhooking the buttons of his linen shirt one by one, exposing the warm skin beneath as she trailed slow kisses along his neck and down to his collarbone.

"Show me your fun bags!" Perry screeched as he bobbed up and down on his perch.

"Maybe we should take this upstairs?" Margaux whispered into the warm crook of his neck, feeling him stiffen against her thigh. "Seems your bird is a bit of a peeper."

"Yes. Let's," he whispered as their lips collided, and he was consumed by his need for her.

She felt the rush of power fill her as he took her by the hand and led her up the stairs and down the hall to his bedroom. The bed was piled with fluffy pillows and luxurious throws in dark navy with hints of silver. She surrendered to the searing rush of sensation, letting it crash over her in waves. Sex had never been their problem; it was always incredible, but the angst added a raw, intoxicating layer to the act. He was the only man capable of making her lose control, of pushing her to the edge of oblivion. Her body arched against his instinctively, drawn into the heat as she used him to trigger the release she craved.

The next morning, while she pretended to sleep, he kissed her gently and then slipped away to return to his studio and paint. As soon as the door clicked shut behind him, she felt the thrill of victory rush through her. Margaux sprang out of bed, pulling one of his soft t-shirts and a pair of boxers from the dresser, and slipped them on in a hurried, triumphant blur. She scanned the bedroom, drinking in the opulence of the furniture he'd had imported from France. Two three-drawer dressers flanked the bed, each with ornate lamps sitting on top, and mirrors reflected the light flooding in from the windows.

She pulled open the drawers of his bedside table, unsure what she was looking for, and made her way through his walk-in closet, tucking one of the credit cards she found stashed inside into the waistband of the boxers. It was one of twelve, and she doubted he would ever notice it had gone missing.

Disappointed by her findings, Margaux made her way back out to the bedroom and was drawn to a canvas that covered one entire wall directly across from the bed. It leaned against the drywall unframed. The paint was thick, applied by a skilled hand wielding a palette knife, and she reached out one hand to brush her fingers against the stippled texture.

She leaned closer, studying the small pattern of circles that made up the composition when a thin line on the wall next to the edge of the canvas caught her eye. Running her index finger down the length of it, she wondered what it was. Intrigued, she slid the canvas aside two feet, revealing the continuation of the line. To her astonishment, it formed a perfect rectangle, one that unmistakably resembled the outline of a doorway.

Margaux pressed her fingers along the length of the seam, probing the wall with gentle strokes. When she found the right spot, a faint click echoed through the room, and the rectangle shifted, popping open a fraction of an inch. Her breath caught in her throat as she wondered what lay behind it. Margaux tugged at the exposed edge, pulling until the makeshift door opened completely to reveal a shadowy, hidden room.

She slipped inside, her pulse quickening as she felt her way along the walls, her fingers brushing over rough surfaces until they connected with a switch. With a flick, the overhead light buzzed to life.

The room was cramped, filled with half-finished paintings leaning against each other and a chest overflowing with sketches and smaller paintings on raw, unframed canvases. Her eyes scanned the clutter, her heart racing. She tore through the drawers, the tension rising with every pull, discarding piles of sketches as worthless, when she found a small leather-bound sketchbook. Margaux flipped it open. The first page was a detailed pencil sketch of a nude blonde woman reclining on a chaise lounge.

"He always had a gift for capturing the female form," she whispered to herself as she drank it in. It was well-executed but lacked the repeating patterns of Ruben Angelica's signature style.

She continued to flip through the book, each page an iteration closer to his trademark patterned impressionist style. But then, halfway through the book, a signature in the corner of a very detailed sketch stopped her cold. It wasn't Ruben's. She held it up to the light, straining to make out the letters. There was an unmistakable letter "c" followed by a line of loops. Perhaps a dotted "i."

Margaux's breath hitched in her throat as she turned the last page, her pulse quickening as the truth rushed in. When she'd been released, she'd quickly uncovered Martin's meteoric rise in the art world under the name Ruben Angelica. She had immersed herself in his work, becoming an expert in his distinctive style. At first, she'd believed he had simply evolved as an artist. It had appeared his transformation from the formulaic female forms he painted right out of art school matured into a far more complex and revolutionary style. His new body of work, instead of being overlooked, had suddenly become relevant and highly sought-after.

Ruben's latest pieces employed a groundbreaking layering technique, one that required more paint and longer curing times but offered a depth that was uniquely his own. The avant-garde technique that had catapulted Ruben to fame involved using a palette knife to scrape away layers in tiny, deliberate circles. Once finished, he would add a transparent glaze over the entire canvas, amplifying the colors and creating a mesmerizing three-dimensional effect.

It was a style reminiscent of pointillism, but with a twist that had never been seen in the art world before. Each circle, a speck among millions, contributed to a larger, unified whole. Viewed up close, the individual circles formed an intricate, repeating pattern, but from a distance, they merged seamlessly, transforming into a cohesive image that seemed to breathe and shift with every glance.

Margaux's heart raced as she flipped through the book a second time when the truth hit her like a thunderclap.

Camille.

The genius behind his current style wasn't his. It was all Camille's, and she was holding the proof in her hands. A self-satisfied grin spread across Margaux's face. She closed the sketchbook slowly, her fingers brushing over the worn leather cover, feeling the rush of pure satisfaction. It was all coming together now.

Ruben wasn't the successful contemporary artist he claimed to be. He'd just made a minor pivot, leaving the forgeries, and her, behind and had stepped into the spotlight of Camille's greatness. She cradled the sketchbook to her chest and tied the robe securely around her waist. As she made her way out of the room, Margaux couldn't help but let out a justified chuckle under her breath. Ruben had always underestimated her. He thought she was stupid, that she had no ambition. But now, she held the keys to his undoing, and Margaux would not hesitate to leverage them if she needed to.

***

That night, after dinner, Margaux casually leaned back against the tufted leather couch in the study, a glass of wine clutched in her hand. Ruben was on the phone, as usual, chatting animatedly with an art dealer. He was so absorbed in the conversation that he didn't notice her observing him, assessing his every move.

As he finished his call, he hung up, wiping a hand over his face. "Sorry, Margaux. That was my agent, Orlando. The deadline for the auction is in two weeks, and he needed an update on the final pieces."

Margaux simply smiled and leaned closer, infusing warmth into her voice. "You're always so busy. It must be exhausting being such an artistic genius."

He gave her a wan smile, dropping into the chair

across from her. "You have no clue. Everything is riding on this auction. I am under immense pressure."

"I know you are," she murmured as she covered her Cheshire grin with the rim of her wineglass and batted her eyelashes at him. Composing herself, she forced her glee to recede, and swirled the wine in her glass for a moment before fawning over him. "I was just thinking I'd love to watch you work. Your technique has evolved so much over the years. I'd love to get a glimpse into your new process."

Ruben chuckled, stretching his legs out. "Though I thoroughly enjoyed last night's festivities," he took a sip and continued, "I must maintain my focus until the deadline is met. With you in the room, that would prove quite difficult."

Margaux leaned forward, her creamy cleavage on full display along with a glimpse of a darker nipple playing peekaboo beneath her off-the-shoulder top. His sharp intake of breath told her everything she needed to know about where his mind was. She kept her tone flirty and purred, "What if I promised to behave?"

Ruben let out a snort of laughter. "I'm not sure you know how."

Margaux flashed him another dazzling smile. "Don't you want someone to witness the genius that goes into your work firsthand?" She was buttering him up, and it seemed to be working. "You've always loved to watch me." She spread her legs ever so slightly, hiking up her miniskirt. Margaux let the salaciousness dangle on the word "watch" just long enough before adding, "I'd welcome the opportunity to watch you create your latest masterpiece."

Ruben stood abruptly, setting his glass down with a decisive ring, and narrowed his gaze. "I said no. I don't need any more pressure right now. You can see it when it's finished at the auction along with the rest of the world."

Margaux's smile remained, though it wilted slightly. "Of course. No need to get irritated."

Ruben shot her one last icy glare before striding away. "I'll be in my studio," he muttered over his shoulder.

"Moody bastard," she mumbled under her breath, raising her glass to his retreating form. "*Quell surprise!*"

The next few days felt like a game of cat and mouse to Margaux. Ruben, oblivious to the storm brewing just beneath the surface, went about his usual routine, painting in his studio, making sporadic appearances at their shared dinners, and ravaging her at night.

She continued to feign curiosity about his work, always asking just the right questions. On the surface, they seemed innocent, even complimentary, but in truth, they were meant to test the waters. Ruben, ever the master of deflection, answered with practiced ease, but his discomfort was starting to show. It was subtle at first, a slight stiffness in his posture when he spoke, a flash of irritation that flickered behind his dark eyes.

Ruben had been clever, covering his tracks, but she knew him better than anyone. She saw through all of his tired tactics. He was teetering on the edge of a confession, and she knew if she pushed just a little harder, he would reveal everything, and then they could get back to business. Long ago, Ruben taught Margaux that power was never handed to you. It had to be taken, piece by piece, until you had it all. And she wouldn't stop until she did.

CHAPTER

THIRTY

THE NEXT MORNING, Neve was dusting the shelves in the study when she overheard part of a one-sided phone call that made her heart rejoice.

"Liam, please come collect Ms. DuBois at ten o'clock and take her wherever she wants to go."

There was a stretch of quiet as Ruben listened, then answered, "Use my black Amex, but do not, under any circumstances, give her physical access to the card. No limit. Let her get whatever she wants. There will be a bonus in it for you if you can keep her out all day."

At ten o'clock, Neve was dusting the floorboards, crouched down out of view, in the great room where Margaux and Ruben were just finishing their breakfast.

"I have a surprise for you," he said over the rim of his coffee cup. "I've arranged for Liam to take you shopping today."

"Fantastique!" Margaux exclaimed. "I need a gown for the auction next week." She clapped her hands

together as joy spread across her face. There wasn't much that she adored more than an afternoon spent shopping.

Ruben sniffed and then set the cup on the white tablecloth before lacing his fingers together. "Before you go, we need to talk about the auction."

She took a final bite of her eggs and laid the silverware across her plate, dabbing the corners of her mouth delicately with a napkin. "What about it?"

"As much as it pains me to say this, you cannot attend," he said softly, then added, "I can't risk being associated with you in public."

"What?" Margaux's mouth fell open in shock. "Why not?"

His chin jutted back in surprise. "Are you really that daft? You are a *convicted felon* who served five years in a French prison for art fraud. It would undermine all my hard work and open me up for scrutiny."

Intrigued, Neve popped up and tiptoed closer to the open passageway, stealing glimpses of the couple as Margaux's tone grew pitchy.

"*Your* hard work?" she hissed. "I took the blame while you walked away, rotting in that prison, and now you want to pretend I don't exist? I refuse to be your dirty little secret."

"*Non, mon coeur*, You have it all wrong, I am doing this for *us*." He emphasized, as he reached out to squeeze her hand and begged her with his eyes. "This event could set us up for a decade. All I am asking from you is a bit more patience."

Fuming, Margaux yanked her hand back and set her shoulders. A pinched look aged her face as she tried to come to terms with what Ruben was demanding of her. There was a long silence that stretched on forever before Margaux gave him an answer.

"Fine!" she spat at him and stood. Then she gathered her handbag, and with her head held high, stormed out of the house.

Ruben watched the town car pull away, and when they disappeared out of sight, Neve watched his shoulders finally relax. The tension that seemed omnipresent lifted, and she heard him mumble under his breath, "Finally, a moment's peace." Noticing the maid for the first time he addressed Neve, "I'll be with Camille all day. We have to messenger the final two paintings to the auction house tonight."

When his footsteps had faded away, Neve returned to the kitchen where Amos was cracking eggs into a pile of flour, humming to himself.

"Can I ask you question?"

"Of course," Amos answered, turning to meet her gaze as he flicked on the stand mixer.

"How you think about Ms. Margaux? She always in kitchen with you."

"She's cool, why you ask?"

"She say some things make me think."

"Like what?"

"Well, she say Mr. Ruben take two-million-dollar life insurance on Camille."

Amos pursed his lips, stopping the mixer he was

using to create his homemade pasta. "Dude is probably just trying to protect his investment."

"It too much for woman who has no family and no assets, don't you think?"

"Maybe," he said.

"But what more trouble is Ms. Margaux told me be careful around him."

"You know that fool is fickle as the day is long." Amos frowned, adding, "But I can't afford to lose this job."

Me same. Neve heard Rosa's fear and hung her head. Still trying to convince both of them she said, "Ms. Margaux is two-face. One way with us, another with Mr. Ruben. I very worried about Camille. She say be careful."

"Maybe she's just trying to look out for all of us?"

Neve exhaled a hot breath, frustrated she couldn't get through to him. Amos always saw the good in every person. Deciding to drop it for now, she said, "I go dust study, then feed Perry." Neve tightened her apron, gathered some fruit Amos had prepared, and left the kitchen.

Upon reaching the study, she found Perry warbling cheerfully in his covered cage. With a gentle tug, she pulled the fabric away, and he responded with a delighted chirp, flapping his wings in greeting. Neve smiled as she opened the cage door, filled his dish with pellets and nuts, and offered him a juicy chunk of bright orange mango.

"Nevermore! Where have you been? I thought you'd never return!"

"It been eight hours," Neve retorted, looking down at her watch, rolling her eyes at his hysterics.

He shook his feathers and, after finishing the mango in record time, dove into the dish, picking out the nuts around the pellets. When he was finished, he squawked with contentment. Picking up on Neve's conflicted energy, he asked, "What perplexes you?"

"I think Mr. Ruben up to no good."

"I concur," Perry said thoughtfully. "I will say Margaux appeared rather captivated by the files Ruben keeps locked in his desk. Perhaps the answers you need are hidden within." Then he gave her directions to locate the concealed key ring. Within moments, Neve was rifling through the files alphabetized in the desk drawers, her curiosity fully piqued. One in particular caught her eye. Her fingers paused on a tab labeled "Transfer Agreements" in Ruben's handwriting.

Pulling the thick manilla folder free, she slid the contents onto the desk. The first document captured her attention immediately. It was an Assignment Agreement, signed by Camille Sinclair.

She mumbled as she read the remaining documents under her breath. They were drafted with exacting detail, with paragraphs outlining the "complete and irrevocable transfer" of intellectual property rights from Camille Sinclair to Ruben Angelica. The language was mostly incomprehensible legalese but didn't prevent the truth from trickling in.

Camille had signed over not just her paintings but her very identity as the artist who created them. Below the signatures, a notary's seal was embossed into the thick paper. The uneven pressure of Camille's signature had a vulnerable, child-like quality that spurred Neve's protective instincts. The deeper she delved, the more damning the evidence became. There were letters, correspondence from Ruben to Camille, thanking her for her collaboration and reassuring her that he would handle all public-facing matters in the future.

At the bottom of the pile, she found a note scrawled in looping, uneven penmanship addressed to Ruben:

I don't understand what all these papers mean, but if it's what I need to do to succeed in the art world, I trust you.

Outrage built in her belly as the realization hit so hard, it took her breath away. Ruben wasn't nurturing and inspiring young artists to make their mark on the world. No, he was stealing their work, claiming it as his own, and profiting from it. The geode in her pocket crackled against her skin, and she felt a rush of heat and energy zing through her.

"He taking credit for Camille work," Neve said to Perry when she was finished reading. She locked the drawer and replaced the key in its hiding place. "He been control her all time, forcing her to stay here and do paintings make him famous. If he have chance, he do same for Nevermore. We must stop him!"

"Ruben's a fraud! Ruben's a fake!" Perry whistled, getting caught up in the excitement.

"What did you say, bird?" The door burst open, and Neve gasped as she spun around and her eyes locked on Ruben. His lanky frame filled the doorway, and she felt the first fingers of fear scrape up her spine.

He rushed into the room, closing in on Perry. "Too smart for your own good." he scowled, inching closer.

Neve stepped between them, shielding Perry with her hands. "Calm down. He just bird…"

"Just a bird?" Ruben's eyes burned with fury as he turned on her. "This 'bird' and his wild accusations! Do you think I'll let some dim-witted parrot ruin me?"

Before Neve could answer, Ruben lunged toward the bird, who squawked in alarm and flapped his wings wildly.

"Rosa! Do something!" Perry cried as he dodged Ruben's grasp.

Thinking fast, Neve darted to the nearest window. Her hands fumbled with the latch as Ruben advanced on Perry, a twisted look of determination on his face.

"You'll pay for this, you dirty bird!" he screamed. "I'll kill you with my bare hands!"

"Not today!" Perry screeched, flitting up and gliding out of reach.

With a final tug, Neve flung the window open. Humid air rushed into the room, carrying with it the scent of fresh rain. Perry circled and Ruben jumped and latched onto the claw on Perry's foot. He pecked at Ruben's exposed skin, making him shriek in pain as his beak drew blood. Ruben released his tightened grip, flinging the bird toward the ground. Two awkward flaps and Perry righted himself before soaring above Ruben's head, back to safety.

"Ruben's a fraud," Perry squawked, egging him on. "Ruben's a thief."

The insults only fueled Ruben's fury. He lunged toward the window, eyes locked on the taunting bird. Forced to dip lower, Perry flapped frantically as Ruben leapt, fingers snatching at the air before closing around red tail feathers. With a desperate, last burst of adrenaline, Perry twisted free. He shot a parting glance at Neve before launching himself outside the window, his wings catching the wind as he soared to safety.

"No!" Ruben roared, his hands clawing at empty space.

Before Perry disappeared from her sight, he chirped once more, a code word he knew Neve would understand.

"Sheila's!" Perry crowed, then disappeared and Ruben was left heaving jagged breaths. With a scowl of disgust, he shook the loose feathers still clutched in his fist to the ground and swiped at his face where the fresh wound was bleeding. Ruben slammed the window shut, then stormed out of the room, but not before barking, "Rosa, you're on notice. When I've found an adequate replacement, you're fired."

THIRTY-ONE

ROSA'S HANDS trembled as Neve placed a white gardenia in a bud vase and waited for Amos to finish the eggs, bacon, and toast.

I fire? What happen to me?

She couldn't help but sympathize with Rosa's rising anxiety about her uncertain future. Anxiety was an emotion Neve knew intimately. "Don't worry. Perry and I will figure it out," she promised softly under her breath, but it did little to calm the storm of turmoil raging inside her.

Amos turned from the stove, the sizzling sound of the eggs fading as he slid them onto the plates and covered them with a stainless steel cloche. Neve's mind was elsewhere. She glanced at her watch. Only a few more hours and she could catch the bus headed to her childhood home to find Perry.

With the tray in her hands, Neve climbed the stairs

and was poised to knock on the door when she heard the murmur of strained voices inside. Though the words were difficult to decipher, Ruben's pleading tone came through loud and clear. Neve pressed her ear to the door, holding her breath, as the muffled words began to take shape.

"We agreed you would work under my name because it's more marketable, Camille. Be honest with yourself. Do you think the world would line up to see your work if they knew it came from someone like… like you?"

"Someone like me?" she echoed, her voice wavering. "What do you mean?"

"An eccentric painter who is awkward and weird? A timid little mouse who can't even attend gallery openings, let alone entertain high-profile collectors?" Ruben released a theatrical sigh. "I've done everything I can to make your dreams come true. I put my reputation, my connections on the line, all in order to show your work to a greater audience. And *this* is the thanks I get? You questioning every move I make?"

"No…" she stammered. "I *am* grateful. I just…"

"We have to play the game. That's why you signed the contract, remember? So you could focus on painting without worrying about the world outside."

Neve felt her breath hitch in her chest. She felt a tide of rage building, and the geode in her pocket released another surge of energy that shored her resolve and helped Rosa's fears subside.

"I didn't… I didn't realize the contract meant I…"

Camille stuttered, and then the rest of the sentence died on her lips.

"We've been through this so many times," Ruben cut in smoothly, carefully concealing his irritation. "You create the paintings and I sell them. I agreed to be the public face of your work because you were too afraid of the spotlight. It is a win-win. Isn't that what you wanted?"

There was silence. Then, softly, Camille said, "I just wanted people to see my work."

"They have and, more importantly, they *will* continue to do so," Ruben said, his voice warm and reassuring. "We offer them the best of both worlds. I can offer them a personal experience, where the collector is not just investing in the art but also in the artist. And you never have to face the pressure of public appearances. You never have to deal with critics or journalists. I've taken all that off your shoulders. All you have to do is paint."

"Paint," Camille murmured as if testing the word.

"Exactly. This is a partnership, Camille. All I need you to do is trust me."

"I do. But sometimes," she began, her voice small, "it feels like it's not mine anymore. The work, I mean."

"Don't say that," Ruben said sharply, then softened his tone again. "It's always yours, in spirit. But it's my job to make sure it's seen and appreciated. Without me, your work would sit in a dusty studio, unnoticed and uncelebrated. Is that what you want?"

"No," she whispered.

"Good," Ruben said, eager to move on. "Then let's focus on what matters. These changes I'm suggesting will make your work even more extraordinary. I know what the market wants and what will drive the price up. I am only asking for a few small tweaks, and then they will be perfect. You'll see."

"Okay," Camille finally agreed, though her response lacked conviction.

"That's a good girl," Ruben said warmly. "Now, I've drafted some notes for you. Here's what I need you to adjust on the final paintings." Papers shuffled again, and his tone shifted, becoming brisk and businesslike. "This one needs more vibrancy in the foreground. Use the reds and golds. They are bold, eye-catching colors. The pattern in this one is too obscure. Rework it to be more uniform. And this one…"

Neve clenched her fists as Ruben's voice continued, rattling off demands like a punishing taskmaster. The way he spoke to Camille was so calculated, so manipulative. He painted himself as her savior, all while stifling her voice and exploiting her talent.

"And Camille," Ruben added, his tone dropping to a low warning, "try to pick up the pace, will you? The auction house is expecting the final pieces by the end of business tomorrow."

"Tomorrow?" she squeaked, her voice rising in alarm. "I don't know if I can paint that fast."

"You can," he interrupted firmly. "You have to. Do you think I've built all of this for us to fall short now?

You're extraordinary, Camille, but you need to believe in yourself as much as I do. Don't let me down."

Neve's stomach churned. She couldn't let him continue to degrade Camille. Gripping the tray tightly, she knocked on the door and stepped in, cooling her expression into neutrality. It was an act that took considerable self-control.

Her gaze landed on Camille standing at the easel with a brush in her hand, adding the last strokes to *Inheritance of Grace*, Ruben's most famous masterpiece. In a single breath, the final shocking truth came crashing in. Ruben's masterpiece wasn't his at all. It never had been. Neve had refused to see it, based on her allegiance to the man who'd championed her artwork as a child. Now there was no denying he was a fraud. A talentless grifter who was profiting from Camille's hard work.

Neve lost her grip on the tray, and it fell from her hands and hit the floor with a crack, breaking the ceramic plate into pieces and splattering eggs onto the floor and walls.

Neve's stomach flipped into a sickening twist that seemed to drop straight to the floor. The revelation hit her like a physical blow as her eyes scanned the room and the façade crumbled. *None* of the canvases that ringed the walls of the art studio were his. They were all Camille's. She took a step back, her hands trembling as she leaned against the wall, gasping for breath.

Seeing their breakfast on the floor, his nose wrinkled in disgust. "Jesus, Rosa. You're becoming more worthless by the day," Ruben scolded, shooting daggers at her with his eyes as he flipped through a glossy issue of GQ. "Clean up this mess and bring us something to eat. Camille needs to keep her strength up."

Later that evening, Neve took the bus, switching back and forth between them, paranoid she was being followed. When she was satisfied that she was alone, she walked the final few blocks to her childhood home just as the sun was setting.

She crossed the street, slid to the yard adjacent to her father's house, and whispered, "Perry!" When there was no answer, she hissed louder, "Where are you?" Above her head, she heard the rustle of palm fronds and called out again a fraction louder, "Perry?" Knowing he was food-motivated, she rattled the container. "I bring nuts!"

There was a flap and a rustle as the gray parrot alighted on her forearm. Her heart lifted, gazing at his glossy feathers glimmering in the muted light. She poured a heaping pile of seeds into her hand, wiggling when he dove into it, chomping away.

"Quit squirming," Perry demanded as he plunged his beak into her palm again, and the bird seed drifted to the ground between her splayed fingers. He crunched with delight and, after finishing the seed, she handed him a large Brazilian nut that cracked when he bit it in half.

"Sorry take so long, Ruben watch me like hawk, and

Rosa very scared. I need find way out this mess that doesn't hurt Rosa future. She not ask for this."

"Agreed," Perry said, his intelligent eyes studying her with an air of knowing. He cocked his head to the side, picking up on Neve's apprehension. "What happened?" he asked in a shrill voice.

"Many thing." Neve pinched the bridge of her nose, trying to fend off a tension headache. "First, Ruben, he no paint a single thing. Camille, she do all. He was my idol, *comprende*? He no artist at all. And Margaux, she be too friendly with me, make me suspicious. She say, when man get life insurance, woman should be nervous."

Perry flicked his wings playfully as his beak dipped to a smirk. "She didn't look very nervous in the study the other day. In fact, she was quite the opposite, pressing her glorious ta-tas into Ruben's quivering hands. And might I just say they were spectacular?"

"Eeww," Neve said. "Only if you promise never say word ta-tas again."

"I don't know if I can make that vow," Perry squawked. "You might have forgotten, but I was once a man who embraced carnal pleasures."

Neve felt bile rise in her throat at his admission. "Nope. We not going there." She shook her head back and forth in repulsion.

"Fine, Nevermore, be a prude." Perry chirped a chuckle, getting right back on track. "I highly doubt Ruben's ex-wife has returned simply for the sake of rekindling their romance. Margaux has an agenda, of that, I am certain. But is she an ally or an adversary?"

"I not know." Neve shivered. "And I find more money in paintings. *Mucho, mucho dinero.*" While cleaning Ruben's bedroom, she'd uncovered his secret storage room that had been a goldmine. Her underwear drawer was now completely full, and she'd started wrapping it in plastic and securing it to the underside of the toilet tank in her bathroom.

"That could prove quite advantageous," Perry remarked. "Money makes the world go round. You'd be wise to extricate it from that house immediately. A safe deposit box at a reputable institution away from greedy fingers would be the sensible choice."

"Good idea."

"Margaux said she has proof from their past that could ruin Ruben. Destroy everything." Perry ruffled his feathers, clearly mulling it over. "She also seems like the jealous type, and with that monumental chip on her shoulder..." He hopped on the ground, pacing as he thought. "...it doesn't bode well for Camille."

Neve took a deep breath. Her mind raced, but she couldn't help feeling a strange tug of guilt as she admitted, "Right now, Rosa and Camille *both* be collateral damage in their war."

Perry whirred, thinking over the new insight. "We must protect them."

"*Sí,*" Neve agreed. "All this time, I wondering why we were sent back here. At first, I thought to find some clues about what happened with my father, but when I shift and wake up inside Rosa, it make me think different." She pulled the geode crystal out of her pocket. It was glowing and hot in the palm of her hand, vibrating so fiercely it practically levitated.

"Whoa," Perry chirped. "Has it been acting like that this entire time?"

"No," Neve answered. "It glow brighter when I shift and fill me with energy. I think it a sign. I sent here to help Camille. She like me. I think she on spectrum."

"I concur," Perry said.

Neve nodded, feeling the weight of responsibility settling in. She wasn't sure if she was ready for the journey ahead. The challenge hung heavy on her shoulders and the stakes were high. Neve said her goodbyes, left some food, and then turned and walked away from the trees, her mind a whirlwind of thoughts and fears. There was no easy path forward, no clear answer. There was only one truth she knew for sure. She must stop Ruben from exploiting Camille's talents for his own gain.

Darkness settled in like a blanket over her childhood home, and she saw a flicker of movement inside. Neve's heart tightened as she watched her father standing at the window, wearing gloves with a pair of shears in his hand. He was tending to the bonsai tree that lived in the sunroom. Ellis was focused intently on selecting which fronds to clip and which to twist with copper wire to shape the miniature tree. A few feet away, Nevermore rested on the sofa watching *Jeopardy!* with a large stainless steel bowl of popcorn settled in her lap.

Dinner at 6.
Bath.
Jeopardy! at 7 with popcorn and lemonade.
Bedtime at 8:30 after two chapters of reading
together. Then lights out.

Seeing elements of her childhood nightly routine
playing out in front of her made Neve's heart flutter. She
yearned to reach out and feel the comforting ring of her
father's arms around her, to feel the warmth and safety
of his warm body against hers. Where was this
unexpected swell of emotion coming from? Was it
Rosa's influence?

Her breath caught in her throat as she stepped back,
retreating deeper into the shadows.

Neve had never felt that way. Not even once as a
child.

Neve wasn't supposed to be here.

She wasn't supposed to feel this.

A strange mix of emotions churned inside her—
nostalgia, regret, love. For the first time in forever, Neve
ached for her childhood as this new experience of it
took her breath away. Neve's mind blurred between
reality, her childhood memories, and the ones she'd
made recently. She was a stranger here, witnessing a life
she could never be part of again, and the sensation was
completely overwhelming and disorienting.

Her eyes grew glossy with tears then flicked over to
her father, and a wall of anger roared over her as she
mourned the life that had been stolen from her. Neve's

breath hitched, and a whimper escaped from Rosa's lips as she watched them from the shadows.

"You not his daughter no more. Not in this body," she muttered under her breath, trying to self-soothe and talk herself out of ringing the doorbell and flinging herself into his embrace. With great effort, Neve stood her ground. She had already crossed too many lines and pushed too many boundaries. To reveal herself now would only confuse everyone, herself included.

The ache deepened. Neve swallowed the lump in her throat, wiping away the tears gathering at her lashes. She had to stay away. She had no right to be here, to want to slip back into this life, yet she yearned to do so. Neve clenched her hands at her sides, desperate to steady herself, desperate to stop the tide of emotions that threatened to overwhelm her.

"Rosa?"

Neve jumped as Isla walked up behind her. Her shimmering hot pink sequined dress hung down one shoulder to the wrist and had a slit to the thigh. Neve caught a peek of a metallic stiletto, and her dangling chandelier earrings sparkled in the moonlight. "I'm sorry to startle you. What are you doing here?" Isla asked with a warm smile, her sweet laughter tinkling in the humid night air. Neve studied her for a long moment before breaking her own heart. Her next words had the power to change the trajectory of her childhood with consequences that could reverberate well into her adulthood.

"I come to tell you, Ruben is bad man."

"What?" Isla asked, her chin jutting back in surprise, confused already.

"Nevermore not safe with him. You must find other way for her to go to École Artiste."

"How?" Isla leaned closer, turmoil pinching her brows together. "I don't have the connections to get her in. Nevermore is going to be crushed, and she's so talented. She deserves this opportunity."

Hearing Isla's championing of her talent, Neve melted, and another lump formed in her throat. She'd never known Isla was such a staunch supporter of her artwork. Neve closed her eyes before she continued, mourning the loss of attending the prestigious art school. Her time spent at École Artiste was one of the most pivotal experiences of her entire life. It had laid the foundation for the career that now supported her as an adult. Neve hated to sacrifice it, but she could see no other way to ensure Nevermore's safety. She stepped out in faith that her talent would see her through.

"*Sí.*" Neve nodded sadly, imploring Isla with her eyes. "She be disappointed, but she understand."

"You don't know Nevermore." Isla gave a low chuckle. "When she wants something, she's like a dog with a bone."

Neve felt Rosa nudge her to grab Isla's hands. Her voice became grave. "I need you promise me. I know you care about Nevermore."

"I do." Isla nodded. "I would do anything for her."

"Then keep her away from Mr. Ruben. In time, you

understand why." She looked at Isla. "I wish I could tell you more, but it not safe."

Isla hesitated while she considered the request for a long beat. Then she let out a resigned whisper of agreement, "Okay."

"I must go," Neve told her, retracting her hands and stuffing them into the pockets of her apron, cradling them around the geode. "Promise me."

"I promise."

THIRTY-TWO

THE HOUSE WAS EERILY quiet for a Sunday. Rosa and Amos had the day off, and Ruben was out dining with the auction house manager. When he casually informed her that he'd be going alone, Margaux had pouted, but it was more than disappointment she felt. A chill curled around the wrath building in her chest. It was becoming obvious Ruben was distancing himself from her. A familiar dread stirred to life, and she felt the distinctive tingle of déjà vu.

"He will not get away with this again. Not on my watch," she muttered under her breath as she pulled a micro-recorder from her purse and popped in a fresh cassette tape, tucking it into the pocket of her oversized blazer. Her stint in prison taught her to always hedge her bets.

The study was empty as Margaux stepped into it and inhaled the scent of leather and lemon furniture polish. She made her way to the bar cart and poured two fingers of whisky into a glass before knocking it back, exhaling her building rage through flared nostrils. She was grateful when the alcohol began to unravel the pit of self-doubt in her stomach. Margaux wanted to give him the benefit of the doubt, but it was becoming more difficult by the day.

On the desk, a sealed envelope bearing the return address of a travel agency caught her eye. Curious, she lifted it to the light before tearing it open. Inside, she discovered a single first-class ticket to Spain with Ruben's name printed in bold letters. The departure was set for just ten days after the auction.

Holding the irrefutable evidence of his impending betrayal in her hand, she seethed, waiting for him to make an appearance. An hour later, she heard footsteps drawing closer as Ruben hummed to himself. Clearly, his meeting had gone well, and he was in a relaxed state of mind. Margaux quickly pressed record and tucked the micro-recorder behind a plant, angling the built-in microphone between the bar cart and his desk, making a mental note to stay within range.

She arranged herself on his desk, her long tanned legs draped down the front of it as she sipped on a second drink, waiting for him to appear for his evening nightcap ritual.

"What are you doing in here?" Ruben's amiable tone veered cautious, hovering on annoyed as he filled the doorway.

"Waiting for you," she purred, offering him a glimpse of the lace on her garter belt and stockings before she gracefully stood and strode back over to the bar cart. Margaux tipped the amber-colored contents of the blue labeled bottle into another crystal glass and offered it to him.

"Helping yourself to the Johnnie Walker, I see." He sighed ruefully as he accepted the glass. "You always had a thirst for the finer things in life." His fingernails were stained with paint and he loosened his tie and unbuttoned the top button, leaving it open at the neck. Margaux let her gaze walk up his torso and felt her resolve begin to wither in the heat of desire. She steeled herself against it. Why had this man always had such an effect on her? She really wanted to know. Combustible and tumultuous was the dynamic that defined them, and she was careful not to let herself overindulge in it. It had been her undoing once, but she would not let it happen again.

He sat down in the leather desk chair, and she crossed over to him and straddled his hips with her legs. Before he could object, she pressed her lips to his. He was hesitant at first, but she continued her pursuit until she felt him melting under her touch. The backs of his hands stroked her cheeks, then spread down her long, elegant neck. His thumbs pressed gently into the hollow of her throat, and she moaned, which produced a deep groan of desire from him.

She pulled back and wrapped her fingers behind the curve of his neck, scraping her fingernails lightly over his scalp, knowing it would further relax him.

"Rough meeting?" she murmured in question, and he exhaled a heavy breath.

"*Non*. It was productive, but I am exhausted. Orlando said they expect to draw a record crowd at the auction house, but it's been an absolute mountain of work. I cannot wait until it's over."

She leaned closer to commiserate with him. "It must feel absolutely incredible to have your work recognized by important collectors and to have museums clamoring for more."

He nodded, closed his eyes, and leaned back into her hand as she stroked and scratched the back of his head. "But I won't be able to relax until I know it's well received."

Margaux pressed her lips to his favorite spot on his neck before pulling back and asking, "Once the auction is over, can I count on you to start working on our project? I already have some ideas about where we should begin." Ruben remained still, eyes shut, unaware his next response would seal his fate. She'd wanted to believe he would keep his promises, but seeing the plane ticket destroyed what little faith she had in him. Now, Margaux just needed confirmation.

"The forgeries?" he murmured softly, still blissed out by her nails gently scratching his scalp. "Why would I want to waste my talent mimicking old dead men when I am beloved by the art world for my own creations?"

Margaux seethed, then swallowed her rage. She had her answer. It was time to put her plan in motion.

Without skipping a beat, she rocked closer, grinding down on his erection, and murmured into the warmth of his ear, "That would be true if they *were* your own creations."

His eyes popped open, and his brow furrowed. A furious scowl pinched his expression into a tight ball.

"Who is Camille?" she whispered, then licked her lips in anticipation. She was eager to push his buttons until she drew blood.

Ruben roughly pushed her off his lap and stood, and Margaux knew she'd hit her mark.

"You must remember Camille, *mon coeur*. After all, you took out a two-million-dollar life insurance policy on her."

Ruben's face paled, and his jaw ticked. He gritted out through clenched teeth, "You don't know what you're talking about."

"Don't I?" Margaux asked innocently. "*Mon coeur*, it wouldn't be the first time you used unscrupulous methods to further your ambitions."

His jaw tightened. "Those are some wild accusations. I suggest you watch yourself."

"Are they, though?" Margaux pressed. "The last five years have proven otherwise."

"You knew the dangers. We both did."

"*C'est vrai.*" She shrugged.

"You took too many risks," he offered as an explanation. "The hardest part of a successful con is knowing when to walk away. I could feel the noose tightening around both our necks, but you never did.

You pushed and pushed for more. The final straw was the lost Matisse I painted for the Wexler Collective. Do you remember it?"

"Of course, how could I forget the painting that sent me to prison for five years?"

"I needed more time to finish the canvas. It hadn't aged properly and wasn't responding to UV rays, as expected. The colors didn't mix well with the formaldehyde wash, and under a microscope, the fakery was too obvious. I wanted to fix these issues, but you rushed my process. Then, to make matters worse, the Provence paperwork you provided was shoddy and incomplete. The truth of the matter is, you got sloppy, and you got caught."

Margaux slapped his face with her open palm, relishing the warmth from where she'd stuck him as his cheek reddened. Instead of pulling away, he yanked her by the wrist. Ruben stepped closer. Now they were just a breath apart. "Careful, you're playing with fire."

Her pulse quickened, but she held her ground.

His eyes darkened as a flicker of lust passed between them. "*Très bien.* I like it hot and so do you."

His lips crashed against hers, and he devoured her with his tongue. Margaux gave herself over to it. She'd never met another man who could raise the beast in her like Ruben could. The air pulsed with a dangerous energy. For Margaux, it was the most potent aphrodisiac.

Cradling her face in his hands, he whispered more lies into the air between them, "Business is booming. If you stay quiet and let me take the lead, I will make you another promise."

"What's that?"

"I will cut you in."

"You're a liar," Margaux called him out, pulling away from his grasp. "I know you're over-leveraged. Your life is all smoke and mirrors."

He ran a hand through his curls, clearly frustrated. "No, the auction will make me whole… make *us* whole again."

Margaux tilted her head back, feigning curiosity. "You really expect me to believe you'd share? After what you did to me last time?"

Ruben let out a low chuckle, his voice dropping to a dangerous whisper. "It was just business. We both know how this world works."

"If I agree, there will be one non-negotiable condition."

"What is it?" Ruben asked.

"Total honesty," Margaux said softly. "Starting now."

"What do you want to know?"

"All of it." Margaux slipped closer and walked a hand down his torso to tug at his belt. She reached back up and laced her fingers through his thick curls, careful to hide her delight in his response.

"The forgeries opened us up to scrutiny. Replicating another artist's work is dangerous and a dead-end endeavor. Yes, we discovered it was temporarily lucrative, but ultimately it led to our downfall." He brushed a series of small kisses from her collarbone to her jawline before he continued. "After leaving France, I was determined to make my mark in the art world with a fresh body of work. I painted for a year before I found Camille. I was teaching an adult education class for Pathways of Light, and she was one of my first students. The very first day, I saw it. There was greatness within her waiting to be realized."

"Why the life insurance?"

Margaux watched the gears turning as he tried to offer her a plausible explanation. "It's simple. She's become an asset, and assets are often protected by insurance."

Ruben pulled her close, discarding her shirt and burying his face into the center of her lace bra, making circles on her nipples with his thumbs. She closed her eyes and let him pleasure her on the sofa relaxing as euphoric satisfaction spread across her features, but it wasn't the result of his prowess in the bedroom. It was because of the micro-cassette recorder hidden just a few feet away and what had just been recorded on it.

CHAPTER

THIRTY-THREE

THE MOMENT RUBEN stepped out of the house to deliver the second to the last painting to the auction house, Neve seized her opportunity and rushed to the studio. The room was silent except for the rhythmic swish of Camille's paintbrush as it moved with confident strokes across the canvas. The image emerging was a masterpiece in progress. Each stroke she made added to the vivid, impressionistic study of a child standing in a field of flowers. Camille was completely absorbed in her work, her body hunched over the easel protectively, sheltering it from view.

From the doorway, Neve watched her work. Witnessing her heightened focus, she knew intimately what it felt like because she felt the same immersion when she held a pencil in her hand. It was as if she became one with the medium, able to finally unleash the creativity stuck in her head. It was the only place Neve felt a sense of total belonging, and she wondered if it was the same for Camille.

Her presence went unnoticed until Neve cleared her throat softly, at a volume calculated not to startle the woman but to gently interrupt. "I brought your snack," Neve murmured.

"Chai tea with one sugar cube, steeped for four minutes, with two chocolate biscotti?"

"Yes," Neve confirmed, keeping her tone reassuring and low. "Exactly as you like." She stepped into the room and set the tray down on a cluttered side table loaded with half-empty tubes of oil paint. "You need eat something, or you work yourself into exhaustion."

Camille turned toward Neve, the brush still poised in her hand. Her paint-smeared smock hung off her slight frame, and dark circles smudged under her eyes. "I can't stop now. The auction..." She trailed off, her gaze darting around the room as if the words were hiding somewhere among the scattered paints and sketchbooks.

"Of course, Ruben's deadline, it coming," Neve finished for her, perching on a stool. Her movements were slow, careful not to get too close, giving Camille ample time to adjust to her presence.

Camille nodded, the tension in her shoulders easing just a fraction. "Yes. He's counting on me."

Neve's lips tightened. She'd rehearsed this conversation in her mind ad nauseam, but now, in the presence of Camille's fragile temperament and knowing how much was at stake, the words felt cumbersome on Rosa's tongue and she didn't know where to begin.

After considerable indecision, she blurted, "I want talk to you about Ruben."

"What about him?" Camille asked, her tone guarded. She returned her attention to the canvas, though her strokes were slower.

"I think he use you, take advantage," Neve began, feeling a twinge of guilt rear up when she realized how blunt she'd been.

The brush paused mid-air and Camille's gaze flicked over to Neve. "Taking advantage, how?"

"He no just mentoring you," Neve said, leaning forward slightly. "He use your talent to make his name in art world. Ruben put his signature on your paintings, say they his."

"I know," she said matter-of-factly. "Statistically, paintings from male painters are more sought-after and command a higher price at auction. We have an arrangement. He handles all the business details, and I paint. Ruben says it's a win-win."

"I bet he did," Neve muttered under her breath.

Camille's head snapped toward Neve, her eyes narrowing. "You don't understand. He's helped me. Ruben's the only one who's ever seen promise in my work. Without him, I…"

"You still be extraordinary," Neve interjected firmly. "Your work speak for itself. You no need him to say you good. You need stand up for yourself, else he take credit for all you make." Neve struggled to piece the right words together, in Rosa's broken English, to convince the artist.

Camille's breath quickened, and she turned away, picking up a palette knife and clutching it in her fist. She continued to add strokes to the canvas, unable to meet Neve's direct gaze. "I don't want… I don't like the attention. I am happy here." Her voice was strained, her words coming out in staccato bursts.

Neve took a deep breath, steadying herself. "Believe me, I know how the world too much. The noise, the people, the pressure. The voices in your head saying you different. But you deserve to be seen for your work. Your art can make people feel. Think how many could be moved by your story, your vision."

Camille shook her head vehemently. "It's too much. I'd have to talk to people and go to galleries. I can't do it." She looked away, her fingers twisting the hem of her paint-stained smock. "It's easier this way. If people knew it was me, they'd expect things. Interviews, appearances… I can't do that. I just want to paint."

"You no have to do it alone," Neve said softly. "We find people who understand and can help you."

Camille's grip on the palette knife loosened, and she stared at the floor, her brow furrowed. She set it down and crossed her arms, her voice growing defensive. "It's not that simple. There's a contract. Everything I paint here belongs to him. I agreed to it."

"You agree because you think your work not good enough alone. But it is, I see firsthand," Neve implored, choosing her next words carefully. "Contracts can be challenged, especially if they wrong, and I think the one you sign is wrong. Ruben got no right to exploit your talent for his own gain."

Camille looked up at Neve, her eyes shimmering with unshed tears. "Why does it matter to you? Why do you care?"

Neve's expression softened. "Because I see you. Not just your art, but you. I know how it feel to be invisible. People ignore or not understand you. But you deserve to be seen, not just as artist, but as person."

"I don't want the world to see me." Camille's voice was barely above a whisper. "I don't like the limelight. Ruben handles all that so I don't have to."

Neve nodded slowly, her expression softening. "I understand that. I do. Crowds, strangers, all that noise… it hard for me, too. But hiding not help. When you got amazing gift, part of what you must do is share it with world."

For a long moment, silence filled the room. Camille's gaze shifted between Neve and her painting, her fingers twitching restlessly. Then she laced her fingers together in front of her waist, and stared at the stack of finished works leaning against the wall. Her face was pale and her lips tight. "But what if I can't handle it? What if I can't be what they want me to be?"

"You no have to be what *they* want," Neve said, taking a small step closer. "You just need to be *you*. That enough. Always been enough."

Camille bit her lip, her shoulders trembling. Finally, she whispered, "I wouldn't even know where to start."

Neve widened her stance, feeling the weight of

Camille's worry fill her and wanting to do right by the woman. "We figure it out, together, one step at a time. First, we document your work, then talk to someone who can help with legal side of ending contract."

Camille let out a heavy exhalation. "This *is* the final piece for the auction."

"Then it perfect time for new start. You done what you promise, now you can go separate ways amicable."

"Amicable? Ruben is going to be livid when he finds out." Camille shivered, her eyes widening as the gravity of Neve's proposition now loomed large in her mind.

Neve wanted to cheer when she heard the word "when." "Is that yes?"

Camille was silent for a very long time, and Neve was careful not to push. She hated being rushed when making important decisions, and for Camille, this was the most important decision of her life. Finally, Camille flicked her gaze to Neve and squared her shoulders, giving her a nod of approval. "It's a yes," she whispered.

The tingle of the geode in the pocket of her apron circuited through Neve's body, and she felt a rush of happiness energize her as she thought through the next steps. "We keep this from Ruben 'til we sure it safe. You can do that?"

"I am not very good at deception," Camille said with a doubtful grimace. She paced and began to wring her hands as her anxiety rose. "Lying makes me uncomfortable."

"You know Dalai Lama?"

"Yes!" Camille confirmed, brightening. "He's in Tibet."

"Yes, he is," Neve said, nodding. "You know he believe in yearly silent retreats, no speak, just meditate and pray for weeks?"

The light bulb went on, and Neve saw her relax into understanding. "I see what you are proposing. I will go on a silent retreat, then I won't have to lie to him."

"Exactly!" Neve praised. "Now you drink tea before it cools!"

With a solution in place, Camille exhaled deeply as if releasing a weight she'd been carrying for years. She turned back to the tray and took a sip of the tea, then stuffed the biscotti into her mouth.

"It okay to chew. You not being timed at eating competition."

Camille grinned and a few crumbs shot out of her open mouth. Neve handed her the teacup one more time and watched her gulp it down. Then she returned to the easel, but this time, her strokes were confident, more controlled. As she worked, Neve quietly tidied up the studio, then let herself out carrying the empty tray.

It felt like a win.

CHAPTER

THIRTY-FOUR

THE AUCTION HOUSE thrummed with anticipation, its plastered walls glowing under the spotlights focused on the paintings. The air was saturated with the scents of luxury fragrances, aged leather, and cognac. Ruben stood poised at the edge of the room, his heart quietly hammering beneath his double-breasted suit. Though his paintings had long commanded critical acclaim, tonight marked the pinnacle of his career. As he scanned the elegantly dressed crowd, a tremor of apprehension danced in his belly. Somewhere among these polished smiles and glittering eyes were the bidders who would save him from the brink of financial ruin. He was certain of it.

All around him, white-haired collectors and sequined socialites gathered in circles, sipping on champagne and previewing the collection. During events, Ruben preferred to work the room, stopping to graciously speak to each pod of wealthy patrons, sparking conversation and regaling them with the stories and symbolism behind each piece. He'd learned long ago, if a collector felt a personal connection to the artist and was sufficiently lubricated by liquor, they would become paddle-happy, creating bidding wars that could set records.

And he'd never needed a record-breaking sale more than tonight. The tension in the room had been building all evening, but now, a fresh wave of excitement rippled through the crowd. Ruben's curiosity piqued, and he turned toward the buzz just as the crowd parted like the Red Sea. His eyes locked on Ana Castanova, striding confidently toward him in a stunning crimson gown with long red gloves ending at her elbows, her bold red lip matching her dress.

She flashed him a dazzling grin, and Ruben felt a surge of pleasure ripple through him.

"Ana!" He cried, without missing a beat, leaning in to brush kisses on both of her cheeks. Then, with an exaggerated flourish, he offered her his arm.

"Smile!" the photographer hired for the event barked.

As the flash momentarily blinded him, Ruben straightened up, his smile still wide but his mind already calculating his next move. He could feel the adrenaline racing beneath his skin, knowing her appearance could tip the scales in his favor. Every word, every gesture had to land perfectly.

"You have a way of stealing the spotlight wherever you go," he said smoothly, leaning in just a bit closer.

"I think you'd make the perfect muse for my next piece."

Ana raised one eyebrow, the hint of a smirk playing on her full lips. "I'm flattered, but it's beneath me to pander to a starving artist."

"Starving?" Ruben was offended as he waved a hand behind him, indicating their luxurious surroundings. "I'd hardly say I'm starving."

Ana rocked her head back and forth. "Don't be coy with me, darling! You're practically penniless. At least that's what I've heard."

A flash of fiery rage crossed his features as he raked his hand through his hair. "It is a slanderous lie. I must ask where you heard it."

She waved her gloved hand here and there, bored with the question. "It's of no consequence to me." He was ready to pull away when she gripped his forearm with one gloved hand. "Don't be so defensive, darling. I will buy one of your little paintings tonight. After all, I *am* a patron of the arts."

He pursed his lips together to stop an insult from spewing from his mouth. Her caustic retort lingered in the air, leaving him feeling smaller, less certain, as if her snark had toppled the pedestal he had placed himself on. He stood there for a long moment, watching her walk away and disappear into the crowd, suddenly questioning everything about his carefully crafted plan.

A jingle of bells chimed, indicating the auction was about to start. The crowd filed into the main room through the red velvet rope and filled the chairs to capacity.

"Standing room only," he whispered under his breath, giving himself an impromptu pep talk to combat his faltering confidence. "They are all clamoring to own a sliver of my genius."

From the podium at the front of the room, the auctioneer welcomed the crowd, and then the first piece was brought out by two white-gloved men in tuxedos. When the bidding began, the air became electric. Ruben was unable to sit still, preferring to watch the bidding from a distance as he paced at the back of the room.

The auctioneer worked the crowd like an expert, his witty banter just enough to spur the bidders into action, coaxing bids higher with every playful jab. What began as a steady rhythm quickly gained momentum, and as the winning bid for each painting climbed higher, Ruben could hardly contain himself. He practically vibrated with joy, his pulse quickening with every raise of a paddle. The collection was selling, and with each strike of the gavel, Ruben felt the weight of his fears melting away. When the fifth lot soared past one million, driven by the decisive raise of Ana Castanova's paddle, a rush of vindication flooded through him.

"I'll take one-point-one million for my 'little painting' any day," he scoffed under his breath.

The rest of the auction sped by in a blur, and as he calculated the running total in his mind, he felt a calm peacefulness wash over him. It might be enough.

When the final piece was brought out, a hush fell

over the crowd. It was the painting of Isla with the child, a tender masterpiece titled *Inheritance of Grace*. After a tense, three-minute bidding war, the room burst into thunderous applause. It had sold for an unprecedented $4.1 million, making it the highest-grossing art auction for a living artist in Florida's history. Cameras flashed, reporters clamored for interviews, and Ruben basked in the limelight.

After the champagne reception, he left the auction house, tipsy and eager to continue the celebration. Ruben was flying high, feeling like he'd just crossed the finish line of a lengthy marathon. He'd cemented his legacy and would enjoy the immortality that went along with it. While Camille had done most of the heavy lifting, it was *his* genius that had shared it with the world. Without him, her paintings would have languished in the shadows, never seeing the light of day. *He* was the one who had ensured they were appreciated. *He* was the one who had molded her ideas and curated them into masterpieces. *He* was the one who directed the strokes as much as if he'd painted them himself.

When he arrived home, Margaux was irritated, seated in the great room, her arms crossed at her chest. She'd been waiting impatiently, flipping through the TV channels before landing on Miami Vice, letting the dapper Don Johnson provide a nice visual distraction.

"It was a perfect night!" Ruben exclaimed, popping the cork from a bottle of champagne. He poured two flutes and handed one over to her, trying to butter her up. "*Mon coeur*, please don't pout. We made history tonight!"

Margaux accepted the bubbly with a tight smile and lifted it to tap against his before taking a small sip. "I'm pleased to hear you use the word 'we'. Out of curiosity, how much did *we* make?"

"A little over six million, after expenses."

The number stunned Margaux speechless.

"With the proceeds, it might be time to retire. We could move anywhere you want. Live any life we choose to live."

"Provence?" she whispered. Ruben knew it was her favorite city in the world. A trickle of naïve optimism welled up. *"J'adore Provence!* The lavender fields have been calling me home."

"Perhaps," he said, waffling and unwilling to commit. "I was thinking somewhere a bit more cosmopolitan? An apartment on Avenue des Champs-Élysées?"

Her nostrils flared once and her chest heaved as reality set in. Ruben was, and always would be, a selfish bastard. She blew out a hot breath between her teeth and let the spur of irritation pass. Then, deciding to give him enough rope to hang himself, she grinned. "One more auction like we had tonight and we could have both. Why limit ourselves?"

He let out a morose chuckle. "Because gluttony will put you behind bars. I thought you learned your lesson."

His comment incensed her, and her lips set in a hard

line. She felt the first spike of indignation warm her insides like cognac.

"Perhaps you're right." He took a sip, then continued, "We might as well take advantage of my new zenith in the art world. Camille can create a few more paintings that we could use as an insurance policy while I figure out how to extract us from this situation. I will need to make arrangements with my accountant and lawyers. It's going to take some time."

Margaux stared at him, searching for signs of deception, but she'd never been good at reading Ruben. He lied as naturally as he breathed. She swallowed the consternation along with the rest of the champagne. It was time. She had arrangements of her own to make.

CHAPTER

THIRTY-FIVE

A FEW DAYS LATER, Margaux stood in the foyer wearing a chic black dress cinched at her waist paired with a silk scarf knotted at her neck. She glared down at Ruben's wide grin, pressed cheek to cheek with Ana Castanova. Her fingers clenched the newspaper so hard the edges crumpled, smudging the ink, as her eyes locked on the photo, unblinking, wishing she could set it on fire. A muscle in her jaw ticked and her lips snarled into a frown as jealousy consumed her.

She crumpled it into a ball and flung it down onto the growing collection of newspapers and magazines from the last two days, next to a vase filled with birds of paradise. Headlines mocked her, shouting in bold capital letters: "Record-Breaking Auction: Ruben Angelica declared a modern-day Michelangelo."

She read every word, and a flame of indignation ignited in her belly. The articles painted him as some sort of artistic savant. It was difficult to stomach all the accolades that were making his head balloon when she knew the truth. He wasn't any more special or talented than she was.

Turning her attention away, her stomach growled at the aroma of roasted duck mingled with the buttery scent of garlic mashed potatoes.

"Smells divine," Margaux gushed as she swept into the grand kitchen, beaming at Amos, who was giving her final instructions.

"I've just finished plating the main course as directed. Keep the dishes in the warmer until you are ready to serve. The wine is aerating in the decanter, and dessert, a chocolate mousse, is in the fridge."

"You've done more than enough. Now go, enjoy the night off. I insist." She offered him a crisp one-hundred-dollar bill she'd lifted from Ruben's wallet. Then she punctuated her command with a sweet, yet pointed smile. "I know *we* will, thanks to your hard work."

Amos beamed with pride, then accepted the cash and washed his hands. He slipped out of the kitchen, and Margaux waited by the window, watching until his taillights burned red down the driveway and disappeared. She'd already alerted Rosa to her plans that included serving the meal *au natural,* and by the horrified grimace that creased Rosa's lined face, she knew they would be left alone for the rest of the evening.

The house was eerily still, the only sound the low hum of the air conditioner cycling on and off as Margaux waited, her impatience growing with every passing second. She drummed her fingers on the table, listening for footsteps. When she was certain she was alone, she moved quickly, her pulse quickening as she slipped into the kitchen.

From behind the stack of Christmas mulled wine spices, she retrieved the pouch of glucosamine powder she'd hidden. She'd had Liam stop at GNC under the guise of buying vitamins and purchased the powder with the credit card she'd pilfered, careful to pocket the receipt quickly instead of signing it. Her breath hitched as she remembered how simple it had been, the guilt already ebbing away as she focused on her next move.

"No time to waste," Margaux murmured to herself as she pulled the Alfredo sauce Amos had made from the fridge, twisting open the glass jar with ease. Her hands worked quickly as she tore open the pouch of powder, dumping most of its contents into the sauce. With a flick of her wrist, she whisked the white powder into the creamy sauce until it completely dissolved. Then she sealed the lid with a soft click, gave the jar a good shake, and checked once more to ensure it was velvety smooth. Pleased with the results, she shelved it back in the refrigerator.

Next, she grabbed a washcloth from the stack Amos kept by the sink and wiped the handles of the refrigerator, then the countertop, and tossed it into the laundry. From her handbag, she pulled out an orange bottle of prescription sleeping pills. Her smile sharpened into a predatory smirk, and her eyes darkened as she dumped four pills into a mortar. She ground them using the pestle into a fine powder. Then she poured two glasses of wine and stirred the powder into one glass until it fully dissolved.

Satisfied, Margaux set the table, dimmed the lights on the chandelier to a romantic glow, and slipped a .38 Special CD into the player to set the mood. Humming to it, she carried the wine glasses to the table and set the plates down. Then she quickly disrobed and donned a black apron and heels.

"*Mon coeur!* Dinner is served!" she called up the stairwell, sexiness oozing into every syllable. A few minutes later, she heard the door to his study open and then his footsteps on the staircase as he descended. At the bottom, Ruben got his first glimpse of her and a devilish grin lit up his face.

"*Quell surprise!*" He drew her in for a wet kiss, his knuckles grazing her breast before his thumb circled a nipple through the fabric of her apron. When he cupped her bare bottom with both hands, a delicious shiver ran through her. Margaux recoiled, hating herself for the hold he always had over her body.

"I don't know what I want to devour first. You or the food! *Mon coeur,* is this your way of telling me you are ready to leave the past behind?" he whispered as the CD shifted to the chorus of *Second Chance.*

Margaux shot him a coy smile as she turned away to give him a view of her greatest asset, then spun around to reveal the latest newspaper article about his success. "I just wanted to do something special for the artist of the century." She held it up, gushing as she read,

"Historic Sale Propels Ruben Angelica into the Stratosphere." She handed it to him, and he skimmed the article, his grin widening by the second. Margaux waited until he was finished reading and then laced her fingers through his hand.

"Sit, sit." She guided him to his chair at the head of the table with a flourish. After he was settled in his chair, she let her hands roam across the expanse of his shoulders as she leaned in close, breathing into his ear and playfully biting and licking his earlobe.

Ruben pulled the lid from his plate, and the duck was still steaming. He leaned down and inhaled. "This looks incredible. Did you make all this yourself?" He let out a braying laugh that got on her nerves. "What am I saying? Of course you didn't!"

Margaux laughed with him, the act softening the frown that quirked the corners of her mouth. As they ate, she kept Ruben's wine glass perpetually full, her eyes gleaming with anticipation as she watched him drink deeply from it. "This vintage," he mumbled with a grimace. "Remind me to have Amos remove it from the cellar. It's bitter? *Non*?"

She scrunched up her forehead. "It doesn't taste bitter to me at all. Perhaps your palate for good French wine has suffered during your time in America?"

"Maybe." He took another drink.

By the time they reached dessert, his eyelids were drooping and his head nodded forward as he struggled to remain upright.

"Are you feeling alright, darling?" Margaux asked, careful to ensure he felt her concern.

Ruben blinked slowly, his words slurring together as he shifted in the chair. "I… I'm… just tired…"

Margaux murmured in sympathy, "You've practically worked yourself to *death* to prepare for the auction. Now that it's over and the world has declared you a genius, it is time to relax."

"Yes." He nodded in agreement, his eyes at half-mast. "Relax."

Margaux pulled out the plane ticket she'd found and waved it in the air. "Never fear. It looks like you'll be basking under the Barcelona sun soon enough," she purred, her voice dripping with saccharine sweetness.

His chin lifted, dark eyes narrowing as a flicker of recognition dawned on him. Margaux leaned back, savoring the way the realization seeped in, slowly, like ink spreading through water.

"But there's one tiny detail you overlooked," she added, her smile sharpening.

"Detail?" His tone was confused, the word slurred.

She let the moment stretch, her pout exaggerated as she circled the rim of her glass with her finger. "You forgot to buy a ticket *pour Moi*," she said, her voice lilting with mock reproach. "And I *do so adore* the Mediterranean coast. It would be a pity to enjoy it alone, don't you think?"

"Yes… I mean, no…" Ruben swallowed, and she watched him squirm, trying to gather enough wits about himself to form a logical explanation. He was starting to sway in his chair. Leaning forward, he propped his chin up on his hand as his blinks became slower. He pushed away the glass of wine, and it spilled onto the white tablecloth, staining it red. "What did you do to me?" His words were sluggish and slurred. He wiggled his fingers in front of his face and let out a weak chuckle.

Margaux began to hum a French lullaby, and within a minute, a content smile softened Ruben's lips as he blinked one last time. He sighed, then slumped forward, his head hitting the dirty plate with a dull thud.

Margaux stood, her lips curling into a triumphant smirk. "Sweet dreams, *mon coeur*," she murmured, her words dripping with venom. She rushed to the kitchen and pulled the EpiPen from the glass cabinet. She wiped it clean with a dishcloth, then carefully walked it to a sleeping Ruben. Holding it by the cloth, she cupped Ruben's fingers around it and squeezed. Then she walked up the stairs of the mansion to Ruben's suite and buried it deep inside Ruben's nightstand, underneath his bedside clutter. In the closet, she placed the almost empty packet of glucosamine inside a satchel he often used for meetings. Then she helped herself to his credit cards, putting back the one she'd lifted and choosing another. It would at least pay for a room for the week at the Hyatt House near the shore.

Pleased with herself, she pulled off the apron and took a long hot shower, leaving Ruben face-planted in the dining room, snoring and dead to the world. Then she packed up her things and called a taxi to take her to the hotel, but not before clipping the phone line leading into the house.

CHAPTER
THIRTY-SIX

"Sɪʀ?" Amos shook an unconscious Ruben, who was still passed out in his mashed potatoes the next morning. He jerked up and palmed his face, spreading the cold mixture around before scowling into his palm. Congealed sauce formed a crust on his curls, and when he stretched, his neck popped.

Still in a daze, Ruben glanced around the dining room, trying to get his bearings. Early morning light flooded in through the windows, illuminating empty wine glasses and dried-out duck.

"What happened?"

"Man, I just got here. I don't even know." Amos made quick work of gathering up the serving platter and taking it to the kitchen.

"Where's Margaux?" Ruben turned to ask Neve, and Rosa's eyes were the size of dinner plates as she took in the spectacle.

"She leave," Neve answered, busying herself with

gathering the silverware from the table. Last night, she'd been stunned when Margaux had knocked gently on her door, her eyes red-rimmed from crying. She stood there wringing her hands with her suitcases on the floor behind her.

"I have to go, Rosa. And if you know what's best for you, you'll do the same before it's too late."

Neve was suspicious. "What wrong?"

"Ruben booked a one-way ticket to Barcelona. Now, he just needs to tie up all the loose ends here, and I fear Camille is one of them."

"Wait," Neve said, trying to convince her to stay.

"The taxi is here. I have to go." Margaux rushed down the hall and out the front door. Neve didn't know what to make of it, but something was undeniably wrong. First came a cryptic warning, then Margaux's hasty exit, and finally Ruben, slumped over his plate in the dining room. This was no coincidence. There was more to this story. Much more.

Ruben picked up a napkin and wiped his hands and then his face. His nose wrinkled in repulsion at the dried bits of food in his hair. "I need to shower. In the meantime, please check in with Camille and confirm that she's aware I'll be meeting with her at eleven to discuss our next project over lunch." He walked away, and Neve cleaned up the mess in the dining room, scraping the wilted salad into the trash and tossing the tablecloths that had been stained with wine.

At eleven, Neve brought Camille's lunch tray to her room. She drew back the curtains, lifting the window sash to let the salty sea air flood in. As she did, a flash of red caught her eye at the tree line.

"Perry?" she called out, her voice carrying. He responded with a sharp whistle, the sound cutting through the quiet. The instant Camille heard it, she rushed to the window, eager to see the bird.

"I missed him!" Camille pinched her fingers together, open and closed, as he flew closer. Neve removed the screen and held out Rosa's tanned arm, and he flapped twice, then landed on it with a warble of joy.

Camille grinned, her eyes lighting up as she hesitantly extended a finger to gently smooth the feathers on top of Perry's head. The bird responded with a soft churring sound, nuzzling deeper into her palm.

"Feed the baby!" Perry trilled in a playful, sing-song voice. "Feed the baby."

Neve reached into her pocket and produced a bag of mixed nuts, offering one to Perry. She glanced at her watch. "Ruben be here any second. Find a place to hide." She turned toward Camille, and her voice dropped to a somber tone. "No talk about bird. Ruben no like him."

Camille nodded quickly in agreement and Neve returned to the tray, "Let's see what Amos make you for lunch."

"Silly Rosa, it's the same thing every day. Fettuccine Alfredo and a single kiwi peeled and cut into eight slices," Camille said as she shifted back and forth on the balls of her feet.

Neve pulled the cloche off the steaming pile of

fettuccine, and she set the plate on the table. "You right again!"

"Yes!" Camille said, tapping the tips of her fingers together. "Thank you, Rosa!"

Camille had barely sat down on the chair, a pleased expression quirking up the corners of her mouth, before Ruben joined her. His skin was pale and his eyes were bloodshot, but he was freshly showered. He shook out a napkin and placed it on his lap, allowing Neve to place his plate in front of him and remove the cloche. Neve returned to her usual place, hovering by the door, waiting for them to finish so she could remove the empty plates.

"Let's talk about the next steps," Ruben stated without preamble, spearing a slice of kiwi with his fork.

"Next steps?" Camille asked, her forehead puckered with exasperation. "I thought you said after the auction I could take a break."

"I did, I did," he repeated, dismissing her concerns. "And there will be plenty of time for that later, but we need to strike while the iron is hot! The world is hungry for the next Ruben Angelica masterpiece."

Camille's mouth set in a hard line, and Neve watched her chew on the inside of her cheek. It was obvious the woman wanted to respond, but she was frozen with fear of the confrontation. Ruben had steamrolled Camille for years, and she didn't have the confidence yet to stand up for herself.

"After lunch, perhaps we can go over some of your recent sketches?"

"But I'm tired," Camille said, her voice heavy with exhaustion. "I need a break."

Neve's heart clenched as she watched Camille stand her ground against Ruben, her frustration bubbling to the surface.

"Don't whine, it's unbecoming." He cut into his seared steak and popped a bite into his mouth, propping his elbows on the table as he chewed.

"I *deserve* a break," Camille insisted, her tone firm, unwavering. Her gaze flicked to Neve, who offered a nod of encouragement.

Ruben's eyes narrowed, his tone icy. "You'll get a break when I say so, and not a second before. You have to earn your place around here. This is not a charity!" After a long pause, he calmed himself down and restored the forced smile to his face. "Go on, eat. You know how you get when your blood sugar dips." Ruben's tone was condescending as he reached out to pat her hand. Camille recoiled and pulled her hand away, busying herself with the napkin wrapped around her silverware.

She dug into the pasta, twirling the noodles with a fork until they were neatly twisted together, and took a large bite. Her cheeks puffed out like a chipmunk hoarding nuts for the winter. Without missing a beat, she shoved two more oversized bites into her mouth, barely pausing to breathe. Suddenly, a harsh cough burst from her, and a rogue speck of noodle flew from her mouth, landing squarely on Ruben's hand.

He froze, his face twisting in disgust before he grabbed a napkin and wiped it away.

"A lady should always…" he said coldly, his gaze cutting to her, "…chew with her mouth closed."

Camille opened her mouth to retort, but no words came. She took a sip of cool water, then coughed and cleared her throat, fighting her way through it. A few bites later, her hand instinctively pressed to her chest as panic flickered in her eyes. A cold sweat broke out at her hairline, beads of it tracing down her forehead. The discomfort spread like wildfire, crawling up her hands and down her neck, making her scratch furiously until deep pink lines marked her skin. She reached up to touch her lips and froze in shock when her fingers met swollen skin.

Ruben rose from his chair, his earlier frustration replaced by urgency. "What's wrong?"

She tried to speak, but the words came out strangled. "I… I don't know. My throat feels… tight." Her breaths became shallow and rapid, panic setting in as her airway seemed to close further with each passing second.

"Mr. Ruben, I think she having another allergic attack!" Neve rushed to her side. Camille clutched her throat, her eyes wide with panic.

"What? How?" he cried. Ruben cursed under his breath and ran toward the open doorway. "Amos, bring the EpiPen!" he shouted down the staircase.

Camille's pulse pounded at her throat. "I can't see! It's blurry!" she cried. Her chest heaved and made a rattling noise as she struggled to draw in air. Ruben barked at Rosa standing by the door, "Get the EpiPen in here now and call an ambulance!" Neve nodded and disappeared down the hall at a run.

A few seconds later, footsteps echoed up the stairwell and Amos entered the room, but his hands were empty. His eyes darted to Camille, whose lips were swollen and turning faintly blue.

"I can't breathe," she rasped, falling from the chair and collapsing to the floor.

Ruben was at her side in an instant, his face a mask of terror. Pinching his fingers together in a gimme gesture, he shouted at Amos, "Give me the EpiPen!"

"It wasn't in the cabinet." Amos stood at his side, frozen in fear.

"Did you move it?" Ruben snapped.

"Of course not."

"Then it should be there! Go look again!"

Camille let out a small, strangled sound, clutching her throat as her body began to tremble. Her skin was blotchy now, patches of red spreading across her neck and arms.

"The phone is dead." Neve burst through the doorway again, out of breath from running up the stairs on Rosa's strong legs. "Pick her up, we drive her to hospital ourselves. We can't afford wait no longer."

Ruben sprang into action and rushed down the stairs with Camille in his arms while Amos pulled up his car. "Camille, stay with me," Ruben begged, lowering her gently to the backseat while Neve settled into the front seat. Her breathing was thready now, each inhale a desperate hiss. Her fingers clawed weakly at his sleeve as her legs twitched and her eyes fluttered. "Stay with me," Ruben repeated, his tone softer now, almost pleading. It sickened Neve. He was only afraid of losing his investment. It had nothing to do with Camille's well-being.

"DRIVE!" He turned and barked the command at Amos, who slammed the pedal to the metal, dodging around traffic and running red lights. He was hell bent on making it to St. Pete's Beach Memorial Hospital as fast as possible.

Amos's knuckles whitened on the wheel as he spun to look over his shoulder. "We're almost there. Just hold on. It's not far now."

"If anything happens to her, I am holding you directly responsible," Ruben yelled, as he smoothed a tendril of hair from Camille's cheek. "FASTER!"

Ten minutes later, the car screeched to a halt in front of the emergency bay of St. Pete's Beach Memorial Hospital. Camille's head hung limply to the side, her lips a frightening shade of purple, and her breathing had slowed to a terrifying crawl. Neve was out of the car before it even came to a full stop, her feet pounding the pavement as she sprinted toward the emergency entrance. She ran inside the hospital and shouted. "Young woman in my car. Need EpiPen. She in anaphylactic shock! Hurry, she no breathe!"

A doctor and two nurses ran toward the town car, rolling a gurney between them, its wheels squealing in protest. The urgency in their movements made cold fear rush through Neve.

Ruben never let go of Camille's hand, his grip so tight his knuckles were white. "Hold on," he murmured, though his words felt hollow.

The doctor uncapped the EpiPen and jabbed it into the muscle of Camille's thigh. Time froze for a heartbeat. Neve's pulse pounded in her ears as she willed Camille to take a breath. Her body was still, frozen in place, then her chest rose sharply. She gasped for air with a ragged wheezing inhalation and a shudder ran through her body. A few minutes later, color began to return to her cheeks, and the angry swelling in her face and neck started to recede. Ruben let out a huge sigh of relief, stepping back to allow the nurses access to lift her onto the gurney.

"She needs to be monitored," one of the nurses said as they prepared to roll her inside the emergency room. "What is she allergic to?"

"She's had a previous reaction to shellfish, but nothing like this," Ruben said, scrubbing his face. "I've forbidden my cook from bringing seafood into the house. It's got to be something else."

"Maybe," the doctor said, "but we'll have to figure that out when she's more lucid."

Ruben looked down at Camille, who was now conscious but groggy. "Please. Take good care of her. She's very important to me."

Neve was silent, unable to mask the raging storm

inside her. Margaux's warnings echoed in her mind, setting off a cascade of alarm bells.

Ruben has taken out a two-million-dollar life insurance policy on her, naming himself as the sole beneficiary.

Leave before it's too late.

He needs to clean up the loose ends, and Camille is one of them.

What if it wasn't just an accident? What if Ruben had given Camille the allergen on purpose? The questions gnawed at Neve, relentless and chilling. Had she just witnessed an attempt on Camille's life? She knew Ruben was rotten to his core, but could he truly be capable of murder?

CHAPTER

THIRTY-SEVEN

TWO DAYS LATER, Margaux leaned back in her chair, eyeing the door and drumming her red lacquered fingernails on the metal table. The fluorescent light of the police station interrogation room cast green shadows across her quilted leather Chanel handbag resting on the table. A few minutes later, a detective in a wrinkled suit opened the door and slid into the seat across from her. She leveled her gaze on him, registering his white button-down shirt straining across the expanse of his belly and the coffee stain on his chest pocket. He was a slovenly caricature of a police investigator, one donut away from being a cliché.

"Alright, let's get started," he addressed her as he punched the record button on the cassette player that rested on the table between them. "For the record, this is Detective Eric Keegan, badge number 1267, with the Tampa Bay Police Department. The date is March 29th,

1989, and the time is 10:47 AM. We are currently in Interrogation Room B at the 5th Precinct. This session is being recorded for documentation purposes."

He turned toward Margaux. "Ms. DuBois, please state your full name and date of birth for the record."

"Margaux DuBois. November 11th, 1949."

"Thank you. You are here voluntarily as a witness to assist in an ongoing investigation. You are not under arrest and are free to leave at any time. Do you understand?"

"Yes."

"Good. Now begin wherever you are comfortable."

"Last week, there was a fine art auction that shattered records. A collection of Ruben Angelica's artwork sold for a record-breaking seven million dollars." Margaux leaned forward in the hard chair across from the desk. "But none of it was actually his."

"Hmm." The detective was wary. "Tell me why you think that."

"He presents himself as a mentor to young artists," she explained. "But I think he coerced a talented painter into signing over the rights to her work and selling her paintings as his own."

"How do you know this?"

"I know his work intimately. I was married to the man for over a decade." She paused for emphasis. "I know his style, his process, and I know for a fact those paintings were not his."

"Why isn't the artist here making these accusations?"

"Camille is living as guest in his home, and Ruben seems to have some type of control over her."

Keegan's pen scratched against the notepad. "Do you have any proof of this in writing? Contracts, letters, gallery paperwork?"

She pulled the sketchbook from her purse and opened it, walking the officer through each drawing, and pointing out the signatures. "Many of the early stage sketches for every painting he sold at the auction appear in this notebook signed by Camille Sinclair."

"You might have a reasonable case for fraud," Keegan said, hemming it over. "*If* it can be proven, but it would be difficult to prosecute. We'd need copies of any agreements, or the artist would have to give a statement. Otherwise it could end up being a civil dispute over ownership."

"But Camille is in danger!" she cried, losing her patience with the dullard. "I found a life insurance policy in his desk taken out on her for two million dollars, with Ruben listed as the sole beneficiary. I believe he wanted to sever their arrangement permanently before fleeing the country."

Detective Keegan's shrewd eyes narrowed. "It's quite a leap from life insurance to murder."

"Let me close the gap for you," Margaux offered evenly. "What if I told you I believe Ruben administered a supplement containing shellfish, then conspired to conceal the antidote?" She was leading the horse to the poisoned water, hoping he would take a long drink. "If you don't believe me, check with her doctor." Keegan scribbled a note while she asked, "What are the odds a person would suffer two 'accidental' ingestions in as many months?" She used finger quotes as she let the damning tidbit dangle in the air. "That's not a coincidence. It's attempted murder."

The detective's pen paused. "Am I to believe you are simply a concerned citizen looking out for the well-being of another?" He leaned back and studied her before asking, "What's in it for you?"

Margaux's expression darkened. "Nothing. I simply want justice for Camille."

"Of course you do." His sarcasm sent a chill through Margaux. This wasn't how she thought this conversation would go. "Mr. Angelica has already made the department aware of your criminal record. He said you were the first artist he mentored, and he was devastated that you squandered your substantial talent. He said you were obsessed with carrying out your vicious vendetta to destroy his career."

For the first time, Margaux's composure wavered. A flicker of unease darted across her face before she recovered. "He's lying and I have proof!" She twisted the brass clasp on her handbag, pulled out the micro-cassette tape, and slid it over to him with two fingers. "I think you'll find the conversation on this riveting."

Keegan picked it up and tucked it into his pocket for safekeeping. He was silent for several minutes, tapping the folder with the relentless precision of a metronome. "Let's talk about the elephant in the room. The incident in Paris several years ago?" Margaux gasped in surprise as he continued to lay out the facts of her incarceration. "We contacted the officials in Paris. They confirmed you served five years for fraud tied to the sale of counterfeit art."

Her jaw tightened, and she shifted in her chair, finding it difficult to find a comfortable spot to perch. "Ruben painted those forgeries, not me." She spat the information out, feeling her cheeks burn with indignation. "And we conspired *together* to sell them. That man destroyed my career and made me a pariah in the art world. And yes, maybe I am *slightly* motivated by revenge because it would feel incredible to finally see him held accountable for what he's done."

"If these allegations are true, at the very least, you are an accomplice."

She balled her fist and struck the table. "*C'est incroyable!*" she exclaimed, leaping to her feet and pacing the room in frantic strides. The detective remained still, arms folded, his sharp eyes tracking her every move as she poured out her fury.

"Ruben Angelica isn't even a real person! It's an alias, a fabrication Martin dreamed up to start fresh after he implicated me. And now he's going to get away with it? Again?" Her voice cracked with equal parts anger and righteousness, her accusations ricocheting off the walls like gunfire. The scowl on her face deepened as she implored the detective. "I served my time and repaid my debt to society. I will not take the fall for him this time. There is no evidence I was connected to these fraud allegations. There is no paper trail that leads to me, no bank transfers or wires, no emails or other exchange of information. Margaux was bitter, her words laced with venom. "As a matter of fact, I did not even meet Camille. Ruben practically kept her prisoner at his home." She sat back down and swallowed hard, trying to regain her composure. "You must realize Ruben is in damage control mode, and he's ruthless when it comes to protecting his reputation. He'd do anything to secure his future."

"That's funny. He said the same about you."

Her jaw ticked, then she laughed, low and dark. "*Touché*, Detective. Ruben's testimony sent me to prison as the sole mastermind behind his counterfeit operation, and he left me to rot in that cell for five years. Was I out for *blood*? Sure. But murder? No way. That's his territory." She settled back in the chair, folding her arms across her chest.

Keegan studied her for a long moment, his expression unreadable. "They say hell hath no fury like a woman scorned," he murmured under his breath as he stood. "Thank you for coming in. You've given me some things to think about." He slid a business card over to her. "If you think of anything else, please let me know."

She stuffed it into her handbag. "Listen to the tape. Everything you need to know is there."

"I won't make any promises," he said gruffly. "It might not even be admissible in court."

"While that may be true, it confirms he engaged in a pattern of illegal activity," Margaux reasoned as she stood, thrusting her shoulders back. "The truth is, I don't need to orchestrate his downfall. Ruben is perfectly capable of destroying himself. But promise me this, Detective, if he goes down, I get a front-row seat!"

"Okay," he agreed. "I'll make that promise, but if you're lying, I'll drag you down to hell with him."

<hr>

When she got back to the hotel, Ruben was in her suite, pacing. Margaux raced over to him, all of her cells sparking with rage. Her full lips curled into a sneer, and she beat on his chest with her hands balled into fists as hot tears gathered at her lashes. He encircled her wrists with his own, dodging her punches.

"Enough, Margaux!" He pushed her away and ran one hand through his hair.

"You can't dispose of me so easily this time!" Margaux snarled. "I made sure of that!" She stalked toward him and gritted out, "How's your little artistic genius? Still breathing?"

"What did you do?" he shouted at her as he paced, coming to grips with the truth. "*Mon Dieu!* Camille's allergy attack wasn't an accident. It was you!"

Margaux's lips curved into a smile that didn't reach her eyes. Her reply smacked with sarcastic saccharine. "I simply eliminated your problem and paved the way for you to get what you deserve. You're welcome."

Ruben recoiled as if struck. "Are you insane?" he hissed as he grabbed her arms with both of his hands, shaking her. "She could have died!"

"But she didn't," she replied coolly.

Ruben's chest heaved with anger and disbelief. "You're psychotic!"

Margaux's bubble popped, and rage spilled out. "*Comme ci, Comme ça,* but you should know I've given Detective Keegan enough circumstantial evidence to send you to prison."

He laughed at the outrageous statement. "Whose word do you think they will take? The word of a convicted thief, or the word of a beloved artist with a flawless reputation?" He let her go, tossing her to the bed and stalking to the other side of it.

"Not so flawless anymore! I told Detective Keegan everything and even provided a recording in your own words. I will not be your scapegoat a second time," she snarled at him, yanking her clothing from the dresser and throwing it into her suitcase in a haphazard pile.

He poured himself a drink from the minibar and raised the glass to her. "I will give you extra points for creativity this time, *mon coeur.* Exploiting Camille's allergy to frame me for murder was, and I don't say this lightly, a chef's kiss!" He kissed the tips of his fingers dramatically, and it made her blood boil. "That was low, even for you." He tossed back the rest of the whisky and swallowed hard. His jaw ticked as he said ruefully, "We could have had it all, but your jealousy ruined everything. We're done."

Margaux's composure faltered for a moment, but she quickly regained it. She wanted to claw his eyes out of his self-important head. "You're right about one thing, *mon coeur*. We *are* done. Now get out!"

CHAPTER

THIRTY-EIGHT

BACK AT HIS SEASIDE MANSION, Ruben was in his bedroom, frantically stuffing clothes and toiletries into suitcases. Avoiding him, Neve was hiding out in the kitchen with Amos when she heard him roar with fury, then bellow, "That conniving bitch stole my money!" With her heart in her throat, Neve climbed the stairs to the master bedroom where Ruben was surrounded by a pile of scattered paintings and empty frames. He'd torn the backing paper off several in a frenzy, clearly searching for the envelopes of cash, most of which Neve had locked away in a new safe deposit box just days ago.

The doorbell chimed in a relentless loop, and Neve rushed down to answer it when Detective Keegan burst through the door clutching a thick wad of legal papers. "Where is Ruben Angelica? We have a search warrant to execute."

Neve said nothing, instead pointing up the staircase where Ruben was wheeling out his carry-on luggage.

Keegan rushed up the stairs with two other officers, handing him the paperwork. "We need you to come with us to the station for questioning."

"I've answered all your questions already," Ruben protested.

"Seems after talking to your ex-wife, Margaux, we have a few more," Keegan said, adding, "Hands behind your back."

"That whore," Ruben spat out as they dragged him away in handcuffs. When the door was closed behind him, Neve rushed to her quarters and tucked a banded stack of hundred-dollar bills she'd found hours ago into the elastic band of her bra to secure it.

The rest of the investigators spread out through the house like a virus, yanking open drawers and taking photos. Cabinet doors banged against the walls, and the rustling of papers filled the air as officers rifled through every possible hiding place. Footsteps pounded up and down the stairs, their frantic energy spiraling with the occasional muffled curse or barked command.

In the study, the whir of a drill twisting through metal screeched as the officer drilled through the lock on Ruben's desk. Once inside, they labeled and boxed up the contents and carried them away. A shout came from the bedroom when the EpiPen was discovered in his nightstand, and the almost emptied packet of glucosamine powder was placed into a plastic evidence bag and sealed shut.

The sheer destruction unfolding around her made Neve freeze, and the noisy chaos overwhelmed her frayed edges as Rosa's aversion to law enforcement only amplified the tension. She focused on a tree just outside the window, using it to still her galloping heartbeat. Inside the pocket of her apron, she fingered the geode, finding its warmth comforting. When a flash of gray and red filled her vision, her heart lifted as she rushed to the window to open it. Perry alighted from his hiding place in the trees, and the soft whisper of his feathers sliced through the mayhem. He landed on Neve's shoulder, and she turned her face and buried it into his soft feathers.

"There, there, Nevermore," he churred softly, trying his best to comfort her.

After inhaling a shaky breath, she finally said, "Ruben not here, he with the *policía*."

"Good riddance," Perry squawked.

In the distance, Camille's distressed shouts were damped behind doors, her anguish evident. Somewhere, a metal tray clattered to the floor with a sharp crash, and her loud cry followed it.

"Hurry! Camille needs us," Perry said as he led the way, flapping out of the study and toward the back staircase. Neve quickened her steps, staying close behind. She knocked gently on the door, but Camille didn't hear it, lost in her sobs. Neve turned the knob and slipped into the bedroom. There, in the corner of the closet, Camille rocked back and forth, using her thin arms to ball her knees into her chest.

Neve instantly understood she was overstimulated. "It Rosa, Camille. I here to help you."

"Loud, so loud," Camille cried as she heard the officers shouting from room to room while they conducted their search. She pressed her hands to her ears and trembled, her skin pale.

Neve glanced around the bedroom, feeling helpless until her gaze landed on the pair of headphones attached to a yellow Sony Walkman. She rushed over and delivered them to the terrified young woman, careful not to crowd Camille. After a long pause, Camille reached out one shaky hand and placed them on her head. When her ears were covered, Camille's screaming slowed, then finally stopped. She hiccupped and her gaze fixed on Perry, who crept closer, careful not to startle her. When Camille reached out one tentative hand, he leaned into it, burying his head in the middle of her palm, an act that seemed to further calm her overstimulated brain.

When she was certain Camille could handle it, Neve gently offered her one hand and led her out of the bedroom and to her studio, knowing it was her place of greatest solace. Neve crossed to the wall of windows and drew open the blinds, letting the last threads of daylight spill in. Camille stood there, motionless, eyes locked on the sun's reflection shimmering across the water. The serene view seemed to soothe the artist as her shoulders eased and her breath slowed. Neve stepped closer and tapped gently on her own ear. Camille blinked, then pulled off her headphones and turned to listen. Her gaze locked on Perry, who never left her side.

"I need check some things and feed Perry. I bring you snack?"

Camille nodded enthusiastically, then seeming to turn a corner, she swiveled back to her paint palette and squeezed out dollops of color along the wells, readying herself for work.

"Can you keep watch?" Neve asked Perry. "She mind not strong, no can handle more loud noise and interruptions. Best thing for her now is paint. Routine make her feel better."

"Yes. Don't worry," Perry agreed, and his iron-clad conviction puzzled her. "The only way someone is getting in here is over my deceased avian body!"

Neve descended the back stairs and made a quick stop at her bedroom, pulling the rolled-up canvas from its hiding place in her closet. She walked it down the stairs and over to where Detective Keegan was boxing and labeling evidence the team was collecting. "I think I have something help your investigation into Mr. Ruben."

She handed it to him and he unrolled it, his brow furrowed. "This a Renoir he say he love, but I know it fake," she explained. "Mr. Ruben make me destroy others when Ms. Margaux come. He say he tell immigration if I not help." She turned away, feeling Rosa's fears starting to climb. Suddenly desperate for clarity, she asked, "Should I be worry?"

"No," Detective Keegan said, putting her fears to rest. "I have no interest in reporting a hardworking person to immigration when they are forthcoming with information to aid an investigation."

Neve felt the burden on her shoulders ease, heightened by Rosa's relief. She turned to leave, telling the officer, "Please excuse, I must get back to Camille."

Hours later, the house was finally silent but looked like it had weathered a hurricane. Chairs were tipped on their sides and the drawers of cabinets were either flayed open or upside down on the floor with their contents spilled. Neve and Amos stood frozen, gaping at the chaos law enforcement left behind. Then Amos returned to the kitchen, pulled out a bottle of rum and mixed up a fruity concoction, offering one frosty mug to Neve.

"Tomorrow. We'll deal with the mess tomorrow," he said, with a resigned sigh. "Tonight, we drink."

She nodded sadly, taking a sip of the cocktail before she righted two overturned chairs and offered one to Amos. They sat in companionable silence for a long time. "I have plan…" Neve blurted, leaning into her typical nature to work solo, but the alcohol lowered her inhibitions and softened her rigid nature. She studied Amos for a moment. Neve knew he was trustworthy, but it still felt uncomfortable to ask for what she needed. Finally she admitted, "I need your help."

Concern knitted up Amos's brows as he locked his gaze on her.

"Follow me?" Neve said, as she stood and walked down the hallway. The soles of her rubber shoes squeaked as she led him into the bedroom lined with

Ruben's mediocre paintings. Some were splattered with vibrant colors and unfinished, others meticulously detailed. They'd been rifled through during the search and were scattered face-down on the floor.

Neve paced nervously, wringing her worn hands together, calloused from years of scrubbing as she glanced at the tall, broad-shouldered man leaning against the wall. "I need you understand," she whispered urgently. Her eyes darted toward the doorway as if expecting someone to burst through at any moment.

Amos paced, feeding off the nervous energy cresting in Neve. "You know this room is off-limits. If Ruben knows we've been in here, we're both cooked."

"He fire me already," Neve snapped, her voice cracking under the weight of Rosa's fear. She took a deep breath and gestured around the room at the piles of toppled canvases. "I find most of it in here."

Amos followed her gaze, frowning. "What?"

"The money," Neve said, her voice barely audible. She turned around modestly, unbuttoned her smock, and pulled the cash from its hiding place. When she turned back around to show him, Amos let out a whistle, taking the stack of bills from her and shuffling the corner like a deck of cards.

"This is the most cash money I've ever held in my hands at once." He said with awe.

"Remember when Ruben make me destroy painting in garage? That is where I find first bundle. Then Ruben tell me clean in here weeks ago. I move all paintings to mop floor. One painting felt so heavy, much more than others. Back was loose, so I open it, find cash inside. It wasn't just one painting. Many had hidden spaces. Ruben been hiding money around house in back of art. I go through them one by one when he gone."

Amos let out a heavy breath as his eyes locked on the neat stack of cash. "Why are you showin' me this?" Amos asked after a long pause. "What you want me to do with it?"

Neve reached out, gripping his arm with surprising strength. Her dark eyes burned with intensity. "You only one I trust. You care for Camille. I see it. The way you make her favorite food, how you listen when she talk about her paintings when nobody else care."

"I'm just doing my job," he protested.

"No," Neve disagreed. "It more than that, my friend."

He closed his eyes. "She's vulnerable, and I can't help it. She just brings out my protective side."

"I counting on it." Neve grinned. "You got pure heart, and Camille need you now more than ever." He nodded, lost in thought. "I want you take this money, use it to help her. Get her away from him."

"He's caught up already."

"For now," Neve cautioned. "Snake like him always slither away." She pointed to the thick stack of cash. "But this give Camille what she need for start fresh."

Amos stared at her, stunned. "Woman, you hear yourself? This ain't a few hundred bucks. This is… what, five G's? Ten? Where am I supposed to take her?"

"We go hotel tonight. It not safe here. Then we figure out plan."

"And how do I explain this?" He waved the bills in the air. " You know a brother can't be walkin' around with fat stacks without drawing attention."

"I not know!" Neve's voice broke as her nerves frayed and tears welled up in her eyes. "I do know, if he get out on bail, he trap her more. He keep using Camille, make her paint for him while she get nothing. She don't see what he do to her."

Amos stood, pacing the room. His mind raced as he tried to process the situation. Neve watched him anxiously, her fingers twisting the hem of her apron.

Finally, he stopped, turning to face her. "This is straight-up crazy. We talkin' about stealing. Even if it's for a good reason, it's still theft. I am a black man in America, man. If I get caught, it ain't gonna be pretty for me."

Neve implored him with her eyes. Her voice steadied, filled with determination. "You not get caught. I help you. I not ask you if there was other way."

Amos exhaled sharply, his hands on his hips. "Look, even if I'm with you, a hotel ain't nothin' but a band-aid."

Neve's eyes brightened with a flicker of hope. "I know. Camille need new home. She do good near ocean. How about Aura Cove? It small town, only thirty minute from here. I find rental?"

"I dunno." Amos battled with his reservations.

"Change hard for Camille, but together, I think we can convince her make new start."

"Okay," he said reluctantly, then pulled his hat off his head and palmed his face with one hand. "Ain't nothin' for me here. Let's do it. But we gotta move smart, plan every damn step. We can't slip up."

Neve let out a shaky breath, relief flooding in. "*Gracias!*"

He gave her a small, wry smile. "I must've lost my damn mind! You talkin' me into stuff I got no business doin'."

THIRTY-NINE

THE FOLLOWING AFTERNOON, the conference hall of Tampa Bay's Plaza Hotel buzzed with activity, teeming with reporters from every prominent East Coast media outlet. Cameramen hoisted their bulky video cameras onto their shoulders, while on-air personalities in brightly colored blazers maneuvered for prime positioning. Their thin, wired microphones jutted forward, eager to capture every soundbite as the room pulsed with the frantic energy of a high-stakes news event. At the podium, Margaux clutched the edges of the wooden lectern with crimson-tipped fingers.

She was dressed in a tailored burgundy suit, the neckline cut scandalously low to show off her exquisite figure. She adjusted the silk scarf at her throat, and as she lifted her chin, her high cheekbones caught the light while she waited for the room to fall into a hushed silence.

"*Merci*," she said, her accent becoming thickened

under duress, her voice carrying a tremor of fear. "Thank you all for coming today. My name is Margaux DuBois." She paused, letting the name hang in the air. "I was married to Martin DuBois, whom you may know under the alias, Ruben Angelica. He is the contemporary modern painter whose piece *Inheritance of Grace* sold at auction for $4.1 million earlier this month." The room was so silent you could hear a pin drop.

When she spoke again, her voice was a register lower, as though what she was about to disclose physically pained her. "I stand before you today because there is a lie that must be exposed," she began. "For far too long, I have been silent. But now, I must speak." She exhaled sharply and placed a trembling hand on her chest. "Ruben Angelica is not the man you think he is. He is a thief, a fraud, and a man accused of attempted murder to keep his legacy in the art community intact."

The room collectively gasped. Pens scratched across notepads, and cameras whirred to life.

"Five years ago, I went to prison," Margaux said, her voice quivering. "I was convicted of art fraud, a crime I committed *with* Martin DuBois. At the time, we were married. We were partners, in every sense of the word." She laughed bitterly, shaking her head as if marveling at her own gullibility. "We were both guilty of the crime," she continued, her gaze hardening, "but I was the only one who paid for it. I served five years in a French prison, while Martin walked away."

She lifted her chin defiantly, and the room seemed to collectively hold its breath.

"He relocated to America under a new name and befriended a local artist, offering to become her mentor." She paused for a long moment, then continued, "The paintings sold at last week's record-breaking auction were *not* his masterpieces. Not a single one of them. They were hers."

The silence in the room broke like glass shattering. Reporters shouted questions over one another, camera flashes popping like lightning strikes, but Margaux held up a hand, asking for decorum before she continued.

"The true artist," she clarified, her voice rising, "is Camille Sinclair. She is a brilliant young woman, a savant, if you will, with a palette knife and a brush." Her voice cracked slightly, and she gripped the lectern tighter. "Ruben discovered her through the Pathways of Light organization and moved her into his residence where he could control every aspect of her career. She was naïve and trusted Ruben when he promised to help her share her artwork with the world."

Margaux's lips twisted into a grimace. "Instead of fulfilling his promises, he betrayed her trust. Ruben took her paintings, signed his name, and claimed them as his own. Over the last several years, Ruben Angelica made millions off of her genius."

"Why didn't she speak out?" a reporter shouted from the back.

Margaux's dark eyes darted toward the man. "Camille is reclusive and prefers to stay out of the limelight. Ruben Angelica manipulated her for his own gain." She paused, letting the weight of her words settle over the crowd. "But that's not all this despicable man is capable of," Margaux continued, her voice icy with fury. "A few months ago, he took out a two-million-dollar life insurance policy on Camille. I have reason to believe the evidence will reveal that Ruben Angelica exploited her known shellfish allergy, using it as a weapon to try and end her life in order to keep his secrets intact."

Her eyes narrowed, the weight of her words heavy in the room. "Just two days ago, Camille suffered from a case of life-threatening anaphylactic shock and might have died if it weren't for the doctors and nurses at St. Pete's Beach Memorial Hospital."

The room erupted again. Margaux's hands trembled visibly now, and she took a deep breath to regain her composure.

"Why come forward now?" a female reporter near the front asked, her tone skeptical.

Margaux forced her eyes to soften and let shame infiltrate her voice. "I should have spoken up sooner, but I was afraid of Ruben. I was also a victim of his abuse and manipulations. But I am here today because I refuse to sit by and watch him destroy another woman's life."

"Do you have evidence of these accusations? How do we know you're telling the truth?"

Margaux opened her handbag and produced the sketchbook, holding it up in the air while flashbulbs blinded her, but she continued anyway. "Inside are sketches by Camille, with her signature, that match the paintings he claims are his."

The room broke into chaos again. Voices shouted over one another, asking questions she had no intention of answering.

"I am making this statement of my own accord and imploring law enforcement to act swiftly and bring formal charges against this vile man. I want justice for Camille. I want people to know the truth about the artist they all admire. And I want to be free. Free from the past, free from Ruben's lies."

The room buzzed with whispers and frenzied note-taking. With that, she turned and walked out of the room, her heels clicking against the linoleum floor. The reporters surged after her, shouting questions, but Margaux did not look back, afraid they would see the wide grin spreading across her face. Her spine was straight, her head held high as she navigated to the waiting taxi. At last, she felt completely vindicated.

CHAPTER

FORTY

WHEN A FRONT DESK clerk called the *National Enquirer* and revealed Camille Sinclair's whereabouts, reporters descended on the hotel like locusts. For a solid week, Neve fought to keep Camille from drowning in the relentless media storm. The press had swarmed, their insatiable hunger for details pulling Camille into a whirlwind of interviews. Their cameras and microphones were obtrusive, never giving her a moment's peace. Neve handled it all with uncanny composure, coordinating her schedule and coaching Camille on how to respond. They role-played questions together late into the night until Camille finally felt a shred of confidence in answering them. It was exhausting but necessary.

Thankfully, just as they were nearing their breaking point, a new scandal exploded. The mayor and several high-ranking government officials were allegedly linked to a prostitution ring that, bizarrely, involved donkeys.

The outrageous story dominated the headlines, and the media, ravenous and titillated by every lurid detail, pounced elsewhere. At last, their bloodthirsty focus shifted away from Camille.

Unable to post bail with his financial assets frozen, Ruben had been detained all week, giving Neve and Amos the time they needed to pack up their things and find a new home for Camille.

It had been a whirlwind, and Neve stretched as she stood on the front steps, holding the keys to the rental in her hand. She dropped them into Amos's large, outstretched palm with a sigh that spoke volumes of the toll the week had taken on all of them.

"Should we get her settled?" Amos asked, glancing back at the white-paneled van where Camille was waiting, sketching quietly.

"In a minute," Neve said, waiting for him to unlock the front door. He cracked it open, stepped inside, and immediately let out a low whistle of appreciation. The space felt warm, alive with the soft glow of sunlight streaming through large windows, casting a golden hue on the beach cottage's cozy interior. "First year rent, all paid," Neve said in Rosa's choppy English. She could feel Rosa practically sigh with relief.

The walls were painted a soft white, and Camille's artwork, with its bold colors and repeating patterns, adorned every wall. The fully furnished beach home was comfortable and inviting, yet it felt familiar. Amos worked at the mansion to box up all their things, and Neve unpacked them in an effort to ease Camille's transition. It had taken every minute of the last forty-eight hours to ready the house for her, and they were both bone weary.

Neve led Amos down the hallway to the series of bedrooms. "This Camille's," she said, opening the door. Inside, Camille's organic cotton bedding covered the queen-sized bed, and her two favorite paintings were hung prominently on the walls. On top of the coverlet, her plushies were lined up in order of most to least favorite as they had been at Ruben's. Knowing how important these details were to Camille, Neve did everything she could to make her new house feel like home.

"It's perfect," Amos said, delighted. "She's going to love it."

With a pleased smile, Neve shut the door and walked further down the hallway toward two more smaller bedrooms. "Mine." She opened the door to the smallest bedroom, then crossed the hall and opened the other door, "And yours."

When Amos got a look inside, he tried to protest.

"You shoulda let me have that one and taken this bigger room for yourself."

Neve shut his objections down immediately. "After all that space to clean at Ruben's, trust me, I happy."

Before he could make another argument, Neve beckoned him to follow her back into his bedroom and over to a full-length mirror that was on the wall closest to the ensuite bathroom. With a swift, practiced motion, she pressed her fingers against the edge, and the mirror swiveled open with a soft click. It revealed a hidden recess concealing neatly stacked piles of cash. "Emergency fund," she said. "Until Camille's work start earn money, and legal fees to fight contract?"

Amos exhaled a hot breath between his crooked teeth. It seemed he still had his reservations. "Looks like you really thought this all the way through. I don't know if I should be impressed or low-key scared." He shot Neve a small smile, then asked, "But uh… what we gon' do when Ruben come lookin' for it?"

Neve make a quick sign of the cross and then kissed the top of her praying hands. "God willing, he be too busy fighting own legal battles for now, not worry about us. I think he be charged soon." The answer seemed to placate Amos's deepest fears, and Neve saw his jaw unclench as she continued to explain their next steps.

"Next week, we go appointment with Jamison Bach at Dorsay, Smith, and Bach. He come highly recommended. He help us with the legal fight. Our whole focus, make sure Camille feel safe and protected. Make sure her life not change. And also we keep away from media circus when Ruben's case go to court."

"Agreed." He nodded solemnly. They were both lost in thought for several minutes before he brightened, rubbed his palms together and said, "Now, let me at that kitchen!"

"Of course!" Neve said, and she walked him to the other end of the house that faced the sea. A wide expanse of windows framed the view, which wasn't as magnificent as at the mansion, but it still overlooked a sliver of the aqua-colored ocean and rippling swaths of sea grasses. The room was a wide open space where Neve had positioned an easel in front of the window. Instead of a sofa, the room had two smaller chairs pushed against the perimeter. Next to the easel, Neve set up a station filled with Camille's paints and a horizontal rack for drying her finished pieces. The gilded cage hulked in the corner of the room, looking out of place surrounded by the builder-grade finishes and the cove popcorn ceiling.

On the perch, Perry squawked out a greeting when he saw Amos enter the room. "All hail, the King of the Kitchen! The Master of the Mixer has arrived!"

Amos broke out into a wide grin. "Yes, sir, you in the presence of royalty!"

"Peregrine is hungry. Feed the birdie!" The bird warbled and stirred, getting agitated on the perch.

"Hold on, it not always about you, Perry," Neve interjected. "You wait. Let me finish his tour." She turned back to Amos and explained, "The kitchen, I know it not same level you used to, but I make sure it got everything you need."

Opposite the windows, the kitchen was expansive and spanned the other side of the open space.

"Now we're talking!" Amos enthused, his voice full of excitement as he ran his hand appreciatively over the smooth laminate countertops and the suite of pristine white appliances. With a crank, he turned on a gas burner, and the sharp crackle of the flame made his grin stretch even wider, his eyes lighting up with satisfaction.

"I stock fridge with Camille's needs and some things you like, too." On the outside of the refrigerator, a whimsical stingray magnet pinned a list of emergency contacts. Beside it, a calendar was tacked in place with handwritten appointments already scheduled. In a drawer closest to the easel, she pulled out a brand new EpiPen and showed it to Amos. "Just in case."

"Perfect." Amos nodded, his eyes darting away as if unsure of what to say next. Neve studied his face, the weight of the awkward silence between them growing heavier with each passing second.

"Feed the birdie!" Perry chirped again, his voice cutting through the tension like a lifeline. Neve felt a wave of gratitude for the interruption.

"Can you cut up apple or something for Sir Squawk-A-Lot, and I get Camille settled?"

"You got it," Amos replied quickly, a little more at ease now as he moved in the kitchen, pulling a paring knife out of the block.

Neve watched him work, taking a moment to exhale deeply. She turned to face the ocean view, feeling a shift in her energy. She pulled out the geode and studied it in her palm as it pulsed with delight, and she felt a calm sense of peace wash over her. It wasn't perfect, but it was a safe space for Camille to start over and claim the success she deserved, and for that, Neve was grateful.

FORTY-ONE

A FEW DAYS LATER, the afternoon sun was lowering on the horizon line and the ocean breeze ruffled through Rosa's coarse black hair. Neve pulled her sandals off and trudged into the sugary sand that led to the ocean, stopping to call his name.

"Perry!"

Since they'd moved to the rental house, Perry seemed to grow more restless. The smaller space seemed to suffocate, and the open sky called to him more than ever. No longer content to perch on her shoulder while she tended to the house and Camille, Perry was becoming a master escape artist. The parrot preferred to spend most of his days outdoors, high in the palm trees that flanked the house, his gray feathers blending with the swaying leaves as he watched the world below.

A few hours ago, a strong gust of wind whipped open the back door that hadn't been fully latched, and off he went, wings flapping furiously. Perry had been gone for hours, and Neve was becoming increasingly worried about him. Heat inside her pocket burned at her hip. She reached in and fished out the shard of geode. It pulsed in her hand, brilliant and shimmering, alive with inner light. She squeezed it between her thumb and forefinger, its jagged edge biting into her skin as a sudden flare of heat surged through her.

Neve had discovered Ana Casanova was right. The geode wasn't just a pretty stone. It was a talisman, a mystical guiding force, leading her to her destiny and giving her strength when she needed it most. She didn't have all the answers but knew intuitively that it would never lead her astray. Her father had given it to her for a reason.

The sudden shift in light and heat was either a signal or a warning. Her pulse accelerated as a new confidence thrummed through her. Whatever came next, she was ready to face it.

In the distance, a low rumble of thunder made her quicken her pace.

"Storm's coming," she said under her breath. Neve glanced back toward the path that led to the house, torn between returning home and pressing on. But the thought of leaving Perry out in a storm, alone and vulnerable, spurred her forward. Neve called his name louder. "Peregrine!" She craned her neck, listening for the familiar rustle of feathers or his chirp, but there was nothing but silence. The gathering clouds had long chased away the families with their wet towels and frisbees, and Neve was alone on the beach. A gust of wind sent grains of sand blasting to her face, and she braced against it, gripping the small tin of sunflower seeds in her hand. She shook it to entice him as she called out again.

"Perry! Stop playing around. Storm coming!"

The sky darkened to an ominous shade of deep pewter as she pushed on, her irritation increasing with each step. Perry was really testing her patience this time.

"C'mon, Perry!" Her voice carried over the surf but failed to coax the parrot from his hiding place. "Silly birdbrain," she muttered under her breath, scanning the horizon for the flash of scarlet tail feathers that she'd watched disappear near the dunes only moments ago. One glimpse of him had been enough to propel her into a run.

The tide lapped higher as the waves began to churn, becoming opaque and foamy, crashing over each other. It wouldn't be long until the approaching storm unleashed, and Neve was desperate to find him before that happened. Perry was more than a pet. He'd become her sounding board, and after all they'd been through at Ruben's, the thought of losing him now gnawed at her.

A roar of thunder growled in the distance, and Neve paused to catch her breath, pressing a hand to her chest and scanning the sky. The air felt heavier now, charged with electricity. Over the ocean, a fork of lightning split the horizon in two and made goosebumps rise up on her arms.

"Oh, bird-man," she whispered. "Why you not stay

in your cage today?" Her fears were swallowed by the crashing waves. She paused again, scanning the dunes in the fading light. The ocean stretched before her, its surface glittering like cut diamonds, but the beauty of it was lost on her. A smarter woman might have turned back at this point, but she pressed on, feeling pushed forward by an invisible force, her tin of seeds rattling rhythmically in her hand.

The clouds churned above her, dark and oppressive, and the air grew thick with a metallic tang. She called his name again, her voice cracking as the first fat drops of rain began to fall. "Perry! Stop being drama king and let's go!" she shouted into the gale. A streak of red and gray caught her eye, and for a moment, her heart soared.

"There you are!"

But when she hurried closer, it was only a broken kite tangled in a piece of driftwood. Neve sighed, the weight of disappointment pressing down on her shoulders.

"Perry! Please!" she begged.

Another flash of gray feathers appeared in the distance, this time unmistakable. Neve's breath hitched as she saw him perched on a piece of driftwood near the shoreline. His scarlet tail flicked once, and he cocked his head at her approach.

Relief washed over her, momentarily eclipsing the storm's growing fury.

"There you are, you little troublemaker!" She crouched, holding out the tin of seeds. "Come here, silly boy. Let's get you home."

"Fine! But I expect nothing less than the choicest fruits and the finest silken perch upon my arrival!"

"Of course you do." Relief flooded Neve's chest, and she let out a shaky laugh. She stepped closer, extending a hand. "We need go inside. Not safe out here."

The moment her fingers brushed the bird's smooth feathers, the sky lit up in a blinding flash. The storm was upon them now, the rain coming down in sheets that soaked them to the bone. Lightning forked across the sky, illuminating the beach in stark, terrifying glimpses. Neve shielded Perry's body with her own, her heart pounding. Underneath her feet, the sand felt unstable. The air was electric, charged with a palpable energy that made her skin prickle.

Another flash of lightning struck, this one closer, so close she could feel the searing heat from it. She stumbled but remained standing, her breath coming in shallow gasps. Perry gripped her forearm tighter with his talons.

"Once more into the breach!" he squawked, raising one wing in proud defiance.

The storm answered with a roar of thunder that shook the ground.

"Not again," Neve whispered, her voice trembling. Her hip was on fire where the geode connected with it, and she could smell the acrid scent of her own burning flesh and hair. She clawed at it, eventually pulling it free. The stone burned brilliant in her hand, and when it connected with her skin, she felt the first wobble.

Then, before she could take another step, a blinding white light consumed her vision. The lightning struck the sand just feet away, its raw energy arcing toward her and Perry in an unpredictable burst. It hit her like a freight train, the force of it knocking her off her feet. Neve clamped her eyes shut, protecting them from the brilliant light that erased everything around her.

A crack split through her bones, echoing through her skull. Every muscle in Neve's body contracted at once as the flow of electricity completed its circuit. It seared every nerve traveling her veins and burned her from the inside out. Pain exploded through her, blazing every cell in her body. She didn't scream. Her mind went blissfully blank as her senses overloaded.

And then, the entire world went still.

PART 3: POST RETROGRADE LATE APRIL 2024

FORTY-TWO

Neve's limbs were impossibly heavy as if they had been turned to stone, and her eyes refused to open. A creeping terror slithered through her veins as her limbs locked in place, and she realized she was trapped back inside her own body. There was a tearing sensation as she felt Rosa slip away into the mist, leaving her adrift in an eerie void of nothingness. Until that moment, she hadn't realized how much of a calming presence Rosa had been to her mind.

"Perry?" Her question was a trembling whisper that went unanswered. The loneliness that came next made panic claw up her throat, sharp and suffocating.

"Shh." She heard a man's voice whisper from the mist, then felt the gentle press of a cool palm on her forehead. "You are safe." The whisper was familiar, threading through the haze of her mind like an ephemeral melody. She strained to grasp it, to hold on to the timbre and cadence, certain she had heard that voice before. It lingered at the edges of her memory, just out of reach, teasing her with the certainty that it belonged to someone she knew. Someone she *loved.*

A wave of agony crashed over her. Every muscle and synapse were on fire, and she was distracted by the intense pain. She felt his comforting hand press its cool surface to her face again, and she sighed in relief as she faded in and out of consciousness.

A few moments later, Neve struggled harder to get her uncooperative limbs to move, relieved when she felt her toes wiggle inside her hiking boots. Her chest was tight, and her lungs struggled to inhale. She attempted short, staggered breaths, consumed by the task of acquiring air.

"Who are you?" she coughed out. Words were difficult to put together, and she let out a strangled exhalation before succumbing to the pain again. "Stay…" she whispered as she drifted away, feeling the sensation of being pulled and then sucked down into a well of silence as she settled into delirium.

When Neve's eyes fluttered back open, she was lying on her back in the sand, staring up at a sky that was no longer stormy but painted in shades of pink and gold, and the air was fresh and clean.

Disoriented, she sat up slowly, her movements stiff and unsteady. Her breath came in shallow gasps as she looked around, trying to piece together what had happened. Neve looked down at herself, expecting to find scorched clothes or some visible mark of the lightning's wrath, but her outfit had changed entirely. Gone were the shorts, t-shirt, and sandals she remembered dressing Rosa's body in before she left to find Perry.

Now Neve was wearing her leggings and familiar hiking boots. She brushed her hands over her body, savoring the comfort of its familiarity. Rosa's stocky torso had been left behind in favor of her own longer limbs. They weren't the mile-long coltish legs of Isla either. She let out a chuckle of delight as she settled back into her own skin and felt a wash of self-love surface. She hugged her arms to her chest and swayed with joy, reveling in it. It was a homecoming in a sense, and she'd gained a new appreciation for herself.

A headache pinched at her temples, and she pressed her fingers there to relieve it. Her hand slid down the length of her braid, but when it traveled farther than she remembered it reaching, a fresh wave of muddled confusion swept over her. Pushing the odd realization away, Neve staggered to her feet. A few steps away, she found her geode. The piece she'd traveled with was missing, and she brushed her finger over the hole it left behind as a confusing sense of loss trickled in. Scanning the sand, she laid eyes on her messenger bag and tucked the remains of her geode deep inside. Her headache was starting to pound in unison with her heartbeat as she draped the strap across her body and stood on wobbly legs. Her *own* wobbly legs.

Neve turned to the ocean, the waves now calm and

sparkling in the sunlight. Beyond the surf, paddle boarders and swimmers frolicked in the water, their laughter echoing for miles. She glanced around, her eyes locking on the people. No longer were they sunbathing with paperbacks or playing frisbee. Instead, they were absorbed in their glowing smartphones, wearing cordless earbuds. A group of teenagers stood near the water's edge, not laughing together but texting furiously on their devices and taking selfies. Above her, a drone whizzed past, its buzzing barely audible over the sound of ocean waves. She heard the faint hum of electric scooters whizzing past on the boardwalk, and a pang of realization hit her. They weren't stuck in 1989 anymore.

Her throat was dry and rough when she finally choked out a single word. "Perry?" Relief rushed in when the familiarity of her own voice registered. It centered her scattered thoughts. A rustle of gray feathers nearby made her heart leap.

"This is an unfortunate turn of events," Perry called out, clearly disappointed as he glided closer to her. "You seem to have found your way back into your own body, but here I am, still trapped in this one. How splendid."

"My hypothesis was correct." Neve hit him with a truth bomb as he neared. "It's simple. You had no body to return to."

"I refuse to believe I will be stuck as this stupid bird forever." He let out a surprised squawk and jutted his chin back and forth as he seemed to wrestle with himself internally. He rolled onto his back in submission, letting out a screech of pain before he muttered an apology. "Please forgive me."

"What is happening?" Neve asked, confused by his actions as Perry righted himself and shook off the altercation.

"Seems my Siamese twin would prefer to see a bit more gratitude from me. The bird is ruled by his more basic instincts," Perry chirped with a judgmental scowl.

He skipped across the sand closer to Neve, letting out a surprised chirp when his beady eyes landed on her. "We might have a small problem," he churred out, taking a few hops away but continuing to dart furtive glances back at her.

"What?" Neve glanced down, confused by the deeper wrinkles in her hands and the proliferation of sun spots that speckled them now. She held them up to Perry. "Have my hands always looked this old?"

"Um. I don't know how to answer that question."

"What do you mean?" She absentmindedly tugged on the end of her braid, tightening it as a coping mechanism. Her braids were so long now that the ends grazed the backs of her thighs. The sight of it made her stomach lurch as a strange dissonance knotted in her chest. A sharp ache throbbed in her back and out to her joints as her nose began to run. Neve reached for a Kleenex from her bag and wiped her nose absently, still trying to make sense of what was happening. When she glanced down at the tissue, her breath caught in her throat. It was stained red.

"I think we should wait to have this conversation at

home. Do you think you can walk?" His concern set off warning bells in her mind.

"Of course I can walk. I'm not a little old lady!" she muttered, adjusting the bag, and then she turned to begin the short walk home.

FORTY-THREE

A BURST of relief made tears prickle at her eyes when Neve laid eyes on her front door. She was exhausted. She couldn't remember a time when she'd been more physically drained. Her back ached and she couldn't wait to unburden herself from the messenger bag. On the doorstep, a stack of mildewed mail was collecting, addressed to Sheila. On the top was a wrinkled copy of Mother Earth News. She estimated it was several weeks' worth and stepped over it for now, knowing she would have to haul it to the recycling bin eventually.

"Sanctuary saccharine sanctuary," Perry cawed with a chuckle, perched on her shoulder.

His pretentious way of speaking made Neve crack the smallest grin as she pulled the carabiner of keys off her bag and opened the front door. Just inside, she dropped the bag to the ground and rolled her shoulders, massaging her lower back with fingers that felt knobbier and knuckles that twinged with pain. She scrubbed her hands over her face, and the looser texture of her skin felt strange under her touch.

"I need three ibuprofen and a hot shower, so go entertain yourself for a minute, Freeloader."

"I prefer free bird!" he cried, then swooped inside, heading to the sunroom to roost on the top of his cage in search of food. Only a few dusty pellets remained in his food dish, and he turned his beak up at them with a scowl of disgust.

Neve stepped into the bathroom and flicked on the light switch. She sucked in a sharp gasp when she saw her reflection for the first time. Staring back at her was a face she did not fully recognize. Her blue eyes, which always seemed a little too intense, were framed by deeper lines that had not been there previously. The skin around her mouth sagged ever so slightly, and the network of wrinkles on her forehead had deepened into noticeable creases. Most unsettling of all was her hair. Once brown and streaked with hints of silver, it had transformed into an almost uniform platinum silver cascading down to the backs of her thighs.

Her scream sent Perry flying to the rescue.

"Nevermore? What is it?" he asked, his concern evident.

"Look at me! It's like I've aged five years overnight!" she cried. He narrowed his beady eyes at her, taking in the physical changes. Neve ran her fingers over her face, tugging at the looser skin whose elasticity was shifting into crepe-like territory. The logical part of her brain began spinning. The sheer impossibility of it did not alarm her the way it should have. Instead, she methodically cataloged the details of the transformation.

Her lips parted slightly, her tongue darting out to wet them. Dry. That was new. Not the usual morning dryness, but a papery sensation she had only recently begun experiencing during the colder months. Had this aging been a side effect of the lightning strike? Or was this something else entirely? Was the time travel responsible for this disruption in her biological continuity? She tugged at the loose skin on her neck and watched it hesitate before snapping back into place. No, she wasn't seeing things. This was real.

Neve exhaled a measured breath as she debated her options. Panic would be an ineffective response. What she needed now was information. She walked out of the bathroom and picked up her cell phone. Staring at the date and time, she said, "We lost three weeks, but why does it feel like five years?"

Her nose prickled, and then a trickle of blood dropped onto her hand.

"You're bleeding again," Perry squabbled. "Tip your head back." He glided over to the tissues and pulled three out with his beak before flying them over and guiding her back into the bathroom to sit on the toilet seat. She pinched her nose closed and focused on evaluating the rest of her body. She flexed her fingers and lifted one foot off the ground. Her mobility was intact, but her bones creaked. Her back was tired and her mind was foggy.

Neve ticked off plausible explanations one at a time. "Am I having hallucinations?"

"I mean, you could be. Perhaps the last three weeks were simply one long hallucination?" Perry reasoned.

She scrunched up her forehead, clearly disagreeing with him. "A dual hallucination with another species? Highly unlikely. I haven't taken any psychotropic drugs."

"That we know of," Perry squawked out a chuckle.

"Not helping," Neve blurted. "What about the mirror and lighting? Maybe it's an optical illusion?"

"If that is what you need to tell yourself to accept what you see."

"Geez, Perry, that's harsh, even for you."

"Maybe an undiagnosed medical condition that presented quickly? Like Progeria?" she asked out loud, then discounted it immediately. "No, that's genetic and usually manifests very early in life." She googled for several more minutes, then read, "A severe disruption in cortisol levels or a rare autoimmune disorder could accelerate aging."

"Seems like a stretch," Perry discounted.

"Yes. Five years in three weeks is a bit excessive." She scanned more medical articles, ruling them out one by one before she asked the question that mattered most. "Is it reversible?"

"Doubt it," Perry chirped.

"Would it kill you to give me a glimmer of hope?"

"It may."

Neve groaned. Her heart rate remained steady, her

breath even, but she recognized the familiar sensation of cognitive overload creeping in. She felt the weight of uncertainty pressing against the logical framework she favored. Neve needed more data before drawing conclusions, but data required time, and time was currently an unreliable variable in this equation.

Remembering her father's love for data collection, she decided to document the phenomenon. Grabbing one of his empty notebooks from her desk, she scrawled down her observations in neat, precise bullet points.

- Marked increase in wrinkles, particularly on the forehead, around the eyes, and near the mouth, signaling accelerated signs of aging.
- Dramatic graying of hair, with approximately 80% transition occurring almost overnight.
- Hair growth patterns consistent with a five-year time lapse.
- Loss of skin elasticity and noticeable dryness, with the skin appearing thinner and less supple than before.
- Intermittent joint pain, with occasional stiffness and discomfort.
- No discernible changes in strength, mobility, or cognitive function.
- External environment remains unchanged, with no visible alterations in the

surroundings, suggesting that reality itself remains stable despite internal changes.
- Potential explanations: The changes could be due to an unexplained medical anomaly, an unknown biological phenomenon, or external interference beyond immediate comprehension.

Neve paused, tapping the pen against the pad. Should she see a doctor? That would be the conventional choice, but she was wary. Doctors often dismissed her concerns or, worse, fixated on the wrong details. They would likely focus on stress factors, psychosomatic explanations, or push unnecessary tests that wouldn't get to the heart of the problem. Still, ignoring the possibility of a medical condition entirely would be negligent. She would schedule an appointment.

The phone vibrated in her hand, and Neve dropped it on the floor. Her back twinged as she squatted down to pick it up. When she stood up, she saw Talulah's name flash on the screen. She took a deep breath and tapped to answer.

"There you are!" Talulah sighed with relief. "I've been worried ever since you missed our check-in last week. Where have you been?"

It was a loaded question. Part of Neve yearned to share it with Talulah and unburden herself. The bigger part of her pulled back, deciding to keep the journey she'd taken to herself for now. "Just busy here at the house," she said, being as vague as possible.

"I've been busy, too. Chakra and I have finally moved into the new house. I would love to have you come for a visit! And you can meet my new roommate."

"Roommate?" Neve winced.

"I know you hate meetin' new people, but I think you would like her. Her name is Yuli and she makes incredible chocolates."

"It's too far of a drive."

"Nevermore," Talulah scolded in her sweet drawl. "Too far of a drive? You love gettin' out on the open road. I feel like you're hidin' somethin' from me."

"I prefer my own itineraries."

Talulah let out a small chuckle. "I know you do, but it's been too long since I've seen my favorite niece."

"I'm your only niece."

Talulah let out a tinkling laugh before she pressed on. "I've booked a readin' at the Omni next month. It's only twenty minutes from you. Say you'll come and then I'll leave you alone."

Neve grimaced, trying to put her off. "I don't know."

"I know you don't like crowds, but I will put two tickets aside for you in the VIP section."

"Can I bring Peregrine?"

"Who's that?"

"My bird."

Perry let out a surprised chortle of delight in tandem

with Talulah. "Sure. I'll tell the hotel he's your emotional support animal."

"I don't know. Maybe." Neve was noncommittal but knew Talulah would not back down. She was going to have to face her aunt sooner or later.

"Besides, we need to celebrate makin' it through another Mercury in retrograde."

"Mercury in retrograde?" Neve asked, eager to shift the conversation back to Talulah. "Remind me what that is again?"

"It is an astrological phenomenon where the planet Mercury appears to move backward in its orbit from our perspective on Earth. It is an ideal time for introspection, reviewing plans, and reconnecting with past projects or relationships. They happen about four times each year."

Backward. The word stuck in her mind like a splinter as she tried to stay present in the conversation with her aunt. Neve responded to questions and asked a few of her own, careful not to arouse suspicions, but her aunt was insistent. Talulah wouldn't end the call without securing Neve's promise to attend the reading. Reluctantly, she agreed, eager to end the call and escape. Any explanation for the drastic changes to her appearance would have to wait for another day.

As soon as she hung up, her fingers flew over the keys, typing frantically into the search bar with her thumbs. Mercury in retrograde. The phrase had seemed so insignificant at first until she noticed the pattern. The dates perfectly aligned with their trip back to 1989. And then the epiphany hit her, slamming into her with the force of a freight train and rattling her bones. She froze, staring at the screen as the weight of the revelation crushed down on her. What would happen during the next one? And at what cost?

Afraid of what lay ahead, she googled the dates of the next Mercury in retrograde and added a warning on her calendar. The next event was only four months away. She had four months to figure out what the hell was happening.

FORTY-FOUR

THE NEXT FEW days passed in a blur, each moment steeped in the anxiety of looking for answers she wasn't sure she was ready to find. Neve couldn't stop thinking about it. She'd traveled backward, and it was easy to get stuck ruminating on the reasons and the possibilities, but she knew it was dangerous to remain stuck in the past. She needed to move forward.

Early for her one o'clock appointment, Neve was parked in front of Elysian Atelier. She pulled the keys from the ignition and glanced at her reflection in the rear-view mirror. She'd had several inches of her hair chopped off, and a stylist worked her magic to dye the remaining strands into a shade that was almost exactly like the one she'd worn when she attended the opening. The changes to her skin were undeniable, but she was hopeful it would be close enough to pass inspection when she saw Talulah.

"You deserve this. You worked hard. Go pick up

your check." She gave herself a pep talk as she counted the steps to the front door and then into the building. The sold out show was an unexpected victory in the midst of upheaval, and she clung to it like a lifeline.

The warm, ambient glow of the gallery welcomed her, and she heard a gentle undercurrent of quiet conversation. She passed the front desk, then turned the corner and let out a gasp. On an easel, a placard for an exhibit read, "Camille Sinclair: A Textural Impressionist Romp in the Twenty-First Century."

She followed the curve around the corner and heard soft voices murmuring together.

"Nevermore!" Lisa closed the distance between them with a warm smile. "Perfect timing! Camille Sinclair is here, and she's been asking for an introduction."

"Camille?" Neve whispered, stunned at the turn the universe had taken. The older woman stepped closer, her hands laced together and her thin frame dressed in a cotton shift. Long sleeves covered her arms, and a cobalt blue headband pulled her white hair from her face. Thirty-five years had passed, and the time was etched on her face, yet she retained her gentle spirit. Neve wanted to ask so many questions but knew she couldn't dare. When their eyes met, Camille's face lit up as if she'd been waiting for this moment.

"I've been looking forward to meeting you. Your drawings are extraordinary."

"Camille would like to acquire several of your pieces for her private collection," Lisa said.

"Wow." Neve was speechless. "I don't know what to say."

"You have a very bright career ahead of you. It's time for you to step out into the world and be seen," Camille said. "It's a lesson I learned many years ago, thanks to my dear friends, Rosa and Amos."

Neve swallowed hard. Tears welled at her bottom lashes and she blinked them away.

"I'm sure you've heard my scandalous backstory. The truth is, I used to be quite ashamed of it, but Rosa and Amos helped me see the strength in my journey. They saved my life and gave me a brand new start. In their memory, I'd like to pay it forward to another deserving artist."

Neve felt her heart lift. Her actions in 1989 reverberated across the decades after, and here she was, standing in front of the proof.

"Ruben tried to silence me. He tried to steal my life's work, and when that wasn't enough, he tried to kill me."

Neve gulped as Camille waved her hand toward the walls adorned with her paintings, each practically glowing under the gallery lights. It was breathtaking.

"I never wanted the spotlight," Camille finally said, her voice full of realization. "But now I feel like I've earned my place in it. Amos and Rosa convinced me not to hide anymore." Her gaze darted to Neve's before she added, "And now it's my turn to inspire you. Your art deserves to be seen. *You* deserve to be seen."

Neve nodded, feeling the truth settle deep into her

soul. Curious, she couldn't resist asking, "What happened to Ruben?"

"He was arrested," Camille replied. "The police uncovered everything, the life insurance policy, the stolen sketches, the lies he had told to cover his tracks. He was convicted of fraud, money laundering, and attempted murder and sentenced to eighteen years. Before he could get out on parole, he got into an altercation and died in prison." She paused, then added, "I had my rights reinstated to all of my work, and as you can see, things went pretty well after that."

"That's an understatement!" Lisa cried. "Camille is currently the most collected contemporary female painter in the world!"

Neve's mind swirled as she staggered to accept the ramifications of her visit to the past. They had a ripple effect for decades that made her heart swell. She could finally see all the sacrifices she'd made had been worth it.

Camille placed a gentle hand on her shoulder, guiding her attention back to the present. "Enough about the past. Let's focus on your future. The world needs to know your name, and soon they will." Neve felt her shoulders square as she absorbed Camille's confidence in her.

Camille grinned ear to ear, exchanging excited glances with Lisa. "Go on! Tell her!"

"Tell me what?" Neve braced for overwhelm, squeezing her eyes shut.

"You were awarded the TMOM grant!" Lisa was practically bursting with joy.

"What?" Neve staggered back in shock.

"Isn't it incredible?" Lisa said, "Ana Castanova is on the board, and she single-handedly championed your selection. I've got all the details in the back with your check. Excuse me, and I'll return with the paperwork."

"Congratulations!" Camille said as she flicked her gaze back up to Nevermore. "Having the space and time to dedicate to your art is such a gift, one that you deserve. Do great things with it!"

A few hours later, Neve was back at her childhood home, filling Perry in on her visit to Elysian Atelier.

"We did it," Neve said. "Seeing Camille at the height of her success has washed away every moment of doubt I wrestled with during our trip to 1989. At the time, I believed we were sent to spend time with my father, to rediscover who he was, and to piece together what happened to him. But now, with a clarity I didn't have before, I realize the journey was something far more profound. We were sent to help Camille, to restore what had been taken from her, and it was rewarding to see the long-term effects of righting that wrong." Then a dazzling smile crossed Neve's features, and she blurted, "And... I won the TMOM grant!"

There was a long silence, and it made Neve prickle with frustration.

"You have nothing to say? Aren't you happy for me?"

"Of course, I am. I love that for *you*," Perry chirped

as he swooped closer and alighted on her shoulder. "But what about me?" He burrowed his head into the side of Neve's neck, hiding the embarrassment of his selfish response. She reached over and brushed her thumb over the top of his head to reassure him.

"Don't worry. I'll figure something out," Neve said, surprising herself with her answer. "I never thought I'd say this, but we're a package deal. You've grown on me."

Hearing her response, he chirped and hopped, perking up instantly.

Neve's tone grew somber. "You know, it was a gift to be able to spend time with my father on another timeline, and I'd gladly sacrifice more crow's feet, gray hair, and angry joints to see him again."

Perry jutted his chin back and forth and shook his tail feathers in what Neve could only describe as a ridiculous mating dance. "*I'd* sacrifice my tail feathers to see Isla again. That was one gorgeous female specimen!"

"Perv!"

"What? I just happen to have a healthy adoration for the female form," he argued, then mused, "I wonder what happened to her?"

Neve pulled out her phone and beat him to it, googling Isla Warner. The results were a Wikipedia page, and she read it aloud.

Isla Warner

Born: 1969-2022

Nationality: American

Occupation: Businesswoman, Philanthropist, Autism Advocate

Years Active: 1990s–2000s

Isla Warner was an influential American businesswoman, philanthropist, and autism advocate, best known for her leadership in the corporate world and her unwavering commitment to autism awareness and support. Throughout her career, Warner built a successful empire in the fashion and lifestyle industries while dedicating her resources to advancing autism research, funding educational programs, and supporting families affected by autism spectrum disorder.

Early Life and Background

Isla Warner was born in 1969 in Tampa, Florida, to a middle-class family. She was raised in a supportive household by her mother, who was a schoolteacher, and her father, who worked as an electrician. Warner's early life was marked by her role as a nanny to a family with an autistic child, which she later cited as an influential factor in her deep connection to the autism community.

Rise in the Business World

In the mid-1990s, Warner launched her first business venture, a boutique retail store specializing in sustainable fashion and locally sourced products. Her innovative approach to ethical consumerism quickly gained traction, and by the early 2000s, her brand had expanded nationwide.

Her ability to anticipate market trends and adapt to consumer needs earned her accolades within the industry, and she was frequently invited to speak at global business summits.

Philanthropy and Autism Advocacy

Despite her demanding career, Warner was deeply committed to philanthropy, particularly in the field of autism awareness and support. She established the Warner Foundation, which focused on funding autism research, creating educational resources for families, and providing grants to schools specializing in ASD education. Her foundation played a crucial role in launching early intervention programs and increasing accessibility to therapy services for children with autism.

Warner collaborated with leading autism organizations, including Autism Speaks and the Autism Society of America, advocating for better policies, increased funding for research, and greater public awareness. She was a passionate speaker at autism conferences, using her platform to amplify the voices of individuals on the spectrum and push for meaningful societal change.

Personal Life

Isla Warner kept much of her personal life private, but it is known that she married in the early 2000s. She was diagnosed with cancer in 2022 and passed several months later.

Legacy

Isla Warner's influence extended far beyond the

boardroom. Her philanthropy left a lasting mark on both the corporate and nonprofit sectors. She is remembered not only for her sharp business instincts but also for her unwavering commitment to using her success to create meaningful change for the autism community. Her foundation continues to support autism research, education, and advocacy, ensuring that her legacy of empowerment and inclusion lives on.

When Neve finished reading the last word, her eyes brimmed with tears that cascaded down her cheeks. Perry glided over to land on her lap and, for once, she didn't wave him away. He burrowed closer to her neck and his softness was comforting.

"What an impression you must have made on her," Perry exclaimed.

Neve felt her heart flood with love for Isla, and it carried her away, making her retreat into herself to understand it. She'd been loved, not just by her father, but by Isla, and the tender realization filled her with joy.

CHAPTER

FORTY-FIVE

A FEW DAYS LATER, Neve sat on the creaky wooden floor of her childhood attic as dust motes swirled around her in the dim light filtering through the rain-spotted window. She had been going through boxes for hours, trying to piece together the fragments of her father's life. Neve was surrounded by his belongings, desperately searching for answers. The time they'd recently spent together stoked the fire in her heart to understand what happened to him.

Neve sifted through another box, her fingers brushing against faded receipts, yellowed letters, and strange keepsakes that didn't seem to fit. But then something caught her eye.

A stack of polaroids. The edges were worn, and the colors had shifted due to the extreme heat of being stored in the attic. Neve flipped through the photographs. At first, they seemed ordinary. A few pictures of her father in a white coat, smiling in the lab with the evidence of his nerdiness on full display. He was genuinely happy surrounded by petri dishes, microscopes, and the colleagues he worked with.

But then she came to one that stopped her cold. It was a photograph of a pregnant woman standing beside her father. A sinking feeling slithered through her, tightening around her ribs. The woman's face was familiar in a way that made Neve's stomach twist, an echo of her own. She had brown hair, pulled back into a loose ponytail, and the same serious yet contemplative expression Neve had seen nearly every day in her own mirror.

Neve's breath grew shallow as her gaze shifted to her father. His arm was draped casually around the woman's waist, his fingers resting lightly against the curve of her hip. There was warmth in his eyes, an unmistakable tenderness as he looked at her that made Neve's heart gallop in her chest.

Neve's mind spun as her heart hammered against her ribs. A curious thought flickered through her mind, wild and impossible.

Who was she?

Her fingers, suddenly clumsy, fumbled to another photograph. The same woman, standing beside her father, holding a folder while he studied it intently. It was the *way* they were standing, just a fraction too close. It hinted at an intimacy that couldn't be denied.

Neve swallowed hard and flipped through a few more before freezing. Another shot of the same woman, her belly more pronounced now. Her hands rested protectively over it as she and Neve's father sat across from each other at a table strewn with scientific papers. The sight of them together, absorbed in their work yet undeniably connected, sent a shiver through her.

Neve's breath hitched.

Could this woman be her mother?

Ellis always told her she'd been adopted and her biological mother died when she was four months old. But this photograph turned that story inside out, unraveling everything she thought she knew.

An uncomfortable truth coiled in her gut, whispering that the woman in the picture wasn't just some random lab assistant. There was something more, a connection that had been hidden from her all these years. The resemblance was undeniable. The familiarity of the woman's face gnawed at the edges of her memories like a fever dream.

Neve stared at the photograph, her mind racing. Her hands felt clammy as she flipped through the rest of the stack, but they were more of the same. Image after image flashed by, her father and the woman together in a sterile medical research lab, heads bent over microscopes, and an unspoken bond between them captured in every frame.

Her fingers shook as she shoved the stack back inside the box. Her internal axis had shifted. Suddenly, the attic felt suffocating, the walls pressing in on her as the realization hit her like a freight train.

Her father wasn't the man she thought he was.

A shudder ran through Neve as she forced herself

to take a centering breath. She had spent her whole life accepting the story she'd been told, but not anymore.

Neve reached for the next box, her heart pounding.

Her world had come undone. Where there was once order and understanding, a web of lies and unanswered questions formed, and she was tangled inside it. Desperate for answers, Neve vowed she would not stop until she uncovered the truth, even if it destroyed everything.

Thank you for reading *Nevermore*! Get ready for the next thrilling installment of the Aura Cove Temporal Traveler series with *Never Lose Hope*—Book Two, packed with unexpected twists, excitement, laughter, and heartwarming moments! **Order here.**

Before You Go… Claim Your Sneak Peek!

Can't get enough of Aura Cove? **CLICK HERE for an exclusive 3-chapter preview of *Hawt Flash*. The magical series that started it all.**

Turning 50 is supposed to be a milestone, but for Katie Beaumont, it's the beginning of a supernatural adventure that will change her life forever.

Devastated by her husband's infidelity, Katie discovers she possesses powers beyond her wildest dreams. But as she embarks on a journey of explosive self-discovery, a century of ancestral secrets begins to unravel and threatens to upend everything she thought she knew.

Guided by her sassy best friend, a talking dog, and a ball-busting lawyer, Katie embraces her new life. But she soon realizes that her magical abilities come with a price and enemies who will stop at nothing to claim them.

WANT MORE GOOD BOOKS?

Scan the QR Code Above or Tap **HERE** to unlock my entire backlist & find your next great read!

🎁 JOIN MY BOOK CLUB

- **Read FREE Extended Sneak Peeks**
- **Unlock Exclusive Bonus Content**
- **Private Subscriber-Only Discounts**
- **Handpicked 5-Star Book Recs**
- **Delicious, Healthy-ish Recipes**

☞ JOIN THE BOOK CLUB HERE

bookclub.tealbutterflypress.com

About the Author

I've always been a risk-taker, so at 44 I decided to write and publish my own books. It has been a roller coaster ride with a punishing learning curve, but if it were easy, everyone would do it. I write under the pen names of Ninya and Blair Bryan.

I love to travel and a trip to Scotland with a complete stranger was the inspiration for my memoir. I also seem to attract crazy experiences and people into my life like a magnet that gives me a never-ending supply of interesting storylines.

If you love a good dirty joke, a cup of coffee so strong you can chew it, and have killed more cats with your curiosity than you can count, I might be your soulmate.

Join My Book Club